T0278628

THE WILD HUNTRESS

BY EMILY LLOYD-JONES

The Drowned Woods

The Bone Houses

The Hearts We Sold

THE ILLUSIVE SERIES

Illusive

Murder on the Disoriented Express: An E-Novella

Deceptive

His Hideous Heart

THE WILD HUNTRESS

EMILY LLOYD-JONES

LITTLE, BROWN AND COMPANY
New York Boston

This book is a work of fiction. Names, characters, places, and incidents are the product of the author's imagination or are used fictitiously. Any resemblance to actual events, locales, or persons, living or dead, is coincidental.

Copyright © 2024 by Emily Lloyd-Jones
Map copyright © 2024 by Kathleen Jennings
Baroque pattern copyright © Gorbash Varvara/Shutterstock.com;
ornaments copyright © HiSunnySky/Shutterstock.com

Cover art copyright © 2024 by SPIDER.MONEY (Wansiya Visupakanjana).
Baroque pattern copyright © Gorbash Varvara/Shutterstock.com; black grunge texture and brown paper texture copyright © Krasovski Dmitri/Shutterstock.com.
Cover design by Jenny Kimura.
Cover copyright © 2024 by Hachette Book Group, Inc.
Interior design by Carla Weise.

Hachette Book Group supports the right to free expression and the value of copyright. The purpose of copyright is to encourage writers and artists to produce the creative works that enrich our culture.

The scanning, uploading, and distribution of this book without permission is a theft of the author's intellectual property. If you would like permission to use material from the book (other than for review purposes), please contact permissions@hbgusa.com. Thank you for your support of the author's rights.

Little, Brown and Company
Hachette Book Group
1290 Avenue of the Americas, New York, NY 10104
Visit us at LBYR.com

First Edition: October 2024

Little, Brown and Company is a division of Hachette Book Group, Inc. The Little, Brown name and logo are registered trademarks of Hachette Book Group, Inc.

The publisher is not responsible for websites (or their content) that are not owned by the publisher.

Little, Brown and Company books may be purchased in bulk for business, educational, or promotional use. For information, please contact your local bookseller or the Hachette Book Group Special Markets Department at special.markets@hbgusa.com.

Library of Congress Cataloging-in-Publication Data
Names: Lloyd-Jones, Emily, author.
Title: The wild huntress / Emily Lloyd-Jones.
Description: First edition. | New York : Little, Brown and Company, 2024. | Audience: Ages 12 and up. | Summary: Branwen, Gwydion, and Pryderi, a huntress, a trickster, and a prince, band together in the dangerous tournament, the Wild Hunt, to win a magical wish granted by the Otherking, but unbeknownst to them, winning may cost them more than losing.
Identifiers: LCCN 2023052853 | ISBN 9780316568142 (hardcover) | ISBN 9780316568166 (ebook)
Subjects: CYAC: Hunting—Fiction. | Monsters—Fiction. | Ability—Fiction. | Magic—Fiction. | Fantasy. | LCGFT: Fantasy fiction. | Picture books.
Classification: LCC PZ7.L77877 Wi 2024 | DDC [Fic]—dc23
LC record available at https://lccn.loc.gov/2023052853

ISBNs: 978-0-316-56814-2 (hardcover), 978-0-316-56816-6 (ebook)

Printed in Indiana, USA

LSC-C

Printing 2, 2024

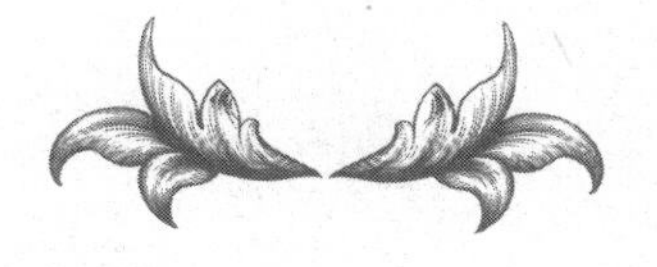

For my wonderful readers.
Don't worry, the cat survives.

N
W
E
S
Ynys Môn
Caer Dathyl
Caer Sidi
Colbren
Gwynedd
Gates of Annwvyn
Annwvyn
Argoed
Bae Ceredigion
(formerly
Cantre'r Gwaelod)
Powys
Seisyllwg
Rhwng Gwy
A Hafren
Dyfed
Brycheiniog
Gwent
Morgannwg
Caerdyf
THE
Isles

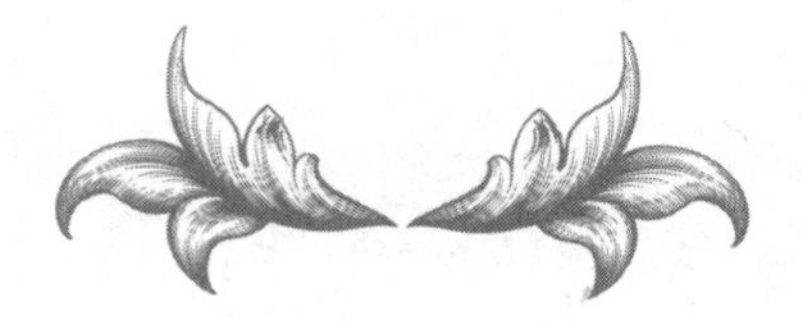

IT WAS WHISPERED *that the otherfolk stole children, but one autumn evening they came for the midwife instead.*

She was a slim woman with pale hair and strong hands. A small iron charm hung on a leather cord and rested in the hollow of her collarbones—a ward against magic. One did not live so close to Annwvyn without keeping to the old ways. Which was why the woman hesitated when a stranger knocked thrice at her door. Evenings were dangerous. Magic flourished in moments when the world was in flux: when the sun rose or fell, when seasons shifted, and when the days were at their shortest or longest.

"Yes?" said the midwife, speaking through her door. "Who is it?"

It was a man who answered. "Please. I have need for a midwife."

Compassion overcame caution, and the midwife unlatched the door.

The man that stood before her was not human. His eyes had the flat pupils of a goat, and his clothes were spun from oak leaves and lichen. He was beautiful and unsettling, and at once the midwife took a step back, her hand going to her iron charm. She knew of the otherfolk, but one had never crossed her path. She was half tempted to shut the door on this magical creature.

"My lady," said the man of the folk. "Please. My wife is laboring with our child, and I fear I will lose them both." He looked pained. "I do not have gold, but I promise a favor of equal measure."

The midwife straightened. This was familiar. She strode back into her home, gathering her supplies. Her own babe, a child of six months, was napping by the fire. The midwife bundled her into a sling and settled the babe against her shoulder. "I have no one to watch her," said the midwife.

The man nodded. "I will provide safe passage to you both."

The midwife lived on the edge of the wild country, where the forested mountains of Annwvyn cast shadows across the mortal lands. The man led the midwife past the fields and toward the wood. He moved with the unsettling grace of a deer, finding paths that the midwife would never have seen. She held her babe close, glad that her daughter was a heavy sleeper. Perhaps it would have been safer to remain indoors, to stay where iron and fires drove back the wilds. But she had been a midwife too long to let a mother suffer alone.

The man approached two ancient yew trees. Their branches were woven to form an archway—a living gate.

The gates of Annwvyn.

The man hesitated, casting a glance at the midwife. "While you are within the forest, do not speak your name. Nor your daughter's. There are those who would remember, and they would have power over you both."

The midwife hesitated for half a heartbeat. Taking a tighter hold on her daughter, she stepped through the wooded gates.

At first glance, all seemed ordinary. The forest was dusky; small creatures found their way by weak moonlight; owls called out overhead; a creek burbled nearby. But when the midwife glimpsed a bird, its wings glittered as though it had been made of spun gold.

"This way," said the man. He led her down another unseen path until they came upon a small home. It was tucked in the roots of an old oak tree, and the man made a gesture. The roots moved obligingly, revealing a doorway. The midwife stepped inside.

At once, she smelled the blood. There were two of the folk inside: A very pregnant woman lay on a bedroll, laboring with uneven breaths and sweat staining her moss-green hair. A woman knelt beside her, holding a bandage over the pregnant woman's shoulder. The bandage was soaked through with half-clotted blood.

"A hunter's arrow struck my sister," said the kneeling woman. "The iron—it caused her labor to begin before it should. And none of us can dig out the iron."

The midwife nodded. This was why one of the otherfolk had sought out a mortal midwife rather than one of their own. She set her own sleeping babe on a table, and then she began to work. The midwife found and removed the arrowhead from the folk woman's shoulder, but the labor was too far gone to halt. The mother had little breath to cry out. The midwife tried her best to save mother and babe.

Her victory was only half won.

She bore a bloodied child to the table. She cleaned him and made sure the babe could breathe well enough on his own. He was a small thing, with briar-green eyes and wickedly sharp canines. The lad's father sat beside his still wife, hand in hers. The sister had gone outside to howl her grief to the forest. "What can I do?" asked the midwife quietly.

The man let out a small hiccuped sob. "There is an oil," he said dully.

"The bottle on the shelf, with the green stopper. We anoint all our children with it."

The midwife found the bottle. The liquid inside was a thick brown, and it smelled herbal and sharp. She touched her fingers to the liquid, then brushed it over the newborn's brow. The lad blinked up at her, bewildered by the touch. He squealed sharply.

That noise startled the midwife's young daughter. She let out a surprised sob. Hastily, the midwife went to her child.

But her fingers were still stained with the strange oil.

Unthinking, the midwife touched her child's right eye, wiping away her tears.

Her daughter's eyes had been the blue of a summer's sky—but as the midwife watched, gold flooded through the iris. Gold as the strange birds in the forest. Gold as the late-autumn leaves.

Gold was not for people like the midwife. Gold meant coin or magic. It meant power.

Then, as abruptly as it had appeared, the gold faded away. The babe sobbed harder, her face scrunching and chubby fingers rubbing at her right eye. Panicked, the midwife tried to use her sleeve to wipe away any traces of the strange oil, but it was too late.

Behind her, the man drew in a sharp breath. The midwife looked up, suddenly fearful for herself and her child.

"I didn't mean to," the midwife said, but the man spoke over her.

"Listen carefully," said the man of the folk. "You saved the life of my son, and now I shall do the same for your daughter. I will tell no one of what happened, and neither shall you. You both need to leave."

The midwife picked up her daughter and followed the man through the forest and toward home. When they stepped through the wooded yew gates, the man bowed to her. He reached for the babe, his hand hovering over her. "The trick is not in the seeing," he murmured. "But in knowing where to look."

His words made little sense to the midwife. But before she could ask, he returned to Annwvyn.

The midwife dared not chance a look backward until she was home. She locked her door, dragged a chair beneath it, and then placed her sleeping child in her cradle.

Magic had touched her babe, marked her. She knew what happened to those with magic—they were taken by nobles or royals, bound into service. She would not let that happen to her daughter. The midwife yanked the iron charm from around her neck. She stitched that charm into a small cloth and folded it across her babe's right eye. Then she bound the cloth in place.

She considered leaving her village, to go as far from Annwvyn as she could. But she did not have the coin. Instead, the midwife moved to a home beyond the boundaries of her village, where there were fewer neighbors to watch them. She delivered children and found herbs to ease the pregnancies of her neighbors, all the while keeping an eye on her daughter.

The girl grew up like a weed. She was quiet and watchful, a determined little thing. Her mother told her to always wear the iron-stitched cloth around her eye, and most of the neighbors assumed she had lost her eye in an accident. The midwife told her daughter again and again that she needed to keep her right eye hidden from the world.

And the girl did as she was told.

Until she was seven.

The girl was out in her neighbor's fields, having been offered a coin to count the lambs born in the night. As she worked, a few strands of sweaty hair snagged in her blindfold. The girl looked around to be sure she was alone, then yanked the cloth away. She knew the tale of what had happened to her eye; her mam had told the girl over firelight, whispering the story. But the girl only half believed it.

She blinked the world into focus, enjoying the early-morning sun on her face.

That was when she caught sight of a man walking along the distant road. Merchants, messengers, and travelers were not an uncommon sight. But this one made her look again. A creature was following the man.

A hound. Long-legged and fearsome, with eyes that glowed like embers. It stalked the man with predatory grace, and the girl's heartbeat tore into a gallop.

She called out to the distant traveler, warning him. But he merely looked at the girl as if she were telling tales. "There's no dog," he shouted back, pulling his cloak tighter around himself. "Go back to your mam, girl."

"He's right there," cried the girl, pointing at the hound. It looked to be a skeletal thing, hungry and gaunt, but again, the man did not seem to see it.

The girl frowned. She raised her iron-stitched blindfold to cover her magicked eye—and the hound vanished from sight. When her hand fell away, the hound reappeared.

The traveler waved the girl off. The hound followed, silent and unseen. As it approached, the world grew unnaturally quiet. The girl shivered and ran back home, not stopping until she was safely behind a locked door, her iron-stitched blindfold firmly in place.

The next day, villagers found the man dead on the road. He had been mauled by some animal, it was whispered, but there were no tracks near his body.

In the following weeks, the girl began to steal moments when she looked at the world with both eyes. It was how she saw the kindly bwbach that lived at her neighbor's home, helping keep mice and rats from the grain. She saw an aderyn y corph as it soared overhead, casting a long shadow over the fields. She saw the way the otherlands glowed on some nights.

And that was when she understood.

Her left eye saw the world as mortals did; her right eye saw the world as magic.

During the late-summer harvest, the midwife and her daughter went to the village markets. They browsed wares—woven baskets, iron charms, dried seeds. A man played a crwth while a woman sang, and several children danced to the tune. The smell of honeyed cakes and sweet drinks made the girl's mouth water. She danced with a few other children until sweat trickled down her back. The blindfold itched, and she pulled it up for a moment, scratching at the corner of her eye.

A flicker of movement caught her gaze.

And then she saw the otherfolk.

There were three of them, children all. They darted in and out of the crowd like minnows in a stream. They were taking small treasures from pockets, unknotting cloaks, shoving pebbles into boots. They were folk children playing at mischief, and only the girl could see them.

She tried to turn away, she truly did.

But when one of the folk tried to slip his hand into the girl's pocket, she seized his wrist. She had only a few coins, and she would not let herself be robbed.

It was a dangerous mistake.

The folk boy looked at her. He had the eyes of a cat, and his hair was red as old blood. "How did you—" he began to say, but then his voice caught. He reached out and pushed the girl's pale hair aside, revealing her right eye.

"Look!" he said, and the otherfolk children flitted through the crowds. Before anyone could notice, they dragged the girl into an alleyway.

"She's got an eye like one of us," said one of the folk, a girl with flowers crowning her head and a voice like a burbling stream. "Did you steal that magic, human girl?"

A second folk boy watched her from a few steps away. He had briar-green eyes and a raspy voice. "She looks like a white crow."

"We should cut out that eye," said the first boy. He held a knife made of the fang of an afanc—long and wickedly jagged along one edge.

Cold terror flooded the girl. She was helpless, outnumbered and trapped, with no one near enough to help her. It was the first time she had ever felt such fear.

Fear sharpened into anger, crystallized into action.

The girl slapped the folk boy's hand away. Tucked into her palm was the iron-stitched cloth. The iron stung the folk boy, and he stumbled back, snarling in agony. The afanc dagger clattered to the ground. The girl seized it, clumsy but determined, and backed away from the otherfolk.

"Try to take my eye," said the girl, baring her teeth.

The otherfolk hissed, but she had iron in one hand and a knife in the other. The folk retreated.

One of them looked back—the boy with briar-green eyes. "What is your name?" he called.

The girl knew all the tales of Annwvyn. She knew of humans gone missing in the woods, of prophecies, of diviners of magic. And she knew better than to give one of the folk her birth name. She thought of what these folk children had called her.

"I'm a white, thieving crow," she said flatly. "Call me that, if you are to call me anything."

The boy flashed a grin. "So be it, Branwen."

Then the midwife called out to her, rounding the corner. She saw her daughter holding a knife at nothing, and her brows drew tight. Hastily, she took her daughter by the hand and bustled her away. The girl looked over her shoulder and saw the folk watching her with those inhuman eyes.

They would not forget her.

She would not forget them.

She slept with the knife for a week until she went to one of her neighbors. He was an older man, with aches in his joints and a grumble in his voice. But he had served in the cantref's armies for many years, and his eyes were still sharp.

The girl brought him fresh eggs to sweeten his mood. Then she pulled out the dagger, placing it on his kitchen table. "Can you teach me how to use this?" she asked.

The neighbor picked up the dagger, examining it with a practiced eye. "That's quite a weapon for a child."

"I'm seven," said the girl stubbornly.

He scoffed. "Why do you want to learn?"

The girl thought of the skeletal hound. Of the corpse-bird in the sky. And she thought of hands on her, dragging her into an alley to be threatened with this very knife.

"There are monsters in the mountains," she said. "And some of them do not stay there."

He nodded. "Aye. Is that why you've come to me? You afeared of monsters?"

The girl shook her head.

The power of monsters was that they could go unseen. Their magic shielded them from sight and sound, so they always struck the first blow.

But the girl had a power all her own. She unbound the iron-stitched blindfold, letting it flutter to the table. The world came into focus. There was an enchantment upon the afanc-fang dagger, a wicked gleam that would cut through anything. Her fingers settled around the hilt.

"The monsters," she said, "will fear me."

The Huntress

CHAPTER 1

MONSTERS HAD LITTLE respect for mealtimes.

Branwen crouched behind a thicket of briars. The late-autumn sunlight cast the forest into shades of crimson and gold. The lush scent of sun-warmed blackberries made her stomach clench with hunger.

It had been hours. Perhaps she should give up this hunt and return in the morning. She was reaching for her small lantern when she heard it.

A whisper of leaves. The murmur of a footfall against damp earth.

Branwen swallowed, her tongue suddenly too dry. She touched the knife at her belt. Her bow was at home; the thick undergrowth and close trees ensured that this hunt would need to be at close range.

A woman rounded a bend in the path. Sunlight caught in her

red-brown hair. She carried a basket brimming with loaves of bread, apples, and cheeses.

Or so it seemed.

In the immortal lands, one could not trust mortal senses.

Branwen reached up, her fingers alighting on the iron-stitched cloth she wore across her right eye. Quietly, she pulled it free.

And then the world changed.

The forest glittered with unseen power. Branwen blinked several times, waiting for her eye to adjust. Then she looked at the woman. She half expected to see one of the folk: hair woven with vines, inhuman eyes, or too-sharp teeth. It was not unheard of for one of the folk to visit the village wearing the guise of a mortal.

But nothing about the woman changed. Her hair was still a ruddy brown, a flush on her cheeks as she carried her day's shopping.

It was just a human woman.

Branwen blew out a breath and sat back on her heels. She would wait another hour, then return home. One did not remain in the forests of Annwvyn—even the outskirts—after dark. She slid the blindfold back into place. Using that eye for too long left her with a headache that throbbed through her whole skull, made her flinch away from light and sound. It was best to use her power sparingly.

The traveler continued along the path. There were always a few willing to risk the edges of Annwvyn. Most of the time, they came out unscathed. Some emerged with bloody injuries or enchanted trinkets. And some simply vanished.

A noble, Barwn Ifor, lost his son a few weeks ago, after the young man ventured too near Annwvyn. The hunt to find him had led Branwen to this briar patch and this very ordinary-looking traveler.

The traveler stumbled over a root in the path and grumbled quietly to herself. Sweat beaded on her brow, and she paused, setting down her burden long enough to swipe at her forehead. She knelt beside a stream and cupped one hand, reaching for a drink. Sunlight danced merrily upon the water. It looked so clear and refreshing that Branwen dragged her dry tongue across her lips. It was easy to imagine how sweet that water would taste, how refreshing it would feel against her dirt-smudged fingers. The traveler cupped a handful of water.

And then a hand surged from the stream and seized her.

The woman shrieked. She thrashed like an animal caught in a snare, but the grip was unbreakable. It began to drag her toward the water. She reached for roots, for ferns, for any handhold. But it was a useless struggle, and slowly she was dragged into the stream.

Branwen surged to her feet. Her legs tingled with disuse, and she stumbled as she ducked out from behind the briars.

There were a few charms against magic. Iron was the most common, but to scatter iron into Annwvyn was akin to walking into a prince's great hall with a cup of poison. It was an insult at best and a declaration of war at worst.

Branwen shoved a hand into her pocket and withdrew a handful of dried gorse. It was less potent than iron, but it would also decay and leave no trace. She tossed the leaves into the water, where they bobbed merrily in the current. One of them touched the hand emerging from the water, and it flinched in pain.

The hand slipped back beneath the waves, and the traveler scurried to the path on hands and knees. When she saw Branwen, she let out a startled noise.

"Run," snarled Branwen.

The traveler did not need telling twice. Leaving her fallen basket, she rushed up the path. Branwen listened to the thud of footsteps, to the ragged breathing, to those last mortal sounds. And then Branwen was alone with the monster that rose from the water. That stream should have been far too shallow to hide anything larger than a fish or frog. An illusion must have hidden this unseen creature.

Nothing beneath the trees of Annwvyn could be trusted, save for names and oaths.

The woman who stepped from the stream had hair black as obsidian, skin pale as sun-bleached driftwood, and the kind of beauty only glimpsed in paintings. She wore a white gown sodden with creek water. She looked like a maiden spun from magic and tales, just waiting for the right hero to save her from this place.

Branwen inhaled deeply a few times, blowing out each breath in its entirety—the way she prepared to dive beneath choppy waters. Then she pulled a small flask from her belt and tipped it into her mouth. Alcohol burned at the corners of her chapped lips, and she had to resist the instinct to swallow it down.

The corners of the woman's mouth curved into a gentle smile. She opened her mouth and began to sing. It was as lovely as the rest of her: clear and perfectly pitched. Slow and gentle. The kind of melody that should have rocked babes to sleep.

Branwen dug her nails into her palms. She did not have magic.

She had something far more dangerous—knowledge.

She yanked away the cloth that covered her right eye. And Branwen saw the woman for what she was.

The creature was thin. Her stomach was hollow—not as one

who was starving, but the flesh was simply not there. Her torso was all ribs and tattered cloth.

A cyhyraeth. A maiden of bracken, bone, and driftwood. It was whispered that they foretold death with a wailing song.

She was a nightmare. And yet somehow, when Branwen saw the truth of her nature, her song became all the more beautiful.

The creature approached on bare, skeletal feet. Branwen saw something glittering through her torso. A gleam of silver—no, not silver.

Iron.

An iron-tipped arrow had pierced the maiden's chest and lodged there.

The cold weight of fear dropped into Branwen's belly. She swallowed instinctively, and a few drops of the spirits slipped down her throat.

Iron was poison to the otherlands and to all those who dwelled within them. It smothered magic, like dirt poured on flames. It could drive monsters to madness. Iron sickness, the folk called it.

And this maiden of death had an arrowhead buried in her chest.

"Sweetling," whispered the cyhyraeth. The melody was so lovely that it hurt. The song held all the ache of lost loves and faded flowers.

"What is your name, sweetling?" asked the cyhyraeth. Her voice was soothing as the touch of cool fingers against a fevered forehead. It made Branwen yearn to answer, to give this monster the power it needed to destroy her.

There was a cold touch at Branwen's throat. Fingers that were half-bone and half-branch stroked her skin with such tenderness that a shiver of pleasure ripped through her.

"Tell me your name," the cyhyraeth crooned. She had hold of Branwen, fingers curled around the young huntress's throat.

It would have been so simple to tell her. To whisper the word that Branwen had forbidden herself to say. It was a name Branwen had tried to bury, to leave behind with the failings that accompanied it.

The cyhyraeth was so close, and she smelled of oceans and misty nights. It was intoxicating, as easy to slip into as a warm bath.

She opened her mouth—

The cyhyraeth's song grew sharper, higher, *hungrier*.

—and Branwen spat her mouthful of spirits into the monster's face.

The creature recoiled, its jaw gaping wide in a wordless scream.

Branwen's left hand reached for her lantern, and she swung it upward, catching the cyhyraeth on the edge of her jaw. And this was why Branwen never stilled her tongue with mouthfuls of bread or iron.

Alcohol *burned*.

The moment the flames touched the strong drink, the cyhyraeth ignited. Fire caught in the wisps of her cobweb hair and the threadbare clothes dragging from her skeletal frame.

Her song sharpened into a screech. The cyhyraeth's hand flashed toward Branwen's stomach. Her long nails were jagged as broken barnacles. Branwen leapt back, but those nails sliced through the loose fabric of her tunic. It parted, a few threads fluttering through the air.

The cyhyraeth shrieked again, pressing her advantage. Branwen stumbled. Her feet were on damp, uneven ground, and this creature was swift as a fish in water. The fire guttered in the cyhyraeth's damp hair.

Fighting back a surge of fear, Branwen ducked and rolled away, reaching into her pocket. When she came up, she threw another handful of gorse leaves into the cyhyraeth's face.

But the cyhyraeth was too swift. She ducked beneath the flutter of leaves, her mouth pulled back into a snarl. Her teeth were jagged chips of river rocks and a terrible light burned in her eyes. Before Branwen could swing her knife, the creature had her by the throat again. She felt the wind gusting out of her as she slammed into the hard ground. Creek pebbles dug into her back. Her hand was pinned beneath her, knife sinking into the ground. She dared not thrash, not with her own blade pressed flat against her back.

The cyhyraeth hissed, her slender fingers tight around Branwen's throat. "What are you? A mortal with a fang in her hand and fire in her mouth?" Even those hissing words had the cadence of a song. "The iron-blooded should know better than to touch our lands, our streams."

"You've iron in you, too," gasped Branwen. Her gaze flicked down to the arrow embedded in the creature's torso.

"Iron, iron, iron," sang the cyhyraeth. "It burns in our bones, sings in our veins. We used to fear it, you know, but now it's in the streams, in the rains, in the trees. We will never escape it—and so, we shall drown the ones who made it. A young man came into the forest looking for legends and glory, but all he brought was iron."

The barwn's son. He must have been the one to fire the arrow.

"Let me take it from you." Branwen rasped out the words; she had one hand around the cyhyraeth's wrist, and the other was twisted beneath her. Her heartbeat throbbed in her temples as the cyhyraeth squeezed her throat. Every time she blinked, the cyhyraeth's visage shifted. First, she saw the creature with her mortal eye—beautiful, cold as a starlit night—and then her right eye focused on the monster—bone and sinew, river and murk. "I will free you from the iron if you tell me where to find the one who shot you."

"Take it?" The cyhyraeth's grip tightened, and Branwen could barely hold back the animal panic of suffocation. "You offer mercy with a blade in your hand."

"You're—a—monster." It took the last of Branwen's breath to utter the words.

The cyhyraeth leaned in closer. "Want to know a secret, mortal girl?" Her voice softened, losing its giddy ire. She sounded suddenly, terribly lucid. "I may be a monster, but you are the most dangerous creature in this forest."

Branwen went limp.

The cyhyraeth loosened her hold, satisfied she had wrung the life from the mortal. But as her bony fingers slackened, Branwen bucked like a startled horse. She twisted, wrenching her arm out from beneath her, and drove the afanc-tooth dagger up. She cut the creature from pelvis to collarbone, shattering ribs and driftwood.

The cyhyraeth *screeched*. She pulled back, retreating into herself, but the damage had been done.

The cyhyraeth died like a pitiful spider: thin limbs pulled tight, her body drawn up, suddenly so much smaller than before. Only once she had gone utterly still did Branwen sheath her dagger and slump into a crouch. Her throat burned, and she could feel bruises forming on her back.

I may be a monster, but you are the most dangerous creature in this forest.

Some hunts let Branwen sleep better at night...while others gave her nightmares.

This would likely be the latter.

Branwen nudged the creature over. Wincing, she shoved her hand into the creature's ribs and withdrew the metal arrow tip. She tucked it into her pocket. The ironfetches—humans tasked by the otherfolk to seek out and remove iron—would have found this arrow eventually. But Branwen might as well save them the trouble.

She picked up her lantern. The fire had gone out, candle fallen into the damp earth. Her cloak was stained with mud, and she smelled like burning driftwood.

All she wanted was a meal and a bath. But her job wasn't done, not yet.

Branwen carefully picked her way down the embankment. Without the cyhyraeth's magic to enchant the water, its luster had faded. The stream had a tinge of green algae, and beneath that—

Bones.

Bones and fine cloth. There was a leather boot and glove, and what looked horribly like the remnants of blond hair. Tangled around one of the finger bones was something heavy and silver.

Forcing herself not to retch, Branwen reached down and took hold of the bones. Attached was a heavy ring, embossed with the seal of a noble. She recognized it at once: the signet belonged to the barwn's household.

Well, that was that. The barwn's son was dead, and Branwen's hunt was for naught. All she had to show for it was a silver ring and a broken lantern. She straightened, giving the drowned bones one last glance before she picked up the traveler's fallen basket. It brimmed with apples, cheese, and bread.

"It would be a shame for this to be left behind," murmured Bran-wen, hefting the basket into the crook of her arm. At least she wasn't going home entirely empty-handed.

She turned toward home, choosing one of the folk trails. She could see the traps, the enchantments, the lures. She knew which trees had false roots, ones that could be pried open with the right whisper. She knew where to step and where to avoid.

It had always been this way, as long as she could remember. One eye was mortal, the other immortal.

It was why she could hunt magical monsters. She could see them for what they were.

Human monsters were not so easily discerned.

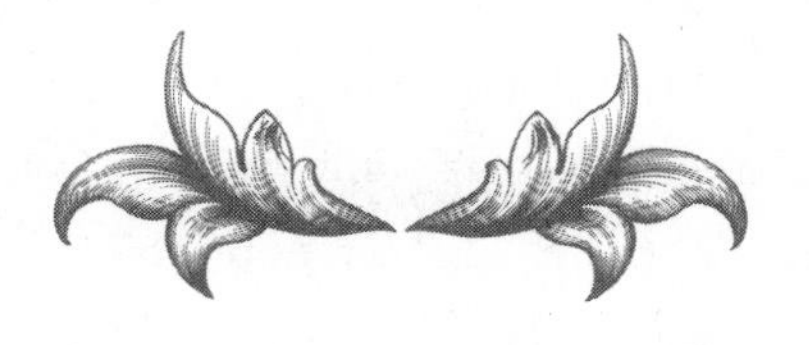

CHAPTER 2

GWYDION, SON OF DÔN, moved through the forest like a wraith.

He went barefoot, every step softened by the moss that rose up to meet him. These lands may have belonged to his uncle, but the woods answered only to Gwydion. He knelt amid the grasses, brushing his bare fingers against the roots of an oak. "Talk to me, friend," he murmured.

When the morning sunlight touched their leaves, the trees *sang*. The song rose and fell, a murmur of appreciation and comfort—unheard by all but him.

The wind rustled through the browning leaves, and there was an answering groan. It might simply have been the creak of wood, shifting as sunlight warmed tree bark. But Gwydion could hear something flitting beneath the trees, rushing in a desperate attempt to escape.

Gwydion rose. He did not run; he did not even quicken his pace. He simply walked barefoot through the wood, and when he pushed the ferns aside, he saw the creature.

The fox was small, with fear-wild eyes and heaving breaths.

"Hello there, little one," said Gwydion softly. He kept his voice low, the way he did when his nephews woke from nightmares. "You look as though you've had better mornings."

The fox trembled. It was a beautiful creature, with sleek fur and dark eyes. It looked at Gwydion, unsure of which way to run. There came the distant bay of a hound. The fox flinched, its ears low against its head.

Gwydion heaved a sigh. Of course the hounds would catch the scent *now*.

"My brother would enjoy having your pelt as a trophy," Gwydion said. "But he ruined my morning, so I'm inclined to return the favor." He rose to his feet and hummed softly. The roots of the tree parted, becoming a narrow corridor. The fox looked at the new path, unconvinced.

A howl rang out. The fox's ears flattened in panic, and it bolted.

Gwydion followed. He had never been good with long distances; too much exertion left him winded and exhausted for hours. But he was a swift sprinter.

And in a forest, no one could catch him.

He divined a path through the oaks and alders, over tangled vetch and through late harvest wildflowers. The morning air was sweet in his chest—sun-burnished grasses, the tartness of blackberries, and a last whisper of autumn. As he ran, Gwydion guided the fox. He opened paths through the growth, keeping the creature going in the right direction.

From behind came the thud of hooves, the cries of hunters, and the barking of hounds. The sounds spurred Gwydion on. His brother had been the one to drag him from the castell. *It's not as though you're doing anything useful*, Amaethon had laughed as he pulled Gwydion from a desk full of coded correspondences and scattered notes.

The fox darted through Gwydion's path, tired but determined. Perhaps it was the creature's will to live that made him sympathize with it.

He hummed again, and the forest shifted, opening another path. This one led into a thicket of briars so tangled that the gardeners must have given up. Gwydion murmured, and the briars opened—just the slightest bit. The fox hesitated, looking into the depths. Once the fox vanished into those briars, nothing would catch it.

"Go on," said Gwydion.

The fox glanced at him, its eyes wide. Perhaps it was his imagination, but Gwydion thought he saw gratitude in the creature's gaze. It flitted into the thicket. Gwydion waited a heartbeat, then he closed the path behind the fox.

He had chosen briars for a reason. He reached to pluck several tufts of fur from the thorns. He turned them over in his fingers and darted in the other direction. He let a few strands fall as he sprinted around a thick oak. The bay of the hunting hounds echoed all around him.

With a whisper, Gwydion called to the tree. The old oak dozed in the morning sunlight, its golden and brown leaves fluttering in the breeze. At Gwydion's call, the oak slowly lowered one of its branches. There was an unhurried grace to the gesture; this tree had seen centuries—kings and princes, hunts and fights. A lone diviner that smelled of fox and walked barefoot was of little consequence to the oak.

Gwydion took hold of the proffered branch and heaved himself upward. He took care to put weight on his left hand; his right hand bore the old wood-and-leather brace that kept his index and middle fingers from bending too far. Once he was secure, the oak shifted again, lifting him the way an adult might heft a child to their shoulder. Soon, the oak would be sleeping for the winter; now, it would be shelter for yet another hunted creature.

When the tree went still, Gwydion was shrouded by leaves and morning mist. He waited.

He did not have to wait long.

Three horses cantered along a well-worn path. Their hounds hastened after them, barking and nipping at one another as they chased the scent of prey. One of the hounds, a long-eared creature with a sagging face, sniffed diligently around the roots of the old oak. The other hounds seemed to catch on, and then all of them were circling the tree and barking—at first in eagerness, then in confusion. These creatures had been bred to hunt and give chase, but they could not find their prey.

The hunters drew their horses to a halt. The first, a golden-haired noble with freckles along his pale cheekbones, gazed at the tree. "Has the fox taken refuge among the roots? An old den, perhaps?"

"I don't see one." The second noble had dark skin and hair bound into intricate braids. She frowned. "Did the hounds pick up a second trail?"

The last hunter slid from his horse. Amaethon, son of Dôn, had burnished red-gold hair, fair skin, and all the warmth of a hawk watching for mice. Only he knew to look upward. "Brother," he said the word like a curse.

Gwydion grinned down at him. "I wondered when you would arrive."

"I should have known you would take the place of the fox," said Amaethon. "Rather fitting, considering your temperament. And I admit, skinning you does have a certain appeal." There came a low chuckle from the other hunters.

"But would I end up a rug before your hearthfire, or would you wear me like a cloak?" asked Gwydion, raising his brows. "I could live with the former. A little rest, a little warmth."

This brought forth a louder bout of laughter. A victory in Gwydion's favor.

"Come down, Gwydion," said Amaethon, voice like simmering coals.

Gwydion did not go down. The last time he'd come down when Amaethon sounded like that, Gwydion had been nine and Amaethon sixteen. Gwydion had hidden in a hay loft, having stolen his older brother's clothing after finding him and a girl rolling around in the stables. Gwydion still bore a scar in the shape of a man's hand on his upper arm where Amaethon had gripped him.

"I rather enjoy the view from here," said Gwydion lightly.

Amaethon snapped his fingers—and it was as though he had used firesteel. Flame bloomed in his hand.

The other two hunters fell into a quiet hush, their expressions torn between apprehension and wonder. Magic had that effect.

"Come down, brother," said Amaethon. "Or I'll do away with your hiding place."

It was not a bluff. When Amaethon's divining manifested itself, the king's commander had taken the young boy to apprentice. Amaethon had been trained with steel and maps, battles and blood. And when his skill with flame proved to be deadly, the royal blacksmith crafted him a sword that could be stained with pitch and set alight. It wasn't a practical sword, but the fear it instilled was a weapon all its own.

At the sight of the fire, unease flared in Gwydion's stomach. He could feel the oak tree, the strength and the life beneath his fingertips. This had been a jest, a simple trick, and the tree should not burn for it. All around them, the song of the forest went silent.

Amaethon reached out, ready to set the oak alight—

And then his arm was jerked back, as though by some invisible force, cracking the back of his hand into his nose. There was a sickening crunch, and Amaethon dropped to his knees, both hands flying to his face. The fire dropped from his fingers and caught in a few fallen leaves. Amaethon looked more startled than pained, his gaze darting around him. But there was no one close enough to hurt him.

"What did you—" he began to say, fury in every word. But before he could react, a fourth figure stepped from the trees.

She wore a dress of copper—not dyed threads but *copper*. The metal flowed down her neck and shoulders like snake scales. A scar was etched through her right brow and her dark hair was threaded with silver.

"Hello, brother," she said, stepping on the fire. The flames guttered beneath her heel.

Amaethon glowered at her. He pulled his hand from his bleeding nose, glaring at his rings as though they had committed a deep betrayal. As fire answered to Amaethon, metal answered to his sister.

"Arianrhod," Amaethon gritted out from behind his broken nose.

"Younger brothers," she said, with a sidelong look at the visiting nobles. "They never stop squabbling, do they?"

That brought forth the loudest laugh, but Gwydion heard an undercurrent of relief beneath the mirth. They were glad to return to the thrust and parry of a verbal spar, rather than the threat of a wildfire.

"Come along," said Arianrhod. "My uncle sent word that his baker has spun together some new delight, and he wishes to share it with you." She inclined her head toward Amaethon. "You, as well."

"Of course," Amaethon said, recovering his temper. His moods burned away as swiftly as his divined flame, and he looked as amiable as any young man on a fox hunt. He led the hunters away, their voices and the hounds' barking fading into the quiet sounds of the forest.

Arianrhod crossed her arms. The copper scales of her dress glittered in the morning sunlight. "Come down, Gwydion."

This time, he did.

"Before you say a word," said Gwydion, his bare feet softly hitting the earth, "I would like to remind you that I just gave you the best gift you will receive this autumn."

Arianrhod's mouth was set in a disapproving line. "Did you?"

Gwydion grinned. "No one else at the festival next week will have the joy of breaking Amaethon's nose."

Her frown fractured into a begrudging smile, one that she hid behind her hand. She had a smith's hands—flecked with burn scars and calluses.

"Admit it," said Gwydion. "You've wanted to do that for years."

"He'll snore worse than ever now," said Arianrhod.

"When he finally gets his wish to invade Dyfed, they'll hear him coming."

Arianrhod made a sound that was half exhale, half laugh. "I'm sure he'll tell everyone that it was broken in a valiant battle with an afanc. And not that his older sister made him punch himself."

"You could use the rumor to your advantage," said Gwydion. "Story has a power all its own. A few whispers, and all will know you as the powerful diviner that drove the would-be prince to his knees."

He was only half joking. While Amaethon was practicing with swords and spears, Gwydion had been learning how to listen at keyholes and spread rumors. Magic aside, his voice had always been his best weapon.

The kingdom of Gwynedd had no spymaster—and it did not need one.

It had a trickster instead.

"The rumors," said Arianrhod with a prim little grimace, "already say that I am a wicked diviner who lives in a magicked fortress and plots King Math's demise. And that my twins were born on the floor of the great hall. I've had enough of your stories." She sighed, tilting her head back. "Did you truly have to taunt Amaethon? What if I hadn't come along? All you had to do was sit on a horse and watch him chase a fox. And now, I'll have to explain to Uncle why I felt it necessary to maim his heir."

"He's not the heir," said Gwydion at once.

Arianrhod gave him a tolerant look. "Not yet." She blew out a breath. "Why *did* you sabotage the hunt?"

Gwydion shrugged. "The fox was sentenced to death for the crime of being defenseless. I thought it rather unfair."

It was a light answer but with a ring of truth. What Gwydion did not say, would never say, was that when he saw that fox, he'd felt a prickle of empathy. He knew what it meant to be easy prey.

If Gwydion had been born to any other family, he would have been beloved. With his divining, he could have charmed crops, sung fields to life, whispered harvests into glorious yield.

But the family of Dôn was a family of magic.

Arianrhod and her twin brother, Gofannon, had power over metal. Amaethon had his fire. Only Gilfaethwy had been born without magic, and he had been exiled to a distant friary after his... indiscretions.

The other children of Dôn carved themselves a place in the kingdom of Gwynedd: Arianrhod created elaborate works of armor; Gofannon commanded boats and worked with shipwrights; Amaethon was groomed for war.

When one's siblings divined metal and fire, being able to grow a fern was not a feat to boast of. But Gwydion knew that power was more than magic or weapons. Power was simply another word for *advantage*. If he could not best his enemies in battle, he would do so from the shadows. His voice and sleight of hand were his weapons.

And if everyone overlooked him, they would never see him coming.

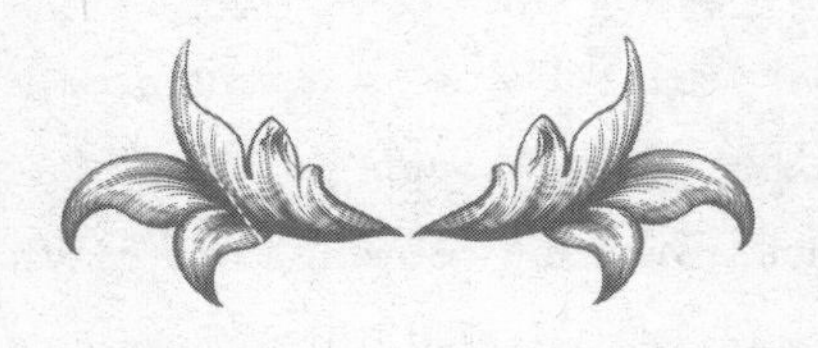

CHAPTER 3

BRANWEN BEGAN HUNTING when she was nine.

It began with an unruly flock of sheep. The shepherd complained to Branwen's mother that his herd was avoiding a large swath of pasture and grazing the rest to the ground. Branwen listened from her place in the corner, where she had been trying to mend a torn shirt. Seeing an opportunity for more excitement, she slipped outside.

She went to the pastures. True to the shepherd's word, the sheep were avoiding the eastern edge of the fields. Branwen looked for the cause but found nothing. Finally, she unbound her iron-stitched blindfold.

That was when she heard the screaming. It seemed the magic that touched her right eye had changed her other senses, as well. Without the touch of iron, she could sense that which other mortals could not.

Branwen had hastened to a clump of bushes, where she found a coblynau caught in a hunter's snare. It looked a little like a tiny man with astonishingly ugly features. It was said coblynau haunted quarries and mines, and they could find the richest veins if treated kindly.

The iron had snagged on one of the coblynau's sleeves, rendering it helpless. The creature was exhausted and near starving. Branwen could have slain it. But the coblynau was no great monster. Carefully, she reached down and freed it. It bit Branwen for her troubles and then scurried into the bushes.

But the next morning, she found an uncut, beautiful red crystal on her doorstep.

After that, Branwen earned a reputation as the girl who could find and deal with magicked troubles. She kept quiet about her eye and simply let the villagers think that she had a knack for finding the unseen. She discovered a stray but friendly pwca—a shape-changing creature—disguised in the form of a goat and brought it to her poorest neighbor, advising them to feed it well. In return, the pwca had blessed their farm with milk and good harvests. One weaver was haunted by an owl and feared that it was an ill omen. Branwen climbed a tree to find an irate and wholly ordinary owl with a nest of eggs. She had returned to the weaver with bleeding arms and reassurances that the owl meant no harm.

When she was thirteen, she began to hunt the true monsters. There had been a llamhigyn y dwr that had nearly drowned her in a murky lake—and Branwen bore the scars across her left shoulder. An iron-mad pwca took the form of a wolf and killed two men before Branwen slew it with an arrow.

She *had* attempted less dangerous means of earning coin: She worked as a messenger, using her sight to navigate the outskirts of

Annwvyn without falling into traps. But that did not pay enough. Then Branwen tried her hand at being a mercenary—until one of the men said something rather unsavory, and Branwen knocked out three of his teeth with her dagger. There was the month she spent as a ring fighter. Then a single week of serving drinks before the tavern-keeper, Glaw, declared her too restless for indoor work.

Branwen was not a mercenary, nor a messenger, nor a server of drinks.

She was a huntress. And she was tired of pretending to be anything else.

"What do you mean he's dead?"

Ifor's house was far more luxurious than Branwen was used to. The rugs were plush and thick, the air sweetened with burning herbs and the smell of fresh bread. As barwn, Ifor collected taxes, defended the village and its surrounding lands, and would be required to raise troops if Gwynedd commanded it. But even with his lavish house and servants, he was merely a vassal to nobles of higher rank.

One of the servants had led Branwen into a sitting room, whispered into the barwn's ear, and scurried away. In hindsight, that servant had been wiser than Branwen. She should have sent a written note and a request for her fee. But Branwen knew how it felt to lose family, and she had wanted to do him a kindness.

Barwn Ifor stood before her, hands clenched and mouth drawn tight. Grief radiated from every quiver in his voice. "My son can't be dead."

Branwen reached into her cloak and withdrew the heavy signet ring. "This was all I could bring back."

"I don't believe you," said Ifor. He was well past middle age, with silver hair and a brittleness about his eyes. "My son is alive. You're—you're wrong."

"No," she replied, keeping her voice soft. "I'm not." She set the ring down on the barwn's table.

"I paid you to find him!" snarled Ifor.

"And I did," said Branwen. "What was left of him."

It was the wrong thing to say. She knew it the moment the words left her tongue.

Ifor's grief crystallized into anger. And before Branwen could so much as blink, he struck her across the face. The shock had her staggering, and instinctively, her hand rose up to protect her cheek. Her fingers came away bloodied. His own signet ring had scratched a shallow cut across her face.

"Get out," Ifor snarled.

He did not have to ask her again. Branwen turned on her heel and strode from the room. To her surprise, the servant appeared as though she'd been waiting. "This way," said the servant, putting a hand on Branwen's shoulder.

It was not in Branwen's nature to take orders, but the gentle weight of the older woman's hand and the warmth of her voice were irresistible. She could not recall the last time anyone had taken care of her. She found herself being guided into a well-kept kitchen. A cook was tending to a cawl simmering above the fire, and when she saw Branwen, sympathy flashed across her face.

"Come here," said the servant. She picked up a cloth, dampened it with cool water, and pressed it against Branwen's cheek. "You're lucky he missed your eye. It's not as though you have one to spare."

Branwen snorted. Most people were under the impression she had lost her right eye in a childhood accident. It was a safer explanation than the truth.

"Did you find the barwn's son?" asked the cook.

Branwen nodded. She did not have to explain; both the cook and the servant grimaced.

"I heard the lad before he left," said the cook. "He was blathering on about joining the Wild Hunt."

Branwen jerked in surprise. "What?" She thought the son had simply wandered too near Annwvyn, not that he had been fool enough to try and enter the Hunt.

The Wild Hunt was held on the last day of autumn every fifth year. It was a hunt for the immortal King Arawn and the mortal King Pwyll, in celebration of their friendship between their two kingdoms—Annwvyn and Dyfed.

No one knew what they hunted, but there were rumors aplenty: monsters, legends, even mortals. Those who lived near the village of Argoed knew better than to trespass into the woods on a Hunt year, lest they go missing.

"Why?" asked Branwen. "He must have known that was certain death."

"He was saying that the winner of the Hunt was granted a boon," said the cook. "And he wanted to be the greatest fighter in all the lands."

The servant snorted. "As if a noble from Gwynedd would be allowed two steps into Annwvyn."

"I know," said the cook, with a long-suffering sigh. "He's a daft one."

"Was," said the servant quietly. "He *was* a daft one."

They all went silent for a moment, bowing their heads in acknowledgment.

Branwen shifted on her feet. "I should be going," she said, pulling the damp cloth from her cheek. "It's an hour's walk home."

"You give your mam these from me," said the cook. She hurriedly bundled up an assortment of hard cheeses, salted fish, and a loaf of bread. "She helped deliver my niece a few years back. Tell her Olwenna still thinks well of her."

Branwen took the food gladly. "I will."

The gift meant she would not spend what little coin she had on food. While she could hunt for her meals, there were other necessities: cloth for mending and sewing, tools, and medicinal herbs. So many herbs. She had meant to visit the village apothecary, but without the barwn's payment, Branwen could not afford it.

She left the village, ducking between houses until she was in the familiar countryside.

The sun sank toward the western seas and evening stole across the golden fields. She quickened her step, her hand resting on the hilt of her dagger. With Nos Calan Gaeaf a week away, it was best not to be out at dusk. The last night of autumn was known to be rife with magic.

As she rounded a bend in the path, she saw a creature waiting in the branches of an oak tree. For a moment, Branwen's heartbeat quickened... and then she recognized the familiar black-and-white fur.

It was a cat. Her cat, to be specific.

"What are you doing out here?" said Branwen, frowning. "I locked you in the house."

Palug stood, stretched, and then darted down the tree. Even among cats, he was a gorgeous creature. His black-and-white fur was long and well-groomed, his eyes were like cut emeralds, and he was quite large for a cat. But he had a kitten's mew when he wanted food.

"Come out to greet me?" said Branwen, but concern tightened her belly. He should not have been outside; the neighbors had seen a pack of stray hounds wandering the countryside, likely escaped from Gwynedd's soldiers. Branwen knew it was only a matter of time until a shepherd scraped together what coin they had and came knocking at Branwen's door. Stray hounds were more dangerous than wolves because they did not fear humans. Sooner or later, they would attack livestock. It would be a dangerous and ill-paid job, but Branwen would take it. In the wild country, one needed the goodwill of their neighbors. And Branwen needed it more than most.

Palug batted at her bundle of food and gazed up at her adoringly.

"Oh, no," Branwen said. "This cheese is not for you."

Palug's tail lashed in irritation. Branwen did the only thing she could: She scooped up the cat. He squirmed for half a heartbeat before he seemed to decide that the indignity of being picked up was worth a few chin scratches. He purred, relaxing against Branwen's shoulder.

"Monster," said Branwen affectionately.

Her home looked as it always had: stone walls, thatched roof, and windows that remained firmly closed during the fall and winter months. A small wooden fence rounded the home and tree. Gorse grew up along that fence—a valuable protection against wild magic, even if she did have to cut it back every year. Branwen opened the gate, allowing Palug to slip from her shoulder. The cat trotted to the front door and meowed back at her, as if insisting she hasten her pace.

The door was ajar.

Fear slid into Branwen's belly. She hurried into the house. "Mam?" she called.

There were no signs of violence, nothing out of the ordinary. Dried bundles of mint hung near the windows, a three-legged stool rested by the hearth, a half-written letter sat on the small table and a cup of tea beside it. Branwen touched her fingertips to the cup. Still warm—which meant it had not been abandoned for long.

She stalked outside and gazed at the tangled web of footprints in the dirt of the yard. And there it was—the delicate shape of a woman's foot.

Barefoot, Branwen thought, a sympathetic shiver running through her.

Palug meowed as though he could not understand why he was not being fed.

"If you were a hound," said Branwen, following the footprints toward the gate, "you could find her for me."

Palug sat back on his haunches and looked away, haughtily indifferent.

"Keep the mice out of the food," said Branwen, "and I'll give you a bit of cheese."

The trail led south. Branwen's boots were worn so thin that she could feel every ridge in the road. A sheepdog watched her pass;

a few small chickens scampered across the trail, heading home to roost. The shadow of the mountains loomed on her left. In evenings, Annwvyn looked as murky as a dark sea. Even Branwen dared not venture beneath its branches after the sun had set; her magicked eye wouldn't protect her. She would just be able to see what came for her.

Despite the dangers, Branwen preferred Gwynedd's wild countries to its cities. She liked the stillness of a forest, the beauty of a spiderweb beaded with morning dew, and the breath of cold mountain air.

A distant howl made Branwen quicken her pace. She hurried along the path, rounding small hills and swerving past thickets of trees until she stepped around a large alder.

Ahead was a familiar silhouette. Branwen's heart lurched in relief. "Mam," she called.

Branwen's mother had been beautiful in her day—straight-backed, with hair like snow and bright eyes. Some said that Branwen looked like her, but Branwen couldn't see it. Where her mam was soft and welcoming, Branwen was sinewy and scarred. Mam had the delicate beauty of a pressed flower, and Branwen was as sharp and pale as the white crow she'd named herself for.

"Mam," said Branwen again.

Mam halted. She wore a loose dress for working around the house; it was far too thin to be worn outside. Her bare forearms were prickled with gooseflesh, and her feet were bare and muddied. There was a line between her brows, a distance to her expression.

Mam said a name that wasn't Branwen.

Branwen winced, glad that they weren't too near Annwvyn. Mam was one of the few who remembered her birth name. Branwen had forsaken it long ago, only using it once when she hunted a murderer. On that hunt, the name *Branwen* would have alerted her prey that she was after him.

"Your cousin invited us for a meal," said Mam distractedly, her gaze roaming over the fields. "We should have left earlier—we'll be late—"

Derwyn had not lived near the village in years. That Mam could not remember . . . it made Branwen feel ill. Mam was forgetting more and more.

"Mam," said Branwen, voice gentling. "Derwyn sent word that he cannot meet us tonight."

Mam went still. "He did?"

"Yes." Branwen took her mother's arm, gently steering her back toward home. "We'll see him tomorrow."

A year ago, Branwen would have balked at telling such a lie. But since Mam had first begun to forget, Branwen learned that evenings were the worst of it. Something in the shifting light seemed to make Mam restless and uncertain, her memories waning.

Evenings were a time for magic and forgotten things.

Mornings brought remembrance.

Branwen woke early, boiling water for tea and grumbling when Palug wound between her legs and meowed for cheese.

Mam was awake. She was bright-eyed, sitting beside the fire as she braided her white hair. "Good morning," she said. "When did you return from the village?" There was no hint of the confusion from last night. And perhaps that was the most painful part—these moments when all was well. Branwen wanted to cling to them, to hold on to these mornings tightly enough that they might never slip away.

To keep her hands busy, Branwen picked up a small knife and an apple and began to slice. While she did not *lie*, she chose her truths. "Late," she replied, popping a bit of apple into her mouth.

"And did you find the barwn's lad?"

Branwen grimaced.

"I can't tell if you're making that face because you found him or not," said Mam, raising one pale brow.

"I found him." Branwen twirled the small paring knife through her fingers. "... Or rather, parts of him."

"Poor lad." Mam finished the braid, letting it rest against her lean shoulder. She gestured for Branwen to come closer. "He should have known better than to venture into Annwvyn on a Hunt year."

"According to Ifor's cook, the Wild Hunt *was* his aim," Branwen said as her mother began to braid her hair. Mam's fingers were swift and sure, and the slight graze of fingernails against Branwen's scalp made her shiver. Mam had been the one to teach Branwen how to braid her hair, how to keep it from being snagged in a bowstring or falling into her eye. When she had been a child, she had sat between her mother's knees while she plaited her hair every morning. These days, Branwen mostly tended to her own hair. But the touch was familiar and comforting, and she leaned into it. "He thought he could win it."

Mam shook her head. "Foolish child. I pity his father, though. No one should ever live through the loss of their child." She folded the braid, making a crown of it, and pinned the hair in place. She nodded in satisfaction.

It was such a small little expression, but it made a lump rise to

Branwen's throat. These moments when her mam mothered her were becoming rarer and rarer. Part of her wanted to cling to them, to cling into her mam's lap and be a child again. And another part of her wanted to recoil, to brace herself for the inevitable loss when Mam no longer remembered her.

Branwen's nails dug into her palms. "I need to bring a few things to Rhain. Can you feed the chickens?"

"Of course. And then I have a few shirts to mend," said Mam, waving her off. "How do you rip so many of them? Do you swim through briars?"

Branwen thought of the clawed fingers of the cyhyraeth.

"Yes," she said airily. "Briars."

Rhain had lived on the next farm over for as long as Branwen could recall. He had always been cantankerous, old, and yet surprisingly formidable. He taught Branwen how to hunt and fight. He had taken a liking to her when she was a child. While her bluntness seemed to irritate some villagers, Rhain only let out a hoarse chuckle when Branwen returned one of his barbs with her own.

Branwen brought a basket of apples and a loaf of bara cymysg. The maslin bread was a little stale, but the apples were crisp and sweet.

Rhain was weeding in his garden. He had fashioned an overturned barrel into a table, and a few of his tools sat upon it. His back and shoulders were a little bowed, and his hair looked like old cobwebs, but his eyes were sharp. "Morning, girl," he said. His gaze settled on Palug. "You brought the monster, I see."

"Be polite or he might devour your sheep," said Branwen solemnly. Palug regarded the old hunter for a moment, then headbutted Rhain's knee. Rhain reached down to rub the cat's ears.

"Can't you use that eye of yours to tell if he's truly magic?" he asked. He was one of the few people who knew the truth. He was trustworthy—and besides, he had no one to tell but his chickens.

Branwen tapped the corner of her right eye. "I could. Only trouble is all cats are a little bit monstrous. Hard to tell if he's more monster than the rest."

Rhain grumbled softly beneath his breath. "What brings you here so early?"

"Mam wandered off again," said Branwen. "Last night."

A flicker of sadness touched Rhain's face. "Oh. I'm sorry." He brushed some of the dirt from his hands. "I was in the village last night. When I looked in on her beforehand, she was at home."

Rhain had promised to do his best to keep an eye on Mam when Branwen was hunting. But she could not expect him to be there at all hours of the day. "It's not your fault," she said. She leaned against the barrel, letting some of her exhaustion creep into her shoulders. There were very few people she allowed to see her weakness, but Rhain was one of them. He would never hold it against her.

"I cannot keep leaving her," said Branwen. "One of these days, she will wander someplace dangerous."

Rhain's face was grave. "You need to hire someone," he said, with a blunt honesty that Branwen appreciated. "I'm not spry enough to follow her at all hours of the day. And I have my own home to tend to. Find a young servant or one of the farmhands."

"As though I could pay them."

"You need more coin," said Rhain.

Branwen snorted. "Truly an inspiring insight."

Rhain gave her a tolerant look. "You need to take that pride of yours and put it aside." He crossed his arms; he had rolled his sleeves to his elbows, showing off old scars. "Monster hunting is all well and good, but you need steady work."

"I have tried other work," said Branwen. "Hunting is the only skill I have. I thought perhaps working for nobles would help, but all the barwn paid me was this." She touched the bruise at her cheek.

Rhain shook his head, grizzled gray hair falling across his eyes. "Girl, the nobility are as temperamental as cats and twice as likely to bite you. I'd find a wealthy merchant or those newly come into coin. They'd pay well for the taste of a hunt... even if you're merely chasing foxes."

Branwen bit her lip. Her gaze fell on Palug, who had begun grooming himself in the morning light. She thought of the warm place above the hearth where she slept, the familiar smells and tastes of home. If she did as Rhain advised, she would have to leave them. There were no wealthy merchants near the village of Argoed; she would have to venture into one of Gwynedd's cities. She feared her mother would take a turn for the worse in Branwen's absence. Mam thrived in the familiar. An upset in her day would unbalance her. But if leaving was the only way to pay for Mam's herbs...

"I will think on it," she said finally.

Rhain nodded. "Call on me, if you need help," he said. "I'll do what I can."

"Thank you," said Branwen.

They remained in comfortable silence for a few moments before he said, "What *did* happen to the barwn's son?"

Branwen made a sour face. "I found a few bones in a cyhyraeth's lair."

Rhain's battle-scarred hands froze on a weed. "That's a fate I'd wish on no one. I thought they didn't come this way?"

"The iron's driving them into Annwvyn." Branwen reached down to pick up Palug. She wanted the warmth and softness of him. Palug meowed in annoyance, but he allowed it. "With all the kingdoms trying to grow their territory, iron is leaking into the rivers now. Soon, I fear we'll have monsters from all the isles retreating into those mountains. And crossing our fields to get there."

"It's too early for that kind of talk," said Rhain. He shook his head. "Someone will have to send word to Caer Dathyl if this keeps up. King Math is bound by duty to protect all of Gwynedd's people from Annwvyn. Even a village like ours."

Branwen raised a brow. "Would you go to the royal court yourself?"

He shuddered. "I'd rather walk into Annwvyn blindfolded and naked."

"That would be a sight," she said teasingly. "Might be enough to make all the monsters flee."

"Jest all you want, girl," replied Rhain, "but royals are far more bloodthirsty than any water wraith or magicked cat. Mark my words. Stay away from the lot of them."

Branwen laughed. Rhain spoke as though he expected a king to ride over the hillside at any moment. "What kind of royal would have anything to do with me?"

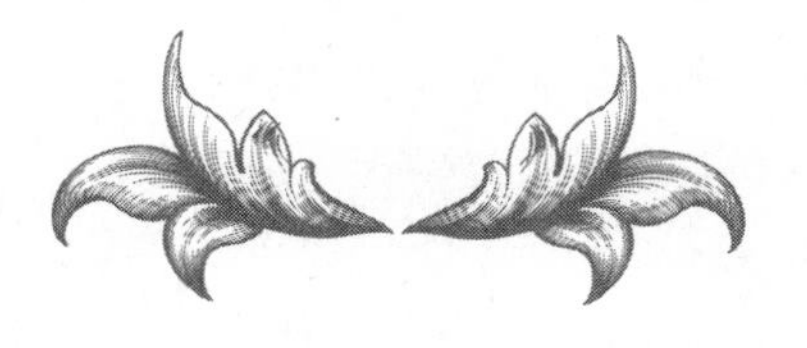

CHAPTER 4

EVERY FIFTH YEAR, King Arawn of Annwvyn summoned the Wild Hunt.

It began at autumn's end, on the night of Nos Calan Gaeaf when the boundaries between magical and mortal were thinnest. In bard-song, the Hunt simply appeared from nothing. The immortal hunters of Annwvyn and the mortal hunters of the kingdom of Dyfed met deep within the forest. And then they took to the Hunt in a revel of blood and magic and madness.

Those bards would have been rather disappointed to see precisely how much *work* went into the Hunt's preparations.

Hunting camps took time to assemble, and this was no exception. Tents were constructed, tables and chairs hauled by wagon, weapons unpacked, food prepared, and barrels of drink rolled into place. The servants were sent ahead first, followed by the hunt master and those that tended the hounds. King Pwyll of Dyfed and a handful of chosen nobles arrived a week before the Hunt, to settle into their tents and see friends that had made the journey. And it was rumored that King Arawn and King Pwyll took those seven days to reaffirm their friendship.

The otherfolk welcomed the nobles of Dyfed. They moved among the humans with a wild grace, their mortal guises discarded. They had hair braided into flowers and eyes the delicate shade of violets; there were shape-changers that flickered from form to form, singing tales of long-dead heroes; corgis trotted among the camp, carrying messages attached to their collars; a handful of mortal ironfetches drifted among the folk.

In the bustle of the hunting camp, no one noticed a single young man. He worked alongside the servants, helping carry tables and arrange chairs. Those who knew his name pretended not to see him, and those who didn't thought he was just another servant.

A voice rang out from above him. "Hiding again, my lord?"

The young man looked up. Straightening, he tried to convey a sense of easy confidence. Which was not easy when he held a chair in each arm. "I'm not a lord," he said.

One of the otherfolk sat in the branches of the tree, one leg dangling and arms crossed over her chest. She perched with an easy poise. "My apologies," she said. "Prince Pryderi, son of King Pwyll and heir to the throne of Dyfed... are you hiding again?"

Pryderi fought back a smile. "I'm not hiding. I'm helping."

She tilted her head. It made her even more birdlike. "You are aware my kind can sense untruths, are you not?"

Pryderi gave her a shallow bow. "It is considered a kindness among my people to allow certain lies to go unremarked upon, Lady Cigfa."

Cigfa slipped from the tree branch and landed beside him. Like all the tylwyth teg, she was gorgeous. The first time he had seen her, Pryderi thought Cigfa looked like a quail: short, rounded, with delicate features and keen eyes. Her cloak was lined with dark feathers, and she had a laugh like birdsong.

She was also King Arawn's champion, which made her the second deadliest person in camp.

"Do all mortal princes help carry furniture?" she asked.

Pryderi shrugged. "I wouldn't know. I have more experience with goats and chickens than princes."

Cigfa laughed. "Unfortunately, I did not seek you out for your expertise with chickens and goats. The king sent me to find you."

Pryderi forced his lips into a smile. "It would be a joy to speak with my father again."

Cigfa offered him an indulgent look. "I don't need magic to tell you're lying," she said. "Your face speaks more loudly than words."

"I shall endeavor to make my face more believable," he replied.

He liked Cigfa. She had an infectious smile and a wicked sense of humor, but there was no cruelty in her. She had been given the task of shepherding him through the formalities of the Wild Hunt. Even if she wouldn't tell him precisely what the Hunt consisted of. No one had told him. His father, King Pwyll, said it was tradition. None but the kings ever partook in the Hunt more than once, and everyone else learned the rules as they hunted.

"The problem is that I have nothing to do but move furniture," said Pryderi, falling into step beside Cigfa. "I've no diplomatic duties, and most of my own people are too wary or too eager to befriend me. The chairs don't ask uncomfortable questions, at least."

"The Hunt will begin in seven days' time," Cigfa said. "Then you might lose yourself in the woods rather than hide in your tent."

Pryderi sighed. "The problem with the Wild Hunt is that... well, it's a hunt. I will be expected to hunt something."

"Have you never hunted?" she asked. "I would have thought..." She let the sentence trail off delicately.

"That because I was raised common, I would be hunting for my own meals?" He smiled to demonstrate her words had not offended him. "My foster father was a farmer. The only hunting I ever did was shooting the foxes that dared try for the chickens."

"You can fight," she replied, her eyes sliding to the blade tucked into his belt. "I heard the reason you were invited into the Hunt was because you beat a young noble in a duel."

Pryderi shook his head. "I don't know how to duel."

Cigfa frowned, likely confused by the truth in his voice. "But I heard—"

"I can fight," said Pryderi. "I never said I could duel." He resisted the impulse to rub at the back of his neck. He still bore the bruises of that fight. "I was cornered by a noble's son. He wished to test me, to see if I truly am the prince of Dyfed. He did so by trying to hit me upside the head and shove me into a river."

"So you defended yourself," said Cigfa.

"I did," said Pryderi. "By breaking his arm." The memory of cracking bone and snapping sinew made him wince. In that moment, he had not been thinking—his only instinct had been to survive.

He continued, "And as my attacker could no longer join the Hunt, my father invited me to take his place. I was not even supposed to be here." He looked at Cigfa. "Does that disappoint you?"

"My prince," said Cigfa, her eyes agleam. "You just became far more interesting."

He looked away. Taking pride in violence seemed wrong. Even now, he wanted to crawl out of his own skin. He felt stained by the fight, rather than proud of it. Back with his foster family, he would never have reacted so violently. But in the royal court, he was always on edge.

The camp was brimming with activity. Every tent had its own banner to mark a noble house—and soon, those nobles would be arriving at the gates of Annwvyn. The royal tent of Dyfed was larger than the house Pryderi had grown up in. When they reached it, Cigfa gave Pryderi a merry little bow. "Good luck, my prince."

Pryderi returned the bow with far less grace. Taking a steadying breath, he stepped into the royal tent. Old tapestries gilded the walls, and candles burned merrily. A table, laden with bottles of wine and plates of dried fruits and cheese, sat untouched. An overlarge chair—the makeshift throne for Dyfed's king—sat at the head of the table. Pryderi expected to see his father there, his warm face creased with years of responsibility.

But it was not a human that resided in that chair.

Pryderi stiffened, his heartbeat stuttering in his chest. At once, he realized his mistake. Cigfa had told him that he'd been summoned by a king... but she neglected to mention which one.

King Arawn, ruler over the tylwyth teg and the otherlands, sat before him.

Assumptions would kill him as surely as any blade, Pryderi thought. Particularly in Annwvyn, where words were true, dangerous, and ever-binding.

It was said that the Otherking wore a crown of bones, that he possessed all the beauty of the otherfolk and all the mercilessness of a monster. He had red hair, golden eyes, and a wolf's prideful countenance. Time could not touch him; he stood amid the ebb and flow of the world like an unchanging mountain. Pryderi knew better than to believe all the rumors. But the first time Pryderi had met King Arawn, he had seen that bone crown. It was no mere tale.

But for all the terror he instilled, Arawn had impeccable manners. "Heir of Dyfed," said King Arawn, inclining his head politely.

Pryderi realized his mistake and hastily dropped into a bow. "King Arawn. It is an honor."

Arawn chuckled. His voice was warm and rich as spiced wine. "I'm sure that is why you paled when you saw me."

Pryderi bit back a denial. The king would sense the untruth.

"Apologies," he said, keeping his head bowed. "I intended no offense. I expected a different king."

"Ah, I see." There was a rustle of fabric, and Pryderi looked up. Arawn had stood, one hand resting indolently on the back of the throne. He was a head taller than most men, with shoulders as broad as an oak. His crown was nowhere to be seen, but an old sword rested on the table.

"You wished to speak with me?" said Pryderi.

"I wished to take your measure before the Hunt." A human might have softened the words with a bit of flattery, but the folk did not bother. It was almost reassuring. In his father's court, Pryderi had come to expect the elegant dance of conversation, the half lies and insinuations. The otherfolk were dangerous, but none of them could lie. Not with their words.

Pryderi spread his arms. "Go on, then. I've disappointed lesser men. I might as well disappoint a great one."

That earned him a full-bodied laugh. Arawn stepped around the chair, circling Pryderi. "You have your father's charm."

"At least I possess something of his," said Pryderi wryly.

"Not his tact, though," Arawn added, his eyes warm. He reached for a bottle of wine. He poured two cups, offering one to Pryderi.

Pryderi took the drink with a nod of thanks. "I favor my mother in looks," he said. "Or so all the servants say when they think I cannot hear them."

In truth, Pryderi was not sure if he believed it. His birth mother, the queen, had welcomed him home with shaking hands and sobs, with whispered apologies and a desperation that made him want to pull away. She always seemed to want something from him—some nameless thing he could not give. It made him feel impossibly guilty.

Arawn let out a breath. "Unfortunate what happened to her."

Pryderi drank to drown out his reply. *Unfortunate* would not have been his choice of words. She had been imprisoned for nearly fifteen years for a crime she had never committed.

"Tell me," said Arawn, refilling Pryderi's cup. "What do you make of my kingdom?"

Pryderi said, "I have seen very little. But what I have seen is beautiful, Your Majesty. Your people have made me welcome. Cigfa has done a fine job keeping me out of trouble."

"Now there is your father's tact," replied Arawn. "It only took a little wine to draw it out."

Pryderi snorted. "My father's advisers will be thrilled to know that I should be attending council meetings with a cup in hand."

Arawn threw back his head and laughed again. "You remind me a little of myself when I was young. Hard as untempered metal. You will settle, young prince. A few years and the role will not seem so daunting. In the meantime, enjoy yourself. Your burdens will only grow heavier—but you will grow with them."

Pryderi blinked in surprise. He had imagined King Arawn had always ruled in Annwvyn. But there was a wistful remembrance in the king's voice.

"That is a relief to hear," said Pryderi. "I was not raised to rule."

Amusement glimmered behind Arawn's golden eyes. And before Pryderi could react, Arawn drew his sword. The scabbard was made of scarred leather, and the blade was heavy and unadorned. It was not a decorative weapon but one that had tasted blood—and King Arawn swung it at Pryderi's collarbone.

If he had been raised a prince, Pryderi would have frozen. Fear would have flooded his mouth, cascaded into his stomach, and held him hostage.

Pryderi was prince-born—but he was monster-raised.

It was not magic but instinct. The bone-deep memories flared to the surface.

And for the first time since walking into camp, he was unafraid.

He fell to one knee and rolled. In the same movement, he lunged toward Arawn. There was a dagger at the king's belt—and quicker than thought, Pryderi ripped the blade free. It was not iron but some gleaming metal he did not recognize.

The second time Arawn brought his sword down, Pryderi met blade with blade. Then he seized Arawn's wrist and dragged the Otherking closer, in reach of the short dagger. He had the tip at Arawn's ribs, ready to slide in if the king made a move.

But there was nothing. Arawn was utterly still, his breath even and unhurried. And he was *smiling*. Not a polite smile, but the bared teeth of a wolf.

Before Pryderi could react, Arawn spun his sword around, slamming the pommel into Pryderi's wrist. The dagger dropped from his suddenly numb hand.

Pryderi fell to his knees as he came back to himself. He had attacked a king. *He had attacked a king.* This was no mere scuffle with another noble lad; this was a diplomatic disaster. His fingers dug into the plush carpet as shame rolled over him like a wave.

"Majesty," he gasped. "I apologize."

This was why he should never have been brought to court, he thought miserably. In the court, he could never let down his guard. Because the moment he did... he became *this*. Pryderi licked his dry lips—and thought he tasted uncooked fish and falling rain—but it was merely an old remembrance. He yanked himself back to the present with a force of will. He did not want to return to those times in his waking hours; they haunted his dreams often enough.

Arawn's eyes flicked over Pryderi. "Why would you apologize? I attacked first."

Pryderi shook his head. "You are a king. One of my father's dearest friends. I should never have raised a weapon against you."

"I am your father's friend and a king," said Arawn with a gentle twitch of his brows. "But when I swung a blade at you, I became none of those things. I was a threat. You defended yourself. And you have nothing to be ashamed of. I wanted to take your measure, and I did."

Anger flickered through Pryderi. "This was...this was a test?"

"I heard of how you entered the Hunt. I thought perhaps it was simply rumor," said Arawn. He slipped his sword into its scabbard. He looked utterly at ease, untouched by the violence. "And I should be the one apologizing. I wished to see how you would react. Kings may talk all they like, but when their life is in danger, their true nature emerges. Some freeze; some cry out for help."

The words made Pryderi's stomach clench. "So that is my true nature?" he said quietly. "To see a challenge coming and answer in kind?"

Arawn gave an elegant shrug. His fine red cloak rippled, spilling across his shoulders like blood.

The Otherking said, "As I would. As would your father. Whether you like to admit it or not, you were raised to rule. Kings and monsters are grown from the same soil."

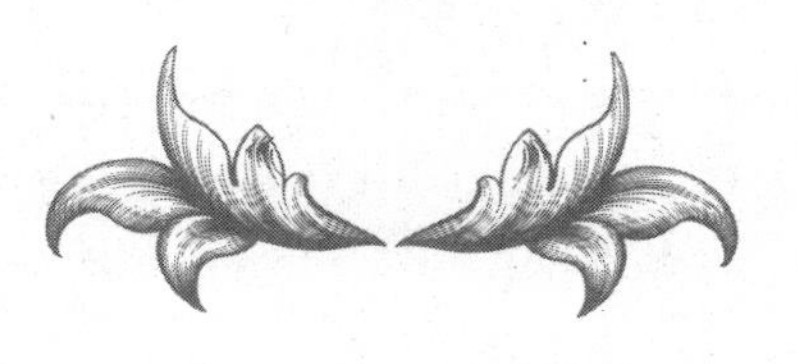

CHAPTER 5

GWYDION NEVER ENTERED Caer Dathyl through the main gates.

The northern kingdom of Gwynedd had a wild beauty: a rugged coastline, roughly hewn mountains, forests dripping with moss and lichen, and waterfalls that cascaded down sheer drops. It was a kingdom of bardsong and enchantment, of whispers and legend. And Caer Dathyl was the beating heart of the kingdom.

The city was crafted of human ingenuity and diviner magic. There were markets brimming with everything from oysters to spun wool; bards entertained passersby for a coin or two; and guards in finely crafted armor watched the crowds with benevolent fondness.

But when Gwydion looked at the crowd, he saw the beggars in the shadows, the children with bare feet and ragged hems, and the way one guard's purse was heavy with a recent bribe.

Those who visited the city would likely never notice. They would only see the grandeur and the wealth. They saw a fortress and a throne that would never fall. They did not see the rot that crept through the foundations, the petty cruelties, the dangers, and the inequality of it all. Gwydion saw all of that—but he also saw the potential of the city. Caer Dathyl was far from perfect, but in the right hands it could have been *more*.

Gwydion slipped into the city unseen. He had long ago drawn up his own maps of the secret places that one might come and go without being noticed by the city guard. This time, he used a well-worn tree to lift him up and over the high walls.

He walked down the street in a rough-spun cloak, his gaze roaming over the shop fronts. One did not let their guard down in the outskirts of Caer Dathyl, where lives and loyalty were cheaply bought. He ducked into one of the familiar eating houses. The smell of hot griddle stones and cider had sunk into the walls. Candles burned merrily at small tables—which were truly just barrels with some wood nailed into them. A boisterous group of soldiers were eating a midday meal; a drunken old man with a southern accent was mumbling that he was a champion of the Wild Hunt and someone should buy him another drink; two lovers from opposing noble houses were tucked away in a corner, their hoods raised and hands clasped.

Gwydion headed for a table near the back. A young woman sat there. She had short black hair and clothing that would make no sound when she walked. Two empty tankards sat before her, and she was on her third. "You're late," she said.

Gwydion slid onto the stool beside her. "I was unavoidably detained, Eilwen."

Eilwen cast him a sidelong look. With her keen eyes and instinct for survival, Eilwen was a remarkable thief. They had met when she'd tried to pickpocket him...only to find her hand trapped by a vine in his pocket.

Gwydion kept two gardens—the first was of herbs, poisons, and a few rare flowers. He had carved out a place on the castell grounds to grow his plants. He loved that garden for its quiet and its peace; he could spend a few hours with earth beneath his nails and fresh greenery all around.

The second garden consisted of a different kind of plant: thieves, gamblers, beggars, and a handful of children. Gwydion had grown this garden of eyes and intelligence for years. Some he paid in coin and others in food, while a few requested healing herbs. He knew each and every one of them, knew what they desired most dearly, and he used that. From them, he harvested secrets. He knew which guards took bribes, which nobles visited brothels, which gambling houses drugged their patrons to steal coin from their pockets, who tried to avoid taxes, and so much more. He memorized it all, refusing to put such power to paper. He knew too easily how such things could be stolen.

Eilwen reached for a plate of oggies and pushed one toward Gwydion. "Eat something. You look pale."

"Every time I need a compliment, I should come here," said Gwydion.

"You want flattery, try the brothel down the road," she replied. "You come to me for stolen truths."

He acknowledged that with a nod. Then he picked up an oggie, because he *was* hungry. Eilwen nodded in approval. They were not friends, but they were allies, and he had come to trust her. If only because he knew her secrets.

Gwydion took a careful bite of the pastry. He had to suck in a few breaths so the hot filling did not scald his mouth—chicken and leeks—but at least the food quieted his unruly stomach.

"What news have you gathered?" he asked.

Some of Gwydion's plants required threats or blackmail—but Eilwen's needs were simple. She had two younger brothers and a sister, and she wished to keep them out of the mines. Stealing had been Eilwen's way to keep them fed until Gwydion had discovered her. Now those same siblings were being trained as servants. It would be a safer life for them... and when they did work for noble houses, they would report all they saw to Gwydion.

Eilwen was bound to Gwydion as tightly as a person could be: His gold kept her family fed and housed, and the unspoken threat of arrest was never far from reach. Eilwen was a thief and a spy, and she would betray him if a better patron came along.

But even so, Gwydion liked her.

"Amaethon returned before you did," Eilwen said, wrapping her fingers around a tankard. "There was an incident in the courtyard."

Gwydion grimaced. He should have realized that Amaethon would find another outlet for his temper. "What happened?"

Eilwen shrugged. "He set a small fire."

"Not the horses," said Gwydion, alarmed. Even Amaethon would not go so far.

"No," agreed Eilwen. "There was an ambassador who said Amaethon was looking ragged after his hunt."

Gwydion waited for the rest of the tale. And then the horrible implication struck him. "He set an ambassador on *fire*?"

"Oh, of course not," said Eilwen. A moment of quiet. "He set the ambassador's *daughter* on fire."

Gwydion covered his eyes with his left hand. "Fallen kings. Is she all right?"

"She's fine," said Eilwen. "Her gown was burned right off her back without scorching a hair on her head. The fire was intended to frighten and shame. I'm no expert in magic. But it reminded me of when my siblings would put a snail down my shirt when they were frustrated about something else." She gave Gwydion a keen-eyed look. "Brothers, right?"

Gwydion did not agree nor disagree. He came here to buy information, not to give it away. "Anything else?"

"You remember that shipment of black powder that went missing?"

"Of course." Gwydion tasted his own drink. The cider was terrible, but at least there was no trace of poison. "I thought you knew nothing about that."

Eilwen's mouth went tight in irritation. "We didn't pull that job. Wish we had—would've made a tidy profit. No, some other crew did, and they're planning on dropping small jars of the powder in some of the bonfires of Nos Calan Gaeaf. Not enough to blow anything up," she added, seeing Gwydion's alarm. "But when those fires are lit, there'll be enough fizzle and flare to distract some fat-pursed lordlings."

"And then someone takes their valuables in the chaos," said Gwydion.

Eilwen tapped her nose, winking at him. "The princeling understands."

"I'm not a prince," he murmured.

Princes inherited thrones. Princes ruled lands. Gwydion was the youngest nephew of a king. He was neither heir nor spare—not with three older brothers and a sister. He was an afterthought, at best.

"You want us to stop them?" asked Eilwen. "Or leave the powder, then rob the crew afterward?"

Gwydion considered. "Find the jars, have the powder delivered to one of my safe houses. I'm sure I'll find a use for it."

Eilwen gave him a little salute with her oggie. "All right."

"My thanks." Gwydion set down his cup and half-eaten food and made to rise.

"One last thing," said Eilwen, and he went still. This was her way—to leave the most important bit of knowledge to the last moment.

"Yes?" said Gwydion.

Eilwen let out a breath. "Your nephews have snuck out of the castell again."

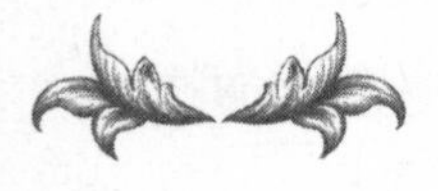

Gwydion left the eating house through a side door. Pulling his hood over his brow, he hastened down the street. He navigated the city with easy practice, darting between shops and homes. He knew where every fern had roots, where ivy could be used as a ladder, and where moss found a home in rotted wood.

There was a beggar at the intersection of two streets. He was one of Eilwen's watchers, observing the flow of travelers through the city.

Gwydion tossed two coins into his bowl. "Two boys," he said quietly. "Eight years of age. Which way did they go?"

The beggar jerked his head northward. "Heard 'em talking about some game, mayhap ten minutes ago."

A sickening chill went through Gwydion. His right hand clenched, and pain flashed through his cold-stiffened knuckles.

Without bothering to thank the man, he hastened up the street. It led to a row of houses owned by visiting nobles. They would come in the summertime to pay their respects to the throne, boast of new heirs, and buy fine things before returning to their cantrefs.

Two men stood near one of the empty houses. They wore the garb of gardeners and servants, but something in the way they held themselves made Gwydion's footsteps slow. Their skin was too soft, their hair lush and fingers unmarred by calluses. Spies, then.

Which meant two things: First, he was in the right place. And second, he had no time to lose.

Gwydion heard the twins before he saw them. There was a whisper of familiar voices, then a hushing sound. The noises came not from the houses but from *below*.

A sewer grate had been pried free of the street. The underground passages were wide enough to traverse with ease. Thieves, spies, and those that wished to go unseen found them useful. Unease flared in Gwydion's stomach. He would have preferred the twins had climbed a tree. He had never been fond of dark, small spaces.

With a muttered curse, Gwydion knelt. He carefully settled his feet on the rungs of an iron ladder. Instantly, it was as though someone had stuffed his ears with cloth. The quiet song of the trees, grasses, moss, even the lichen—all were plunged into silence.

Iron drove back magic. Diviners like himself had to be careful of jewelry and armor, choosing pieces without traces of iron. It was why Gwydion's hand brace was leather and wood, why all his family's signet rings were silver and gold, and why Amaethon never challenged Arianrhod. Only she was trusted to craft his armor.

Magic was rare among humanity. Commoners called such people *other-touched* while the nobles referred to them as *diviners*. Those divining magic could call to some part of the world, and that element would answer in kind. Diviners discovered young were often taken from their families and given to a noble patron—someone with the resources to find a tutor and keep the diviner safe until they were of an age to use their magic. In exchange for that education and protection, diviners would often work for those patrons willingly. And those that were unwilling... *well*. Divining was a valuable tool. Too valuable to be let go.

But power was not without cost. Every divining drained the diviner. Fire diviners used the heat from their bodies to kindle flame; stone and metal diviners sapped the metal from their bodies; wind diviners could suffocate themselves if they were not careful; and water diviners could die of dehydration. But some costs were higher than others. When Amaethon overused his magic, all he needed was a warm hearth and heated blankets. Arianrhod's meals were heavy with liver, eggs, and meats.

Gwydion did not know what his own divining cost. He was the only living diviner of trees and plants. When he drew on his magic for too long, he grew tired and pale, and dealt with headaches. Wounds and broken bones were slow to recover fully, *if* they recovered. One of the healers had pondered that perhaps his magic drew away Gwydion's ability to properly consume his food. Another was certain that sunlight was all that Gwydion needed. One wanted to bury him in freshly tilled earth up to his chin. After years of being an object of study, Gwydion had stopped going to the healers. They gave him no answers, only frustrations. He crafted his own brace for a hand that had never healed from the hard slam of a door; he planned his own meals; and he spent his power with care. Every divining was a choice with the knowledge that the price would be paid at a later time. And he never knew how steep the cost would be. But even if he never reached for his magic, he could always *hear* plants. They sang and whispered, murmured in tongues so old that even the tylwyth teg had no language to answer.

Surrounded by the iron of the city sewers, Gwydion's world of magic fell silent.

The twins' voices echoed hollowly from the stone and metal walls. Gwydion rounded a corner, and there they were—two boys studying a piece of parchment.

"I think we took a wrong turn," said Lleu. He held a lantern high, and the light wavered in his unsteady hand. He was smaller than his brother, with finer features and a curl to his golden hair.

"We need to go up one more grate," said Dylan. His hair was a dark blond, and his stubborn chin gave him a roguish look. "Then we'll go up into the courtyard."

Gwydion cleared his throat.

The twins' reaction was perhaps a little overblown. Dylan swept Lleu behind him with one arm, and with his other, he thrust a hand at the ankle-deep water. A laughably weak wave lapped at Gwydion's boots. He snorted and stepped into the circle of lantern light.

"Uncle," said Dylan, relief evident in the word. "It's just you."

"It is," agreed Gwydion. "Luckily for you. Using your magic in a place like this?"

Dylan's brow furrowed. "It should have—I mean—" He gestured at the water, and it stirred sluggishly. Sweat broke out across Dylan's brow.

"Don't strain yourself," said Gwydion. He reached for the water flask he kept on his belt and handed it to the boy. "There's a reason the kings of Gwynedd built the sewers to be large enough to be traversed by humans and folk."

It was Lleu who figured it out first. He reached out to touch one of the walls. "Iron?" he said.

Gwydion nodded. "Any diviners or tylwyth teg who dared try to enter the city through its sewers would be rendered powerless. As you are right now." He gave Dylan a sharp look.

As befitted the family of Dôn, Dylan was a diviner. A water diviner, and as far as Gwydion knew, the last of his kind. There had been four others in the isles, but three were slain by a murderous spymaster. The fourth had—rather ironically—drowned. King Math had gone to great lengths to keep Dylan's powers a secret. Those in rival kingdoms might simply assassinate the lad rather than let Gwynedd keep him. They would see him as a threat. But when Gwydion looked at Dylan, he saw only the young boy that liked horses, boats, and sweets. He was boisterous and friendly. Gwydion wished he could protect him a little longer, but those days were swiftly coming to an end.

"We were being careful," said Lleu. "We brought rope and a lantern."

Lleu was quiet and small, a rabbit in a family of wolves. His lack of magic marked him as unusual within their family, and Gwydion worried for the boy. Lleu was kind and sharp-witted, but neither kindness nor intelligence would protect him.

"Does your mother know you're out of the castell?" said Gwydion, crossing his arms. Arianrhod would be less than pleased when she discovered them sneaking out again.

The twins shifted uneasily.

"I didn't think so," said Gwydion. "Now why are you in the sewers?"

The twins glanced at each other. There was a silent exchange, and then Dylan held out the scrap of paper. "Great-Uncle sent us a message, a game. He said we're supposed to bring back a letter from the house of the barwn from Rhufoniog. If we did, Great-Uncle said we could sit by his side at the festival. I heard one of my friends talking about how he could go anywhere by using the sewers, and I thought with my magic…" He scowled. "I didn't know they were made of iron."

Gwydion swallowed. The twins were eight—young enough to be enchanted by horse races, puppies, and tales of monsters at bedtime. But they were swiftly growing, and the realization that they were old enough to take part in King Math's games…that chilled him.

This was how it began. With small risks and wagers, challenges and rewards. It was like wading into a river—the clearness of the water disguised the dangerous depths. It was all too easy to drown.

"So you snuck out of the castell?" said Gwydion sharply. "What if you got lost?"

"That's why we brought the rope," said Lleu earnestly.

Gwydion pinched the bridge of his nose.

"Uncle," said Dylan, "why are you angry?"

Because this was not the childhood he wanted for them. Because they should not have had to fight for their great-uncle's favor. Because he did not want them to grow up as he did.

He forced his hand down, making an effort to smooth his face into neutral lines.

"I'm not angry," Gwydion said. "Just tired. This game is for young children. You're not children, are you?"

Dylan and Lleu shook their heads.

That was the trick. To make the games less appealing, less forbidden.

If only someone had done that for Gwydion, perhaps things would have been different. His right hand throbbed beneath its brace. The familiar ache was little more than background noise, but surrounded by cold iron and chill waters, he could not ignore the discomfort. "Come," he said. "We should—"

It was Lleu's sharp intake of breath that warned him.

Gwydion flung himself to one side, catching the twins with his arm and spinning so that they were behind him. Something sharp and metal hit the sewer wall where he'd been standing mere heartbeats before. The arrow glittered in the wavering light of Lleu's lantern.

Two men stood twenty paces up the sewer. The spies from the street. One had an arrow nocked. The other man held a sword. *Not spies, then*, Gwydion thought. *Killers.*

Dylan raised one hand and thrust it forward, calling upon his magic. The water tried to answer. A weak little wave flickered up the sides of the sewer, then faltered. Dylan made a soft, pained noise. It was a valiant effort to defend them, but the assassins had chosen this ambush well.

Panic flared hot in Gwydion's stomach. "Who sent you?" he said tightly. When he survived this, he needed to know where to aim his retribution.

He had every intention of surviving this.

The first man stepped forward. He carried his sword with an easy grace, and he flicked the blade so that he cut a line in the water. "Your brother has so many enemies," said the man, "you likely wouldn't even know her name."

"I enjoy making new friends." Gwydion's hands remained at his sides. Visibly, he was no threat. But his fingers twitched toward a pouch on his belt.

"Then die disappointed," said the man, and stepped forward, raising his blade.

Dylan was young and inexperienced with his magic. He couldn't overcome the heavy press of the iron sewers. But Gwydion had spent his whole life at a disadvantage: youngest, smallest, with a power that most people disregarded. With a snarl of contempt, he reached deep within himself to that place where his magic dwelled.

Other diviners summoned their power with a gesture—a flick of the wrist, a clench of the fingers. With his dominant hand encased in a wood-and-leather brace and his left keeping the twins behind him, the spies did not expect Gwydion to attack. But Gwydion's power did not lurk in the spaces between his fingers, in the muscle and sinew of his palms. The magic of growing things, of trees and plants and flowers, was found in song.

Gwydion opened his mouth and shouted, releasing a wild burst of magic.

It *hurt*. It was like trying to scream through a gag, through the press of an attacker's fingers. The iron dragged at his every breath.

The archer's bow had once been the branch of a maple tree. When Gwydion's magic echoed through the sewer, the bow bucked beneath the archer's hands. He jerked in surprise, releasing the arrow too soon. With another cry, Gwydion tried to push the arrow aside, to use his magic to deflect it. It only half worked; the arrow wobbled in midair, spinning so that it skittered into the shallow water.

The bowstring snapped, slicing a line across the archer's face. He screamed in pain and surprise.

The swordsman twisted, startled by the sound of his ally's cry. Gwydion seized him by the wrist. He did not try to wrest the sword away from him, but rather he stepped into the man's space and pressed his advantage.

Gwydion drove his knee into the man's gut. The swordsman

cried out, the breath leaving him in a rush. Keeping one hand on the man, Gwydion reached into the purse at his belt and pulled out a dried blackberry. He hummed, calling forth his magic a second time. The iron made it an agony—a crack of lightning down his throat, into his chest. He would pay a high price for this magic, but he would protect his nephews no matter the cost.

The blackberry sprouted beneath his fingers, small green tendrils growing and twisting. They locked around the swordsman's hands and arms, thorns driving into flesh and leaves gently rustling. The man made a choked, agonized sound. He dropped to his knees, eyes rolling like that of a pained animal.

Gwydion took a step back. The archer was no threat—he had been slashed open from chin to ear by his own bowstring. And the swordsman would need time to break free of those thorns.

"Lleu, Dylan," said Gwydion. His voice was ragged. Using magic in the presence of so much iron had drained him dangerously. "We're leaving now."

The twins clustered around him, clinging to his cloak like small birds trying to hide beneath their mother's wings. Gwydion would send word to Eilwen, let her know there were two noble assassins to be captured.

"What was that?" asked Dylan, once they had rounded a corner. "Who—"

"Servants of our enemies," said Gwydion tightly. "Perhaps from Dyfed. Perhaps elsewhere."

Dylan looked baffled. "But—but the city is safe."

Gwydion should have warned them, told them that there would always be people that wished them ill. He had wanted them to keep their innocence a little longer. But they were the grandchildren of Dôn and great-nephews of King Math. Their family had countless enemies.

They would never be safe.

Not unless Gwydion made sure of it.

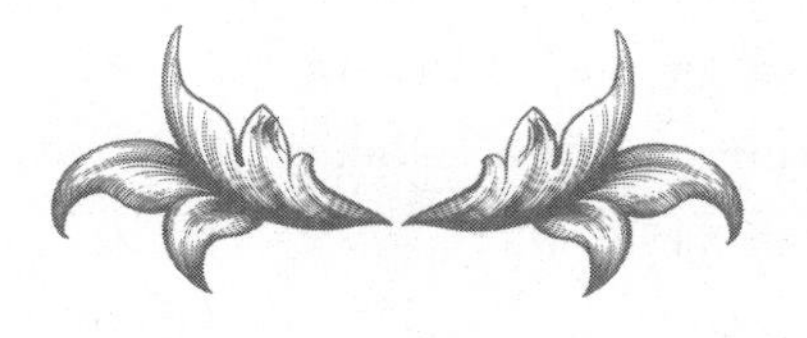

CHAPTER 6

GWYDION BROUGHT THE twins to the great hall.

A small crowd of nobles had filled the room, and Gwydion slipped in among them. Arianrhod leaned idly along the wall, and Gwydion sidled up beside her, angling so that the twins stood between them. She glanced down at the twins, then ruffled Dylan's hair fondly and straightened Lleu's shirt. Luckily the twins did not seem terribly frightened after the attack. Children were remarkably resilient.

"Why do you smell like that?" asked Arianrhod softly. She reached out to brush a fleck of dried sewer muck from Gwydion's sleeve.

"I'll tell you once the twins are in bed," Gwydion replied. The great hall was a wonder of stone—magic was used to smooth out the floor, arch the high ceiling, and add decorative carvings to the doorways. Tapestries of old battles hung along the walls. The throne had been hewn from an old yew tree. It was whispered that the yew tree had once belonged to Annwvyn and a brave woodcutter had crossed the border to bring it as a gift to his king. Whether or not the tales were true, the throne was beautiful, the wood polished to softness and carved in elegant lines.

King Math sat upon the throne, his gaze on the man before him. Despite being well into his seventh decade, he was unbowed by age. His hair was the color of sun-worn slate, and his face had the aged authority of an old sheepdog.

King Math was a diviner of flesh—a rare talent. In his younger days, Math transformed his enemies into animals and let them live out their shortened lives as beasts. Gwydion remembered an incident when he was five and had snuck into his uncle's study. Math had threatened to turn Gwydion into a deer and let the royal hounds have him. It had taken years for Gwydion to return to that study.

Math idled in the throne, his gaze on the nobleman standing before him. Gwydion recognized the man as Barwn Ifor. He was a noble of little importance that oversaw some back country village on the edge of Gwynedd. His face was ruddy, and his voice was hoarse from sleeplessness or grief.

"—demand restitution," he was saying. "If King Arawn will not stop his folk from killing humans—"

"I am to understand," King Math said, "that your son went into Annwvyn of his own accord? No one forced him beyond those borders, and in doing so, he forfeited his life."

Barwn Ifor flushed hotly, and one of his hands balled into a fist. According to Gwydion's spies, Ifor's son had gone missing, and Ifor had pleaded with Math to send scouts to find him. But when the trail led toward Annwvyn, Math had called off the search.

Gwydion knew why—because to send soldiers into those woods would be tantamount to a declaration of war. A barwn's son wasn't worth the risk.

"You are supposed to protect our lands from those—those monsters," said Ifor, his voice shaking with badly repressed fury. "I see little reason for my lands to support your throne if you will sit idle while the otherfolk slaughter humans."

Abruptly, King Math rose. The hall fell silent.

"Your lands," said Math quietly, "belong to you at my pleasure. Your family has long stood in support of Gwynedd's throne, and if that should ever waver, then you will have far more to grieve than the loss of one son."

Fury flooded Ifor's reddened face. He took half a step, and every guard in the hall tensed. Arianrhod slipped her hand free of Dylan's, her fingers at the ready. If Ifor made a move, she would slam him into the ground with a gesture. Gwydion watched, waiting to see how this would play out.

"Strong words," snarled Ifor, "for one with no heir."

Someone near Gwydion inhaled sharply.

Math did not answer Ifor's anger with his own; rather, his expression drained of warmth. He looked upon Ifor the way a butcher might gaze upon meat, deciding the best way to slice it into pieces.

"The matter of my heir has been decided," said Math. His voice was quiet but no less powerful. "And while I have not shared that knowledge with *you*"—his mouth twisted at the corner on the last word—"it will be announced at the festival." He leaned closer to Ifor. "And I suggest you do not take this up with my heir. He has less patience than I."

Gwydion tried to swallow, but his throat suddenly felt too dry.

The matter of inheritance had long been one that weighed upon Gwynedd. Math had no children of his own, but he did have four nephews and a niece.

Arianrhod stiffened. Her fingers went still, and her arm fell back to her side. "So he's decided, then."

Gwydion could not answer. He was not sure he could speak.

"What is it, Mam?" said Lleu, looking up at her.

She shushed him.

Math gestured for the guards to escort the barwn from his hall.

"Fool," Gwydion said quietly.

Arianrhod watched Ifor, her gaze a little sad. "I pity him. Losing a child like that... I understand going to such lengths. He even hired a huntress when his soldiers gave up the hunt." She looked at Gwydion. "One willing to venture into Annwvyn."

Gwydion's brows drew tight. "Truly?"

"She has hunted there before," replied Arianrhod. "One of my maids said she slew a llamhigyn y dwr that had taken to drowning children."

Gwydion snorted. "It's more likely she dragged an overlarge toad from some farmer's well."

Arianrhod gave a delicate shrug. "Well, truth or not, she returned the lad's signet ring. If she were a thief, she might have held her tongue and kept the silver."

"True enough." Gwydion looked at Math. The old king was

retreating toward his study, extracting himself from his advisers. "Are you disappointed?"

"That the barwn's son is dead? I think I shall recover."

Gwydion gave her a sharp look. "You know what I mean."

Arianrhod glanced away. Her attention seemed to settle on the yew-tree throne.

"It was never mine," she murmured, as though speaking to herself. "It was never going to be mine."

"It should be," said Gwydion.

Arianrhod shook her head. "I thought he might have chosen Gofannon."

"That would require Gofannon to set foot on land," replied Gwydion. "We both know how unlikely that would be. Our brother would miss his boats far too much to settle on a throne." His mirth drained away. "You would be a better ruler than Amaethon."

"Do not let our uncle hear you say that. Or Amaethon for that matter." Arianrhod lifted her head, and her polite mask covered her disappointment. "What will be, will be. I've not the time nor the will to rage against unfairness. I've my own household to run, and the twins need a bath."

"I should say all three of them do." A new voice entered the conversation, and Gwydion looked up. Amaethon approached, a buoyant smile on his mouth. Of course he would be pleased with Math's little revelation.

"Brother," Amaethon said, his gaze falling on the muddied Dylan and Lleu. "I see you've finally found a use at court: minding children." He wrinkled his nose. "You smell of manure."

Gwydion kept a tight hold on his expression. "And you of ashes."

A smile touched Amaethon's thin mouth. "A demonstration," he said, snapping his fingers. A small flame appeared between them. "One of the visiting nobles from Gwent wished to see the power of the house of Dôn. So I burned all the clothes from his daughter."

Gwydion made no attempt to hide his disgust. "A wonderful way to forge new alliances."

Amaethon waved his hand, extinguishing the fire. "Power attracts power. Math knows that." His gaze fell on Dylan. "He should learn that."

Arianrhod let out a small chuckle. "I would enjoy seeing him dump water on your next show of power, dear brother."

"Ask him to summon water to bathe Gwydion instead," said Amaethon, his gaze flicking over Gwydion's stained trousers. "Then he won't offend our guests."

With one last cold smile, he strode past them.

Gwydion exhaled.

"I don't think you smell bad, Uncle Gwydion," said Lleu with utmost sincerity.

"I appreciate that," said Gwydion.

"You smell more interesting than Uncle Amaethon," agreed Dylan.

"Thank you, Dylan."

"You could do with clean clothes," said Arianrhod.

"I think I've had my fill of everyone commenting on how I smell today," said Gwydion. He stepped away from Arianrhod. "I'll speak with you later." A headache throbbed behind his eyes. After his show of magic in the sewer, he knew it would be a few days before he recovered.

He would deal with the headache later. For now, he had more important matters.

King Math was walking toward one of the side doors, and Gwydion's heartbeat quickened. He darted through the crowd. He made it just as the door was closing, and he seized the handle before the lock could click into place. He heaved it open and followed his uncle into the corridor.

Math glanced over his shoulder. "Nephew," he said mildly. "Did you wish to speak with me?"

"I did." Gwydion bowed low. "If you would favor me with a conversation, Uncle."

The deference seemed to please the king. A faint smile touched Math's mouth. "Of course."

The king's study brimmed with maps. Math ran his withered fingers over one as he walked, caressing the parchment the way others did a treasured hound.

"Nephew," he said. "Share a drink?"

Gwydion bowed again, holding the position for two heartbeats. "I thank you for the offer. But I can only stay for a short while."

King Math poured a generous amount of wine into a goblet, then sank into a chair. "What did you want to speak about?"

Gwydion drew in a breath. "What you said to Barwn Ifor, was that true?"

"That his son was an ill-tempered creature with more recklessness than sense?" replied King Math. "Every word."

Gwydion smiled—more to acknowledge the jest rather than from true amusement. "Not that. About... about you having chosen your heir." To keep his hands from shaking, he reached out and picked up one of the figurines that rested upon the map, turning it over between his fingers.

Math gave him a chiding stare. "Are you here to confirm your own suspicions or accuse me of lying to one of the nobles?"

"The former," said Gwydion.

Math's mouth quirked. Boldness was a quality he favored, which was why Gwydion kept his tone polite but unflinching.

"I planned on making the announcement at the festival," said Math.

Gwydion nodded. His mind raced even as he opened his mouth. "So there is time, then."

Math took a sip of his wine. "Time for what?"

To alter the course of a kingdom.

Gwydion knew his brother. He knew the kind of enemies he made. Amaethon was like a wildfire. Fire unchecked would rush beyond its boundaries, scorching all in its path.

Amaethon would be a monster.

And the entire kingdom would suffer for it.

Gwydion thought of the small gray fox. Of the panicked rise and fall of its breaths. Should Amaethon become the ruler of Gwynedd, that fox would not be the last creature to flee for its life.

"I believe his skills are better suited to the battlefield than a throne," said Gwydion. "He has little patience for diplomacy."

"The same could be said of many rulers." Math frowned at the wine and gave it a swirl. "Are you suggesting yourself as a suitable replacement?"

There was no mockery to the words, no contempt at all, which made them almost harder to hear. Mockery would have been simpler. "Of course not," replied Gwydion. "I have little interest in ruling."

"That, nephew, is perhaps the first truthful thing you've said," remarked Math. He set down his wine, stepped around the table, and faced Gwydion. "But you do have an interest in who wears the crown. And you think it should be Arianrhod, not Amaethon."

"All of Gwynedd has an interest." It was one of those statements that sounded like an answer but gave away nothing. "Tell me, Uncle. What would it take to change your mind?"

"About my heir?" asked Math. He leaned against the table, idly running his fingers across the map. He traced the line between Gwynedd and Annwvyn, his thumb resting on Caer Dathyl. "A champion of Gwynedd will be crowned the victor of the Wild Hunt before I name Arianrhod my heir."

Gwydion inhaled sharply. His uncle might as well have said that Arianrhod would wear the crown when all the seas dried up.

"A wager, then," said Gwydion.

Math tilted his head. "A wager?"

Gwydion reached out to the map and picked up two small figures: one of a commander and one of a spy. Math frowned, but Gwydion could tell his uncle's interest was caught. Gwydion tossed the pieces from hand to hand, then closed his fists around them and placed those fists on the tabletop.

"If you pick the hand with the commander," said Gwydion, "then you announce Amaethon as your heir next week. If you pick the hand with the spy, you wait until spring."

Math raised his eyebrows. But rather than irritation, gentle amusement warmed his expression. "You always did have a fondness for tricks."

"How can I trick you here?" Gwydion held up his hands. "You saw me pick up the pieces. I did not drop them." This was a truly desperate move, a play for time.

Math's mouth quirked. "All right, then." His gaze fell to Gwydion's fists. He seemed to ponder for a moment, then pointed at Gwydion's right hand. "There."

Gwydion flipped over his hand and opened his fingers.

The spy figurine sat in his palm.

Math let out a chuckle. "Ah. Bested by my own nephew."

"A winter is not so long to wait," said Gwydion. "And perhaps your views on the matter will change in that time."

"I rather doubt that." Math drained the goblet, then set it down. "But you are welcome to try."

Gwydion bowed again. He slipped from the study before Math could revoke his end of their bargain.

The corridor was cool and thankfully empty. Once he was out of sight, Gwydion sagged against the wall. It was done. He had accomplished one small victory—Amaethon would not be announced as the heir until spring.

Gwydion opened his left fist.

A second spy figurine sat there. He had taken it when Math wasn't looking, slipped it up his sleeve. The commander figure was securely in his pocket, where it could never be picked.

Gwydion never left anything to chance.

A champion of Gwynedd will be crowned the victor of the Wild Hunt before I name Arianrhod my heir.

It was an impossible challenge. Gwydion would never be a warrior or a hunter. He could whisper a flower to life, sing fruit to ripeness, or walk through a forest unnoticed. He was a diviner and a trickster. If he could slip into the Hunt, if he could find a way to gain entrance...

Be the victor of the Wild Hunt.

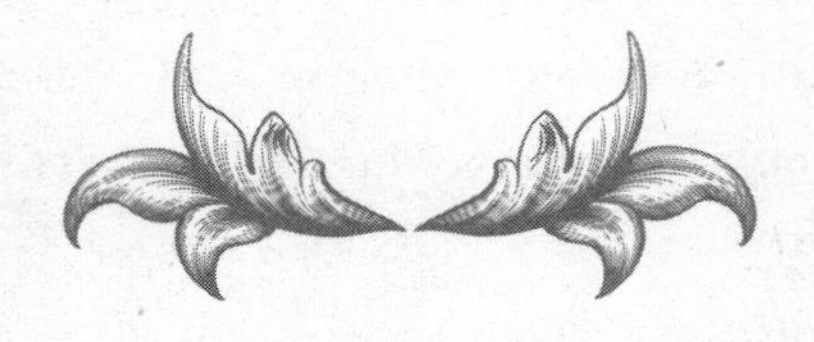

CHAPTER 7

GWYDION FOUND HIS sister on the battlements that night.

The wind tasted of winter. There was a damp bite to the air, and he pulled his hands inside his sleeves, trying to keep his right hand warm. Arianrhod sat with her legs crossed beneath her, the sweep of her gown falling over the edge. The copper caught the last evening sunlight.

Gwydion sat beside her, with his legs dangling over the stone ledge. The world fell away at the tips of his bare feet, the fall from the battlements a sheer drop that landed in cold water. Gwynedd swept out before them: craggy hills, patches of forest, harvested fields, speckles of distant sheep. This high up, it was easy to think of the kingdom as little more than assets to be counted on a map. But the kingdom was worth more than its hills and harvests and livestock.

Cities.

Villages.

People.

A new king would matter little to them, at least until it was time to collect tithes and young people for the armies. But how many of those soldiers would return to their families? How many farms would go hungry to feed Amaethon's appetites?

"I can hear your thoughts spinning from here," said Arianrhod, nudging him gently with her shoulder. "Why did you go to speak with Math?"

Gwydion released a breath. "I asked him not to name his heir until spring."

A frown tugged at Arianrhod's lips. "Why?"

"To give us time to change his mind."

Gwydion told her of the sewer, of the twins and the assassins who had attacked them. When he finished, her face was drawn.

"It was Amaethon's enemies that attacked the twins," he finished. "They mentioned a brother. Gofannon remains at sea, and they were not speaking about me."

"We all have enemies." Arianrhod's frown was a brittle thing.

"But not all of us set people on fire for the joy of it." Gwydion gritted his teeth. "Amaethon sows resentment everywhere he goes. He will bring it home with him—he already has."

Arianrhod said, "Amaethon is not a monster of old."

"You're right. A monster of old could be slain. And the one wielding the blade would be called a hero." Gwydion gave Arianrhod a hard look. "Kings are something far more dangerous."

"You don't need to slay him," said Arianrhod. "Kings come and go. The world changes, and it does not. But what matters is this, little brother." She reached out and settled a hand on his wrist. "Do not trouble yourself over what Amaethon will do. Choose your own path, carve out a place for yourself. The best power you wield is choice."

Gwydion cut a sharp look at his sister.

"Spoken as one who has never been powerless," he said tightly.

Arianrhod's magic would not kill her. It would drain her, but she knew the cost and the cure. He possessed no such knowledge. He could not recall a time when he hadn't been weaker, slower to heal, and mindful of the way his body might rebel if he pushed it too far. It was why he had tried so hard to cultivate his garden of spies. Secrets were a far safer weapon for him. He knew which of Amaethon's soldiers secretly despised him; he knew which of the messengers were spies for other kingdoms; he knew when the blacksmith was soused again; he knew the twins had a secret place to play behind the orchard.

Secrets were his best weapon, but they did not instill the kind of respect that Arianrhod commanded. When she passed, soldiers bowed their heads and servants scurried from her path. Not even Amaethon would raise a hand against her. She would never understand.

Arianrhod shifted in her seat. "You do have choices, even if none of them are what you desire."

Gwydion swung his legs a little, the cold wind numbing his bare feet. His right hand ached in his lap, the familiar throb behind his knuckles. He would need to apply a poultice. The pain frayed his temper, made him want to lash out.

"Math has begun testing your sons," he said. "The way he tested us. Those games he made us play to win his favor."

Arianrhod's lips paled. She, too, would remember the "games" that they had been given as children: stealing signet rings, bits of paper, whispers. It had all been to win their uncle's favor after the death of their parents. Gwydion could still recall the thrill of sneaking a stolen ring from Amaethon's pocket, the triumph when he had bested his brother. The games were a way for King Math to test his niece and nephews... and to gain an advantage over his rivals. Those games had ended rather abruptly—and at the thought, pain flared in Gwydion's knuckles.

Arianrhod said, "I think it might be time to leave Caer Dathyl."

"So you'll run?" he asked, unable to hide the derision in his voice.

"I will take my sons somewhere safe," said Arianrhod.

"They will never be safe," retorted Gwydion. "No place in Gwynedd will be safe if Amaethon is king. Which is why you must take the throne."

She was not perfect, but she *cared*. Those who grew up surrounded by cruelty either took that cruelty into themselves—or they armored themselves against it. If one's family was the foundation from which they arose, then the house of Dôn was that of a briar patch: tangled thorns and hidden hurts. But from that, Arianrhod had raised her own sons with care and love. If she were given a kingdom, Gwydion had no doubt she would dedicate her life to making it a safe place for her sons—and for everyone else.

And his place at her side would be assured.

Arianrhod gazed at the horizon. "You will never convince Amaethon to give up a throne," she said. "Contrary to the rumors, you are neither heartless nor ruthless enough to kill him. And I doubt anything you say will sway our uncle."

"But if there was a way," he said, "would you take the throne?"

Her lips pressed thin, her gaze gone distant. "To spite our brother, no. At Math's behest, no. Even if you begged me to, no." Her mouth softened, and her voice held a quiet warmth. "But for my children, I would. If it meant building a world where they might be safe and happy." She shook her head. "It will never come to pass."

"It will," said Gwydion. "I'm going to make sure of it."

Arianrhod offered him a tolerant little smile. She plucked one of the copper scales from her dress. Her fingers flowed in a gentle motion over the metal. At once, it changed—the shape twisting, the metal gone molten under her touch. In a matter of heartbeats, Arianrhod held a ring. It was twisted into the beautiful shape of an old tree.

"My dear brother," she said, sliding the ring into his palm. "Your path is your own. Stay here or do not. Be Gwydion of Caer Dathyl or Gwydion of the Trees. But do not make the mistake of thinking it is easier to change the world than it is to change yourself."

Gwydion looked down at the ring. It was beautiful and so delicately wrought that it made the dragon signet of Dôn look gaudy in comparison. For a moment, he allowed himself to consider the future if he slid that family ring from his finger and set it on the battlements. If he stood and walked from Caer Dathyl, with no intention to return.

He might have walked away. But the problem, he decided, with looking at the world as a gardener was that he did not see maps and countries, armies and cities. He saw what could grow. What might grow.

He saw how the world *could* change.

Gwydion slipped the copper ring into his pocket.

"Tell me," he said. "Did you catch the name of Ifor's huntress?"

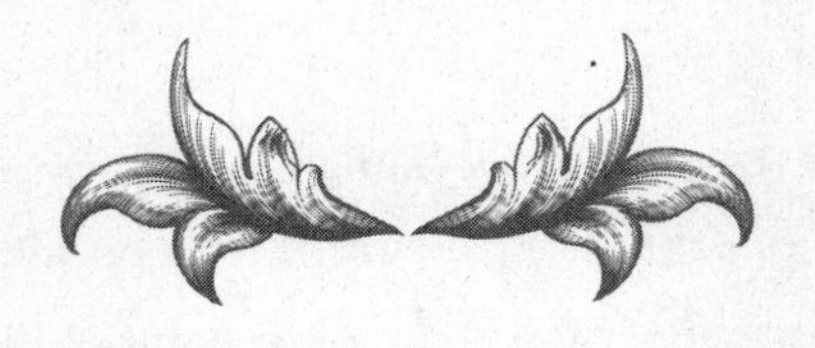

CHAPTER 8

BRANWEN WOKE WITH gritty eyes and a cat's tail hitting her in the face.

"Palug," she whispered, swatting him away. Palug sat beside her, his tail waving indolently. "Stop it, I'm awake."

Palug rose and stretched, his claws gently flexing into the wood of the door. His meaning could not be plainer.

"All right." Branwen heaved herself up with far less grace than her cat. Around the door latch she had bound a rope in a snare that only a hunter—or a weaver—could have untangled. It soothed her worries that her mam would slip out in the night. Quietly, she heaved the door open, and Palug darted outside. A waft of cold air touched Branwen's cheek. The morning smelled of frost and the straw that Rhain had scattered across the mud puddles forming in the front yard.

She dressed beside the embers of the hearthfire, then slipped outside. Dawn crept over the mountains, illuminating mist and fog. Branwen inhaled deeply, tugging her gloves into place. Palug came out of the bushes, tail held high. Branwen leaned down, and he jumped atop her shoulder, turned his face into her warm neck, and purred.

She loved this hour best. The world was caught between waking and sleeping, the pale violet sky flecked with stars. Mam would be safely tucked away in bed; she always slept better in the early morning.

Taking a deep breath, she set off toward Rhain's farm. Something had been stealing from his fields—a few apples here, a patch of barley there. Branwen could not be sure if the thefts were magical in nature, but she set snares at the easternmost edge of his land and checked them every morning. Along each rope she slid a bit of iron—not enough to kill, but enough that it would entrap a lesser creature. It was a common deterrent, a way of letting the folk know that this land was claimed and defended.

Branwen knew more of the folk than most humans. Mortal ironfetches came into Argoed for supplies that could not be found within Annwvyn—herbs, clothing, tools. Two years ago, Branwen had befriended one ironfetch called Fane.

Never give one of the folk a yes or no answer, he had told her. *Words are binding. And they can sense untruths. They have no sense of cruelty—but nor do they understand mercy.*

Which was why Branwen set snares, marked her home's doorway with iron, and kept her afanc knife at her belt. Thus far, her snares had only caught squirrels, a hare, and a few grouse.

On this morning, there were two rabbits. She knelt and unbound the snares. The rabbits would fetch a fair price at the tavern, where their meat would go into the cawl and their fur fashioned into the lining of a cloak. The coin she earned would go to the village healer, who sold small bundles of herbs. Those herbs did little for remembrances, but they would ease Mam's sleep.

Palug darted through the tall grasses, chasing after something. He preferred live prey, hunting rabbits and mice and birds and taunting them with their own powerlessness.

All cats, Branwen thought, had a bit of monster to them. Perhaps that was why cats gleamed gold when she looked at them with her magicked eye. But they also purred and cuddled and kept vermin from granaries, so they were well-loved and well-fed little monsters.

The next snare was empty, and the last was...gone. Branwen knelt beside the fence post where she had hidden the snare, her fingers brushing over the torn earth. Something had ripped it free, stake and all. Perhaps a sheep had blundered into it and was now trailing the snare with every step.

Branwen grimaced; she would speak to Rhain this afternoon. If one of his animals had stumbled into the snare, he would have a few sharp words for her.

Another hunt gone awry, she thought sourly.

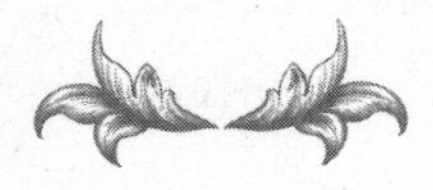

By the time Branwen reached the village of Argoed, the sun had risen. Preparations for Nos Calan Gaeaf were in full force. Space had been cleared in the square for bonfires; a traveling merchant opened his stall to sell wreaths and ribbons; children had been sent out to find sticks for the fires. Branwen stepped around the children, their arms brimming with tangled branches. Two broke away from the others, dropping their bundles to engage in a mock sword fight.

"Careful," said Branwen, ducking as one of the girls thrust her branch with a little too much enthusiasm. The children whirled around, worried they would be scolded. "Don't aim for the face," Branwen said, nudging one of the girls with her hip. "Not unless you want to lose an eye. Go for the wrist. Knock your enemy's weapon away."

The girls' faces brightened, and they began enthusiastically whacking each other's arms. Branwen winced.

One of the young lads eyed the rabbits at Branwen's shoulder. "Did you use the bow to kill them?" he asked eagerly. "My da says he's going to take me hunting next year, when I'm older."

"I bet the cat did the hunting," said another young boy, kneeling down and offering his hand to Palug. "Mine dragged a mouse into my mam's cloak last week."

Palug sniffed the proffered hand, then gently rubbed his cheek against the lad's fingers. "He prefers fish to rabbits," said Branwen.

Seeing their friend petting the cat, a few others surrounded Palug. The cat flicked his tail in mild irritation but allowed the adoration.

"He's so soft," said one of the girls. She chanced on the spot where Palug loved to be scratched—where his neck fur fluffed out against his chest. As though against his will, Palug leaned into her hand and purred. "Where did you find him?"

"On a hunt," Branwen replied.

The children gazed at her with hopeful, upturned faces. Even Palug seemed to be waiting.

"I went to Ynys Môn," she said. She lowered her voice, as though confiding a secret. The children clustered more tightly around her, and she knelt so she could meet their eyes. "There were rumors of a monster prowling the shores. It carried off sheep and goats and left enormous tracks alongside the sea. A hundred knights were sent after the monster, but none returned. Desperate, a noble set a bounty—if anyone could slay the beast, he would pay a fortune."

One of the boys leaned forward, his eyes alight. "Did you hunt the beast?"

Branwen nodded solemnly. "I did. I spent a week tracking it, following tangled paths and bits of the livestock it had slain. And finally, on the seventh night, I ventured into a sea cave. There was a scratching noise, like enormous claws against the rock." She dragged her nails across her bow, and one of the girls shuddered. "I kept quiet, arrow at the ready, and crept through the cave. The air stank of dead things, and the only light came from my lantern. As I went, I saw the bodies of those that had hunted the creature—there was old armor, swords, and one shield. I followed the sound of raking claws... until suddenly, all went silent."

The children all drew in sharp breaths.

"I tried to be as quiet as possible, but the monster must have heard my heartbeat." Branwen shifted, her fingers wrapping around the knife at her belt. "Something rushed past me so swiftly I could not see it, but it knocked me sideways. The lantern tumbled from my hand. I grabbed a shield from a fallen knight."

All the children, and even some of the wreath-makers, were enraptured by her tale. "The shield was well polished, and it caught the glimmer of my lantern. I heard the sound of paws and then a skitter. No matter where I turned, the sound followed me. Then I lowered the shield and saw…"

She dragged the words out, enjoying the way her small audience seemed to be holding their breath. "A large black-and-white cat. It was chasing the reflected light from my shield, the way it might have hunted a mouse. I gave him some dried meat, and he purred and crawled into my lap. I took him home." She held out her arm, and Palug wriggled free of the children. He leapt atop Branwen's shoulder and head-butted her cheek fondly.

"So there was no monster?" asked a lad, sounding disappointed. "Just the cat?"

Branwen stroked between Palug's ears. "Well, something killed all those knights. I suppose the creature might have run before I arrived. But ever since I took Palug from that cave, there were no more vanished livestock. And no more knights were slain."

One of the girls looked skeptical. "You think your cat was the monster?"

"I think he was hungry and alone," said Branwen. "And hunger can make monsters of us all."

The children seemed satisfied by this answer.

"A fanciful tale," came a voice from behind her. The children looked up, then scattered like chickens sighting a hawk.

Branwen rose to her feet and turned.

A young man leaned against the tavern wall, his stance one of easy idleness. He was striking as a tree in winter: dark hair and eyes, pale skin, and a fox's smile. His dark hair was tousled, with a bit of curl, and he wore clothing that brimmed with wealth. But it was not his beautiful face that made her breath catch. It was the way he gazed at her, with a wry smile and a tilt to his eyebrows. He was looking at her as though he were evaluating her.

He asked, "Do you embellish all your stories?"

"I embellished nothing," said Branwen, offended.

The young man shrugged. "Of course."

"Can I help you?" asked Branwen irritably.

"That depends," he replied. "Are you the huntress? Branwen?"

Branwen gave him a flat stare. "I should think the dead rabbits and bow would be answer enough."

The man swept into a small, courtly bow. That made her distrust him all the more. No one bowed to the likes of her.

"I am looking for a hunter," he said. "I heard rumors of you at Caer Dathyl. And if your story has even the slightest bit of truth to it, then you are the huntress I need."

Branwen crossed her arms. Her cheek still bore the fading bruise from Ifor's slap, and now another noble had come asking for her help. "No."

The man's smile was unfaltering. "What?"

"No," she said again. Then she strode toward the tavern.

"I can pay—"

"Whatever the job is, I don't want it," she said, not bothering to look back as she walked away.

"But—"

"No thank you, and I have to sell these rabbits," she said, and walked around to the back of the tavern.

The tavern was one of the larger buildings in Argoed. Branwen rapped on the kitchen door. The tavernkeeper, Glaw, answered. His hair was flecked with flour, and his left hand held a wooden spoon. His right sleeve was buttoned at the elbow. As a former soldier, Glaw had lost most of his right arm to an inflamed wound. If he had been wealthier, he might have paid a metal diviner to craft a replacement. Instead, he poured what coin he had into brewing. The tavern may have been modest, but the ale was crisp and sharp, and there was always fresh-baked bread and cawl. "Branwen," he said warmly. "You're looking well. How's your mam? All right?"

Palug meowed, winding around Glaw's ankles.

"And you, of course," said Glaw. He reached back into the kitchen for a moment, emerging with a scrap of cooked chicken. He offered it to the cat. Palug sniffed delicately, as though considering the offering. Then he took the chicken and retreated a few steps to devour it.

Branwen smiled. "We're as well as ever. And your sister? Has she returned from the city?"

Glaw snorted. "Returned from Caer Dathyl with a stray hound and enough gossip to last until winter."

"That's important for a tavern," replied Branwen, unable to hide her smile.

"I'd rather have a cat," said Glaw, with a nod at Palug. "At least they keep rats from the stores. This hound just naps all day in front of the fire. You ever decide to sell that cat of yours, you let me know."

Palug's tail twitched. He glared at Glaw.

"Palug might eat more than the hound," said Branwen. "Along with a few of your guests." She shrugged her shoulder, allowing the rabbits to slip down her arm. "I brought you something for tomorrow's cawl."

The wooden spoon fumbled in Glaw's hand. All the easy warmth vanished from his eyes. "I... apologies, Branwen. I won't be buying from you today."

Branwen frowned. Glaw had been the first villager to buy her game when she began hunting. He never turned down fresh meat. "Why?"

Glaw looked as though he would rather eat those rabbits raw than answer. "There's been talk."

"Talk?"

"That anyone who buys your game will find themselves an enemy of Barwn Ifor," said Glaw heavily.

Branwen let out a startled breath, as though she had been thumped in the stomach. "No."

"He's been raging," said Glaw. "My sister heard that he spoke out against King Math, of all people, for not keeping our lands safe." He gazed at Branwen with sympathy. "It's the loss of his son. He's trying to spread his grief around because he cannot bear the weight of it. You're getting the brunt of his anger, I'm sorry to tell you."

"So you're not going to buy my rabbits," said Branwen stiffly. "Because word might get back to the barwn." Anger flared deep within her. Glaw was among those Branwen counted as friends. She had never thought he would pull away for fear of being associated with her.

Branwen and her mother had lived outside the village for many years, but they were still a part of it. Her mam had been a well-respected midwife, and Branwen was well-liked. She had saved children from monsters; in hard, hungry winters she came to the village with pheasant, red grouse, and rabbits; she helped her neighbors when they needed it. In the village, one's word and reputation mattered. One could not survive on their own in the wild country.

As though he sensed her growing fear, Glaw said soothingly, "I'm sure the barwn will relent in a few weeks. Maybe after winter."

"I don't have until after winter," said Branwen. She needed the coin these rabbits would fetch.

"Mayhap the butcher," said Glaw. "Or you could try Sawyl's aunt. She's been talking about selling oggies at the bonfires."

Branwen took a step back. She forced herself to say, "Thank you, Glaw."

He nodded back at her.

Her heart heavy, Branwen left Glaw in the shadow of the doorway. She hastened around the tavern, barely aware of her surroundings. There was a terrible rushing in her ears and dread churning in her belly. She needed to go to the apothecary. Her mam's sleep had been growing more restless, and without sleep she would deteriorate all the faster.

"Weren't you going to sell those?"

It was the noble. He stood a few steps away, his arms idly crossed and one eyebrow cocked.

Branwen glared at him. Her manners were worn thin. "I don't suppose you're interested."

The man hesitated, looking awkward for the first time. "I... no. Thank you. I did not come here for rabbits."

She pulled the rabbits from her shoulder, sitting down on the bench by the tavern. "Why did you come to Argoed?"

He seemed to take this as invitation and sat beside her. "I have need of a huntress."

"For what?"

"A hunt," he said dryly.

She gave him an unamused look.

"And here I thought I was being hired to braid your hair," said Branwen tartly.

A grin broke across his mouth. That smile seemed to disarm him—scrunching at his eyes and giving him a boyish look—but he banished it in a heartbeat. His face smoothed out into careful lines, and he was cold and stark and beautiful once again.

"Who are you?" she said.

"My name is Gwydion, son of Dôn," he said. "And I would very much like to buy you a drink."

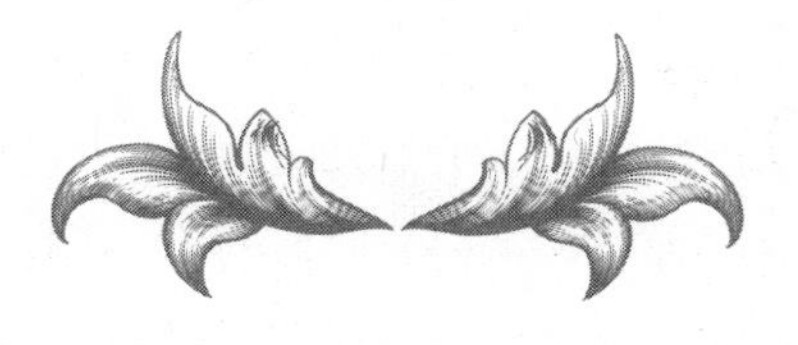

CHAPTER 9

THE HUNTRESS WAS unexpected.

With a name like "the white crow," Gwydion had imagined a woman well into her years. But Branwen could not have been any older than eighteen. Her right eye was covered by a cloth. He wondered if she had lost it in a hunt, but he knew better than to ask. He had dealt with enough pointed questions about his hand.

Branwen ordered drinks and a mutton soup, then settled down in the tavern's farthest corner. Her cat sat beside her, his tail flicking and green eyes fixed on Gwydion. He was glad when a middle-aged man approached the table, easily balancing a tray of drinks and food on one hand. He slid two tankards before them, inclined his head slightly toward Gwydion and far more deeply to Branwen. She picked up the tankard and drained half of it in a few gulps—which gave Gwydion time to study her.

Her hair was so pale it was nearly white. Her eye was icy, and she had a gaze that pierced sharper than any arrow. She was no beauty of the court; she wore no elegant gown, nor jewelry, and her lips were unpainted. But she had a feral, visceral quality about her. He found himself glancing at her again and again, merely for the pleasure of seeing her. Every time, he saw something new—the way her brows were slightly darker than her hair, the strong line of her jaw, and the scar along one cheekbone. Seeing where he looked, she touched her cheek. "Wolf hunt," she said. "Now, why did you want to speak with me?"

Gwydion straightened. He had practiced this speech a few times with his horse on the ride to Argoed, but now all of those words felt wrong. He was prepared for a mercenary, easily lured by coin. But Branwen had dismissed him twice now. "As I said, my name is Gwydion. You might have heard of me."

She ate a mouthful of soup, then said, "Should I have?"

She was a commoner. A huntress. She would have no reason to be familiar with the inner workings of Caer Dathyl. Or that was what Gwydion reminded himself. "I am the youngest nephew of King Math," he said.

Branwen's brow scrunched in thought. Then her face brightened. "Oh. I have heard of you." She thunked her fist against the table. "You stole pigs, right? Tried to start a war or something?"

Gwydion pressed the tips of his fingers to his forehead. "No. No. *No.*" He repeated the word with mingled despair and irritation. Of course she would have heard that rumor.

"So there's no truth to it?" asked Branwen.

Gwydion looked at her through his fingers. "There was an incident. When I was younger. But I have never started a war over pigs."

"That's a relief," she said. "If you're going to start a war, there should at least be a deer, hound, or bird involved." Her face was solemn, but there was a wicked gleam in her eye.

He looked down at his soup. "May I ask you a question?"

"You have bought my attention for as long as it takes me to eat," said Branwen, her fingers curling around the half-full tankard. "I suggest you use that time well."

Gwydion had intended to make his offer at once, but now that he had spoken with her, he had to ask. "How did someone like you begin hunting monsters?"

She set her tankard down. "Someone like me?"

"I meant no insult," he said. "Merely that when I heard rumors of a monster hunter, I thought I would find someone..."

"Older?" she said. "More grizzled? Stares into the distance and broods?"

"Precisely," he agreed. "Not a friendly young woman with a cat."

Her mouth twitched. "You consider me *friendly*?"

Perhaps not with him, but he had listened to her with those children. Many would have simply walked past them, but she had taken a few minutes to speak with them, to offer a story and a little wisdom. The twins would like her, he thought, if they ever had the chance to meet. They would have climbed all over her and demanded more stories.

"Compared to those I normally deal with, yes," he replied.

"I think that's more a statement on the company you keep." Branwen took a slower sip of her drink. "To answer your question, I hunt monsters because it is the only thing I'm good at. I began when I was young because in the wild country, we don't have the luxury of stone walls and iron everywhere. While some of the folk remain in the mountains, others will cross into our lands. Some are friendly and some are not. I've learned how to distinguish between the two." She nodded at his drink. "You should try that."

Gwydion picked up his tankard and sipped. He had expected a watery, stale drink like those he shared with Eilwen. But this tasted smoky and rich. "This is good," he said in surprise.

"Glaw's been brewing for years," said Branwen. "There are rumors that some of the otherfolk will venture into Argoed wearing the guise of humans just to try it."

"I can see why."

Branwen picked a small piece of mutton from her soup and placed it before her cat. The cat gave the meat a sniff before using a single claw to drag it from the table, presumably to be devoured out of sight. "I assume that Caer Dathyl has a monster problem you wish for me to fix," said Branwen.

Gwydion bit back a wry smile. "There are always monsters to be found among the royal courts. But you're wrong as to the particulars." He took a deep breath. This was his moment, the one he had placed so much weight upon.

"Tell me what you know of the Wild Hunt," he said. "If you would be so kind."

Her forehead scrunched. "Kings Arawn and Pwyll hold it every fifth year. It's a friendly hunt between Annwvyn and Dyfed, and it's said that the kings bring their best hunters. It's dangerous. People die. But there's rumors that King Arawn grants some kind of magical boon to the winners, so everyone wants to try. As to what they hunt, I don't know. Those from Gwynedd know better than to go near Annwvyn on a Hunt year. Too many go missing."

Gwydion gave her a nod. "A concise explanation. And you're right. No one from Gwynedd has ever managed to join—or win—the Hunt." He leaned over the table, lowering his voice. "Until now."

He waited for an intake of breath, for the flash of surprise.

But she burst into laughter.

"You?" she said, her shoulders quaking with mirth. "You're going to win the Wild Hunt?"

Gwydion sat there, hands folded on the table, and kept his smile firmly fixed in place.

It was not the first time someone had laughed at him. But if his plan worked, it would be the last. He would make it work. And to do that, he needed this woman. This monster-hunting, beer-drinking, one-eyed woman with a cat she claimed had eaten a hundred knights.

Perhaps this had not been his best-laid plan.

"I'm sorry," said Branwen, recovering herself. Some of his irritation must have flickered through his careful mask, because she made an effort to tamp down her laughter. "It's just—the very idea. Have you ever been near Annwvyn on Nos Calan Gaeaf?"

He hesitated. "No."

She pointed her spoon at him. "Well, I have. Which is why everyone in Argoed binds dried gorse to their fence posts, locks up their livestock, marks their doors with iron, and remains indoors once the sun sets. Monsters prowl the edges of the forest. If a person values their life, they don't go near the mountains when the seasons change." She sat back, her gaze flicking over him. "And forgive me for saying so, but you don't strike me as a hunter."

He gave a small shrug. "I know. Which is precisely why I came to you. I need a champion."

All of her amusement vanished in a heartbeat. "You want *me* to win the Wild Hunt for you."

"I will go with you," he said. "I have a plan to infiltrate the Hunt."

Branwen drained her tankard and gestured for a second. "Has anyone ever told you that your plans are impossible?"

"Every day," replied Gwydion.

Neither spoke for a few moments. To Gwydion's surprise, the quiet felt thoughtful rather than uncomfortable.

Finally, Branwen sighed. "There are two problems."

"Tell me," said Gwydion.

Branwen gave him a look that was almost pitying. "First, what you're attempting is impossible. Only a few days ago, I encountered the skull of someone who attempted precisely what you're proposing now. He was eaten alive. And he was one of the lucky ones. He was found."

"A minor detail," he said. "What's the second problem?"

That earned him a half smile. "The last time I worked for a noble, all I received was a slap and a snarl, and now no one will buy my game for fear of angering the barwn."

"Is that why you cannot sell your rabbits?" he said, taken aback. He recalled Barwn Ifor's fury at Math—and how it had gone unanswered. This young woman must have become the focus of his ire.

"I'm sorry," he said. "I did not know."

Branwen shrugged. "It is my problem to solve, not yours."

"But it could be," said Gwydion. "If you become my champion, I will ensure that Barwn Ifor never threatens you again."

If he had expected gratitude or fawning adoration, he would have been disappointed. She merely ate another spoonful of soup. "How?"

"He would not dare cross a prince," he said.

She speared him with a glance. "You're not a prince, though, are you?"

"My uncle is king."

"But you're not an heir," she said.

He winced. "I am not," he said. Better to admit the truth. "But I still have power."

Branwen opened her mouth, but before she could reply, the door burst open. All heads swung toward it as a middle-aged woman staggered inside. She looked ragged and fearful, her cloak torn at one edge. But it was her eyes that drew Gwydion's attention: They were white-edged and wild like a cornered animal. "Branwen—is she here? I asked and couldn't find her and—"

The tavernkeeper raised a hand toward Gwydion's table. The woman hurried over.

"Please," she said, her voice breaking with panic. "Please—Branwen, they attacked my goats. My husband tried to fight them, but they dragged him into the fields near Rhain's farm."

Gwydion began to rise, but Branwen was already on her feet. "What was it?"

The woman's shaking hands touched her mouth. "A pack—wolves, dogs, I'm not sure."

Branwen cursed beneath her breath. "I knew this would happen." She flung a glance at her cat. Then she looked at Gwydion.

"I have a horse," he said, rising from his seat. "It'll be faster than going on foot."

She bit her lip, as though she wished to argue. "Come on, then."

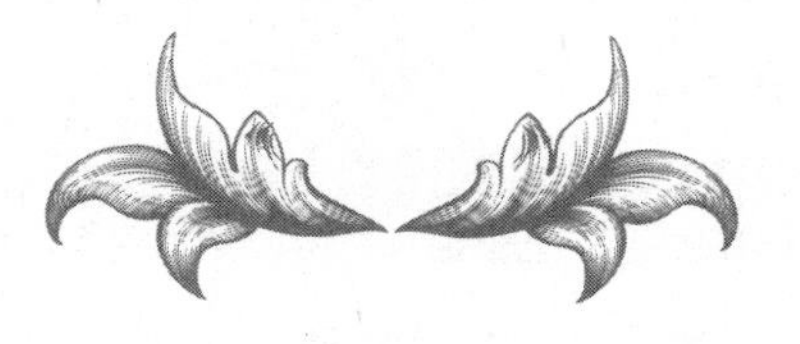

CHAPTER 10

BRANWEN HAD BEEN thirteen the first time she hunted a true monster.

It began with drownings.

There were a few every year. The winter rains lashed rivers into floods. Unwary travelers, careless children, and even a few animals would go missing only to be found when the water receded. It was sad, but it was expected.

But one spring, three village children perished.

There was a lake near Argoed, and children often went there to swim, fish, and sail small boats made of grasses and sticks. The lake had no name, but its waters were clear, and someone had built a small dock.

The drownings happened over the course of a month, and all that was found of the children were their clothes: torn and bloodstained, floating in the reeds.

It set off a small panic. The blacksmith crafted iron charms for frightened parents rather than his usual assortment of tools and horseshoes. A farmer took a long spear and a net down to the lake, determined to drag the monster from its depths.

No one ever saw him again.

After that, no one would go near the lake.

It had been Rhain who gave Branwen the idea to hunt it. They had been helping plant her mother's small garden. "No one knows what the monster is," he said, leaning on his shovel.

The garden had smelled of spring—greenery, clean soil, and possibility. Branwen had convinced her mother to let her plant flowers alongside her feverfew and mint.

"Did someone ask the barwn for help?" she asked.

Rhain gave her a knife-edge smile. "Weeks ago. He said he'd pass word along to the king, but the soldiers are... occupied elsewhere."

Which meant they were raiding the neighboring kingdom of Gwaelod. Branwen frowned. "But the barwn's supposed to protect us."

"He's supposed to do more than sleep, eat fine meals, and entertain guests, yes," Rhain agreed, "but so long as he keeps the taxes flowing toward the royal coffers, no one gives a damn what he does."

Branwen leaned forward. "What can be done?"

Rhain reached down to pull a rock from the garden. "Same as we've always done. Keep your head down, wear some iron, and come home before dark. I might ask about, see if anyone's hounds have had a litter. Wouldn't hurt keeping a dog around."

Sweat trickled through Branwen's hair, and she scratched at the back of her neck. "It's not right, that we're always the ones who have to hide."

Rhain gave her a look that was half pity, half amusement. "If I was twenty years younger, mayhap I could do something. But until I knew what the creature was, I couldn't fight it. That's the real power the otherfolk have—not the magic or the immortality. It's their illusions. Changing how a person sees the world? That's true power."

"You think... you think if the villagers knew what the creature was, they could kill it?" she asked.

Rhain gave a little shrug. "If it's something small. If it's an afanc, we're all going to have to move."

Branwen touched the afanc-fang knife at her belt. She carried it everywhere; its weight was a reminder that she was never helpless.

"Whatever you're thinking, the answer is no," said Rhain. "I know that face. That's a reckless face."

"I don't know what you mean," said Branwen delicately.

Rhain had given her a flat-eyed stare. "Don't be the fourth child lost, girl."

"I'm not a child," she said. "But don't worry. I won't be the fourth."

And she wasn't.

For that night, a three-year-old boy wandered free of his parents' yard. Their gate had been left unlatched.

A search set the village aflame. Torches were lit, parties set out. Even those who lived as far from the village as Rhain and Branwen heard of it, and Rhain told Mam to lock her doors. He had an old sword from his days in the armies and an assortment of hunting supplies. He armed himself and headed for the village.

Mam went to comfort the boy's parents, bringing herbs that might soothe the mother's terror. Once Mam was out of sight, Branwen picked up her dagger and a lantern.

She had never snuck out at night before. As she walked, she pulled her iron-stitched blindfold off. If there were monsters lurking in the night, she needed to see them. She followed the path toward Argoed, but she did not go to the village. Rather, she headed for the lake.

The water looked still and flat as a stone in that windless night. There was no moon, and the stars were blotted out by drifting clouds. Branwen set her lantern on the shore. She walked around the water, waiting. Listening. And looking. But the water remained as opaque as ever. If there was a monster, it did not need magic to conceal itself. The lake was disguise enough.

Frustrated, Branwen picked up her lantern. It was expensive—glass and metal. She pulled off her boots, bound up her hair, and took a steadying breath.

She waded into the water, lantern in one hand and knife in the other. The water lapped around her calves, so cold it stole the breath from her. Once the water was waist-high, Branwen halted.

She twisted the clasp on the lantern to seal it shut. At once, the light dimmed. There would only be a few moments before the fire winked out. With one last gulp of air, Branwen allowed herself to sink beneath the waves.

The world went quiet, the only sound in her ears that of lapping waves. The lantern sputtered but remained alight.

That was how she saw it.

Something was hidden in the silt-soft bottom of the lake. It had buried itself so that only its eyes were visible. Two golden, toad-like eyes peered up at her. It had been waiting.

Terror ripped through Branwen. She hung, suspended in the water, unable to move.

A llamhigyn y dwr. She had heard them called water-leapers, for they had the body of an enormous toad and the wings of a bat. They were wickedly clever, and often fishermen only knew of their presence because of snapped lines and gutted nets. When one had to be slain, it took a group of hunters and an iron net to drag it to shore. Hunters would pin the monster in place while one brave soul used a long-handled spear to kill it.

It was not a creature to be trifled with.

And its attention was wholly on Branwen.

The llamhigyn y dwr blinked. It was her only warning.

The monster surged from the depths in a cloud of silt. Branwen kicked backward, the lantern tumbling from her fingers. Its light went out. She swam as hard as she could, kicking her way toward the surface. She had to tell the village, get help, find—

Something wrapped around her ankle and yanked her down. Branwen thrashed, gritting her teeth against a scream. She could not cry out lest she lose what little breath she had.

She slashed out with her dagger, but the blade cut only water. The grip on her ankle tightened, and she was dragged deeper.

Her chest was on fire. This was how a llamhigyn y dwr killed its prey. It used its long tail to drown a victim and then devoured them.

Branwen thought of her mam returning home and finding Branwen's cot empty. She thought of Rhain searching the reeds, only to find a knife and an iron-stitched blindfold.

No. She would be no one's prey.

Branwen reached down to take hold of the llamhigyn y dwr's tail. Her fingers curled around the slimy skin before she drove her knife into its flesh and severed the tail.

She felt the llamhigyn y dwr scream. It reverberated through the water.

The creature's jaws clamped around her shoulder. Branwen let out a howl of fury, bubbles swirling as she released the last air in her chest. With more luck than skill, she stabbed again and again and again, sinking her knife into slimy, thick flesh. Finally, the grip on her released.

Branwen kicked herself to the surface, and when she broke free of the water, she was sputtering and gagging. She swam to the lake's edge. The knife was still in her hand, dripping with water and golden blood. Branwen rolled onto her side, trying to slow her breathing. Finally, when she was sure she would not fall, she pushed herself upright and looked over her shoulder.

There, in the center of the lake, floated the dead monster.

The aftermath was jumbled in her memories: She recalled walking unsteadily to the village, the story spilling out of her like the lake water she vomited outside of the inn. A blanket was pulled around her shoulders, and several men went to the lake to study the monster.

The missing boy had not been near the lake. He had wandered toward the road and was found unharmed by a passing traveler. Even so, the lad's parents fervently thanked Branwen for killing the monster.

Only Rhain had disapproved. "Foolish girl," he had said, his warm hand steady as he pressed a bandage against her injured shoulder. "One day, your luck will run out."

The world *sharpened.*

It was a unique sensation, one Branwen had only ever found on a hunt. All her thoughts fell away, banished to some distant corner of her mind. There were no people to complicate matters, no lies, no niceties, no worries for her home or mother. It was almost a relief to leave all that behind.

She was a huntress. This was where she thrived.

She and Gwydion rode toward the Davieses' farm. Branwen had little experience with horses, but Gwydion nudged his mare into a canter. The rolling gait made Branwen clutch at his waist for balance. She had stuffed Palug into her pack—much to his indignation—and the cat growled in protest with every step.

The horse's strides ate up the road, and Branwen was grateful for the swift pace. The Davieses' farm was only a short walk from Rhain's.

That snare, she thought. *That missing snare.* She had thought it must have been torn free by some unruly sheep—but it had been something else. A wolf or a hound. And it had attacked her neighbor.

She heard the bleating first. Rounding a bend in a narrow path, she saw the Davieses' small home. The goats were pressed to one side of their pen. The sheep had picked up on the panic and were calling out to one another.

Branwen did not need her magicked sight to see what had panicked the livestock. There was a splash of crimson across the hard earth, and two goats lay unmoving amid the grass.

"Stop," she said, grabbing at Gwydion's elbow.

The mare slowed to a trot, then a walk. Without waiting for her to halt, Branwen slid from the horse. She held out her pack to Gwydion. Palug yowled from inside.

Gwydion looked as though she were offering him a bag of black powder that might explode at any moment.

"My house is farther down the road," she said. "Take my cat, go there. Wait for me. In exchange, I'll hear you out."

The confusion vanished from his expression. He took the pack. Palug's growls grew louder, and claws appeared in the cloth, flexing threateningly.

"Be careful," Gwydion said.

Branwen did not answer; she was striding toward the goat pen. Behind her, the sound of hoofbeats became distant.

She grimaced, took a breath, and stepped over the low fence. One goat fainted at the sight of her, flopping over with its legs stiff and eyes rolled back. The others gazed at her with terror.

"It's all right," Branwen said, in what she hoped was a soothing voice. "I'm not going to hurt you."

The goats did not look reassured. Branwen turned her attention to the dead.

The goats had been mauled and left to die. Not wolves, then. In Branwen's experience, wolves would take stragglers from a field, but they would never come into a pen nor attack a farmer in the middle of the day.

Which left only one option, and it was the one Branwen liked the least: that pack of escaped war hounds. She had known it was only a matter of time until they grew bold. A wolf would fear a human; a monster would fear iron. But a hound had no fear of either.

There were four sets of dog prints she could see. The prints overlapped one another, claws long enough to have torn some of the dirt as they sprinted away. They had been running—all but one, it seemed. Beside those tracks was trampled grass, as though a heavy load had been dragged.

Davies, Branwen thought, her mouth a little dry.

The trail led south into the fields. With a soft breath, she reached up and yanked her blindfold free. She wanted both eyes for this hunt, even if it was not magical in nature. She needed to find Davies and deal with those hounds before any more blood was spilled. She hastened into the long grasses of the fields, searching.

She found him. Or rather, she tripped over him.

Branwen hissed in surprise, sidestepping so quickly she nearly fell into the dead grasses.

She saw the familiar silver of his hair first. Davies lay face down, his arm outstretched as though reaching for home.

Swallowing hard, Branwen knelt beside him.

He had not died well. She could smell the sharp, acrid scent of urine, and she could see where the dogs had torn into him. Near his right hand was a small axe, the blade stained with fresh blood. Davies had wounded one of them, at the very least.

Branwen knelt beside him, reaching down to adjust his cloak so that it fell across his face. "I'm sorry," she whispered. She could not have saved him; he would have been dead before his wife managed to reach the tavern. That knowledge did nothing to assuage the wave of guilt that rose up within her.

She took a step back, trying to see the man's death as a huntress. The bite marks, the tracks—these belonged to those hounds.

She needed to find them before they killed again.

The tracks were messy and confused as though the dogs had fought among themselves. A spatter of crimson had fallen upon the dead grass; when Branwen touched it, the blood was damp beneath her fingertips. They could not be far.

As she half ran through the fields, a sense of unease tugged at her. She could not have named the reason, but with every step, her body seemed to wind tighter. Branwen took a deep breath, trying to let that unease pass through her.

The line between hunter and hunted was fear. The moment she was afraid, she would become prey.

The sounds of barking and howls hastened her steps. It was only as she reached the top of the hill that she realized what was wrong. The noises were not those of a hunting pack. They were the screams of a dog in pain.

Branwen slowed. As she crept nearer, she strained to listen. She peered through the bushes, and she saw them.

There were three hounds. One of them lay on the ground, clearly dead. The other two were pacing around the corpse, snarling to themselves. The late-autumn sunlight illuminated golden tufts of fur in the grass and nearby bushes.

Had the dogs killed one of their own? No, there was a blade wound on its abdomen. Davies must have struck true. The two other hounds sniffed at their pack mate, growling.

Branwen sucked in a breath.

She would need to do this before the dogs realized they were under attack. She drew her bow, heaved the string into place, and plucked two arrows free. She had only a few arrows left; she would need to craft more. She pulled back the bowstring, until the arrow fletching brushed the corner of her mouth. It took strength to hold the bowstring taut and unwavering, and she was glad she had spent years honing her body. She felt the air move around, smelled the scents of the harvested fields. The tension of the bow was a familiar one, almost a comfort, and she held it, aiming at the first dog's throat. It lifted its head, sniffing at the air.

Branwen let the first arrow fly.

It cut through the air with a near-silent hiss, striking true. There was a startled yelp and a thump, but before the second hound could react, Branwen fired again.

The dog whirled.

She was not so lucky this time. The arrow hit the hound in the side, and the creature fell, crying and whimpering. A sympathetic ache swelled in Branwen's chest—she hated the sound of anything in pain—but she forced it back down. If she could have saved these animals, she would have. But these dogs had been mistreated and let loose. They would kill others. A swift death was the best kindness she could offer.

The third arrow slammed home. All went quiet.

With a soft exhale, Branwen sat back on her heels. She had not saved Davies, but she had avenged him. Perhaps her neighbors would find some small comfort in that.

But if she had been victorious, then why was her heart still pounding? Why was her every sense still straining? Why did she see gold flecks in that clearing, like motes of dust?

She blinked. Once, twice, then she remembered. There had been four sets of tracks.

And there were only three dogs in that field.

Oh.

Branwen's eyes flashed wide. She swallowed down a startled little noise, because that was when she heard it: the unearthly baying of a hound that had scented prey.

It felt as though someone had dripped ice water down her back. Biting back a curse, Branwen looked wildly about the fields. There was no place to hide, nowhere to run. There was a short stone wall that separated the divide between Davies's and Rhain's farms. An old sycamore grew there. Heart hammering, Branwen sprinted toward the tree and heaved herself up into the branches. She just needed to be off the ground to get a good vantage point. She drew another arrow—her last.

She licked her dry lips, trying to force her breaths to steady. She had been in far worse situations than this. One last hound and this hunt would be ended.

But even as the thought crossed her mind, everything changed.

The heartbeat in her ears softened, then vanished altogether.

Everything was quiet. No, not quiet. Utterly *soundless*. It was as though someone had stuffed her ears with cloth. Panicked, she reached up and snapped her fingers next to her left ear. Had she lost her hearing?

She opened her mouth to make a sound, any sound, when it hit her: This was unnatural. This was magical.

And it had only happened once before.

She gritted her jaw, clenching every fearful noise behind her teeth, and waited. It felt as though an eternity passed with every heartbeat, but she remained still.

Then she saw it.

The monster slunk out of the tall grasses. It was lean, almost skeletal, with sleek white fur and red-tipped ears.

One of the cŵn annwn.

It was said that they were portents of death. To hear the baying of a ci annwn was to know that one's time had come.

Branwen knew better. A ci annwn did not foretell a death—it *was* death. The cŵn annwn could crack bone with their jaws, could scent blood across forests and fields, and could run as swiftly as a horse. They were the Otherking's hunting hounds. She had been seven the first time she'd seen one stalking a traveler. It was whispered that the closer a ci annwn came to its prey, the softer its howls grew. When death came, it did so quietly.

Of all the monsters she had encountered, only a few inspired nightmares.

The hound paused beneath the tree, its nose lifted to the wind. It drew in a long breath, taking a step forward. Branwen saw the flash of iron at its leg.

The snare. Her snare. The hound had been snagged in her snare and torn it free. Even now, the hound dragged the iron stake behind it. The iron must have driven it to join the mortal hounds and begin a hunt.

This was her fault. She had set those snares. If she hadn't, perhaps the creature would not have gone mad. Perhaps Davies would still be alive.

Her fingers twitched toward her bow. If she could fire an arrow into the monster's heart, at least she would end its suffering. Surely that would be a mercy.

Slowly, ever so slowly, her fingers grasped the bowstring.

The monster sniffed, then sniffed again, its attention caught by an unheard breeze.

The wind was against Branwen's back. Blowing toward the creature.

She went cold.

I'm not here, she thought, hoping against hope. *I am not here, you do not smell me, I—*

The ci annwn lifted its head and sniffed. It circled the place in the grass where Branwen had knelt. As it came nearer, she could see the bristle of fur running down its back and the glitter of iron tangled around its leg; she could smell the fetid stench. It smelled of decaying meat.

She drew the bowstring and sighted down the arrow. She needed a moment of stillness. A single moment—and she would end this monster.

But as though it sensed the movement, the ci annwn looked up and met her gaze.

For a heartbeat, the world froze. She saw the monster, and the monster saw her. Its lips peeled away from bloodstained teeth.

Branwen loosed the arrow. But even as it cut through the air, the ci annwn lunged to one side. The arrow sliced a line along its flank, staining its fur crimson. The hound snarled soundlessly, biting at its own flesh as though it could attack the pain. It whirled around once, twice, then stared up at Branwen. Bloodied foam flecked at the corners of its mouth.

Fallen kings. She was out of arrows and trapped in a tree. She still had her afanc-fang knife, but that would require her to fight at close quarters.

The ci annwn circled the sycamore, eyes never leaving its prey. Branwen bit down on her lip. There was no use in screaming; no one would hear her. Not with this blanket of silence pressing down on her.

The hound snuffled at the grass, then lifted its head. It drew in another long breath, its chest expanding. It was scenting her.

Branwen bared her own teeth in a snarl of challenge.

To her shock, the hound did not lunge for the tree. Rather, it turned and ran, leaping over the stone wall and—

Terror sparked within her, sending fire along her veins.

The hound had caught her scent. And now, it was following that scent back to the source.

The ci annwn was headed toward home.

She did not climb down; rather, she threw herself from the tree and landed hard on her feet. Pain jolted up through her ankles, but she ignored it. She ran as fast as she could. Faster than she had run in years. As the hound gained distance, the silence vanished from her ears.

Perhaps it should have been a comfort to hear again. But it only meant she could hear her own panicked heartbeat.

Mam.

Branwen would not let mortal nor monster harm her mother. She would tear Annwvyn apart if that was what it took. She would hunt down every ci annwn in those mountains. She pushed herself faster, lungs on fire as she rounded a bend in the trail. She would warn Rhain and Mam, get them into her house, and then hunt that monster. It would regret stepping out of the otherlands.

She darted through the fields, cutting across farmland until Rhain's home came into view. Her throat felt raw with every ragged breath, but she did not slow. Her feet slammed into the ground as she rushed past the small flock of sheep.

The quiet bloomed into silence.

And that was when she saw the attack.

The ci annwn had Rhain by the leg. The old hunter had a trowel in hand and slammed the cold iron into the creature's skull again and again, blindly trying to defend himself. Mam was perhaps ten strides away, frozen in terror. She could not see the creature, but she must have known something was there. Gwydion was in front of Mam, trying to put himself between her and the unseen danger. There was a knife in his hand. When he saw Branwen, he opened his mouth—but she never heard what he said.

Rhain kicked out, dislodging the monster's teeth through sheer luck. The hound snarled soundlessly, its fangs stained crimson. Branwen yanked the iron charm from around her neck and flung it at the hound.

The ci annwn seemed to sense the iron. It threw itself away, darting around the charm before plowing into Rhain. It tore into his side, and Rhain was screaming, screaming so loud and yet Branwen could not hear a thing.

She kicked the hound as hard as she could. Ribs snapped beneath her heel.

The ci annwn lunged at her. Its lips peeled back, eyes flashing—

Branwen slashed out with her knife. She felt the blow connect, felt the startled cry of pain as the afanc fang kissed flesh.

Branwen sank into a defensive crouch, knife held at the ready. The dog was limping badly, mouth foamy and red. It sprang at her.

There was no room for fear—she was pure fury.

Branwen screamed. And she drove the afanc knife through the hound's ribs and into its heart.

The hound twitched, then went limp.

Abruptly, Branwen could hear again. Her breaths were loud, a jagged gasp on every exhale. Behind her, Mam was sobbing and Rhain was making quiet sounds of pain.

"What in the otherlands," Gwydion gasped, his gaze on the ci annwn. Now that death had claimed it, its illusion was gone, Branwen realized. They could all see the hound crumpled and bleeding into the dirt.

"Rhain," said Branwen, rushing to his side. The older man was trembling, unable to stand.

Gwydion hastened to Rhain's other side. The young noble was pale, but his hands were steady as he tore off his cloak and bound it around Rhain's leg wound. Within moments, the wool was soaked through. She could see the throb and beat of his pulse.

"The bite must have nicked an artery," said Gwydion.

There was a terrible understanding in his face—a sympathy that made Branwen's stomach clench. She looked away; she couldn't meet his eyes while he looked at her like that. It made everything far too real.

Rhain's shaking hand reached for hers, and Branwen took it. "I'm sorry," she whispered. "I—I'm so sorry."

She should have been here.

Rhain shook his head. "None of that," he said. "Come here, girl."

Grief burned hot at the back of her throat. Everything about this was wrong—the way his hair was rumpled, the pallor in his face, the flecks of blood against his cheek. It felt as though she should have been able to set things aright if she just knew the right words to say.

"You've always been a good girl," he said. "Got no one to take the farm. You'll have to look after the chickens, the goat—"

"I'll take care of it," she said, her voice shaking. "I'll take care of everything, I promise."

His knuckles brushed her cheek. They were rough and too cold, but steady. "Good girl." He blinked, and each time it seemed to take more effort to reopen his eyes. "Always meant it, when I called you that. Wasn't just so I'd forget and use the wrong name."

"I know," whispered Branwen. "You—you were always—" But she did not know what to say. All the words dried up in her mouth. He had taught her how to hunt, how to track, how to craft and use a bow. He'd brought meals after her cousin lost his home and daughter. He had watched over Mam, fed Palug scraps, and treated Branwen with a gruff fondness.

Rhain may not have been of her blood, but he was family.

"I know, girl," he said. "I know."

And those were the last words to pass between them.

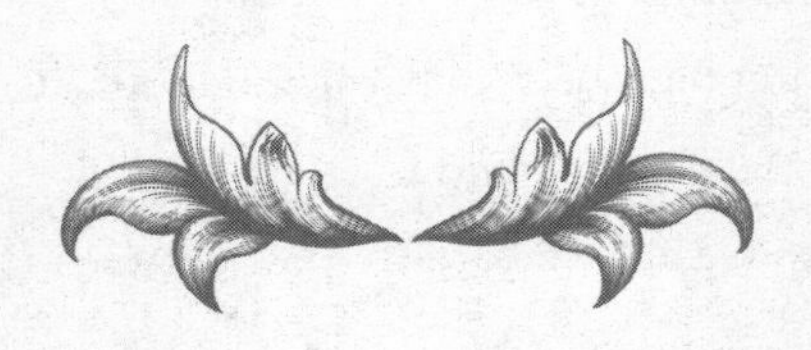

CHAPTER 11

BRANWEN SPENT MUCH of the afternoon digging a grave.

The shovel was old, the blade worn sharp and thin. It cut through the dying grass and dry soil, but the soil was rocky and stubborn. The work went slowly.

Branwen lost herself in the digging. There were other duties to tend to—she needed to return to Argoed and speak with Davies's widow. She needed to tell the villagers about Rhain's passing. Her mam's herbs still needed to be bought. Rhain's animals would need tending.

There was so much to be done; she ached with grief and exhaustion.

Part of her yearned to kneel beside Rhain, to simply sit next to him and pretend the old man was merely napping. But Branwen forced herself to dig.

She picked a place beneath an old oak tree. Rhain had often sat beneath it, enjoying the shade and view of his farm. *It's a nice place to hear myself think*, he once said.

She hoped that he would find this place as peaceful in death as he had in life.

Time passed—hours, though she could not be sure how many. Mam was at home, and Gwydion had gone...somewhere. Branwen could not bring herself to care about anything beyond the shovel in her hands, the weight of dirt, and the lingering scent of death.

It was only when the sun had begun to fall that she heard footsteps. Branwen was waist-deep in the grave. Her work had been slowed by thick roots and a few rocks that would not budge.

"I'm sorry."

Branwen looked up. Gwydion stood over her, kneeling beside the grave. Gone was the polished young man she had met in the market...had it only been that morning? It felt like a lifetime ago. His clothes were rumpled and dirty, and he looked as exhausted as she felt.

"Why?" she said. "This was not your doing."

"Nor was it yours," said Gwydion.

A flicker of anger pierced her numb exhaustion. This pampered lordling did not understand. She had set those snares and, in doing so, accidentally driven that ci annwn to madness. She had tried to defend Rhain's lands, and instead...he had died. "What would you know about it?"

"I know that you tried to save him," said Gwydion.

"I failed," she said dully. She let the shovel fall from her hands, and she knelt there, in a shallow grave with her dirt-stained fingers pressed against her eyes. Both eyes, as she hadn't yet replaced her blindfold. "Damn it."

"Here." When she looked up, she saw Gwydion holding out his hand. She considered not taking it, but there was nothing to be gained by scrambling out of the grave and knocking some of the dirt back in. She clasped his hand—it was the one without the brace, she noticed—and he hauled her upward.

"What happened?" she asked. "After we parted ways?"

Gwydion grimaced. "I went to your home with your cat. Who managed to escape your bag, I might add, and left some rather deep scratches on my arms. Your mother was there, and when she heard of the attack, she wished to warn your neighbor. Then that...that hound. It attacked us in your neighbor's yard."

"It was a ci annwn," Branwen said. "One of King Arawn's hunting hounds. It must have slipped out of Annwvyn so near the Hunt."

Gwydion nodded. "I suspected as much. I've heard rumors of such creatures—the unseen and unheard death, as the bards call them. You should be commended for killing it."

"I should have killed it before it slew Davies and Rhain." Branwen crossed her arms. It felt wrong to accept any praise for her failed hunt.

"I rode back to the village," Gwydion said. "After the attack, I mean. I let that tavernkeeper know what happened—he said he would tell Davies's widow and sent his sympathies about Rhain, and a basket of food. He also mentioned that the apothecary had the herbs you wanted, so I went ahead and bought them." He reached into his cloak and withdrew a small bundle of herbs. Mam's sleeping herbs, she realized. Branwen gazed at the dried flowers and plants.

This morning, it had been all she yearned for. But now, she just felt hollow.

"I can't pay you for them," she said.

Gwydion shook his head. "I did not ask for coin."

"I don't take charity."

"It's payment," he said. "For not letting me be eaten by a monster of Annwvyn. The political ramifications would have been…unfortunate. If one of the otherfolk slew me, my uncle might have been obligated to begin a war."

Branwen blinked in surprise. "Truly?"

"Or at least sent a strongly worded letter." His smile held a wry humor, but all the deprecation was aimed inward.

Branwen looked up. Sunset was less than an hour off. "I'll need to finish this tomorrow," she murmured, mostly to herself. "If I put Rhain in his house…mayhap the body won't deteriorate too quickly."

"That won't be necessary." Gwydion took a step past her. He looked up at the old oak tree, then down at the half-dug grave.

He closed his eyes and drew in a breath. Then he began to sing. It was a soft little song, a lullaby so quiet that the words blended into one another. He had a surprisingly pleasant voice.

Motes of gold appeared at his lips. Branwen took a step back.

Not simply a noble. A *diviner.*

As Gwydion sang, the ground shifted beneath her feet. It was not the ground, she realized. It was the roots of the old tree. They moved beneath the earth. The oak creaked as though waking from a winter's sleep.

The grave widened, the earth streaming away, as hundreds,

perhaps thousands of tiny roots coaxed and pulled at the dirt. Then Gwydion fell silent.

The grave was ready to accept its due.

"Do you wish to say anything?" asked Gwydion quietly. "Is there anyone else who should be here?"

Branwen shook her head. "He had no living family."

"He had you." The words came with surprising gentleness, and Branwen felt a lump rise in her throat. She had not expected tenderness from the likes of a pampered nobleman.

"He did," Branwen agreed.

For all the good it did him, she thought. She did not have the heart to say the words aloud.

Rhain's body was quiet and still. If not for the blood, she might have thought him sleeping. There was a small brooch on his cloak; she reached down and unpinned it. It was no great treasure, but she had seen him wear it every day since she was a child. And she wanted something tangible to remember him.

Once the brooch was in her pocket, she picked him up as best she could, half staggering toward the grave. Before she could say a word, Gwydion made a soft sound.

The roots slipped free of the grave, winding through the air. The roots curled around Rhain, gentle as a parent taking a babe, and settled the old man into the earth.

Branwen knelt. There was so much she wanted to say—and yet no words rose to her lips. When she breathed, her exhale was a stuttering little gasp. The grief cracked her open, gaped like a fresh wound. Rhain would have scoffed if she tried to offer a flowery farewell. So she said the only thing she knew he would have appreciated. "You'll be missed, old man."

They buried him together. Gwydion helped in silence, picking up shovelfuls of dirt and heaving them into the grave.

When they were finished, her fingers were sore, but the work had soothed the ragged edges of her grief. Gwydion's wavy hair had gone curly with sweat, and a flush had risen to his cheeks. He looked better undone, she thought. As though he were more of a person and less of a carefully arranged piece of art.

"Come on," Branwen said. "I need to return home before evening, and you might as well stay at the house tonight. I'll put some blankets before the fire."

If she had expected him to protest, she would have been disappointed. Gwydion gave her a shallow little bow. "My thanks."

Mam was glad to see them. As soon as Branwen stepped into the house, she was drawn into a bone-crackingly tight embrace.

"Oh, my dear," Mam whispered. "You were so brave."

Branwen returned the embrace slowly. She did not deserve thanks or praise, not with Rhain buried beneath an oak tree. "I should have done more."

"You did what you could." Mam brushed Branwen's hair out of her eyes. "You always do. My dear daughter."

Then Mam turned her attentions to Gwydion, clucking and fussing over his dirt-stained clothes. Gwydion made polite noises about the house and their meal of roasted rabbit and day-old bread. But when he thought no one was looking, Branwen glimpsed him feeding a bit of rabbit to Palug under the table.

The conversation was stilted. Mam was mostly concerned with the immediate aftermath: talking to their other neighbors, what to do with the chickens and the late harvest. Branwen simply listened, too tired to do anything else. When the dishes were clean, she brewed hot water, letting the sleeping herbs steep before giving the tea to Mam. Mam took it with a murmured thanks, not bothering to ask what was in it. A few months ago, she would have asked—but at some point, Branwen had become the head of their little household. It was disconcerting to realize that she held most of the power here.

When Mam retired to her bedroom, Branwen turned to Gwydion. He sat before the fire, gazing into the flames. "Sit with me," he said, patting the place beside him. "We should talk."

Branwen plopped down. Palug was in her lap before she could so much as blink. Her fingers wove through his black-and-white fur. He seemed to sense her grief; he head-butted her chin and purred loudly.

"Those herbs you gave your mother," Gwydion said. "They induce deep sleep."

She looked at him sharply. "I would not expect a nobleman to know much of herbs."

"I garden," he said.

She held back a snort. From what she'd seen him do with that tree, it was an understatement. She looked down at the brace he wore on his right hand. It looked like half a glove, wood keeping his fingers from bending too far in either direction. The leather was tanned and soft with age. He had clearly worn it for years. And it was that small detail that made her trust him—he knew something of pain.

"She has the memory sickness," Branwen said quietly.

"I'm sorry," he said. And strangely, she believed him. "She seems fine."

Branwen shook her head. "Evenings are when it starts. She will be restless, forgetful, and she might wander. Once, she went to the village and could not recall the way home. I don't dare leave for too long for fear of what would happen."

"That is why you worked for the barwn," said Gwydion, "because you needed coin to buy herbs that might put her into a sleep before the forgetfulness takes her."

"It's not a perfect solution." Branwen's fingers tightened on Palug, and the cat twitched in protest. He leapt from her lap and settled before the fire. "But even healers can only do so much." She exhaled hard. "Now, since we are being truthful with each other. What you did with the oak tree... I've never seen the like."

"Most haven't," he agreed.

"You're a diviner." He was not the first she'd seen. Branwen had glimpsed a diviner two years before in one of the western port cities. She had been a young woman dressed in a brown cloak and simple blue gown. As she moved, gold seemed to trail from her fingertips—lasting only a few heartbeats before it faded. The young woman had looked as though she yearned to remain unseen, and Branwen had let her go.

Branwen knew the comfort of being able to pass unnoticed. She wouldn't deny another that mercy.

Gwydion warmed his hands over the fire. "You sound rather certain."

"I am," said Branwen. "No one but one of the folk or a diviner could have enchanted that tree." She frowned at him. "Are you an oak diviner?"

He barked out a startled laugh. "Ah—no. Not oaks specifically. Plants and trees." He let his hands fall into his lap. He gave her a sidelong glance. "Now, another truth. You're no ordinary huntress."

It was her turn to say, "You sound rather certain."

"That hound," he said. "I could not see it until it was slain. But you saw it, even at a distance. The way you focused on it... you knew where to strike." Gwydion spread his hands as though in supplication. "And—forgive me for saying it, but I was under the impression you had only one eye."

Unthinkingly, she reached up and touched the corner of her right eye. Her blindfold was still tucked into her pocket. She'd forgotten to put it back on.

For a moment, she considered lying. But untruths had never come easily to her.

"I can see magic," she said.

He frowned. "No human can see magic."

Branwen rose to her feet. She kept pots of mint on the windowsill for tea and to tease Palug.

She plucked two leaves, then sat down before the fire. She held out the mint leaves. "Use your magic on one of them. I won't look while you're doing it."

Gwydion appeared unconvinced, but he took them.

"You want proof," she said. "I'll give it to you."

She closed her eyes and waited. After a long, skeptical moment, he said, "All right."

Branwen opened her eyes and surveyed the mint leaves. There was no telltale glitter of golden magic.

"You've divined neither," she said.

She closed her eyes again—and so she heard Gwydion's sharp intake of breath. A soft whisper and then something nearly like song.

Her eyes blinked open, and at once, she saw the glitter of gold. It danced around the left sprig.

She touched it. "That one."

Surprise flashed across his face. He glanced at the mint, then back at her. "I've...never heard of such a power."

"That's because it was an accident," she said. "My mam was a midwife. She delivered a child of the folk—and in the delivery, I was touched with the same oils meant to anoint the child." She touched her right eye. "Here. I use the iron blindfold to keep the power contained when I don't have to use it."

As she spoke, a light kindled behind Gwydion's expression. He looked like a man who had discovered a great treasure hidden in a heap of sheep's dung.

"Don't look at me like that," said Branwen.

"Why not?"

"Because I'm not as valuable as you think I am," she said tightly.

She did not know how to tell him that she failed far more often than she succeeded. She had not saved that traveler on the road when she was young; she had not saved her cousin's daughter when mercenaries came for them; she had not saved Ifor's son; she had not saved Davies nor Rhain.

The memories welled up like old blood, flooding her mouth with bitterness.

"May I?" he asked, gesturing toward her.

She shrugged.

He leaned into her, his hand hovering over her cheek. She could feel the warmth of his fingers, so close that a breath could barely pass between them. He studied her, a line of concentration between his brows. "I can't see anything abnormal about that eye." He sat back, hand falling away. "Why do you keep your power hidden?"

"Because I would rather not be conscripted," she said tartly, "by Gwynedd's spymaster."

Gwydion opened his mouth, as though to protest that such a thing would never happen.

"All right," he admitted. "That might happen. But we don't have a spymaster—just me."

"The court gardener?" she said skeptically.

"The court trickster," he amended. "I found secrets more useful."

"Pity, that. I think plants are better company than secrets." Branwen sighed. "But now you know why I can hunt monsters. It is why I agreed to look for Barwn Ifor's son. Because I alone can slip in and out of Annwvyn without fear of being ensnared by a spell or one of the otherfolk. But even with my abilities, I'm not sure I could survive the Hunt."

He nodded. "Having seen that ci annwn, I understand your reluctance to join the Wild Hunt. Tell me, what do you want?"

She did not answer. Truths were dangerous as blades if placed in the wrong hands. And her wants were nameless things that she dared not give voice to. To do so would be to give them power over her. "You first," she said. "No lies. Why do you want to win the Wild Hunt?"

Gwydion's gaze flicked away. He seemed to be gathering his

words, pulling them from some deep and painful place within himself. "My uncle is the king," he said. "You know that, of course. What you don't know is that he plans to choose his heir from my siblings. My brother Amaethon is the king's first choice. He is..." Gwydion's right hand twitched. "...Not suitable. His cruelty could doom Gwynedd. My nephews were nearly killed less than a week ago because Amaethon has so many enemies he could not count them all. I fear what he would do with a throne." He inhaled deeply. "My sister, Arianrhod, would be a good princess, but she does not have Amaethon's ambition. But if I bring her the spoils of the Hunt, she could use them to take the throne."

Branwen blinked. She had never truly given much thought to the passing of Gwynedd's crown. For her, rulers were as distant and constant as the sun.

"Does the king know you're attempting this?" she asked.

"No, and he won't know until I win it," said Gwydion. "I'd rather not have him maneuvering against my plans in the meantime."

"So you're here for our kingdom?" asked Branwen. "You wish to save Gwynedd from your tyrannical brother?"

Gwydion smiled thinly. "Is that not enough?"

"For a pig-stealing trickster?" Branwen raised her brows. "Likely not."

That earned her a flash of amusement. "Well, you'd be right, then. I have other reasons to keep Amaethon from the throne. But my reasons are my own and will have no effect on the Hunt, I promise." His face cleared of mirth. "Now, I will ask again. What do you want?"

"Nothing you could grant," she said.

His calm expression did not waver. "What do you want?"

It was the third time he had asked that. In the tales, questions had to be asked thrice for them to be magical. She looked at the bedroom door.

"To keep my mam safe," she said.

He nodded, as if that were a reasonable price to pay.

"Be my huntress," he said, leaning closer. "And I shall give you and your mother a home where you need not fear for her."

Branwen flinched back. "I do not wish to live at Caer Dathyl."

"Nor should you. Horrid place."

She laughed, a snort escaping her before she could silence it.

"If you wish to remain here," he said, gesturing at the house, "I shall ensure the barwn will leave you be. You will never worry about coin again. Any hunts you undertake will be for your own benefit or that of your neighbors. Never because you have no power over your own life."

Those last words struck something within her. She knew what it was to scramble and scrounge. She could never recall a time in her life when she was not planning one meal, one day, one week ahead. Her life was a constant shuffling of resources—whether it be coin or food or time.

"And there's one more thing," said Gwydion. He cleared his throat. "The boon."

Branwen frowned. "The boon? That might simply be rumor."

"It's the truth," said Gwydion. "The boon is real. I have my sources. There was a hunter from Dyfed who used his boon to become a noble. Another asked for a magical ship that would never sink. And there was a woman who used it to cure her daughter of the plague. The boon can be anything you want... anything that magic or power can grant."

Treacherous hope bloomed in Branwen's heart. It was a dangerous thing to hope. It opened the door to so much pain. "You're saying... you're saying the Otherking could cure my mam," she said softly.

"That's precisely what I'm saying," agreed Gwydion. "And if my coin cannot sway you, perhaps that will."

Branwen swallowed hard. She imagined a future in which Mam was herself again—bright and whole and well. They would never have to worry about coin again. They could travel, or rebuild their home, or simply enjoy the luxury of never having to worry over winter-hungry bellies again. All Branwen had to do was win the Wild Hunt.

She couldn't do this.

She couldn't *not* do this.

"We're going to die," said Branwen. "If that happens, there'll be no one to care for my mam."

"I'll write to my sister," said Gwydion. "If we both end up dead, she will ensure your mother is taken care of." Gwydion rubbed his thumb across the dragon of his signet ring. "You have my word."

The Wild Hunt was for kings and monsters, not a trickster and a huntress. But she was no ordinary huntress. She was the only human alive who could pierce the illusion of magic. And Gwydion had a power she had never even heard of. The very trees and plants would answer to him.

Perhaps they could manage this. A hunt to upend her life, a way to find her feet anew.

"If I do this, I'll need someone to watch over my mam while I'm gone," she said.

Gwydion nodded. "Is there anyone in the village you trust?"

She considered it. "The tavernkeeper has a few nieces who could use the work."

Without hesitating, Gwydion pulled his pack between his knees and opened it. Branwen watched, brows raised as he rummaged through the contents. There were clothes, some firesteel, a small purse, and food that would not spoil. They were all of finer make than anything Branwen possessed, but it was all mundane. For a self-proclaimed trickster, she expected... more.

Then he reached into the lining of the bag. It was cleverly hidden, she realized, sewn so that only he could find it. From there, he withdrew a second purse. This one looked to be far fatter.

"Take this," he said, handing it to Branwen. The weight of it surprised her. Startled, she pulled it open. There was enough coin to keep herself and her mam fed for well over a year.

"Consider it your first payment," he said. "Use it to take care of your family while you're away. We have two days until Nos Calan Gaeaf. We must journey to the gates of Annwvyn to join the Hunt."

She gaped at the coin. It was the answer to so many of her sleepless nights, and he had handed it over without flinching. It almost angered her how easily he had fixed her problems with a handful of gold. She took a deep breath; if they were going to accomplish this, she needed him just as he needed her.

"This is folly," she finally said.

"My plans have been called worse," he replied. "Are you in?"

Branwen hesitated. And then she clasped his hand.

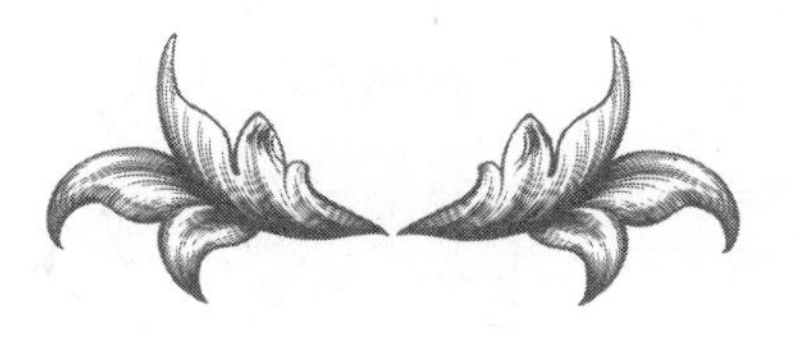

CHAPTER 12

ON THE DAY of Nos Calan Gaeaf, the gates of Annwvyn were guarded by mortals. Mist crowned the old mountains, and the air held the promise of winter.

A gray mare trotted toward the gates, and the rider raised his hand in greeting. His horse wore the colors of Dyfed, and the man was dressed like a noble. He bore a sword that was clearly more ornament than weapon. The soldiers relaxed. Then they tensed anew when they saw the woman at his back. She had an unstrung bow, a full quiver of arrows, a dagger, and enough scars to make them nervous. A cat sat atop her shoulder.

"Good afternoon," called the noble. "We apologize for startling you. I hope we're not too late to join the Hunt."

"Get the scribe," one of the soldiers murmured, before taking a swig from a half-full flask.

A scribe scurried out of a tent, parchment and quill in hand. "Names?"

And Gwydion opened his mouth to tell the first lie of many.

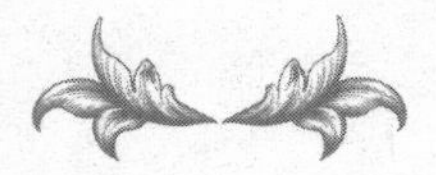

Branwen had been skeptical of Gwydion's plan from the beginning.

"From this moment, I am Nisien, the estranged third cousin of the Iarll of Emlyn," he said as they rode from Branwen's home. She cast one last look at her farm; it was everything familiar and dear, and she hated to leave it. She had told Mam she was going on a hunt, and that was not a lie. Glaw's niece was given coin and instructions, and she would keep Mam safe. They would be all right, Branwen told herself.

Gwydion continued, "I married a woman from Gwaelod and took to living on the coast. I have been invited to the Hunt out of courtesy, with little expectation that I will attend because no one else from my family will be there. However, I *am* attending. And you are the huntress I hired on the way so I would not embarrass myself."

Branwen bit back a snort. She kept one hand on his waist for balance. "That's the story?"

"It's the best explanation I could come up with as to why I attend the Hunt with a... lady lacking in rank."

Branwen did not bother to hide her snort a second time. "Was that little dance all to avoid saying the word 'commoner'?"

Gwydion laughed. "Sorry. It felt rude to say aloud."

"It's true. I am common."

"You are many things," he replied, "but common is not one of them."

She flushed and ignored the remark.

"Nisien," she said, "how did you come up with that story? And why is anyone going to believe it?"

There was a note of pride in Gwydion's voice. "Because I am a very good trickster. And it is not a story. Nisien is a true person with an invitation to the Hunt. I intercepted his invitation."

"And how do you know the real Nisien won't show up?"

Gwydion took a moment to answer. "Because he is dead."

Branwen grimaced. Surely, he hadn't...

"I did not kill him," said Gwydion, after an impossibly long moment. "He and his wife lived on the coast of Gwaelod."

Branwen understood at once. "He drowned when the kingdom flooded."

"He did," agreed Gwydion. "Before word of his unfortunate passing could reach his family, I intercepted those letters. And from there... I simply replaced them with my own. His family thinks he is alive and well. That is why we can sneak into the Hunt when no one else can. Because we have a true invitation... even if it is addressed to another."

Branwen's neck prickled with unease. "So you took a dead man's name? This is... something you do?"

"I keep my own little garden of spies," said Gwydion. "Thieves, mostly. Beggars, children, those who need coin or healing or help. Most of them are in Gwynedd, but I have sent some to other kingdoms." He must have sensed Branwen's displeasure, because

Gwydion added, "After the Hunt, Nisien will suffer an accident of his own. Let his family mourn him properly. But for now the guise is necessary. And if you think Dyfed does not have their own spies in Gwynedd, then you are far more gullible than I thought."

"And what is my name?" she asked. "In this little ruse of yours?"

Gwydion took a moment to answer. "I admit, that same question has crossed my mind."

She swallowed hard.

"When Rhain was attacked," said Gwydion, "I heard what he said... something about calling you 'girl' for fear of using the wrong name."

She had almost forgotten that Gwydion was there for Rhain's passing—and all that it had entailed. She considered her answer.

"Branwen is my name," she said. "Or, it is now. One of the folk called me that when I was a child. Three of them discovered what I could do, and I feared that they would find me and my mam if they knew my true name. They can do that, you know. Names have power." She drew in a long breath, tasting the cold autumn air. "I refuse to belong to another."

Gwydion tilted his head so he could meet her gaze over his shoulder. To her surprise, there was understanding in his expression. "I see." He cleared his throat. "Then you shall be Branwen, huntress of Argoed, lady of the arrow and blade. The huntress I chose above all others."

She rolled her eyes. "Does that sort of flattery work on noble ladies?"

"On noblemen, too," he replied. "Everyone enjoys a touch of well-placed adulation."

Branwen snorted for a third time. "Who else will be at this hunt? Anyone I should know of?"

"Well, King Arawn," he said dryly.

"Of course," she said, her tone equally dry.

King Arawn had ruled Annwvyn for centuries. The king of the tylwyth teg, lord of the otherlands, immortal and untamed as a winter storm. It was said he wore a crown of bones and had hair red as blood. He kept to his fortress of Caer Sidi in the farthest reaches of the mountains.

"And King Pwyll," said Gwydion. "And I heard that his son, Pryderi, fought a duel for the honor of entering the Hunt."

Branwen furrowed her brows, trying to remember what little she knew about the royal family of Dyfed. The southernmost kingdom of the isles was a prosperous one, brimming with trade, mines of copper and lead, sea fishing, and farmland. "Pryderi. Pryderi. Why do I know that name? There was something about a monster, right? Did he try and take one for a pet?"

Gwydion shook his head. "Other way around. There were rumors that King Pwyll wasn't his father by blood, that his mother had taken an afanc as a lover. And the afanc took Pryderi to raise. He was only recovered a few years ago."

Branwen made no attempt to hide her disdain. "I suppose that is a rumor you created."

"I would never repeat such slander," replied Gwydion. Then he added, "The rumor I started was that Pryderi was dead and this new king's son is a convenient replacement."

"You're so kind," she said.

Gwydion shrugged one shoulder. "It's politics. Dyfed and

Gwynedd are rivals, and for decades, Dyfed's closest ally has been Annwvyn. It's why none would dare attack Pwyll openly—he could call on Arawn. And the Otherking has never been fond of my family. We have too much magic for his liking."

She swallowed. "And yet you're still going to slip into his Wild Hunt, invade his lands, and win the entire thing under an assumed name?" She looked at his signet ring; it gleamed upon his left hand. A dragon, as befitted one of the royal family of Gwynedd. "Your ring is very subtle," she added wryly.

Gwydion's thumb rubbed across the ring. "I'll stash it in my cloak. And no one will suspect us."

She raised her brows at him. "Because you're a better spy?"

"Trickster," he amended.

"What is the difference between a trickster and a spy?"

"Spies are paid," he said.

To Branwen's surprise, Gwydion's plan worked.

A harried-looking scribe checked the name *Nisien* against her own records, looked over the royal invitation Gwydion drew from his pack, then waved them past the soldiers. The soldiers eyed Palug with confused frowns, but no one made to stop them. With every step, Branwen tensed. This was too easy. Surely it should have been more difficult to infiltrate the Hunt.

The scribe led them toward the wood. "You cannot take any iron with you," said the scribe, with a glance at Gwydion's sword.

"Weapons will be provided at the hunting camp. If your signet rings are made of iron, those are permitted. But nothing else."

"Of course," said Gwydion smoothly. "Give us a moment?"

The scribe nodded. She seemed used to taking orders from entitled nobles; she retreated out of earshot.

Unbidden, Branwen's hand rose to her iron-stitched blindfold. She had not realized until this moment that she could not take it with her. The same iron that kept her from seeing magic would be forbidden in Annwvyn. With shaky fingers, she unbound the cloth. She felt vulnerable and bare without it.

Even on the fringes of the wood, Annwvyn seemed to pulse and throb with enchantment. A bird cried out, and Branwen looked up. At first, it looked to be a normal swallow—but as her sight adjusted, she saw the bird glitter with gold. Its eyes were oddly human.

"Branwen," said Gwydion. "Are you all right?"

She glanced at him. He knelt a few paces away, unbinding his belt. There was an iron clasp, she realized. "I'll be fine," she said. "It's just... disconcerting, at first. I'll end up with headaches, but that will take a few days."

Gwydion's lips pressed into a sympathetic line. "I have herbs, if you need them. Willowbark, for pain. Others for swelling and infection. A tincture of poppy, if things become unbearable."

"I'll be fine," she said. She would endure the pain. For her mother.

Once they were finished discarding their iron, the scribe returned. "Come with me."

They followed her from the outskirts of the forest, toward a narrow path. It looked as though many people had come this way recently; Branwen saw footprints etched into the dirt, and the nearby grasses were broken. She and Gwydion must have been among the last to arrive. The forest was ancient, the trees worn by wind and time. Roots dipped and curved through the earth like fish through streams. Late-harvest blackberries gleamed in the sunlight.

As they approached, Branwen heard song. It was not birdsong, nor did it sound human. It had the slow cadence of a song sung around simmering embers, when the fire had all but gone out and the stars were bright overhead. She shivered.

The trail rounded a bend, and then Branwen saw a strange sight. At first, she thought someone had planted silver flowers alongside the path. Then her eyes settled on a sword hilt. Someone had plunged the blade deep into the earth and left the weapon to rust. There were others: shields, spears, arrows, a few crossbows, and scattered caltrops.

"What are these?" said Branwen.

The scribe said, "Not all hunters return to claim their weapons."

Branwen's heart lurched.

It was a graveyard.

There might have been no bodies, but these weapons were unspoken grave markers. Her gaze darted across all those rusted swords, those rotting arrows, the blades and the armor. Every single piece had belonged to a hunter who had not survived.

Gwydion drew in a breath as they passed by. His right hand twitched, then he slipped both hands beneath his cloak. Palug trotted along, pausing to sharpen his claws on a tree.

The scribe led them to where the sunlight ended and wood began. The canopy cast the world into shadow.

Two old yew trees stood at the entrance of Annwvyn. Their branches were woven together to form an arch. Branwen's mouth went dry. She had never before glimpsed the gates of Annwvyn. The two ancient trees were spoken of in whispers and bardsong. It was said that King Arawn himself had planted and tended to them. They were bound to him, and he to them. All of this forest was his.

"I leave you here," said the scribe, with a small bow. "Follow the path to the hunting camp. It will take a few hours. The folk have left lanterns to mark your way. Do not leave the path, no matter what you see."

"Thank you," said Gwydion, touching a hand to his heart. Then Branwen realized that he had drawn a gold coin from the purse that hung around his neck. He tossed the coin to the scribe, who caught it easily. The woman gave Gwydion a more earnest smile.

"I hope you return, Lord Nisien," she said, then turned and hastened from the gates. She looked as though she wished to be out of sight of them. Branwen had the feeling the woman would sleep with iron in her pockets tonight.

Gwydion and Branwen gazed at the yew trees. An inhuman song rose in her ears without any true source to pinpoint. It rose and fell, wordless and beautiful, and Branwen found herself straining to listen. Without iron to shield her, that song crystallized into words.

Every fifth year as harvests wane,

Two kingdoms meet in wooded domain.

"Can you hear that?" whispered Branwen.

Gwydion gave her a sharp glance. "The song? Of course."

"Can you understand it?"

His brows drew tighter. "No." Then with dawning comprehension, "Can you?"

She nodded.

And those who cannot hunt nor slay

Belong to your king for a year and a day.

"You still want to do this?" asked Branwen.

Gwydion squared his shoulders. "A little late for doubts."

Something moved in the trees. Gwydion seized Branwen's hand, as though to draw her behind him. They gazed into the trees, and a few heartbeats later, a flock of birds flitted through the branches. Palug chittered at them, tail lashing.

"We'll be fine," said Gwydion. It sounded as though he were telling himself that. His hand was still in hers. Perhaps she should have shaken him off. But it felt good to grip something human, something mortal. Palug trotted ahead, standing between the gates like he belonged there. He glanced back, as if to convey impatience.

With the othersong in her ears and a trickster's hand in her own, Branwen stepped through the yew-tree gates of Annwvyn.

Kings and beggars, trust to your aim—

For in the Wild Hunt, all are fair game.

~~The Monster~~

The Prince

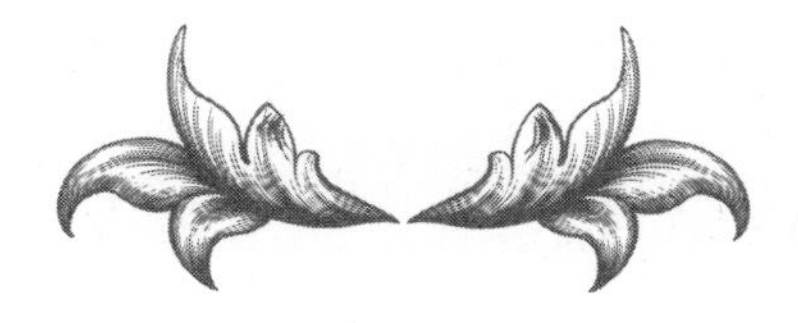

SOME MONSTERS WILL *take children—not to eat but to raise. For not all monsters are born with claws and fangs. Others must be forged with cruelty.*

In the kingdom of Dyfed, monsters lingered in the old places, in the shadows untouched by humans. One night, a monster crept into the king's castell. The king's wife was recovering from the birth of her firstborn son. She slept deeply, her son safe with her maids. But the maids were distracted, and when one of them left the lad unattended, a monster—an ancient afanc—crept into the bedchamber and stole the babe.

It left behind only an empty cradle.

Screams rang out; cries resounded; soldiers and servants alike searched every room, every hidden place. But the child was nowhere to be found. The king turned his wrath upon his wife's maids. Desperate to save themselves, one maid used chicken's blood to mark the cradle while the other claimed to have seen the queen murder her own child. Enraged with grief, the king locked the queen in her rooms and refused to listen to her denials.

Meanwhile, the afanc raced through the night, carrying the babe and leaving a kingdom to mourn.

The afanc raised the boy, teaching him the way of monsters. The boy learned to stalk and hide, learned the taste of fresh lake water and the touch of moonlight. He learned how to fight, how to return every blow with his own.

When the boy was seven, the afanc took him to a farm. It was time for the boy's first hunt—and so the monster decided to make the kill an easy one. There was a sleeping mare in the barn.

"Slay it," said the afanc, in a voice like brackish water.

The boy looked at the mare. She was impossibly soft and peaceful, and the boy yearned to reach out and stroke her nose.

"I don't want to," said the boy.

The afanc hissed and struck him. "Do as you are told."

The boy stumbled back, his shoulder slamming into the stable door. The sound woke the mare, and when she saw the afanc, the horse began to kick and scream.

The commotion woke the farmer. Armed with iron and more foolishness than bravery, the farmer snuck up on the monster. The afanc heard the farmer's footfall and began to turn. The fight would surely end with the farmer's death.

Desperate, the boy looked about, and he saw a comb hanging from the stable wall. It was meant to groom the mare, and the teeth were too short and blunt to do real injury. But it was made of iron. With a scream, the boy seized the comb and drove it into the afanc's side. It whirled on the boy, distracted by the kiss of deadly iron. That moment was all the farmer needed.

The afanc screamed as the farmer's pitchfork pierced its back. It writhed, digging claws into the loose hay and packed earth. But the farmer held on, driving the blades deeper until the monster went still.

And finally, the monster died.

The farmer stood there, chest heaving. His wife came out of their home, kitchen knife in one hand and lantern in the other. When she lifted the light, illumination spilled over the dead form of the afanc. She opened her mouth to berate her husband for risking his life—and then she saw the boy.

He had pressed himself into a corner of the stall, trying to hide, for all he knew was cruelty, and he expected more of the same. The farmer's wife scooped up the boy, comforting him with practice. They had three daughters and one son of their own, all born to work the lands. Another healthy child was a blessing the farmer and his wife would not turn away. And so they raised the lad as their own.

The boy grew up with golden hair and a quiet demeanor. He tended the sheep, the chickens, and the pigs, and worked alongside his adopted siblings. During the day, all was well. But at night, the boy woke in tears. He dreamed of blood, of scales slick with lake water, of something hollow and hungry that dwelled within him. His mother soothed his fears, whispering that all was well, that no monster would ever touch the boy.

But what the boy never told his mother was that in his dreams, he *was the monster.*

When the boy was fifteen, all those in the nearby village knew the lad as a tall, handsome young man. A passing nobleman saw the boy and recognized his resemblance to the king. When he heard rumors that the farmer had rescued the lad from an afanc, he carried word back to the castell.

The king did not believe the story until the nobleman convinced him to look at the boy. The moment his eyes landed on the lad, the king realized his mistake. There was his son, dressed in the garb of a commoner and feeding chickens. Torn between joy and regret, the king paid the farmer and his wife a royal sum for their good deeds and told the lad of his true heritage.

Perhaps the boy should have been glad to know the truth, but he did not wish to leave his home. The farm was familiar and safe—but his adopted mother bundled him in a cloak, hugged him close, and whispered that he could be whoever he wished. A prince had that power.

Wishing to be brave, the boy decided to go with the king. He returned to the castell as a legend, a story, and he was welcomed by his birth father and mother alike.

It should have been a tale with the happiest of endings.

The boy tried to learn how to be a prince. He learned dances and diplomacy, manners and courtesy. But he never quite managed to fit into the royal court. The nobles were uneasy around a prince who had been monster-raised.

When challenged by other young nobles of the court, the prince tried to ignore the taunts. But when the boy was eighteen, he was ambushed by a noble's son. The prince fought back—but not as a prince should. He fought like a monster, all instinct and brutality.

Unease turned to fear.

So when his father asked if he would like to take part in the Wild Hunt, he agreed. There would be danger, but he did not care. This would be his moment, he decided. He would hunt the monstrous and the magical. He would prove himself.

For he heard what the court whispered.

That the monster had taken him because it had seen something of itself in the boy.

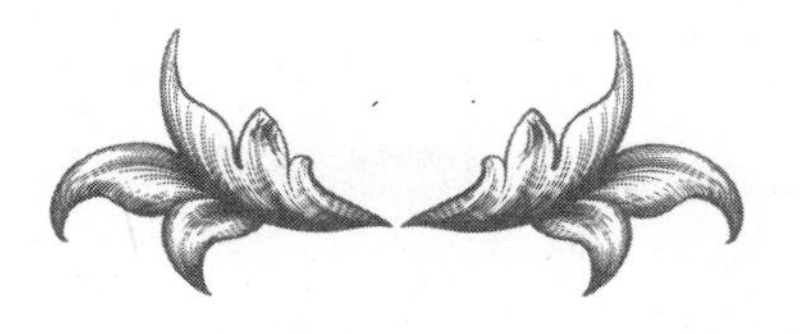

CHAPTER 13

AS LONG AS Pryderi could remember, Nos Calan Gaeaf began with fire.

People spent days gathering wood for the bonfires. Pigs, cows, and chickens were prepared for a feast, and the smells of cooking meats, breads, and sweets would send village children into a frenzy. At least one would try to steal a cake only to be rewarded with a stern glare.

There were old traditions. Some villagers threw marked stones into the bonfires, hoping to find them in the morn. It was considered good luck...although if one's stone could not be found, then the thrower would have ill luck for the rest of the winter. Children ran screaming around the bonfires, testing their courage to see who would brave the sparks. Hedgewitches brought apples and nuts to the fires, divining what they could from their burnt remnants. Older villagers brought chairs to sit near the warmth with a cup of ale.

Everyone looked forward to the festival, but there was always an undercurrent of tension. For the last day of autumn was when monsters roamed the mortal lands. There were rumors of a tree that would crack open to reveal a spiteful woman, a great hog would eat stray travelers, wraiths and ghosts wandered the fields, and even the tylwyth teg would walk among humans in mortal guise. The feast was as much a gathering for protection as it was a celebration.

As night fell within the mountains of Annwvyn, Pryderi felt the thrum of anticipation. Nobles and their chosen hunters were chatting among themselves, greeting friends old and new alike. Pryderi stayed in the shadows; he knew very few, and it felt far too awkward to join a conversation uninvited. So he smiled and fidgeted and tried to look as though he were having a good time.

When a messenger brought a summons from his father, Pryderi breathed a sigh of relief. It was an excuse to slip away. He found King Pwyll in the royal tent, tying a note to the collar of a corgi.

The small dog trotted toward the door, then looked at Pryderi. Pryderi stared back at the dog. It seemed to be waiting for something. Pryderi reached for the tent's cloth door and held it open. The corgi woofed a soft thanks and ran outside.

"They're spies and messengers, you know," said Pwyll, watching the dog go. "Strange little things, but Arawn favors them."

The thought of the formidable Otherking surrounded by a clutch of corgis was enough to make Pryderi laugh. "I like them, too." He could feel his father's eyes upon him, and he tried to stand straighter. "What do you need of me, Father?"

"Nothing," said Pwyll. "I simply wished for you to join me." He walked to the tent's door and gestured for Pryderi to follow.

Pryderi tried to look eager instead of uneasy. It was not his father's fault that Pryderi disliked celebrations. There were too many eyes upon him, too many whispers. "I was not sure what to expect from the festival tonight," said Pryderi. "I've only experienced Nos Calan Gaeaf with humans."

"The otherfolk celebrate the changing of the seasons as much as any mortal," said Pwyll as they walked toward the unlit bonfires. Night fell quickly in the forest, and the cool evening air nipped at Pryderi's bare neck. "More so, even. Tonight is a night of magic for them. They will have their own foretelling, their own dances. And you should take part, so long as you're comfortable. More alliances are forged with a shared drink than through formal meetings."

"Is that a command?" asked Pryderi, only half joking.

Pwyll's hand fell on Pryderi's shoulder, squeezing gently. "Make some friends, son. But do not drink yourself into a stupor. You'll need your wits this night."

Pryderi managed not to flinch from the touch. "I will try not to disappoint you," he said, and he meant it. He *would* try. He always tried to follow his father's word even if his best efforts yielded few results.

What his father did not understand was that Pryderi was not raised for parties and court intrigue. He knew how to navigate the sinews of a winter-barren forest. He knew the taste of fear on a midnight mist. He knew a wounded animal cry—or the imitation of one—would bring forth prey. He knew how to survive.

His foster family had taught him far gentler lessons: how to ask for and accept help, how to slip a hand beneath a nesting hen for eggs, how to bake bread, how to be human. He missed them dearly.

When he had lived with his family on the farm, it had been easier to put aside his monstrous upbringing. There had been no dangers to guard against, save for foxes and hawks that might prey on the hens.

Pryderi had not feared he would become a monster, for monsters needed enemies.

In the court of Dyfed, there were nothing but enemies. Even here, among Dyfed's allies, Pryderi could feel eyes upon him—weighing, judging, regarding.

He did not want to be a monster. He did not even truly want to be a prince.

But he had little choice in the matter.

A dais of gnarled roots had been constructed by magic. Upon it sat two chairs—one wrought of velvet and oak and the second of moss and yew. Two thrones for two kingdoms united in friendship. And beside each throne was a lit torch.

King Arawn and King Pwyll approached the dais from different directions. Arawn was the taller of the two. He looked as ageless as the moon. Pwyll was well into his fifth decade, and while his shoulders were still broad, he had a lined face and silvering hair. As the two kings clasped hands, Pryderi thought he saw a glimpse of how his father must have looked all those years ago when he first met Arawn. For the briefest heartbeat, Pwyll looked buoyant and young.

"My friend," said Pwyll.

"My friend," replied Arawn.

At the sound of their voices, the camp fell silent. All eyes were upon the two kings.

They turned to look at the hunting camp. "Welcome, all," said Arawn, placing a hand over his heart. "To my court, thank you for accompanying me. To my mortal friends, thank you for making the journey. I know it is not a short one."

"You'll find no arguments here," called out one of the Dyfed nobles.

Laughter rippled through the crowd. Even Arawn allowed the ghost of a smile to cross his mouth. "The Wild Hunt is one of our dearest traditions," he said. "It is to reaffirm our kingdoms' friendship. It is to remember how I met one of my dearest friends." His hand fell on Pwyll's shoulder. "We met on a hunt. Or rather, he intruded on my hunt."

"I did not know the stag was yours," Pwyll said good-naturedly. "And it's not my fault your hunting hounds were so much slower than mine."

Arawn waved away another bout of laughter. "I am very glad to welcome you all. Especially Pryderi, first and only son of Pwyll."

Cold nausea swam in Pryderi's stomach as all eyes turned toward him.

Every noble, every hunter, every servant—they were all gazing at him. Taking his measure. It was Pwyll who gestured to Pryderi, beckoning him toward the dais. To turn away or even to hesitate would be a display of weakness.

As he walked, Pryderi tried to glance at the crowds without seeing them, tried to let them become part of the landscape. It was the only way he could stand in front of them without feeling utterly self-conscious. He saw a middle-aged man from Dyfed who frowned and whispered to his companion. Cigfa wore a gown of feathers and velvet. She beamed at him, and Pryderi felt a small bit of relief. At least there was one person here who liked him. As his gaze drifted over the hunters, he saw a woman that made him blink. She had long, pale hair braided into a crown, and her eyes were a pale blue. A black-and-white cat perched atop her shoulder. The cat was such a surprise that Pryderi found himself looking at her longer than he should.

She met his gaze unflinchingly. Most did not. The servants bowed and averted their gaze around royalty; the nobles looked over him, through him, but never at him. But this woman regarded him without fear.

Pryderi was the one to look away first.

He stepped up to the dais. Feeling awkward, Pryderi turned to face the crowd. "This Hunt is particularly important to me," said Pwyll, and there was no mistaking the undercurrent of emotion in his voice. "For it is the first one since I found my son again."

A cheer rose up from the crowd. Pryderi did not know if he should join in it, wave, or simply stand there with his arms at his sides. The choice was made for him when Pwyll picked up the torch beside his throne. "Here," he said. "As my heir, you will light the first of the bonfires."

Pryderi took the torch, fervently hoping he wouldn't drop it. Wouldn't that be a tale to tell? He could imagine how the gossip would reach all corners of the isles.

Gripping the torch, he stepped down. Arawn was beside him, his own torch in hand. The Otherking's face was harsher in the torchlight, the gold of his eyes all the brighter and his smile like that of a wolf.

As one, Pryderi and Arawn tossed their torches into the bonfire. The dry tinder caught, and flames blazed. A cheer rose up from the crowd, and then hunters were thumping Pryderi on the back. It was welcoming, joyous, and he should have reveled in it. But the press of people and the closeness made his jaw clench.

Among the cheers, Pryderi heard drums and fiddles, crwth and song. With the first of the bonfires lit, other nobles were carrying torches to the smaller ones at the edges of camp. The festival of Nos Calan Gaeaf had truly begun.

Pryderi looked around, hoping that in the chaos and bustle he might see that flash of pale blue eyes.

But the huntress was nowhere to be seen.

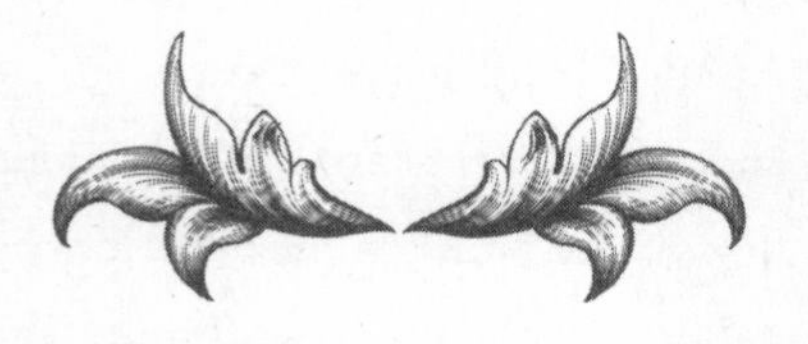

CHAPTER 14

GWYDION HAD SEEN his fair share of feasts, but even he was unprepared.

There must have been at least two hundred people in the camp. They were all dressed in finery—the human nobles wore wool and fur, while the otherfolk wore garments of silk and oak leaves, cloaks of spun lichen, feathers, and scales. He saw a man wearing a necklace of branches, his fingers tipped with elegant claws, chatting with a woman in a wool gown, a cup of wine in her hand. Dancers whirled and spun. Music slithered through the trees, but Gwydion could not pinpoint its source. He understood little, save for a wordless wail. The smell of roasted lamb made Gwydion's stomach lurch. He had eaten naught but dried meat and bread since leaving Branwen's house.

Palug sniffed the air. He had been sitting atop Branwen's

shoulder, but at the sound of the loud music, he flattened his ears and leapt down. He trotted in the direction of the food, his tail curled. Gwydion shook his head, amused. Hopefully the cat wouldn't steal the ham off some noble's plate.

Branwen was watching the dancers, a line between her brows. Her gaze seemed to flick through the crowd as though she could not settle on a single person.

"Tell me," he said, "what do you see?"

When she glanced at Gwydion, her pale eyes caught the firelight. "What?" she said loudly, over the music.

Gwydion huffed out a laugh. He leaned down to her ear. "What do you see?"

"Magic," she replied, turning her mouth toward his ear. "Everywhere. The Otherking... it's like looking at lightning." She touched a finger to the place between her brows. "I can't look for too long. It hurts."

"We'll find something to eat," he said, taking her elbow. He walked through the revel, the music throbbing through him. Others had lost themselves to it; they danced with sinuous grace and little regard for the eyes upon them. He and Branwen hurried past the dancers toward tables brimming with finely prepared fare.

Gwydion gazed at the assortment of food and drink. A tray of goblets had been laid out, and the thick, syrupy cordial smelled of blackberries and honey. He reached for one.

Branwen knocked his hand away. It hurt—the blow rattled through his right hand. His injured knuckles flared in protest. "Ow," he said, teeth gritted.

Understanding and regret flashed across Branwen's face. "Sorry," she said. "It's enchanted. You'd have slept for a week…or longer."

"Oh," he said, surprised. "Thank you."

Gwydion had never lacked for magic. As a diviner, magic was *his* in a way it was to few others. Only his sister, brother, and uncle could rival him for knowledge of it. Branwen had no magic of her own, but she moved through camp with an awareness no other mortal possessed. She would never be tricked by magic.

He would have to rely on her, he realized, in a way that he had not relied on another in years. The thought was not a pleasant one. Trust did not come easily to him.

"Is it an old injury?" Branwen asked, with a look at his hand.

He nodded. "I don't heal as well as I should. And while the bones did eventually knit back together, sinew and tendons are far more fragile."

She winced in sympathy. "I'll carry our food, then. Can you grab that bottle? That one there? It's safe."

He picked up the bottle while she took a plate and piled it high with food. There was a shoulder of mutton stuffed with oysters, onion cakes, chicken in brandy broth, salt duck in onion sauce, and boiled ham. Branwen picked over an assortment of savory pies: marrow, cockles, chicken and leek, and lamb with carrots and mint. Once she carried enough food for three, they retreated from the tables.

They found a bench near the edges of the revel, where they were half-hidden by trees. Bonfire sparks swirled into the air, smoke twining toward the open sky. They shared the bottle of cider and the plate of food.

Branwen gazed at the celebration with mingled wonder and irritation. "This feast could feed my village for a month. Is this how nobles prepare themselves for a hunt? Wear fine clothes, souse themselves silly, and go out looking for deer and rabbits with throbbing heads and dry tongues?"

Gwydion laughed. "In my experience, yes. These hunts . . . they're as much an excuse for excess as they are a competition."

"It's the same in your home, then?"

"Of course." Gwydion caught a glimpse of a woman holding fire in her hands. She exhaled upon the flames, and the sparks flew apart and reformed as tiny birds that flew into the darkness. "Only . . . ours don't have as much magic."

Branwen looked down at herself. "Are the clothes as restrictive as these?" She was dressed in a gown of green and gold, embroidered elegantly and fitted tightly through the waist. It made her look like some forest queen. She seemed to belong to the wilds, to the untamed places of the world. He had the unwise impulse to use his magic to conjure a crown of autumn flowers. But someone might notice that.

"You look beautiful," he said, and meant it.

Branwen rolled her shoulders, as if testing the strength of the fabric. "Beautiful, yes. Practical, no." She twisted around, looking at the bodice. "Just how much did this cost?"

He shrugged.

"Nobles," she said. "Never having to ask for the price of things. Sometimes I don't think you understand the power you wield."

The words struck unnervingly close to home. He recalled his own harsh words to Arianrhod: *Spoken as one who has never been powerless.* It was true that Gwydion had never possessed the power or respect of his siblings; it was also true that he was still the nephew of a king. Gold had little meaning to him; he'd never needed it. It was why he traded in intelligence and secrets.

Two of the folk approached their bench. There was a boy, perhaps a year or two younger than Gwydion, with striking red hair and sharp teeth. The other was a girl with a gown of moss and wispy lichen.

"Well, look who it is," the folk boy said to the girl. "Thieves are not welcome to the Hunt."

Gwydion drew in an involuntary breath. They must have recognized him. How? His mind raced to come up with a lie, an excuse. He felt like he had when Amaethon had held flame in his hand, staring up at the oak tree that Gwydion had taken refuge within. Trapped, cornered, helpless.

He had to talk his way out of this. He had to—

But before he could say a word, the girl knocked the bottle from Branwen's hand. It broke upon the ground, and the sparks of the bonfires glimmered on the shattered glass.

"That's not for you, crow," said the folk girl. "You stole Cydifor's magic."

"And my knife," said the boy.

It wasn't him, Gwydion realized. They had not recognized him. They were after Branwen.

His fear sharpened into anger. He stepped between the folk and Branwen, his words commanding and edged with an unspoken threat. "Touch her again and—"

The boy seized Gwydion's right hand. That grip was inhumanly strong, and pain flared down Gwydion's right arm. He twisted, trying to break free of the sudden agony that consumed him, but the folk boy flung him to the ground. Gwydion stumbled, falling to one knee. "I would really appreciate," he said, through clenched teeth, "if people would stop grabbing that hand."

"Humans," said the girl, making no attempt to hide her disdain. "You're weak, fragile, and so very greedy."

An old fury simmered to the surface. Gwydion had spent most of his life being called *weak*. Weak for a diviner, weak for a brother, weak for a royal. Part of him yearned to reach into his pocket, to take the blackberry seeds he kept hidden and unleash his power upon them. He imagined these two folk hunters wrapped in briars, powerless for the first time in their lives.

But the moment he used his magic, he would be unmasked. There was only one plant diviner in the isles—and he was the trickster of Gwynedd.

"Bold words," said Branwen. She reached into one sleeve of her gown and withdrew that wickedly curved knife. "For one who lost a fight to a mortal child. You never did return for this. Too frightened?"

The boy snarled. "No one frightens us, least of all a mortal. Give me my knife."

Branwen bared her teeth at him. "No. It does well chopping firewood."

Fury glittered in the boy's eyes. He lunged, and Branwen darted aside.

The gown was her undoing. Her beautiful, cursedly long gown. The boy stamped one foot upon the hem, and she fell. She rolled, trying to rise, but the boy's foot came down on her back, pinning her in place.

She clawed at the boy's ankle, trying to free herself. But he was as immovable as a mountain.

"We will have that eye," said the girl. She had a knife of her own.

Gwydion's mouth went dry. He had to stop this. He had to—

But he couldn't stop this, part of him whispered. The moment Gwydion used his magic, his plans would come undone. He had come too far, risked too much. He liked Branwen well enough, but if it came down to a choice of her or the Hunt, he knew which one he had to pick.

There had to be some words to disarm the situation, some way he could stop this without unraveling everything.

"We are here for the Hunt, as are the rest of you," he said desperately. "We are not here for trouble."

"Then give us her eye," snarled the girl, and drove the knife down.

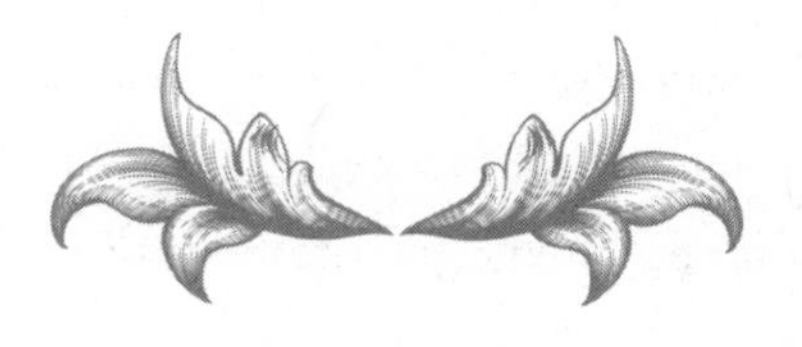

CHAPTER 15

PRYDERI WAS HIDING. This time, he would openly admit it.

The chaos of the revel was overwhelming. There were too many things to see and hear and smell, and it all came together in a din. So Pryderi retreated to the edge of camp, where none would see him.

With a sigh, he sat down on a fallen log. A knot of shame twisted in his gut. He should be out in the revel—making friends, drinking, eating his fill. But the thought was simply too daunting. He closed his eyes, tilting his head back toward the stars. He hoped no one would notice his absence. If they did—

Something brushed his left leg.

Pryderi leapt to his feet, heart hammering. He half expected to see one of the folk or perhaps a human hunter. But there was no one.

Pryderi looked down... and then farther down.

A black-and-white cat stood by his ankle. It had long fur and startlingly green eyes. "Hello," said Pryderi uncertainly.

The cat meowed and nudged at his leg. It seemed friendly enough. Pryderi squatted down and ran his hand along the cat's back. It arched into his palm, a purr rumbling in its chest.

"You're that huntress's cat, aren't you?" asked Pryderi. Perhaps it was foolish of him, but he had always spoken to cats on his foster family's farm. He had enjoyed their company; they were curious and affectionate.

The cat meowed again. The last time he had seen the creature, it had been atop a huntress's shoulder. Surely she would be missing it.

"Should you be out here alone?" asked Pryderi. "Where is your owner?"

The cat turned and trotted away. Then it looked back at him expectantly. Feeling both foolish—and a little relieved to have a task—Pryderi followed. He would make sure the cat ended up safely with its humans again.

But as he walked through the trees, the cat went still. Its fur stood on end, and it growled.

Pryderi frowned, but he heard it a heartbeat after the cat: the sound of raised voices.

At the edge of the camp, partly concealed within the trees, was the huntress. She had white-blond hair, wide-set pale eyes, and a scar across one cheekbone.

Two of the folk stood around her, caging her in. One was a young man with bloodred hair. He stood with a foot against the huntress's back, pinning her to the ground. The other was a young woman, her hair braided and her dress made of moss. They were as lovely as poisonous berries. A human man was on the ground a few strides away, face pale with alarm.

The folk girl lunged for the huntress, driving a knife toward the young woman's face.

Pryderi was moving before he made the decision to do so. He seized the folk girl's arm and yanked her backward. The knife plunged into the earth, and the girl tumbled over Pryderi's shoulder. She landed on her heels, nimble as a cat. She had to leave her knife embedded in the earth—for only a heartbeat. It was enough time for Pryderi to grab it. His fingers curled around the leather hilt, and the moment he touched the weapon, some hidden place within him relaxed. This was what he was meant for. Not for council meetings and diplomacy.

Pryderi bloomed in chaos. He thrived in upheaval and conflict, in those moments when there was too much danger to think. He did not have to worry about impressing anyone. All that existed was this moment: the knife in his hand and the enemy to be defeated.

The folk girl hissed, her fingers digging into the earth as she readied herself to lunge at him.

He let her.

She flew forward, just as the folk boy moved at Pryderi's back. He heard the whisper of movement, and without hesitating, he side-stepped the girl's lunge, grabbed her dress, and flung her. Her own momentum slammed her into the boy. They tumbled together, a falling star of tangled limbs and folk finery. When they landed, Pryderi stood over them.

"You know," he said, "trying to maim a fellow hunter during the feast is rather unfair."

The folk girl bared her teeth at him. "In the Wild Hunt, all are fair game."

"The Hunt has yet to begin," said Pryderi. "So scurry back to your friends and leave these two alone."

"She's a cheat," said the folk boy. "We met her when we were young. She'll steal your weapons and magic."

"If you knew that, then perhaps you should have left your knives in your tent." Pryderi gave the knife in his hand an indolent little twirl. He could kill them. He would have been well within his rights. These two had attacked him, the heir of Dyfed, without provocation. But the thought of sliding this knife into flesh made his stomach turn over.

He took a step back. "Leave. Both of you."

The folk girl and boy grimaced at him, but they did not attack. The girl darted a glare at Pryderi and murmured, "I see why only an afanc was fit to raise you." Then before Pryderi could reply, they both hastened toward the revel.

Pryderi's fingers tightened around the hilt. He forced himself to take deep breaths. *Calm*, he thought. *Be calm.* There were no more threats, no more battles to be won.

His gaze fell on the two humans. The pale-haired huntress was grinning at him. That took him aback—he half expected to see fear. The man stood half a step behind her, one hand raised as though to protectively draw her back.

"Well done," said the huntress. She had large eyes, a straight nose, and a delicate mouth. Her features might have looked waifish, but there was an untamed quality to her. Her smile was all teeth.

"You're welcome. And apologies," said Pryderi, "but I do not know your names."

"Which makes your timely rescue all the more welcome," said the young man. He had the attractive, finely wrought face found so often in nobility. His skin was pale, his dark hair combed away from his face. It was his eyebrows that Pryderi found himself looking at—those brows hung over his eyes like swords waiting to fall. "Nisien of Emlyn. And this is my huntress, Branwen."

Pryderi had spent the better part of a year memorizing the names of every noble family in Dyfed. It took him a moment to pull the memory; it was like trying to find a book he'd misplaced. Pryderi had met the Iarll of Emlyn, but not this wayward cousin. "I apologize. The rules of hospitality should have been honored—their attack broke that rule. I will bring word to my father."

"Your father," the huntress, Branwen, said. Her eyes widened, and he saw the moment she realized. "You're the prince."

"Please," he said. "Just call me Pryderi."

Nisien dropped into a hasty bow, but Branwen remained as she was. "There's no need to bring this to the king. That fight had nothing to do with the Hunt."

Pryderi recognized her desire for it to go unnoticed. It was the same for him when the noble boys of Dyfed murmured to themselves that Pryderi was wrong, that there was something unfit about him. He had never brought those words to his birth father or mother, for fear of bringing them to light. Some hurts were so close to the soul that they demanded secrecy.

"Well, let me bring you a drink to replace the one they destroyed," said Pryderi. "As an apology for your rude welcome to the Hunt."

Nisien said smoothly, "That's kind but unnecessary. We wouldn't want to demand more of your time, my prince."

There was something about these two that made Pryderi's neck prickle. It wasn't quite fear, and it wasn't quite excitement—but something in between.

Pryderi had been a farmer long enough to recognize foxes among the chickens.

"I insist," said Pryderi.

"That's very kind," said Nisien.

It was a short walk to the royal tent. Pryderi slipped inside. Someone had arranged a table of sweets. Among the cwnffets, cyflaith, and teisen fêl, there was a bottle of medd. He stacked a small plate full of the honey cakes and toffees. The mead was golden as the sun. It was a drink of kings, as few commoners could afford the honey. Pryderi had only tasted it on his first night at the court of Dyfed, at a feast meant to welcome the lost prince home.

He hoped that Nisien and Branwen had remained where they were—he did not relish the thought of seeking them out in the chaos and clamor. He hurried through the revel until he broke free near the forest's edge. Thankfully, Nisien and his huntress were where he had left them.

That black-and-white cat sat in Branwen's lap as she stroked his long fur.

"My apologies," said Pryderi, setting down the plate. "I saw that cat earlier and meant to return him to you. I was distracted by the attack."

"You're a prince," said Nisien. "You don't have to apologize to us." His hand hovered over one of the honey cakes, but then he did a strange thing. He looked at Branwen.

The huntress shifted the cat aside, leaning over the plate. Her gaze slid over each and every sweet, then the bottle in Pryderi's hand. "It's safe," she said.

"It should be," said Pryderi. He considered sitting upon the bench, but both Nisien and Branwen were comfortably settled upon the ground. He did not want to imply that he thought himself above them. So he crossed his legs and sat near Branwen. "The food is from my father's tent."

Nisien choked on his mouthful of cake, swallowed, then croaked, "We're honored."

Pryderi shrugged. "I know some of the folk enchant their own meals for enjoyment or trickery. I'd rather not wake in a month, wondering what became of the Hunt." He looked at Branwen. "Are you some kind of poison taster?"

Branwen snorted. "I'd cram a poisoned cake into his mouth before I'd take a bite."

"Such loyalty," said Nisien. If he was offended, he did not show it. Rather, he was grinning.

Many nobles had brought their own servants. It was widely accepted that in most hunts, the actual work fell to hired hunters. Nobles saved their strength for the honor of the killing blow. Skilled hunters were prized in many royal courts. But Pryderi had never heard one speak so informally to their employer.

"Did the two of you know each other before the Hunt?" asked Pryderi. Perhaps they were friends.

"I've known her less than a week," said Nisien.

Pryderi opened the bottle of medd but realized he'd forgotten to take any cups.

"Oh, just drink it from the bottle," said Branwen. "We won't judge."

Feeling a little self-conscious, Pryderi drank a few swigs from the bottle. The medd tasted sharp and sweet as honeyed sunlight. He offered the bottle to Branwen.

"I've never shared drinks with a prince before," said Branwen, taking it.

"Our mouth leavings taste the same as most people, I expect," said Pryderi.

She grinned at him. "I have to say, you're not what I expected."

Pryderi looked down at his hands. He'd folded them in his lap to hide the old calluses and scars; they were not the hands of a prince.

"That's a good thing," said Branwen. "I always thought princes would be more... finicky. Like cats." Her gaze went to the black-and-white cat in her lap.

"What is the cat's name?" asked Pryderi. He offered his fingers for the cat to sniff.

Branwen took her own drink of the medd, then made a sound of pleasure. "He's called Palug." She took another sip. "Where did you find this?"

"The medd is from my father's stores," replied Pryderi. "He brings a few bottles to every Hunt, or so I've heard." He reached into his pocket and withdrew a small hard cheese he'd wrapped in a cloth. He broke off a bit and offered it to the cat. "I took a little for the corgis," he said, when Branwen raised her brows. "I don't normally carry cheese around with me."

Palug sniffed the cheese, then delicately took it from Pryderi's fingers. He devoured it in a matter of moments. When Pryderi held out his hand a second time, Palug rubbed his cheek against his fingers. Perhaps it was the medd in his belly or the cat's acceptance, but Pryderi finally felt at ease. Surely anyone that kept a cat could not be so bad.

"Do you know what the Hunt consists of?" asked Branwen. "No one's told us yet what we'll be hunting."

"No," said Pryderi. "No one knows. The Wild Hunt...well, there are certain traditions. Once you join the Hunt, you never do so again."

Branwen swallowed. Nisien blinked.

"Not that everyone dies," said Pryderi, seeing where he'd gone awry. "I mean, some people do die. But a person can only join the Wild Hunt once. After that, they are magicked never to speak of what happened. I think it's to keep hunters from passing along secrets to their children, giving them an unfair advantage. Only my father and Arawn attend every Hunt."

"So no one knows," said Branwen, her lips pursing. "Not even a prince?"

Pryderi shook his head. "My father would not tell me." He looked at the others. "And why did you join the Hunt?"

"It's an honor to be invited," said Nisien.

"A true honor," agreed Branwen.

Pryderi raised his brows. He was not one of the folk, but some untruths were so blatant one did not need magic to hear them. "Try again," he said.

The line of Branwen's mouth fractured into a smile. "Because he's paying me. And I want the boon."

"Fair enough," said Pryderi. He suspected most of the other hunters would have said the same. He glanced at Nisien. "And you?"

"To win a family argument," said Nisien.

Pryderi was startled into a laugh. Those answers had the ring of truth. "I appreciate your honesty."

Nisien returned the smile with his own. There was something about that smile—it was too practiced, too perfect. "We do strive to be honest."

That was the moment Pryderi finally understood why his instincts were clamoring at him. It was Nisien's accent. The more he drank, the more his accent shifted. His words softened and became melodic.

That was not the accent of a man from Dyfed.

But before Pryderi could say a word, a loud horn rang out.

All of them looked toward the heart of the revel. "Listen well, all hunters!" came the call of a crier. "Listen well!"

"I should probably return," Pryderi said, rising. He gave Nisien and Branwen a polite bow.

"Perhaps we'll see you in the Hunt," said Nisien. His dark gaze rested on Pryderi, as though he were fixing the prince in his mind.

"Perhaps," replied Pryderi. Something in Nisien's face gave him pause, but he pushed aside his own hesitation. He would worry about those two later.

He made his way through the crowds, past humans and folk

alike. Everyone was gathering around the daises. As Pryderi watched, Kings Arawn and Pwyll ascended the steps for the second time that evening.

A hush fell over the crowd.

"A moment, if you please," said Arawn. He had donned his finger-bone crown and bare-bladed sword. His crimson cloak trailed behind him like spilled blood. "I hope you are enjoying the feast."

Cries of agreement broke out; there were cheers and raised cups. A few corgis even took up a howl.

"Good," said King Pwyll. "Now, a few announcements—first, weapons have been delivered to your tents. I know most of you had to leave your iron swords and arrows behind, so replacements have been provided."

Arawn held one hand up, then deliberately and slowly removed the signet ring from his index finger. At this distance, Pryderi could not make out the details, but he knew what the ring entailed: a sun and moon, balanced against each other. A ring for an eternal being, for whom time had little consequence.

Pwyll did the same, holding his own signet ring aloft. It bore the dragon and seahorse of Dyfed.

"These are the rules of the Hunt," said Pwyll. "Listen well."

The quiet drew into a taut silence. Pryderi's heartbeat quickened, and he strained to listen. He did not wish to miss a word.

"Capture an animal," said the Otherking. "Bind your signet ring to it. Then, you will hunt those animals that have been chosen to bear rings. Gather as many rings of value as you can. Bring them to your king. Hunters may work together in groups of no more than three—and those who bring the most fealty to their king will win the Hunt." Arawn smiled, the candlelight glittering in his golden eyes. "And those hunters will each receive a boon from myself."

A quiet rumble went through the crowds. While there were always whispers of the boon, even Pryderi had not been sure he believed in it. A boon from the Otherking would be magic few could ever dream of. It could change the course of a person's life.

Pryderi wondered fleetingly what he would ask for, if he were to win.

To go home, part of him whispered.

To be a good prince, he thought, trying to quash the first impulse.

"Any animal?" called one of the hunters from Annwvyn.

"Any animal," replied Arawn, with a knife-edged smile. "Be it mortal or immortal, so long as its heart beats and you can capture it—it may carry your fealty. I suggest you choose well, lest it be too easily slain. You may send the animal away or keep it with you, but the moment your own ring is captured by another, your time in the Hunt is ended. If you fail to bind your ring to an animal, you will not be allowed within the Hunt."

"How would we know if our ring is captured?" called one of the folk hunters.

Arawn's eyes gleamed gold. "You will know."

"And when we hunt?" said a huntress from Dyfed. "Must we bring the animal back alive?"

Arawn shook his head. "The ring is all that matters. As for your prey... in the Wild Hunt, all are fair game."

"We capture our animal at dawn?" asked another.

"No," said Pwyll. Even in the crowd, Pryderi felt his father's gaze fall on him. "You have *until* dawn to capture an animal."

Cries of protest rang out, but Arawn silenced them with a look. Folk and mortals alike had spent the last few hours drinking, feasting, and dancing. They wore finery and shoes unsuited to a hunt in the woods. And then there were the woods themselves. Outside the circle of torchlight, the world seemed to fall away. Trying to find an animal in the dark was an impossibility.

But this was the Wild Hunt. No one had ever promised it would be easy. This was why Pwyll had warned him against imbibing too readily. The medd in Pryderi's belly burned like a small honeyed fire. But at least he was on his feet.

Arawn raised one hand. His fingers were long, casting spidery shadows. His face held a gentle, wicked amusement.

"Good hunting," the Otherking said, and then he dropped his arm.

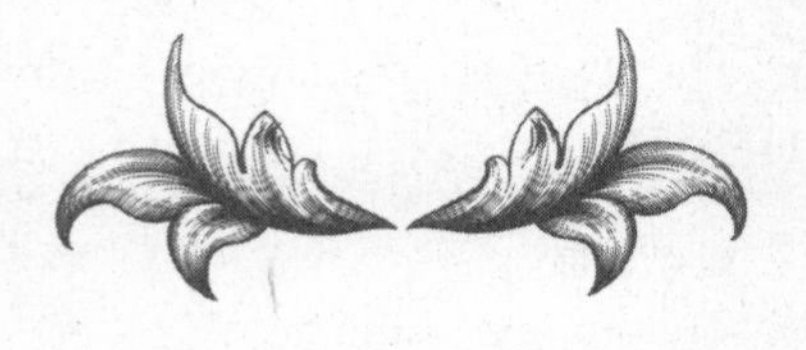

CHAPTER 16

BEFORE GWYDION COULD so much as draw a breath, he felt Branwen's hand close around his left wrist. She half dragged him toward their tent.

Moving through the crowd was akin to being caught in a stampede of panicked deer—everyone was fleeing in every direction, and it was all Gwydion could do not to let go of Branwen. Palug darted between the trampling feet with the ease of a fish navigating white waters. Finally, their tent came into view. Branwen pushed the flap door open, then yanked it shut behind them. It quieted a little of the clamor.

Someone had left an assortment of weapons resting on a bedroll. There was a crossbow, a short bow, bolts and arrows alike, a slender knife, and a longer spear. There were other tools: a lantern, rope, and a flask of water. "Good," said Gwydion. He yanked off his formal tunic and reached into his pack for more practical clothing.

"We should hurry, get as far out into the woods as we can before the other hunters can manage."

Out of the corner of his eye, he saw Branwen hastily untying her dress's bodice. Her fingers slipped on the laces, and she let out a curse. "This is why I never bothered with gowns. They're impossible."

Gwydion considered reaching out to help, but laces required both hands, and his right hand throbbed after the fight. He took a deep breath, closing his eyes. He hummed a soft little melody, drawing from his internal well of magic.

Branwen made a startled noise. "Gwydion!" The dress shifted of its own accord—cloth rippled away from her shoulders, her bodice loosening and laces giving way. The gown almost slid from her, but she clutched at the front. Her bare shoulders gleamed in the torchlight.

"I thought you divined trees," she hissed.

"Plants," said Gwydion, with a gesture toward her gown. "Your dress is made of linen."

She gaped at him.

"It's grown from flax," said Gwydion. "You didn't know that?"

"I'm a huntress," she said, "not a weaver." Then she frowned at him. "Did you buy me linen clothes on purpose?"

He huffed out a laugh. "They're well-made."

"That was not a no."

He shrugged. "I prefer to be around things I can control."

She gave him a skeptical glance. "Do you have many friends?"

"No."

"I can see why," she said. She looked down at her ruined dress. "That cannot be a good use of royal funds."

He silently disagreed. In that gown, she had been a bewitching creature of green and gold.

"Think of it every time you pay your taxes," he replied.

They dressed in haste and silence, yanking on boots and trousers, dark cloaks and belts. Gwydion knelt beside his pack, checking its contents to make sure nothing had been disturbed.

"So we have to find an animal," said Branwen. "Attach a signet ring to it. And then we hunt one another's animals and try to bring as many rings as possible to our supposed king. But if our ring is taken, we're out."

"I think that's an apt summary of the Hunt, yes," said Gwydion. He pulled the pack onto his shoulders. Branwen was picking through the weapons.

"Proving that this is a hunt created for nobles," said Branwen. "Most hunters won't have a signet ring. I don't have one. Does that mean I can't hunt?"

Gwydion had not considered that. He raked his eyes across the tent, searching for... something. Then his gaze fell on the brooch at her cloak. It was a brass circle, simple yet elegant. "That," he said, pointing at the brooch. "That should work."

Her hand went to the brooch. "If you think this thing will fit around one of my fingers, then I have vastly overestimated you."

"I know it's not a ring," said Gwydion. "But it's important to you, yes? You took it from the old man, Rhain. Signet rings are nothing more than who you are. Who your family is. If that man was your family, then take it. It will serve well enough."

Branwen's thumb traced the edge of the brooch. "You sound certain of that."

"I know something of magic," said Gwydion. "Much of it has to do with intent."

Branwen's mouth tightened, but she nodded sharply. "All right. If you think this will work."

"All of my plans work," said Gwydion.

"Even the impossible ones?" she asked.

"Especially the impossible ones."

She flashed a grin. He was not sure if it was the chaos, the danger, or the medd, but he felt a flush rise to his cheeks. The moment they had crossed the boundary into Annwvyn, they had become a team. They were united against the rest of the Hunt. And as much as Gwydion told himself he did not need anyone else, he rather liked that.

It was unwise, he told himself. This Hunt, this huntress—they were all merely part of his plan to keep Amaethon from the throne. He should not become attached to any of it.

"We should move," said Branwen. "Dawn is perhaps eight hours away."

Gwydion straightened his shoulders. "Lead on, huntress."

She turned, reaching for the tent door. Before she could touch it, the flap flew open. A sudden wind made the torch flicker. Something surged into the tent.

Branwen reacted at once, yanking a dagger from her belt.

But the attacker was too swift. It knocked an elbow into Branwen's shoulder with almost inhuman speed, then hooked her leg with his own, yanking her to the ground. Gwydion seized the only weapon he could reach: a long-handled spear. It was a terribly awkward weapon for a close-quarters fight, but it was better than nothing. Gwydion swung it round, hoping it would not snag on the tent wall.

The attacker ducked beneath the spear, one leg slamming into Gwydion's left arm. His elbow went numb, and he dropped the spear, dizzy with the sudden pain. Pain was nothing new to him—he lived with it nearly every day. But this was startling and sudden, and he could not guard against it.

Disarmed and gasping, both Gwydion and Branwen gazed at the monster that had invaded their tent. It wore a dark cloak, and when it rose, it stood taller than Gwydion.

They all went very still.

"Who are you?" said Gwydion, once he could speak. His heart hammered, and his mind was coming up with a thousand lies with every beat.

Their attacker pulled back his hood.

And there stood Pryderi, prince of Dyfed. "I should ask you the same question."

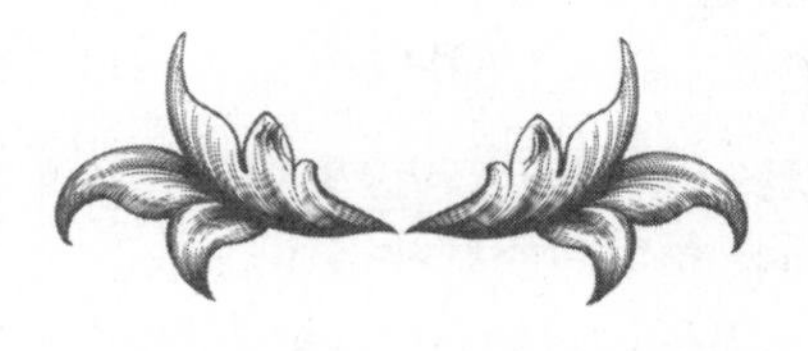

CHAPTER 17

BRANWEN WAS TIRED of being tossed to the ground.

It had happened twice in as many hours. Which was just insulting. She gazed up at Pryderi. He looked menacing standing there with candlelight in his golden hair and eyes flashing like a sea storm.

Palug hissed at Pryderi, his body fluffing so that he looked twice his size. The sound drew Pryderi's attention—which was his mistake.

Branwen bucked upward, locking both of her legs around Pryderi's knee. Then she yanked herself back with all her strength, pulling his knee out from under him. Using that momentum, she flipped them, so that Pryderi lay with his back to the ground, her knee upon his chest and her afanc-fang dagger at his throat.

"I'm Branwen," she said, baring her teeth. "Or did you forget?"

Pryderi's eyes narrowed. His throat bobbed against the tip of the dagger. "You called him Gwydion. I know of only one Gwydion, and he does not hail from Emlyn."

She heard Gwydion sigh behind her. "You did, didn't you?"

"I didn't mean to," said Branwen defensively. "You—you magically undressed me without warning."

"You practically tied your laces into knots," said Gwydion.

"Then perhaps next time, you should hire a true spy instead of a huntress," she retorted. She scowled down at Pryderi. "You followed us here. You were listening. You knew he wasn't from Dyfed, didn't you?"

He met her gaze. "I can recognize dangerous people."

"We're not dangerous," said Branwen.

"You have a knife to his throat," said Gwydion reasonably.

She glared at him. This was his fault; she had known that infiltrating the Hunt would never be as simple as taking a dead man's name. And now she was holding a prince hostage, and they were surrounded by enemies. All Pryderi had to do was scream, and they would be dead.

Determination was written into every line of Pryderi's face. The prince was not unafraid, but he would not be cowed. Even if Branwen cut his throat, he would never surrender. She did not know much of princes nor nobles. But she knew how to face down a foe with only her wits for weapons and stubbornness for armor. Pryderi was no pampered creature; she had seen the calluses worn deep into his hands and the sun-burnished freckles. He reminded her of the young farmers and shepherds from Argoed.

Perhaps she could still salvage this.

"We're not here to harm anyone," she said. "We're here to win the Hunt—like I said. And you're right . . . we're not from Emlyn."

Gwydion made a strangled noise, as though he disapproved of her honesty.

"Gwynedd," said Pryderi. It wasn't a question.

"Yes," she said. "The rest is true, though. Gwydion is here to win some family argument."

"Well," said Gwydion. "It's slightly more complicated than that."

"Gwydion is here to win some complicated family argument," Branwen amended. "I am here for coin. And because . . . because if I win the boon, then I could heal my mam." The words came out a little jerkier than she'd intended. Pryderi gazed up at her, a line between his brows.

"Your mother is ill?" he asked.

Branwen nodded. "Memory sickness. Magic is the only thing that can save her. And Gwydion—he could use that boon to do what no royal from Gwynedd has ever managed."

"Win a war against Dyfed?" said Pryderi dryly.

"Well, that was uncalled for," replied Gwydion.

Branwen glanced at Gwydion and raised her brows. "Tell him why you're here."

Gwydion drew in a breath. "I assume you've learned a little of my family?"

"I have," said Pryderi. "Wasn't there something to do with stolen pigs?"

Gwydion closed his eyes for one long-suffering moment. "Never mind that rumor. King Math is choosing his successor from my siblings, as he has no children of his own. He has decided upon Amaethon."

Pryderi's eyes flickered back and forth for a moment, as though recalling something he had once read. "He is . . . the one who sets fires?"

"That would be the one," agreed Gwydion. "A fire diviner, trained for war, hungry for glory. I imagine even Dyfed would have some trouble with him."

Pryderi appeared unimpressed.

Branwen said, "He wants his sister to be queen instead. And from everything I've heard, she would make a better ruler than the brother picked for the job. Mayhap if she were on the throne, Gwynedd and Dyfed could be allies instead of enemies."

Surprise flashed across Pryderi's face. "I—oh." He looked toward Gwydion. "Is that true?"

"Arianrhod has two sons," said Gwydion, and there was no mistaking the truth in his voice. "She wishes to make a safe place for her children to grow up in. She would never start a war. She favors trade, diplomacy, an exchange of craftsman and knowledge. She would be open to it, I believe."

"But we could not enter the Hunt as ourselves," said Branwen. "We would never have been allowed. Gwynedd isn't welcome here. But all we want is a chance." She pulled her knife away from Pryderi's throat. "That's all we're asking for." She rose, stepping back. Fear beat hotly inside of her.

Pryderi did not move for a few moments. Then he rolled onto his side. His eyes were not on her face but on the blade in her hand. "Your dagger," he said. "It came from an afanc."

Her fingers tightened around the hilt. Most people did not recognize the weapon for what it was—all they saw was a wickedly curved knife, jagged along one edge.

Pryderi stood. "Did you take it from a monster?"

Unbidden came memories of being cornered in an alley. The remembered helplessness twisted her stomach. "Yes," she said honestly.

Pryderi said, "Have you killed before?"

"Yes," she said again. "Monsters."

"How old were you? The first time?"

She racked her memories, gaping at him. Of all the questions he might have asked, she had not expected this. "I—I was thirteen. There was a llamhigyn y dwr drowning children. I killed it with this." She gave the knife a little twirl.

Pryderi nodded. "I was seven."

She drew in a sharp breath. "When you killed a monster?"

"When I distracted the only parent I had ever known," he said, "so that a farmer could drive a pitchfork through its back. I have not slain another since. I have tried to make myself more human. To ignore the thrill of a fight, to pretend that danger does not entice me. You want to know why I came here? It was not because my father invited me. I came to the Wild Hunt to prove that I am the son of a king, not a monster."

Branwen looked at Gwydion. He seemed to be considering the prince, his expression torn between wariness and eagerness. "Groups of no more than three," he said.

Branwen nodded. She had been thinking the same.

Pryderi's gaze jerked toward Gwydion. "What?"

"Join us," said Gwydion. "That way you can keep an eye on us. Make sure we're here for the reasons we said. We'll help you win the Hunt. We can all win. If that doesn't prove you're the son of a king, nothing will."

Pryderi's eyes narrowed. "Aren't you Gwynedd's spymaster? Why should I trust you?"

"Trickster," said Gwydion. "Not spymaster."

"What's the difference?" asked Pryderi doubtfully.

"Spies are paid," said Branwen and Gwydion in the same breath.

Pryderi snorted. "Why should I trust a trickster, then?"

"Because right now our aims align," said Gwydion. "And you could break me in two if you so desired. Branwen is who you should be worried about."

Pryderi's mouth lifted at the corner. "She is quite formidable."

"She is also right here," said Branwen, flushing. "Are you with us? Or will you hand us over to your father?" She reached down and picked up the spear. She held it out to Pryderi, the sharpened tip aimed at her own chest and the shaft extended toward him.

It was a silent offering—her life was in his hands. He could take that spear and kill her before she could draw a breath. Or he could simply shout and alert the Otherking to their presence. She had ceded the decision to him.

Pryderi's eyes met hers. A storm of emotion roiled behind the calm lines of his face. She gave him the smallest of nods. No matter what he chose, she would understand. There were no lies between them. The girl who hunted monsters and the boy who feared he was one.

Pryderi's hand settled around the spear.

"Let us hunt," he said.

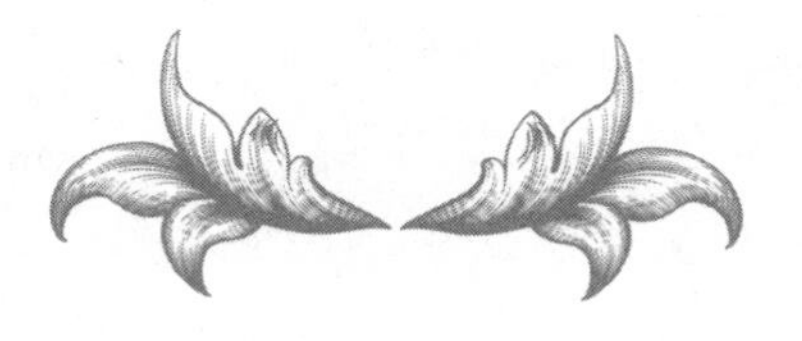

CHAPTER 18

PRYDERI COULD NOT decide if this was a mistake.

He had found two infiltrators from Gwynedd. A king's son would have reported them; a monster's son would have slain them. But Pryderi had allied with them. He did not know what that made him.

A traitor, he thought, *or a fool*.

But he had seen Branwen's desperation when she spoke of her mother—and he could not deny another a chance to save their family. He recalled how his foster mother used to invite passing travelers to their table for meals. When Pryderi pointed out that was a good way to be robbed, his mam had smoothed a hand over his hair and said, "I will not let the evils of the world frighten me out of kindness."

He thought his foster mother would have liked these two—the trickster and the huntress. She would have been amused by them, at the very least. His foster father would have liked the cat; he had always had more of an affinity for animals than people.

Pryderi wished he could have spoken to his foster family. He had sent and received letters, but it was not the same.

The other hunters were gathering their gear and supplies, murmuring to one another. The raucous celebration had died away, leaving a quiet urgency in its wake. Branwen lit a lantern and took the lead. Her cat twined around her ankles, purring softly. Gwydion wore a dark gray cloak and carried an assortment of pouches at his belt. His expression was cool and contemplative, but he nodded at Pryderi when their gazes met.

When they reached the forest, Branwen took a deep breath. Palug stepped up beside her, his eyes fixed on something in the dark. She reached down, picking him up. The cat perched atop her shoulder as she shifted into a hunter's gait.

"Where are we going?" asked Pryderi quietly.

Branwen said, "Away from camp. All the noises will have scared away game. We should look for water."

"There's a stream south of here," said Gwydion.

Pryderi shot him a frown. "Have you visited Annwvyn before?"

"No," said Gwydion, and offered no explanation.

They walked into the forest. The ground was thick with fallen leaves, and the once-lush foliage looked skeletal in the night. The wind carried the scent of cold mist, the bright greenery of conifers, and the smoke of distant fires. When the sun rose, it would be Calan Gaeaf—the first day of winter.

Branwen led them east, deeper into the mountains. They navigated by the pale lantern light. Pryderi snagged his ankle on a bramble once, and even she stumbled over a few loose rocks. Of the three of them, Gwydion moved through the forest with the most ease.

Magic, Pryderi thought. The children of Dôn were all diviners. Gwydion would be no different. Pryderi's fingers tightened around the spear.

Far from the bonfires and the flowing wine, the night chilled. Winter slipped its cold fingers between the bare tree branches. Pryderi's breath fogged around him, and his ears went numb and itchy. The trees were dark, spindly shapes illuminated by moonlight. Wind rustled through the branches, giving the impression of whispering voices. Pryderi took a tighter hold on the spear. It would double as a walking stick, and the weight was a reassurance that he could defend himself.

They spent the better part of an hour picking their way through the forest. The farther they journeyed from camp, the more signs of animals appeared. There were deer tracks, birds' nests in the trees, and freshly tilled earth from rabbits and voles. As they went, Branwen did a strange thing—she gave a little hop, then looked over her shoulder. "Don't put your foot down on that piece of slate."

Pryderi looked down. True enough, a rough rock jutted from the earth. It looked ordinary to his eyes.

Gwydion jumped over the slate. Pryderi did so, too.

Both his companions had their secrets. And while Pryderi would let them keep those secrets, he still made note of them.

Palug trotted ahead, tail curled like a fish hook. Once, he stopped and peered intently toward Branwen's right. She paused, holding up a hand for the others to halt.

Pryderi heard noises. Other hunters were passing nearby, trampling undergrowth and cursing as one of the them stumbled over a fallen log.

Branwen gestured them into the bushes, and they all crouched. As they hid, the sound of voices grew louder.

"—not going to find anything with you making that racket," said a woman irritably.

A man made a huffy sound. His voice had the accent of a Dyfed noble. "I am paying you very well to win this Hunt for me. If you cannot find a wolf—"

"We'll not be finding wolves around here," said the huntress. "Not in the dark, not in these woods. They'll likely find us, if they want to. No, I told you. We need to find a wild hog. They'll defend themselves far more viciously than any wolf."

"I'm not attaching my signet ring to a pig." He sniffed. "Just because you were content to tie your wedding ring to an otter—"

An otter was a good choice, Pryderi thought. They were clever and shy, and one could vanish into a river never to be glimpsed again. Even afancs had trouble hunting them.

The huntress said something that Pryderi did not catch. She and the nobleman were walking away, and their voices quieted. Branwen was the first to rise.

"She used her wedding ring?" said Pryderi, frowning.

"As I told him," said Branwen, with a nod toward Gwydion, "this is how you know the Wild Hunt was created by nobles. Most of us common mortals don't walk around with signet rings. Wealthy merchant families might purchase one, but the rest of us simply use our word as our oath. We have little need of silver and wax."

"I wonder if we get our rings back," mused Gwydion.

"I hope so," replied Pryderi. "A signet ring is a dangerous thing to lose."

"True," said Gwydion.

They continued on. Another hour passed in relative quiet. They heard two other hunting parties, but Branwen managed to avoid them. Finally, they seemed to be so deep within the mountain forest that they were the only three people in the world. A stream burbled nearby.

"We should fill our flasks," Branwen said. "Then we start looking. Many animals will keep to places with fresh water."

While Branwen knelt beside the stream, Pryderi walked alongside the water. The air carried the sickly sweet smell of decay. He pushed aside a bush. Half-rotted into the ground was a dead polecat.

"You could tie your ring to that," said Gwydion, "but I would try for something a little more nimble."

Branwen snorted. "At least we know that we're far enough from camp to encounter predators."

She held the lantern aloft to study the damp earth. Her gaze flickered over indentations in the ground, the broken undergrowth, and the small trails. Pryderi found it fascinating to watch her work; her body loosened as she traced a footprint in the ground, then touched a broken branch. This was where she found her peace, he realized. Others looked for it in drink or stories, but Branwen found it in the hunt.

"Deer tracks," she murmured. "Recent." She rose and began to follow the water.

Gwydion and Pryderi exchanged a glance. "After you," said Pryderi, with a polite inclination of his head.

Gwydion returned the smile—with just as much warmth. "Of course."

Pryderi knew they were both thinking the same: that Pryderi would never let Gwydion walk at his back. It was far too easy to slide in a knife.

Pryderi had heard of Gwynedd's royal family. King Math was a nightmarishly powerful diviner, capable of turning his enemies into animals or killing with a touch. But he had not ventured out of Caer Dathyl for many years. His niece and nephews were rumored to be cruel and capricious, warring among themselves for power.

It could all be tales, Pryderi knew. Kingdoms waged war with words as much as they did with steel. A rumor here, an insinuation there. It all tipped the balance of power. Gwydion could be as dangerous as the tales whispered, or he could simply be a young man with a penchant for trickery. Pryderi did not know—and he could not trust him.

They walked uphill, then Branwen veered from the water. She seemed to be following a trail only she could see.

An eerie cry rang out. They all went still.

"Monster?" asked Pryderi quietly, his gaze roaming the dark wood.

Branwen smiled at him. "From the sound, you'd think so. But no. That is the cry of a roe deer."

"That was a *deer*?" said Gwydion.

"A roe deer," she replied. "Something must have startled them."

Branwen drew her bow. Her hands were steady as she strung it. Pryderi could see why Gwydion had gone to the trouble of hiring her; she walked through the forest as though the wilds were her kingdom.

Several deer had taken refuge within a small clearing. They were small, elegant creatures with reddish-brown coats. A lone buck stood by the herd with his ears pricked and stance wary.

Branwen nocked an arrow. "We can't kill them," she murmured. "But if we could herd them into a trap..."

In the distance echoed the eerie baying of a hound. All around them, hunts were playing out. Nobles and hunters, mortals and folk—they were all in these woods with the same ambition. Alliances were being forged, weapons sharpened, snares set. Against his will, a small fire of anticipation kindled in Pryderi's chest. There was a part of him that wanted to win. To test himself against the best that Dyfed and Annwvyn had to offer and emerge victorious. Perhaps then he would feel worthy of a kingdom.

At the sound of the distant hounds, the deer herd jerked to awareness, shifting and moving like a living thing. They began to flee the clearing, slipping through old brambles and undergrowth. It was like watching water vanish between the cracks of a broken cup—there was no stopping them.

As Branwen stepped forward, hissing in frustration, Gwydion reached out and placed a hand on her wrist. And then he did a strange thing.

He sang. It was a soft little tune, barely audible under his breath.

And the brambles closed around one deer like a fist.

Pryderi drew in a sharp breath. Magic.

The herd was gone. Between one heartbeat and the next, they

had all vanished. All but one. The trapped roebuck thrashed against his bramble cage. The plants moved with him, never injuring the creature, but keeping the deer secure.

The roebuck made panicked barking sounds as they approached.

"Well, that was impressive," said Pryderi, but there was an edge of wariness to his voice. "Plants, then?" He had never heard of such a magic.

Gwydion threw him a rueful smile. "Plants," he agreed. "Not quite as powerful as fire or metal, I'll admit."

Pryderi bit back his disagreement. Fire and metal were both dangerous, but neither compared to this. Plants were everywhere, and they affected everything. He had lived on a farm long enough to know how growing things could carve the very earth.

"This was your victory," said Branwen to Gwydion. "I think you should have this one."

Gwydion slipped a ring from his cloak. Branwen held out a bit of twine, and he took it. "Hello, friend," Gwydion said softly as he approached the deer. Branwen and Pryderi kept back, for fear of panicking the deer further. The roebuck's breath gusted into the night, heavy and terrified.

Gwydion knelt beside the deer. He slipped the twine through his ring, and made to tie it around the deer's antler.

But the moment his ring touched the creature, roots sprang from the earth like skeletal fingers.

Gwydion fell back, but one of the roots took hold of him. Branwen cried out, drawing the dagger at her belt, but Pryderi seized her arm. It would not help Gwydion to rush into a trap.

Before their eyes, the roots curled through Gwydion's ring and the roebuck's antler, tying it into place. And then, gently as a lover's caress, the second root curved around Gwydion's left hand. A small tendril wound itself around his index finger and then broke off, curving into a ring.

All around them, an eerie birdsong rang out. But before Pryderi could pinpoint its source, the roots were sliding back into the earth. They did not so much as leave a scar upon the ground.

Gwydion sat back on his haunches. He held up his left hand, eyeing the wooden ring as though he feared it might bite him. "That was not me," he said.

"It was the Otherking's magic," said Branwen, her eyes on the trees. Her hand remained on her dagger. "He is Annwvyn and Annwvyn is him. These woods are his. That spell must be how he keeps track of us."

With a shaky hum, Gwydion released the roebuck from its bramble cage. The deer shook itself and tore into the woods.

For a moment, no one moved. Gwydion gazed at the wooden ring. "Does this mean...?"

"Welcome to the Hunt," said Pryderi.

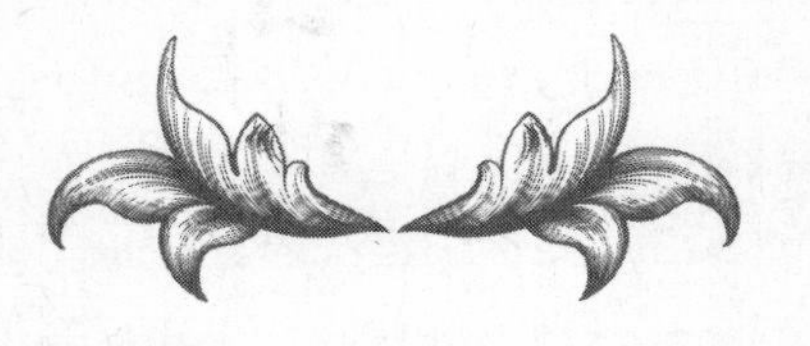

CHAPTER 19

NIGHT HUNTING WAS no easy feat.

If this had been a mortal hunt, Branwen would have risked a torch. She needed to find tracks and follow them to dens and roosts, to the places where animals hid at night. But this was no ordinary hunt—as evidenced by the living ring on Gwydion's finger.

That ring glowed with magic. Tendrils of unseen power plunged into the flesh of Gwydion's forearm like roots into soil. This was how the Hunt worked, Branwen realized. They traded their own signet rings for magical ones—and these replacements would bind them to the rules of the Hunt.

Branwen could not gaze at the ring for too long; it glowed too brightly. At least her sight allowed her to traverse the forest. She could see the magical traps left for unwary travelers—a snare tucked between two trees, a gleam of something gold and watching in the stream, and a bird overhead that sang with a human voice. When she mentioned it to Gwydion and Pryderi, both admitted they heard only owl song.

"I'm going to climb a tree," she said. "See if there's anything to be found."

Gwydion nodded. He kept rubbing his thumb against the strange ring. His expression was distant, as though he only half listened to her. Palug meowed and made as though to climb with her, but Branwen picked up the cat and passed him to Pryderi. "Not now," she said. "You keep them safe."

Palug gave her a flat-eyed, unhappy stare.

She handed her lantern to Gwydion and found a sturdy oak. She took hold of one of the branches and heaved herself up. It took a few minutes, picking her way from branch to branch. But finally, she was high enough to gaze through the canopy. She peered at the forest. By moonlight, it was cast in silver. Night and autumn leeched color from the trees. Something flew through the night—a bat or an owl. Branwen watched its course as it dipped and fluttered, vanishing from sight. As her gaze followed the creature, she saw something.

Her heart jolted in surprise. There was a silhouette two branches away. She blinked, trying to force her eyes to focus in the dark. There was no telltale glitter of gold, which meant this creature was mortal. A cloud drifted, and its absence allowed moonlight to spill across the forest.

A lapwing. It had roosted among the branches of the oak tree.

Branwen had never believed in fate. She believed in tangible things: the strength in her body, the sharpness of her dagger. She knew magic existed, but it was simply a tool like any other. But seeing that lapwing made her stomach lurch. It felt as though the forest had meant it for her.

Her mother loved lapwings. They were beautiful, with long crests and their black and white feathers. When the sun struck those black feathers, they shone with iridescent purples and greens. This bird must have been lost from its flock and retreated to the trees rather than risk the forest floor.

Slowly, ever so slowly, Branwen reached out. She balanced with her weight against the branch, hoping that the bird would not wake and fly into her face. A fall from this height could kill her.

Carefully, Branwen formed a cage with her hands. One for each wing, so that the lapwing could not attack nor flee. It was how she held unruly chickens.

She took hold of the lapwing. It awoke at once, panicked. Branwen thought of the nights when her mam had awoken Branwen from a dead sleep, and she felt a twinge of sympathy for the bird. "I'm sorry, friend," she whispered. "Please, please stay quiet."

She expected the bird to writhe and peck at her, but when Branwen pressed the bird to her chest, the lapwing did not struggle. It made a wary little noise, its talons curled. But it did not attack.

As quickly as she could, Branwen touched her brooch to the lapwing's leg.

The oak tree seemed to come alive. Branches curled, a whisper of dead leaves fluttering to the ground. Even half expecting it, Branwen flinched. She did not relish the thought that this forest was aware of her. Gentle as a parent helping a child, the thinnest of branches curled around her brooch and tied it to the lapwing's leg. In the same moment, a second branch twined around her finger.

She forced herself to breathe as the oak branch broke off and settled on her hand. And before her magicked eye, golden vines grew from the ring and delved into her forearm.

It did not hurt. She would not have even known the enchantment was there, if not for her sight.

But that did not calm her.

There was a magic on her, a spell she had never asked for. It was bound into her very flesh.

"Luck to us both," she murmured, and released the bird. The lapwing wobbled on its branch, spread its wings, and then flew into the night. Branwen watched it go, silently urging it on.

Dawn crept closer and closer—and still, Branwen found no animal for Pryderi. There was a close call with a wildcat, but it scampered before Gwydion could capture it. Branwen almost netted a bat, but a rustle of leaves scared it off. Pryderi spotted a flicker of something in the wood, but they never saw a creature.

The passage of time made Branwen jittery. Soon, morning would warm the mountains, and the Hunt would be underway. If they could not find Pryderi an animal, he would be disqualified before it had even begun. Frustration burned within her as she scouted another set of tracks to an empty rabbit's warren. With a huff, she rocked back on her heels.

"I have an idea," said Gwydion.

Branwen and Pryderi both looked at him. "It's not a good idea," he added.

"Dawn is minutes away," said Pryderi. "I will take any idea."

Gwydion nodded. And then he looked at Palug.

For a moment, Branwen didn't understand. Palug sat on a fallen log, grooming his face. He froze, as though sensing the attention on him. Very slowly, he put his paw down.

"You're right, that's a bad idea," said Branwen.

"Oh," said Pryderi. "You... mean him? Is that even allowed?"

"Any animal," said Gwydion. "Those are the rules. Be it beast or monster."

Pryderi's hand rose to his mouth. "But that means every hunter in this forest will be trying to kill or capture Branwen's cat."

Branwen looked at Palug. As always, she saw that faint glitter of magic around his whiskers and eyes. She held out a hand to him, and the cat nuzzled her fingers.

"I'd like to see them try," she said.

Pryderi's forehead scrunched in confusion.

"He devoured a hundred knights," said Gwydion.

Pryderi's jaw dropped. "I'm sorry, he *what*?"

"Well, he might have," Branwen amended. "I'm not certain."

"Oh, did we forget to mention that?" said Gwydion brightly.

The prince looked back and forth between them. "What other secrets are you two hiding?"

"We could tell you," said Gwydion, "but it would take half the morning. Better to tie your ring to the cat now, and we'll tell you our darkest secrets later."

Pryderi glanced at Branwen. "If—if you are sure."

She nodded. She had no intention of letting any harm come to Palug.

Pryderi squatted before the cat. "Please do not eat me," he said. He dug into his pocket and pulled out a piece of dried meat.

Palug blinked once. Then he took the meat and devoured it.

"I'll assume that means 'all right,'" said Pryderi. With surprising gentleness, he touched his signet ring to the cat's throat.

A vine wound through the earth, fastening around the cat's throat like a collar. It bound the ring into place. The greenery slid around Pryderi's finger. Magic burrowed into his arm.

It was done.

Branwen looked at her own hand, then at the others' rings: Gwydion and his ring of roots; her oaken ring; Pryderi's living ring of greenery. They were bound to this land, to the Hunt, and to one another.

Palug stretched. Branwen picked him up, setting him atop her shoulder. The cat balanced there, his eyes half-lidded.

"If this isn't against the rules, why wouldn't every hunter attach their ring to a hunting hound?" asked Pryderi. "It seems a far easier plan than traipsing through the woods."

"Because they were not clever enough to think of it," said Gwydion, tossing a pine cone into the air and catching it in his left hand.

"We should assume that some of them are," said Branwen, shaking her head. "After all, if we—"

A horn resounded through the forest. She had heard hunting horns before—but never one that rumbled the ground, stirred the trees, and sent every bird shrieking into the air.

Dawn touched the forest.

And with that, the Wild Hunt truly began.

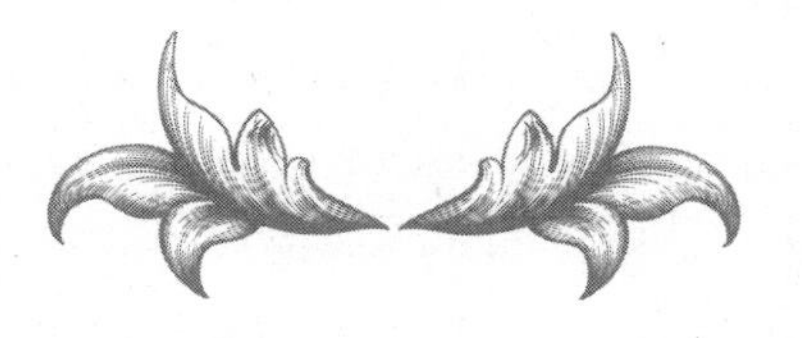

CHAPTER 20

THE TREES OF Annwvyn were so old that they did not sing.

Gwydion had walked old forests, listening to melodies only he could hear: a chorus of oak, hazel, birch, yew, and ash. Annwvyn's trees rumbled like a mountainous heartbeat. The forest had existed long before Gwydion's great-grandfather was born, and it would outlast them all.

Gwydion had slipped off his boots. It took a small effort of magic to soften his footsteps with moss and lichen, but he wanted to feel the ground. It helped attune him to the forest, to feel its breaths and shifting moods.

Talk to me, Gwydion thought. *Warn me of enemies.*

He was not the only one to be cautious. Branwen's gaze was narrowed, her attention wholly on their surroundings. With the sun risen, the Hunt and all of its dangers were underway. They were hunters and hunted alike.

Branwen kept her bow in one hand. She appeared to be following the places where sunlight broke through the canopy and the undergrowth was thickest. She checked for signs of voles and rabbits, murmuring that they would be prey for larger animals.

"You see the deepest parts of the forest?" she said, nodding toward a shadowed thicket. "You'll find smaller game there—birds, voles, maybe a deer. But if you want larger game? Look for the places where the landscape shifts. Where meadow meets forest, where forest meets water, where water touches the grass. In-between places."

"The way magic flourishes at dawn and dusk," said Pryderi. He still took up the rear, that spear resting atop one broad shoulder.

"It does not," said Gwydion, frowning. "Magic has nothing to do with time."

"Your magic, mayhap," said Pryderi. "But in the wild country, most people take measures to protect themselves during moments of change."

"Or perhaps magic *makes* things change," said Gwydion. "For better or worse."

Pryderi pursed his lips. "Most would envy those with magic. Particularly yours."

"Only one raised by a farmer would say that," replied Gwydion with a bitter little smile. A pang went through his right hand. "Magic is all well and good in old legends, but I've seen what happens when a child has power and wants a sweet. The lucky servants escaped with a few burn scars."

Pryderi seemed taken aback. "Is that why you're so determined to keep your brother from the throne?"

"Yes," said Gwydion. "And it is better for Gwynedd and Dyfed if Amaethon never wears a crown."

They walked in silence for a while. Branwen stopped abruptly, kneeling by a broken fern. "Someone came this way recently."

"Should we avoid them?" asked Pryderi. "To keep the cat safe?"

Palug was darting in and out of the undergrowth, chasing motes of dust and shadows.

"We shouldn't seek them out," said Branwen. "But if they attached their rings to animals nearby, the game might not have gone too far."

"How many hunters?" asked Gwydion. All the footprints were a jumble to him, but Branwen read the tracks as though they were words upon parchment.

"Two," she finally said. "One larger, one lighter. You can see the difference in the depth."

"Or one was carrying something heavy," Pryderi said. "Or armored."

Branwen nodded. "Or that."

The tracks dipped south, then southeast. Gwydion tried to find his bearings in the forest, to take in every tree and root. He walked with half-lidded eyes, listening more than seeing. So it took him by surprise when Branwen's arm flung out and caught him in the chest.

There was a polecat standing perhaps ten strides away. It eyed the humans warily, tilting its head.

"Is there a ring?" whispered Gwydion.

Branwen drew in a breath. "That's not a polecat."

Pryderi shifted the spear in his hand. "It's not?"

"No," said Branwen in an undertone. Then, much louder, "Hello, friend."

The polecat sniffed the air.

"It's a pwca," Branwen whispered. "Shape-changed to look like a polecat. They can be helpful, if you do them a kindness." She dug into her pack and withdrew a small honeyed cake. It looked a little squashed, but the sweet scent drew the polecat's attention.

"We won't harm you," said Branwen. She set the cake down. "Step back," she said to the others. "Back, back, back."

They all backed up, half stumbling over roots and grass. The polecat's whiskers pointed forward as it skittered toward the cake.

"There you go," said Branwen. It was the soft, soothing tones that one used for a child or animal. "See? We're not here to hurt you."

The polecat reached for the cake. Then it froze.

Gwydion realized their mistake too late. They had forgotten to account for their cat.

Palug growled. He had fluffed himself up to twice his normal size. He looked like an angry black-and-white storm cloud.

"Palug, no," Branwen said, reaching for him.

The cat yowled a battle cry. The pwca-polecat seized the cake, then sprinted toward a tree and scampered out of sight. Palug tried to follow, but Branwen threw herself at the cat and scooped him up. He howled with impotent fury as she carried him away.

"Well, that was useless," said Branwen. She looked down at Palug. The cat had given up his squirming and sat in her arms with a glum expression. "You can't murder everything we come across, you little monster."

Palug grumbled under his breath.

"I believe that's cat for 'I can try,'" said Gwydion.

Pryderi gazed at Branwen with a cool awareness.

"What?" said Branwen.

"You knew that was one of the folk," said Pryderi. "You did not guess. You knew."

"I'm not sure a pwca is truly one of the folk," replied Branwen. "They're not as conniving as the tylwyth teg."

"You knew," Pryderi repeated. Then he looked at Gwydion. "One of the many secrets you mentioned?"

"It's a long story." Branwen set Palug down and pointed at her right eye. "I can see magic. It's why he hired me. It's why I can hunt monsters. Because their illusions don't work on me."

Gwydion tensed. He was not sure how the prince would react to such a revelation. If Pryderi responded badly, Gwydion would be ready to defend her.

"You can see monsters?" said Pryderi quietly.

Branwen nodded. "Magical ones."

Several emotions flickered across Pryderi's expression. His lips pressed tight, as though he did not trust himself to remain silent. "That seems," he finally said, "a useful skill to have."

"It's served well enough." Branwen turned and picked up the trail. "We should keep moving."

They walked until Branwen gestured them to another halt. They stood at the edge of a small thicket of birch trees and ferns. "I think there's something up ahead," she said softly. "See how those leaves are broken? Something trampled them." She drew an arrow, nodding at Pryderi and Gwydion. "Stay here."

"I can help," said Pryderi mildly.

Branwen said, "All right. Gwydion, you take Palug. I don't want him flushing anything out until I'm ready."

"So I am on cat duty?" said Gwydion.

"No, of course not," said Pryderi, smiling faintly. "You're also in charge of ensuring we don't walk into briars."

Gwydion snorted and turned toward the cat. With a sigh, he reached down and picked up Palug. Then he turned the cat onto his back, cradling him in the crook of his arm like he'd held Dylan and Lleu when they were babes. Palug looked up at him, his feet in the air.

"You've never held a cat before, have you?" said Branwen, choking back a laugh.

"He likes it," said Gwydion, scratching the cat's chest.

Palug began to purr.

"He's a little trickster himself," said Branwen. "No wonder the two of you get on so well." Carefully, she reached for the ferns. She twitched them aside.

Within the thicket was a sleeping deer. A silver signet ring was tied around its neck.

Branwen exhaled. She whispered something to Pryderi, and he nodded, reaching into his pack. He pulled out a small net.

Ah, Gwydion thought. They would try and catch the deer, rather than kill it. Personally, he would have slain the creature; it would have made matters simpler. But he would aid Branwen as best he could. Humming under his breath, he reached for his magic. It trickled through the roots of the trees, delving into the ground. If the deer woke, he would entrap it.

Branwen and Pryderi each took hold of the net, creeping into the thicket.

But as Gwydion's magic sang through the trees, something made him pause. There was a hollowness, an ache through the ground. He had felt that only a few times before, when visiting the mines. Plants would sense when a tunnel had come too near, when their roots met only empty air.

"Wait," he said, suddenly alarmed.

And then the ground collapsed.

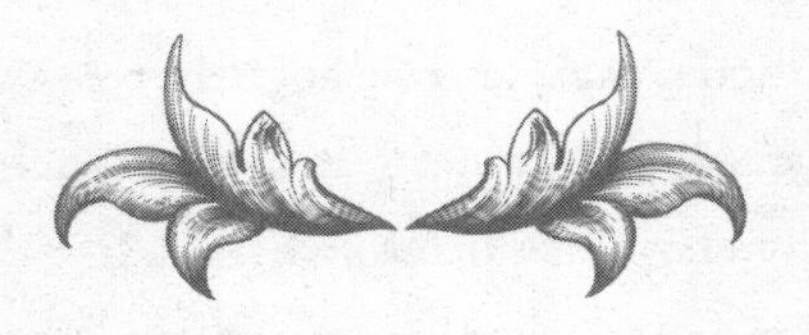

CHAPTER 21

PRYDERI HATED THE sensation of falling.

Even as a child, he had disliked heights. He had been wary of trees and the hayloft, and his foster siblings used to tease him about it. For a moment, he was weightless. Then the ground rushed up, and he slammed into damp earth. He lay on his back, every muscle throbbing and his lungs disconcertingly hollow. He needed to move; he had to move. But his body came back to him with frustrating slowness. Finally, he managed to roll onto his side.

"Branwen," he wheezed. He blinked again and again, trying to clear his vision. Branwen was on her hands and knees, her pale hair wrenched from its braided crown. Dirt stained her face, and she had a bleeding cut across her forehead.

"The deer," she said tightly. Her hand landed on the deer's neck. It lay stiffly between Pryderi and Branwen. "It's dead."

"Did it die in the fall?" asked Pryderi.

Branwen winced. "Too cold and stiff. It died hours ago." She reached down for the signet ring tied to its neck. When she held it up, Pryderi saw it was a bit of wire curved to look like a ring.

Panic tore through him. This was no natural occurrence, no sinkhole. He could see the places where roots had been broken, where rocks were hauled away. Mortal hands had carved this pit.

A trap.

He scrambled to his feet, ignoring the protest of his sore muscles. "We need to get out of here. Right—"

Above them, someone screamed.

It was not a cry of fear. The sound simmered with challenge.

Gwydion answered with a shout. He was alone in the thicket, his companions trapped in a pit.

This was an ambush. And Pryderi had fallen into it. The sound of weapons being drawn made his breath catch. There was a clash of metal upon metal, a grunt, and then the battle yowl of a cat.

Pryderi's first instinct was to leap for the top of the pit and heave himself out. To take apart anyone who dared challenge him. But he could not rush into danger and leave Branwen trapped down here.

He did not know her, not truly. But he wanted to. Perhaps it was because she had a way about her, a wry humor and confidence. Perhaps it was the way she looked at him, not like he was a prince but someone she might share a drink with.

Or perhaps it was because she could see monsters—and she had still chosen him as a companion.

"Here," said Pryderi, lacing his fingers together. "I'll lift you out."

She nodded, stepping into his hands. He boosted her as steadily as he could, lifting her to the edge of the pit. She reached for something to heave herself to freedom, but then she jerked back.

Pryderi stumbled, off-balance, and the two of them fell a second time. He managed to catch her on the way down, keeping Branwen from slamming into the dirt. When he looked up, a face gazed down at them. There was a knife where Branwen's hand had been.

It was a human hunter, a man with a wide grin and a scar through his mouth. He was a iarll's son from Cedweli, Pryderi remembered. Cheerful and boisterous, as sturdy and stout as a wine barrel. "Prince," he said cheerfully, before fitting arrow to bowstring and pulling it taut. He aimed at Branwen.

For a moment, Pryderi could not understand. This was the Wild Hunt. They were supposed to be hunting monsters and game animals, not one another.

In the Wild Hunt, all are fair game.

Pryderi moved without thinking, rolling so that he covered Branwen with his body. An arrow sank into the dirt near his thigh. Close, but it had not hit him. The archer must have flinched at the last moment.

Even he would hesitate to slay the prince of Dyfed.

Branwen squirmed beneath him, seizing her bow and an arrow. "Left," she snarled, and he shifted left. She fired, and there was a cry from above.

Pryderi rolled off of her. His spear had fallen with them, and he picked it up. He met Branwen's eyes.

She seemed to understand; there was a determined set to her mouth. Drawing two more arrows, she took a step toward him. He lowered the spear, keeping it horizontal with the ground. She leapt, landing on the shaft of the spear, and he heaved it up, launching her into the air. As she sailed, she fired one arrow, then landed on the ground above and vanished from sight.

There was another shout and a clash of weapons. With a grunt, Pryderi shoved the tip of his spear into the earth and used it to clamber out of the pit trap. It was ungraceful, but it worked. He scrambled up and out.

A small battle was being waged in the thicket. One hunter was trapped by brambles and trying to cut himself free. One lay upon the ground, an arrow buried in his shoulder. The last held an obsidian sword, advancing on Gwydion. Gwydion stood between the hunter and Palug, a snarl on his mouth and his left hand held out.

"Put down the sword," said Branwen. She had her bow trained on the last man.

The hunter glanced at her. He was an older man with pale hair and gray eyes. His gaze darted from Palug to Gwydion, then to Branwen and Pryderi. Plans seemed to flash across his face, one by one, until he realized he was outnumbered. "Give up," said Pryderi breathlessly. "And we'll let you go."

"Truly?" said Gwydion, jaw clenched. "They'll follow us afterward. Since these vultures cannot hunt prey, they'll steal rings from other hunters."

"We are not vultures," said the man with the arrow in his shoulder. The pain rendered him too breathless to continue.

"That's precisely what you are," replied Gwydion. "You likely put your own rings on the easiest game you could find, then built a trap to steal the rings from others. It's a wonder you managed to bring down a deer for your pit."

He was stoking their anger, Pryderi realized. Making them reckless.

"You're not hunters at all," said Gwydion. "Simply thieves."

The older hunter snarled. He lunged at Gwydion, thrusting that obsidian sword forward. The attack was so swift that Pryderi reacted without thinking. He threw his spear, twisting so that all the strength of his upper body was in that throw. The spear found its mark—the old hunter's sword.

And in the same moment, an arrow pierced the man's heart.

The sword and spear hit the ground moments before the hunter did. There was a sucking inhalation, a look of startled bewilderment on the man's face, and then he fell backward.

Branwen had gone as pale as her hair. Her lips were parted, as though she had begun to ask a question and faltered.

They were moving before Pryderi was truly aware of it. One moment they stood in the thicket, and the next they were running. Some part of him had remembered to retrieve the spear. Branwen darted ahead, swift and nimble as a deer. Gwydion was panting behind him, and then a streak of black fur scampered alongside them. Palug kept the pace easily, his tail held high.

There was a snarl from the thicket, the sound of undergrowth breaking and snapping. Then footsteps—hard and loud. Running.

They were being pursued.

Turn and fight, whispered an old voice from within Pryderi. It sounded ancient as the oceans. *Ensure none can follow you.*

It was what a monster would do; it was what a king would do.

But he was neither.

Not yet.

Gwydion made a sound of frustration. Behind them, the forest began to change. Branches wove together, roots sprang up, and the undergrowth thickened. Moss rose up to meet their every step, muffling the sound of their escape.

They ran until Pryderi's lungs burned, and Branwen finally slowed. Gwydion was wheezing, and when they finally stopped, he sank to the ground. "Just—let—me—die," he managed to say.

Branwen's hair stuck to her forehead, and her tunic was soaked through with sweat. She looked as shaken as Pryderi felt; she stepped from side to side, as though she could not remain still. She had killed that man. It had been in defense of Gwydion, but she had still slain another human.

Gwydion had picked up the obsidian sword. It was beautiful: the bone hilt curved and the blade glittered in the sunlight. It was a weapon that should have been in the hands of an immortal. Perhaps those scavengers had killed one of the folk for it.

"Are you all right?" Pryderi said quietly to Branwen.

She gave him a curt nod. "Fine."

"Well, I'm done hunting for the rest of the day," said Gwydion hoarsely. "We should find a place to set up camp."

Branwen blew out a frustrated breath. "We can't rest now. We still—we have nothing. No rings, no—"

Gwydion reached into a hidden pocket of his tunic and withdrew a small velvet pouch. He tossed it at Branwen. She caught it, despite her surprise, then fumbled with the drawstring.

"The old hunter had that on him," said Gwydion. He finally

heaved himself into a sitting position. "I heard a bit of jingling and thought, 'Who brings coin to a royal hunt?' So I cut it from his belt when he was trying to strangle me."

Within the pouch were three signet rings. Pryderi recognized the heraldry as two from Rhos and one from Gwarthaf. "They're from Dyfed," he murmured. "Are we . . . allowed to take them?"

"All's fair," said Branwen bitterly. Shame was written into every line of her body.

Looking at her was like gazing into a mirror. Pryderi's own instincts had betrayed him more than once—a bruise against his foster sister's cheek when she woke him from a nightmare, a cup smashed in a moment of anger, harsh words that he did not truly mean. He knew what it felt like to be haunted. *He's young,* he once heard his mam murmur to his da. *He went through something none of us understand, and he is still trying to sort himself out. Give him time.*

Gwydion reached down, picking up their flasks. "I can hear water nearby," he said. "I'll refill these. Come on, cat."

Palug had settled on a sunlit patch of fallen leaves. But at Gwydion's words, he stretched and trotted after the diviner. Together, they vanished into the trees.

"Branwen," Pryderi said quietly. Branwen looked at Pryderi, her face smoothing into a mask. "It's all right."

At his words, her mouth twisted. "It's not," she said.

"Have you ever killed before? A person, I mean. Not a monster."

She shook her head. "I tried, once. But I couldn't manage it."

"There are shameful reasons people kill," he replied. "Out of anger or greed or cruelty. But there was none of that in you. You did it to protect a friend. There's no shame in that."

A breeze drifted through the trees. It smelled of pine trees and damp rocks. Branwen lifted her face to it, closing her eyes for a heartbeat. She seemed to drink in the wind, and when she spoke, her voice was calm. "I didn't just do it for Gwydion. I can't... I can't lose this hunt."

He nodded in understanding. "Your mam."

"My mam," she agreed.

And there was truly nothing else to say. Pryderi did not know what he would have done to protect his foster mother.

They sat in quiet for a few moments, simply catching their breath.

"May I ask you a question?" Branwen said.

"We're allies," he replied. "Ask what you will."

"About that." She gestured at him. "Why did you ally with us, instead of turning us over to the kings?"

It was a fair question. Discovering spies and delivering them to his father would have been a fine way to prove his worth.

He nodded at her knife. "Because of that."

Her brows drew together in confusion. "Because of my dagger?"

"You said you took it from a monster," he said. "That is the fang of an afanc." He took a steadying breath. "You've heard the tales."

"I've heard a little." She tilted her head. "But I also know how tales can change in the telling."

"They're all true," he said. "I was kidnapped by a monster. A farmer saved me." His voice softened as he spoke of his family. "He was no warrior, no great hero. But he saw a child trapped by a monster and acted. Anyone with the bravery to fight an afanc has my respect."

She reddened, her hand falling to the knife at her belt. "I didn't kill the afanc myself, you should know. I was very young—and attacked by three of the folk that ventured into my village unseen. When they realized I could see them, they threatened to cut out my eye. To take back the magic they thought I had stolen. I fought back, stole their knife, and used it to defend myself."

He thought of her, young and small, cornered by three immortal children. He knew the folk well enough to realize how terrifying that would have been. "You were still brave," he said.

She shrugged, looking more embarrassed than pleased. "As were you. You helped slay your own monster, did you not?"

The rest of the day passed swiftly.

Gwydion took the lead, his feet bare and eyes half-closed. He hummed under his breath, and it took Pryderi a while to understand it was not because Gwydion enjoyed music—it was part of his magic. He made his way through the forest with ease: He never broke a twig or twisted a branch. Ferns bowed before him, and moss rose up to soften his steps.

It was a gift that Pryderi would have welcomed. He imagined what he could have done with such a power on the farm—their crops would have brimmed over, their family fed and happy. Their entire village would have prospered.

Dyfed did not have many diviners. Perhaps it was the distance from Annwvyn or iron in the ground or some trick of fate. Diviners were more common in the north. If the other children of Dôn were as talented as Gwydion, then Dyfed would do well to make allies of them.

Perhaps Pryderi could. Perhaps this was why fate had led him on this journey.

They went east, climbing into the mountains. The foliage shifted as they went higher, the trees thinning out and the ground giving way to rocks and shorter grasses. As evening crept nearer, Gwydion led them to a cluster of pine trees.

"We can't sleep here," murmured Branwen. "Look."

It took Pryderi a moment to see what she had: a near-invisible trail through the foliage. Something had worn a path into the ground. "Those tracks... well, I have never seen anything like them," said Branwen. "I would not like to meet whatever left that game trail."

Gwydion gave her a mocking little bow. "Who do you take me for, huntress?"

He placed his left hand on a tree. This time, he did not hum. He sang—a soft little song. It was a jaunty tune, and Gwydion carried it surprisingly well. Above them, the pine trees seemed to come awake. Needles whispered, wood creaked, and branches wove together. When Gwydion went silent, the canopy had become its own shelter.

"No one will look for us up there," said Gwydion.

Branwen sighed. "That is a skill I would not mind having."

"Magical tree houses?" said Pryderi.

She grinned. "I would have never come home."

Pryderi did not relish the thought of spending a night in that tree. But he forced his unease into the pit of his stomach and followed the others. He tried not to look down as he climbed higher and higher. The birds around him went quiet and watched with confusion as three humans invaded their domain. Finally, he pulled himself up and over into the shelter Gwydion crafted. He had woven the branches into a tight little net. They were surrounded on all sides, so it would be difficult to fall. And no one would see them from beneath.

There was a scritching noise, and then Palug scurried into view. He had scaled the trunk of the tree, his whiskers pointed forward as he gazed at the birds' nests overhead.

"Oh, no," said Branwen, taking hold of the cat and gently prying him from the tree. "I've had enough of hunting for one day." She reached into her pack and withdrew a smoked fish to distract the cat.

Pryderi ran his hand along the edge of the magicked shelter. "Thank you," he said to Gwydion. "I appreciate this."

"I can tell from the way you look like you want to vomit," said Gwydion.

Pryderi let out a surprised laugh. "I am unfond of heights."

"Safer up here than down there," said Gwydion.

"Which is why I am up here."

They ate a cold meal of dried meats, rolls, and leftover pies. Dusk drained all the warmth from the forest, and Pryderi was glad for the wool of his cloak. He wondered if his father was settling into his tent, back in the comfort and safety of the royal camp. Perhaps he would share a meal with King Arawn and the two would discuss whatever it was that kings talked about.

They fell quiet as night closed in around them. Gwydion settled up on his side, bundled up in his fur-lined cloak. Palug curled against his stomach, and Gwydion lifted the cloak, letting the cat snuggle in. Palug purred loudly.

Pryderi shifted, trying to get comfortable. It felt a little like sitting in an overlarge hammock crafted of woven pine branches. Needles kept jabbing his bare skin.

Branwen did not share his unease. She lay on her stomach, her arms braced on the edge of their makeshift camp, gazing at the forest below. She seemed to be watching for something.

"What's down there?" Pryderi asked quietly.

"Game going home for the night," she replied, equally soft. She reached for her bow, pulling a single arrow free. She fitted arrow to string, drawing it tight.

Pryderi took a deep breath, then chanced a look down. At once, his belly swooped. But he forced himself not to react, to look where Branwen looked.

Something was moving through the grasses.

Branwen inhaled deeply. Her gaze seemed to unfocus, her lips parted slightly, and as she exhaled, her fingers released the bowstring. The arrow cut through the evening, thudding into something far below.

A dead rabbit fell into the game trail, an arrow through its throat.

"That was a good shot," said Pryderi. Looking down at the dead rabbit, he said, "Should I fetch it?"

"No." Branwen tapped a finger against her bow. "You don't eat raw rabbit unless you're truly desperate. And we can't make a fire up here."

"Then why did you—"

"Because," said Branwen, picking up a length of thin rope, "something will always come for the scent of fresh blood."

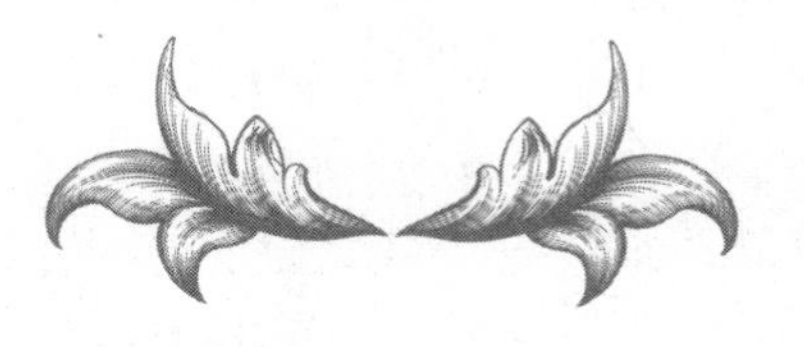

CHAPTER 22

IT WAS NOT a monster that woke her. It was the quiet.

Branwen sat up, her cloak slipping away. Pryderi had fallen asleep with his back to the tree trunk, his head slumped and chin upon his chest. Gwydion was sprawled on his side, one arm still slung around Palug.

Branwen crawled to the edge of the woven branches, peering into the woods. She had set two snares near the dead rabbit. The first she hid near a clump of ferns and the second within the grass. The small knives the folk provided were unfamiliar. The metal was lighter than iron, and when she cut the second length of rope, she had yanked too hard and sliced a thin line down her finger. It was a thankfully small wound, and she'd bound it with a bit of clean cloth.

Now, she peered down at the dead rabbit. The quiet was deafening. Almost as if—

Fear burned through her. The shadows of the tall trees swayed as an unheard wind tugged at their branches.

And then one of those shadows moved.

Branwen's breath caught. It was not a shadow but a large hound. She recognized the pale fur and red-tipped ears. Breath misted around its muzzle, fogging in the cool night. The ci annwn picked its way along the game trail.

It came upon the dead rabbit and snuffled the creature. Then the ci annwn lifted its head and howled silently.

Another hound stepped from the shadows, trotting up to its companion. Then another—and another. An entire hunting pack encircled the rabbit.

Something soft brushed Branwen's arm, and she nearly fell from the tree. A hand seized her arm, steadying her. She looked up sharply. Gwydion was awake, his dark eyes focused on the hunting hounds below. Palug came up on Branwen's other side. The cat glared down at the cŵn annwn, his tail three times its normal size.

Fearful that he might leap at the pack, Branwen scooped him into her arms, caging the cat in place. She felt the vibration of his growl, even as she could not hear it.

The pack shifted and swayed, each of them sniffing at the rabbit. One hound snapped at another, then backed away with lowered ears. Its hind leg snagged in a snare. The hound leapt up in surprise, yanking at the rope. But Rhain had taught her well, and Branwen's snare would only tighten the more the creature thrashed. The hound bit at its own leg, trying to free itself.

A sleek black horse glided from the shadows, cutting through undergrowth without stirring a single leaf. Atop the horse sat an armored figure. He was tall, with a cloak like blood and a crown of bone. He cast a monstrous shadow in the moonlight—some ancient thing arisen from an age before mortals. He did not bow to the laws of this world; gravity did not seem to weigh upon him, and time slid past without ever touching his features.

King Arawn.

Looking at him was like staring into the sun. Branwen's right eye ached, pupil drawn tight while her left eye tried to compensate. He glowed, lit from within by some invisible power. She had seen other-folk with her sight, but it had never been like this.

He did not carry magic; he *was* magic.

Arawn snapped his fingers, and his lips moved soundlessly. The hounds retreated from the rabbit. He slid from his horse and knelt beside the snared ci annwn. He smoothed his hand down the hound's back as though it were a favored pet. Perhaps it was.

Arawn reached down and unbound the snare. Then he rose, turning in a circle. Likely looking for whoever had set the trap.

Branwen knew she should have retreated. She should have shrunk into the shadows, covered the white gleam of her hair with a cloak and closed her eyes. That was the best way to deal with monsters, was it not? To hide under a blanket.

Gwydion's face was drawn, lips slightly parted as though he yearned to call for his power.

Branwen's right hand closed around his left, squeezing hard. A warning.

He returned the grip, his fingers curling around hers. He must have felt her shaking, for his thumb swept back and forth across the soft inside of her wrist. She felt that touch like a shiver up her arm—and heat blazed in her cheeks. She was not accustomed to easy caresses, to the way that some friends seemed to pass touch back and forth like shared drinks. Branwen had been a solitary creature for so long that even the gentle warmth of her hand in his felt scorching.

She did not draw away. She dared not move, not with the Otherking so near.

His horse pranced in place as Arawn looked about the clearing. Slowly, his gaze swept upward.

Branwen could not hear a thing—not even her own heartbeat. Palug's claws dug into her arm, but she only held him tighter.

The Otherking's golden eyes gazed up at the tree where Branwen and Gwydion knelt. He could have fired an arrow, thrown a spear, or called upon his magic. But Arawn did none of those things. Picking up the reins, he urged his horse into a canter. Hunter, horse, and hounds darted along the path and deeper into the forest.

She could have sworn that he had smiled.

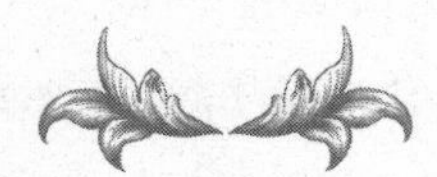

The quiet lasted long after the hunting hounds had retreated.

Branwen sat in the cradle of tree branches, her breathing uneven. Palug had finally wormed his way free and sat on the edge of their shelter, gaze fixed on the place where Arawn had vanished. Gwydion picked up a water flask and poured two small cups, then mixed in a handful of dried blooms. "It will be cold, but it might help," he murmured, handing a cup to Branwen.

She sniffed the water. "Chamomile?"

"I doubt either one of us will find sleep easily," he replied. He offered her a small, forced smile. His gaze fell on Pryderi; the prince's soft snores were muffled into his own chest. "I suppose I shouldn't resent him for resting. He was, after all, the only one of us invited to this Hunt."

Branwen huffed out a quiet laugh. "No rest for the uninvited."

"I'll drink to that," he said, clinking his cup against hers.

It was not tea; there was no fire to warm it. But the chamomile water tasted herbal and a little sweet. The scent plunged her into memories of home. There was always chamomile in the sleep brew that the apothecary sold her. She bit her lip. Mam would be asleep by now, if all was well.

"What is it?" asked Gwydion. His eyes were on her face, a concerned crease between his brows.

She shook her head. "Just thinking of home."

That line deepened, and he looked away. "You miss it?"

"I do," Branwen admitted.

"You'll see it again," said Gwydion. There was something akin to guilt in his face. Perhaps he felt responsible for being the one to drag her into the Hunt. "It might not be for a while, but you will."

"It's not just home." Branwen drained the last of her chamomile. "It's... all of it. The smell of the hearthfire, the sound of Mam waking up in the morning, feeding the chickens, Palug demanding that I feed him first. It's... it's home." There was no disguising the ache in her voice, and she did not try. "Do you miss Caer Dathyl?"

Gwydion let out a startled laugh. "I—no. Not at all."

She gave him a disbelieving look.

"Truly, I don't," he said.

Perhaps it was the late hour or the magic all around them. Branwen felt brave enough to ask, "Then what do you miss?"

His eyes unfocused and his mouth softened, as though he were gazing at something only he could see. "A meadow."

Branwen wrapped her arms around her knees. "A meadow?"

"It was my mother's favorite place," he said softly. "A day's ride from Caer Dathyl. She used to take me there when I was young. She had tended it for years, used her magic to grow herbs and flowers. It was a hidden little meadow—and only she could come and go as she pleased. The trees would welcome her." He cleared his throat. "I inherited my power from her."

"That sounds lovely."

The softness fell away from Gwydion's face. He inhaled, straightening his shoulders. "It's likely gone now. I don't know what became of it after she died."

"What happened?" asked Branwen.

"Illness," he said. "Dôn's power was like mine. Divining takes something from the diviner, you know. Fire diviners lose heat, water diviners are parched, metal diviners drain the metals in their blood. But as for plant diviners... no one truly knows what the magic costs. Mother used the power freely, spending her life with little care for herself. She grew slow to heal and quick to exhaustion. My uncle might have healed her with his magic, but he did not. So she slipped away." His right hand flexed. "The healers tried experimenting on me for a while, trying to find out where my magic came from, but I stopped them. They never helped. So I don't overtax myself. I decide when and where to spend my power. But I still wonder if I will end up the same."

Branwen shivered. Her body had been a reliable thing for as long as she could remember. It was not perfect. She was scarred; her magicked eye gave her painful headaches if used for too long; her once-broken cheekbone ached in cold weather. But she could not imagine living a life where every decision had to be weighed against the cost. "That must frighten you. It would frighten me."

Gwydion shook his head. "It does not. I've known no other life."

It seemed a night for truths. Perhaps the silence of the hounds had left them both hungry for sound of any kind. "Then what do you fear?" she asked.

He looked down at his hands. No, she realized. Not both of his hands—just the right one. The one protected in a leather-and-wood brace.

"Being at the mercy of another," he said softly.

Because he did not trust others. The last time he had allowed himself to be powerless, he had been hurt. He might as well have spoken the words aloud. All of his jests and his wit, all of his charm and his intelligence—it was his armor. He had made himself a trickster because he would never be a knight.

She pointed to the scar along her cheekbone. "You couldn't stop looking at this scar when we met."

His gaze focused on the old mark. "You said it was a wolf hunt."

She exhaled. "It was a man," she said. "Not a wolf. Although he liked to call himself that. He...he slew one of my family. And I could not stop it. Nor avenge it."

His hand came up, fingers brushing over the old scar. His thumb stroked back and forth, as though he were committing it to memory. His brows hung low over his dark eyes; anger embrittled the corners of his mouth. She knew that anger was not aimed at her. His hand fell away, and she felt his fingertips graze her lips.

She said, "Powerlessness. That is what I fear most."

Something flickered through his eyes. It might have been shame; it might have been understanding. He gazed at her as though she were a knot that had just unraveled in his hands.

"Perhaps that's why we're all here," said Branwen. "Because the boon is power. It's a choice we can make for ourselves. Noble or common, hunter or hunted, we all want that."

"Yes," he said softly. "We do."

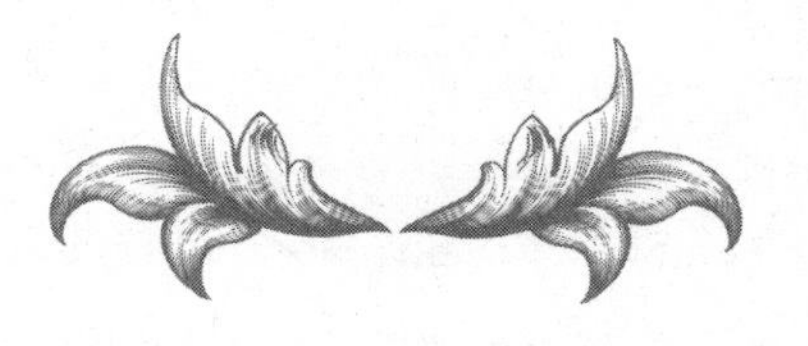

CHAPTER 23

THE MORNING BEGAN with rain.

It dripped from the trees, spattering across Gwydion's hood and dripping down his cloak. The cold made his right hand stiff, and when he tried to stretch the fingers, they throbbed in answer. Palug's ears were pressed to his head, and he glared at the woods as though the rain were a personal betrayal. The rain dampened all of their moods: Branwen muttered about how tracks would be washed away, and even Pryderi looked a little bedraggled. Had this been a royal hunt of Gwynedd, they would have retreated to camp to indulge in mulled wine, game roasted over a fire, and conversation. But in the Wild Hunt, the stakes were too high for indulgences.

"What are you looking for?" asked Gwydion as Branwen led them down a muddied trail.

She shot an irritated glance over her shoulder. "You think you could do better?"

"I didn't mean it that way," he said, holding both hands out. "I am not a hunter."

"I would never have guessed," said Pryderi dryly.

"I don't know what signs you're looking for," continued Gwydion, "and if I did know...I might be of more use. I can sense the forest. It might not be like listening at a door for human talk, but I can discern some things."

Branwen halted. "You make a good point," she said. "Sorry."

"No apologies needed." He could see the taut line between her brows, the clench of her jaw. Pain was written across her face as clearly as if it had been scrawled on parchment. Gwydion had felt enough pain in his life to recognize it in another.

"Should I make a blindfold?" he asked quietly. "I could use part of my cloak."

She touched her forehead. "It wouldn't help. The iron is what drove the magic back, kept it caged. Without that..."

"What's wrong?" asked Pryderi.

"Headache," said Branwen tensely. "Bright lights, sounds—they're beginning to grate. I've never used my eye for this long. My mam made me a blindfold stitched with iron to ward off the magic, but I could not bring it here."

Pryderi touched the pouch he tied to his belt. "If we find a signet ring made of iron, would that work? It might be heavy, but we could put something together. At least so the eye wouldn't pain you at night."

"That's not a bad—" Branwen began to say, then went silent. "Someone's coming."

They hastened off the game trail into a line of bushes. The leaves brushed Gwydion's exposed neck, sending droplets of cold rainwater down his back. He shivered and silently cursed the weather. At least it was not snow.

True to Branwen's word, he heard the sounds a few moments later: the crunch of leaves underfoot, conversation, and laughter. A small group spilled out of the trees, heading westward down the mountain. There was an easy camaraderie among the hunters; one appeared to be telling a tale while the others laughed. They were eating smoked fish and bread as they walked.

The smell of fish proved to be too much. Palug darted from the bushes.

"No," whispered Branwen, horror in her voice. "Palug, stop!"

Gwydion hummed, allowing a small trickle of his power into the ground. Ferns and weeds reached for the cat, but he was too quick. He flitted toward the hunting party.

"That *cat*," said Branwen in exasperation, and rose to follow, knife in hand. Pryderi surged after her, making as much noise as a sheep caught in a fence. Which left Gwydion sitting alone in the bushes.

With a resigned little sigh, he pushed himself to his feet. If this was about to turn violent, he could at least try to protect the cat.

Palug rushed up to the hunters, meowing as though he had never tasted food in his life. "What a handsome cat," said a mortal woman, kneeling.

"I would not," said another hunter. This one had forest-green hair and eyes like moonlight. He gently pulled the woman back when she made to pet Palug.

Branwen and Pryderi scrambled after the cat. "Morning," called Pryderi. "We mean no harm!"

"Morning," called one of the hunters. He was another one of the tylwyth teg, with elegantly pointed ears and a shark's smile. He used those sharp teeth to take another bite of fish. "Prince Pryderi, you're looking well."

"And you," said Pryderi with a polite incline of his head.

"This yours?" The wary green-haired hunter nodded down at Palug.

"He's an ungrateful little beggar," Branwen said, picking him up. "But he is mine. Them, too," she added, with a nod at Gwydion and Pryderi. "And the last hunting party that tried to hurt them ended up dead."

One of the human women shook her head. "Nothing to fear from us," she said. "We're out of the Hunt." She lifted her left hand—and Gwydion felt his breath catch. Curled around her index finger, growing up her arm, was a small bilberry bush. Roots wove through her fingers; leaves curled along her wrist and forearm. Even as he watched, the plant grew up her shoulder. Her magic-given ring must have been made from a bilberry root.

All the hunters bore such foliage—all except for one. He was human, with reddish-brown hair and a leanly dangerous look. His skin was unmarred by sun, but his hands were too worn to belong to a nobleman. Gwydion's gaze flicked over him with practice; he had seen such men before. This man was a blade for hire. Likely a personal assassin belonging to one of the Dyfed nobles.

"Is that what happens when someone captures your signet ring?" asked Branwen, with a glance down at her own oaken ring.

The hunter nodded. "Yes. Once the ring sprouted and took hold of me, I could no longer hunt. We can only walk back toward camp. So we're taking what rings we did collect to King Pwyll."

"And I'm taking mine to King Arawn," said one of the folk hunters.

"I've never seen such magic," Pryderi said, gazing at another of the hunters. Around his arm grew what looked to be a small elm tree.

"It's a binding," said the folk hunter. "I've heard King Arawn constructs the spell every year. Once your ring is given to the Hunt, the forest can take hold of you."

"Because a signet ring is near enough to a name," murmured Branwen. Her gaze flicked uneasily to her own ring a second time.

The folk hunter nodded. "And names have power."

"Are all of you out?" asked Gwydion curiously.

The red-haired assassin shook his head and held up his bare arm. His wooden ring was still intact. "I'm escorting them back to camp."

"Is that necessary?" asked Pryderi.

The assassin gave him a sharp smile. "There are hunters attacking those returning to camp. There is only one rule at this point. Be hunter or hunted. As this group cannot defend themselves, I will keep the scavengers at bay."

"That's kind of you," said Pryderi.

He shrugged. "Any decent sort would."

Gwydion wouldn't. But then again, he'd never claimed to be decent. "How many rings did you collect?" he asked.

One hunter shrugged. "Likely not enough for the boon. Seven rings, mostly found on rabbits and grouse near the camp."

"Impressive," said Pryderi.

"Have you seen the beast yet?" asked one of the women.

Gwydion blinked. "The beast?"

"There's something in the wood," said the other woman. "We never saw it. But...we heard screaming last night. And this morning, we found..."

"Corpses without hands," said another hunter. "They were bound by root and bush, so we couldn't return their bodies to camp. Mayhap that's what happens when you die in the Hunt—you belong to the forest forever."

"Where did you find the bodies?" asked Branwen. Her gaze was hard as the winter sky.

The woman pointed northeast. "An hour in that direction. Take care, if you choose to hunt it."

"Why would we hunt it?" asked Pryderi.

"Because," said the assassin, with a gleaming smile, "what kind of hunter could manage to attach his ring to a beast?"

It was Branwen who figured it out first. "A king of beasts."

"Precisely," said the assassin. "I suspect that a royal signet ring would carry more weight in this competition than ten of lesser value." He shifted restlessly, using his left hand to check the dagger strapped to his other wrist. As he did so, Gwydion saw the rings upon the man's hands. There were five signet rings. This man had captured or killed five animals all on his own.

Dangerous, indeed.

Branwen nodded. "Good hunting."

The assassin returned the nod politely. "You as well."

But as they walked away, the assassin's gaze remained on

Branwen. The look made Gwydion's stomach tighten. It was a gaze of pure hunger, of a starving man a few strides from a feast. Gwydion had the wild impulse to step forward and put himself between Branwen and that man. That was foolish. For one thing, Branwen was a far better fighter. For another, it would reveal his own impulsive loyalties.

He had no loyalty to her, Gwydion told himself silently. He had other loyalties—and those had to come first.

He had little patience for others. His friendships were transactional, like the alliance he shared with Eilwen. True trust, warmth, and companionship were too costly. To let someone near was too great a risk.

There were only four people he was sure loved him: his mother, Arianrhod, Dylan, and Lleu. He was here for them.

As the assassin walked by Branwen, dread filled Gwydion. For the man was not looking at *her* with that naked desire.

He was looking at the ring around Palug's neck. He had seen the prince's signet ring.

When the two groups parted ways, Gwydion's steps slowed. Years of living at the Gwynedd royal court had taught him how to plot and scheme. He could never beat that assassin in a fair fight, so he would not fight fair. He could double back. He could entrap that assassin in a cage of blackberry briars, capture him in the roots of an oak, or simply knock him in the back of the head with a rock. Then that assassin would pose no more threat.

But Gwydion knew that Branwen and Pryderi would disapprove. They had admired the assassin's decency in escorting those others back to camp. They were both good people, wanting to believe in the goodness of others. They hadn't seen the look of hunger on the assassin's face. If Gwydion suggested ambushing him, he knew they would regard him as a selfish, unscrupulous trickster.

Which he was. He very much was.

But there were far worse things to be.

They walked for the better part of the morning, taking a break to wash their faces in a cold stream. Branwen found fresh tracks while Gwydion unearthed a jar of poultice from his pack. His hand was aching, and he knew better than to ignore it. If he left it too long, the joints would swell and burn.

"I'm looking for where game trails meet hunter trails," Branwen said as she refilled her water flask. She shaded her eyes against the sun, wincing. "Then we can follow the game, and hopefully those will be the animals marked with rings."

"Are you all right?" Pryderi asked, frowning. "You keep looking away from the sun."

Branwen's arm fell to her side. "I'm fine."

"I suspect you would say that, even if you were missing a limb," said Pryderi. He shifted so that he stood between her and the sun.

Gwydion half listened to the conversation as he took the poultice, packing it around the knuckles of his right hand. It smelled of oil and fresh herbs, and he covered it with a clean cloth, trying to tie it off with his left hand. It was not his dominant hand, but he had become rather accustomed to using it for most tasks. Unfortunately, the oil of the poultice smeared across his fingers, making the bandage slippery.

Pryderi reached for the bandage, taking the edges from Gwydion. "You're both stubborn, you know that?" He tied off the bandage so gently that Gwydion barely felt the pressure. "If you're in pain, we'll rest."

"If we rested every time I was in pain," said Gwydion. "We'd never get anywhere. We—"

A shriek of birdsong cut him off. Gwydion looked up sharply. Above them, birds took to the air, darting and whirling, crying out.

Branwen had an arrow nocked and aimed before Gwydion could blink. Her gaze narrowed on the flock, assessing. The tip of her arrow swayed as she aimed and aimed again. Then, the corner of her mouth twitched—and she released the arrow.

It cut through the misty air, felling one of the birds. She ran toward the bushes and emerged with it in hand.

It had a golden ring tied around one foot.

"How did you even see that?" said Pryderi, impressed.

She shrugged. "The sunlight reflected off the ring."

"You know," said Gwydion, a note of warning in his voice. "I believe we should find cover."

The forest had gone quiet. Even the trees seemed to be holding their breath. Gwydion did not know what creature could frighten this forest. He suspected it would take something truly monstrous.

A beast.

A cloud passed across the sun. All around him, the forest fell into shadow.

"Something's coming," breathed Branwen.

There was a thicket of blackberries nearby. Their leaves were half gone, green growth edged with the brown of winter. A few desiccated berries clung to the brambles.

"In here," Gwydion said, and with a hum and a gesture, he parted the blackberries. Branwen and Pryderi squeezed into the small space. Palug looked at the brambles, his tail waving uneasily. "You too," Gwydion said, picking the cat up like a babe. Then he ducked into the foliage. With one more whisper, the thorns and half-dead leaves covered them.

They waited, hidden from view, peering through the branches. With his fear-sharpened senses, Gwydion was keenly aware of the taste of the winter mists, the smell of dying leaves, and the warm press of Pryderi and Branwen at his back. Palug shifted in his arms, but not as though he wanted to escape. The cat twisted so that he could see through the brambles. Pryderi's signet ring bumped gently against Gwydion's wrist.

Gwydion closed his eyes, letting his magical senses sink deep into the foliage. Something was running—no, fleeing. Footsteps crashed into the earth, crushing moss and grass, breaking branches, and tearing through ferns.

His mind raced with possibilities. If that assassin was right, then Arawn had chosen a beast to carry his signet ring. What kind of monster would carry the ring of an immortal king? An aderyn y corph? Twrch Trwyth? Or perhaps a creature that had not been named in tales.

But the creature that emerged from the woods was not a corpse-bird nor a giant boar.

It was a young man. He could not have been older than twenty-five.

"Not the monster I imagined," murmured Pryderi. "Unless I am missing something."

"No," said Branwen, just as quietly. "He has no magic. He's like us."

But something prickled at Gwydion. It was an awareness that something was wrong, out of place.

That man wore rough-spun trousers and a tunic. And he was barefoot, his feet bleeding as he ran.

"Who is that?" asked Branwen. In the tight confines of their hiding place, there was no room for her to draw her bow. Gwydion saw her fingers twitch toward her afanc-fang dagger, settling on the hilt.

The man scrambled down the mountainside, tripping over roots and splashing across the stream.

Panic, Gwydion realized. That was why the young man appeared so out of place. Every other mortal in this land had chosen to be here, but this man ran as though all the hounds of Annwvyn were at his heels.

Even the trees could taste the man's terror.

Hunted. The man was being hunted.

"We have to help him," whispered Pryderi. He shifted, as though to rise. Gwydion seized his arm.

"No," hissed Gwydion. He knew the many flavors of fear—he had been the youngest, smallest child in a family that played cruel games. This man was not afraid of something trifling. His eyes were white and rolling like those of a cornered animal. Every breath was a pained gasp, and the stench rolling off him meant he had pissed himself as he fled. Whatever chased this man…Gwydion knew it would be a nightmare.

Pryderi tried to pull his arm free, but Gwydion held on, ignoring the pain. Pryderi looked at Gwydion in betrayal and confusion. He was the kind of person who would run toward danger to help another. Selfless, kind. He would be a good king.

But Gwydion would not allow the prince to rush free of the brambles. That would put both him and Branwen in danger. Perhaps that was selfish, but Gwydion did not care.

The man stumbled over a loose rock and fell to his knees. He pushed himself upright, a whimper emerging from his throat. "We have to," Pryderi began to say.

The stranger managed to take a single step—and then an arrow slammed into his knee.

It happened so quickly that Gwydion had to stifle a gasp. Branwen flinched beside him, and even Pryderi recoiled. The man screamed and desperately tried to pry the arrow free, fingers slick with blood as he pawed at the wound. When that failed, he began to crawl.

It was no use.

The branches rustled, the undergrowth shifting to allow for something to pass. Gwydion held his breath, waiting. He needed to see what kind of creature inspired such terror.

A woman walked from the shadows.

She was short, and her figure was one of shapely curves. Even among the tylwyth teg, she was strikingly beautiful. Her dark hair was bound into a knot, and she walked with a comfortable grace. Her ears came to delicate points, and she wore scale armor. Not armored scales but scale *hide*. It gleamed iridescent in the sunlight. A cloak of feathers was knotted at her throat.

It was Arawn's champion, Gwydion realized. He had seen her by the Otherking's side at the revel.

Pryderi went still. His jaw clenched so hard Gwydion saw a muscle jump in his cheek.

"Cigfa," he breathed.

"Friend of yours?" asked Gwydion.

"Yes." Pryderi's gaze raked over the woman as though he could not believe what he was seeing.

"What is it?" asked Branwen softly.

"That is the hide of an afanc," whispered Pryderi. "Only cold iron can pierce it."

Gwydion swallowed. If Cigfa had slain an afanc and taken its hide for armor, she was a far more dangerous hunter than any they had encountered.

But that was not the most frightening thing about her.

Hanging from her belt were—

Gwydion closed and opened his eyes.

—four human hands.

They had been severed at the wrist. A cord had been tied around each, and their fingertips were dark with pooled blood.

On her belt, those severed hands swayed sickeningly.

Each hand bore a signet ring.

Cigfa had not bothered to take the rings; she had simply taken their hands.

And with a nauseating twist of his belly, Gwydion thought of Arawn's finger-bone crown.

"Fallen kings," Branwen whispered. "Any animal. That's what he said—any animal, mortal or immortal." She seized Gwydion's right wrist, squeezing hard. As though she might make him understand through pressure alone. "Any animal."

He gazed at her, uncomprehending.

She said urgently, "This is why people go missing on a Hunt year. There were rumors. I thought—after I heard the rules, I thought it was just a tale. But it's true. If the barwn's son hadn't been eaten..."

It took Gwydion a moment to recall who she was talking about. Barwn Ifor—his missing son. Gone into Annwvyn and never returned. It was true that a few people vanished every year. Gwydion had heard the same rumors, but he'd never wanted to believe them. It was easier to blame the disappearances on human mistakes.

He felt abruptly cold. His gaze sought the man's hand—and true enough, he bore a dark signet ring.

"What is it?" asked Pryderi.

"The otherfolk," Gwydion said hoarsely. "They're using captured humans as their game animals."

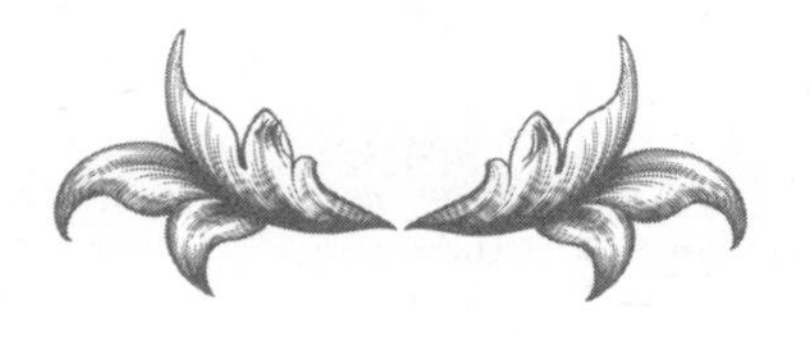

CHAPTER 24

PEOPLE ALWAYS VANISHED on a Hunt year.

It was simply expected, the way snow arrived in winter and wildflowers with the spring. Every fifth year, when the autumn was waning, those who ventured too near Annwvyn would disappear. Some reappeared…and others never did. There were always whispers about the Wild Hunt, about humans being chased through the woods. But at the revel of Nos Calan Gaeaf, Branwen had seen the celebration of mingled mortals and immortals. Surely those of Dyfed would not take part in hunting their own kind.

Of course they would, part of her whispered. *Humans have never hesitated to harm their own.*

Branwen thought of the barwn's missing son. Being devoured down to the bone by a water wraith might have been preferable to this. This man had been stolen, given a folk signet ring, and set loose in the forest like a deer. He was to be hunted and bested—and judging from the bloat of those severed hands, the others Cigfa hunted had not lasted very long.

That might have been Branwen, if not for her magicked sight. How many times had she walked the outskirts of Annwvyn? She had avoided countless folk traps, slipped by the snares, walked freely without fear of illusion.

This poor man had not been so lucky.

"Cigfa can't be," said Pryderi. "She isn't…" His face was bone white, stark against the dark green of the blackberry brambles. "I *know* her."

Gwydion blinked. "Well, there's no accounting for taste."

"Not like that," said Pryderi. "I came with my father and the others to set up camp. She was given the task of keeping me out of trouble, introducing me to folk nobles, and showing me around. She made me laugh. She was never cruel."

"The tylwyth teg aren't human," said Branwen. "I've spoken with an ironfetch about them. The folk are not cruel, but nor are they merciful. Is a hawk cruel for hunting rabbits? Or a storm merciful for passing by a house?"

"They're not monsters," said Pryderi.

"I believe the woman with a belt of severed hands might qualify," said Gwydion.

Cigfa walked toward the fallen man with calm certainty. She held a terribly serrated knife—the kind used for sawing through sinew and bone. There was no chance of escape for that human. He could not run, not with an arrow through his knee.

Branwen could not simply watch. She had seen too much needless cruelty in her eighteen years; she would not bear witness to another death while she stood by. Fury set fire to her blood, giving her a strength she knew she would need.

"Gwydion," whispered Branwen, "let me go."

Gwydion shook his head. "Fallen kings, Branwen. I don't think you can—"

But Branwen was moving before Gwydion could finish his sentence. Heedless of the thick vines, of the dying leaves, of the thorns that looked sharp enough to skewer, she rose from her crouch, yanked the dagger from her hip, and cut her way free. Briars snagged on her sleeve. Gwydion cursed, but he did so in a singsong. With the tune, the briars melted away before her.

The moment Branwen had an arrow drawn, all her disgust and fear and anger seemed to melt away. There was only the hunt.

The fletching kissed the corner of her mouth—and then she let the arrow fly.

Cigfa whirled, slicing with that serrated knife. The arrow fell in two pieces.

The human man saw Branwen, and desperate hope flared in his eyes. "Please," he gasped. "Please, help me. I have a family—please—"

Branwen nocked a second arrow and held a third at the ready. She stalked closer, and her aim never wavered. "You're going to be all right."

"Well, well," said Cigfa, tilting her head. It made her look birdlike. "I do not know you."

Branwen narrowed eyes. "Your people have called me the white crow."

A slow smile spread across Cigfa's face. "That eye of yours. It's gold as autumn leaves."

Branwen's fingers froze on the arrow. "My eye is not gold."

"It is," said Cigfa. "Have you ever looked at yourself in a mirror? You should. You're rather striking."

"Of course I've seen myself in a mirror," snarled Branwen.

Cigfa tilted her head in the other direction. "One without iron?"

Branwen opened her mouth to reply, then went silent.

Cigfa's gaze slid past Branwen. "Hello, my favorite prince. I see you finally made friends."

"Cigfa," said Pryderi as calmly as though they had met in a pleasant courtyard. "What are you doing?"

"Hunting," replied Cigfa. "Same as you."

"No." Pryderi's mouth thinned. "I have never hunted like this."

"You think rabbits do not feel fear?" Cigfa scoffed. "That a deer's heart does not pound when it flees? That fowl cannot feel pain?" She stepped toward Branwen and Pryderi. "Unlike your kind, mine do not lie to ourselves. Every hunt is a cruelty."

Branwen's grip on the arrow never relented, even as her arm muscles burned. "Let him go."

"Cigfa," said Pryderi pleadingly.

"Why this mortal?" said Cigfa. Then she touched one of the severed hands at her belt. "Why not this one, or this one?"

"Because those are starting to look a little ripe." Gwydion had emerged from the blackberries, Palug at his shoulder.

Cigfa took another step. "Kingdoms are not built upon thrones. They are built on blood and bone—the only difference between Pwyll and Arawn is that my king chooses to wear his misdeeds where all might see them."

"I won't tell anyone of this," said the man, his voice shaking. "Please, just—"

Cigfa whirled, took hold of the man's hair, and brought her knife down upon the back of his neck.

But her blade never found flesh. It clanged against Pryderi's spear.

Quicker than thought, Cigfa pulled a second blade from her belt with her other hand. Pryderi lunged, using the spear to drive her back.

Cigfa wielded the weapons as though she had been born with a blade in each hand. Every movement was graceful. She deflected the blow and slashed the spear aside, her dark sea-green eyes alight.

"Well, well," she said merrily. "The lost heir has found his teeth."

Pryderi swallowed. "Don't make me do this, Cigfa."

She smiled. "Come now. You said you could fight. I prefer dancing, but I will settle for this."

"If we fight—" Pryderi began to say.

"Dyfed's champion against Annwvyn's." Cigfa's smile blossomed. She was captivating as a sea storm, and she approached with the same inevitability. "I have heard the rumors of how you were raised. I wish to see them for myself." And without another word, she attacked.

It looked like a dance—Cigfa was all grace and speed while Pryderi moved with the calm surety of a workhorse. When her blades slashed, he caught them on the spear's shaft, then fended her off with his weapon's reach. She could never get close enough to land a deadly blow.

Branwen sighted down her arrow, her aim jerking back and forth as Cigfa moved. She hesitated for fear of hitting Pryderi.

"Branwen!" A sharp voice made her glance back. Gwydion was a few strides away, kneeling beside the injured man.

Branwen inhaled, letting the world slow around her. All she needed was a heartbeat of stillness: She saw the sweat at Pryderi's brow, the glimmer of sunlight through the winter-stark trees, and then the blur as she released the bowstring.

The arrow hissed through the bushes, cutting through the air, and—

Cigfa swung her knife and batted the arrow away. The shards of wood tumbled harmlessly into the ground. And then she was a blur, sprinting so swiftly that Branwen barely had time to bring her own knife to bear. She caught Cigfa's blade with the jagged edge of her own dagger. Cigfa's smile never wavered as she pressed her advantage, shoving forward. Branwen's heels dug in, but for all of her strength, she was still mortal. She would never match one of the tylwyth teg for raw force.

"I like your knife," said Cigfa. There was no strain or effort to her voice, as though she were remarking on Branwen's gown at a royal feast. Her blade crept closer to Branwen, its edge shining in the sunlight.

Branwen's foot slipped, and she crashed to her knees. One ankle tangled in the briars.

She snarled at the strain. Cigfa bore down on her, using her weight to shove Branwen deeper into the thorns.

"DOWN!"

Pryderi's voice was a snarl.

Without hesitating, Branwen flung herself to one side, rolling into the blackberry bushes. Resistance gone, Cigfa fell forward just as Pryderi thrust the spear at her. She barely managed to dart to one side. There was a feral gleam to her smile as she attacked him.

Pryderi drove Cigfa back. There was a confidence to him that Branwen had never seen before. Gone was the young man filled with hesitation, who seemed torn between yearning and wariness.

This Pryderi looked like a prince sent to war.

The violence had Cigfa's full attention. She let out a burble of merry laughter, her knives a blur.

Glad for the reprieve, Branwen managed to pull herself free of the thorns. Pain flared along her leg, but she ignored the discomfort. Gwydion was at the injured man's side. "Help me," he called. "I can't do this alone!"

Branwen nodded, falling to her own knees beside the hunted man. "What do you need?"

"Hold him," said Gwydion. To her surprise, his tone was tight but steady. She would have expected him to be far more frightened by such a wound.

She took hold of the man's thigh and shin. The arrow that protruded from his knee was an ugly sight, and she winced in sympathy. It must have been agonizing.

"This won't hurt a bit," said Gwydion.

The man's pupils were constricted with pain. "It hurts right now."

"Well, what kind of trickster would I be if I told the truth?"

Gwydion moved with surprising ease. He rolled up his sleeves and opened a bottle that smelled of strong spirits. He splashed a little on his hands, rubbing his fingers together. "What's your name?"

The man blinked. "Penbras."

"Don't look at me, Penbras," said Gwydion. He used a knife to cut the man's trousers away. "This is Branwen, and she's a far more pleasant sight. Look at her, all right? Isn't she pretty?"

Penbras looked at Branwen. His throat jerked as he swallowed. "She's beautiful."

"I am not," said Branwen, keeping a tight hold on Penbras's leg. "But I suppose you'd say the same of any rescuer."

"I don't hear him complimenting me," replied Gwydion. He took a knife to the edge of the arrow, cutting the jagged tip free. His voice was soothing, as though he spoke to a spooked horse. "Penbras, I want you to look at her. Tell me what you think of her hair. Tell me all the words you can think of to describe her hair."

"My hair?" asked Branwen.

"Distraction, he needs a distraction," continued Gwydion in that same singsong voice. "Tell me of her hair."

Penbras looked utterly bewildered, but he obliged. "It's... white. Like sheep's wool. Or clouds. Or—" He let out a terrible scream as Gwydion ripped the arrow shaft free. Branwen's grip tightened on Penbras's leg, holding him in place.

"You're doing well, you're doing so well," said Gwydion. He had a flask of water at the ready, and he cleaned the dirt and debris from the wound. Then he was binding it with a clean cloth. "Branwen, there's a tincture in my pack. Clay jar, red wax stopper."

She released Penbras's leg. He was racked with breathless sobs.

She found the jar and handed it to Gwydion. "This is going to help," he said. "I promise." Then he measured a small amount and tipped it into Penbras's mouth.

"There you go," he said, tying off the bandage. "You're doing very well, Penbras. You'll have a story to tell your grandchildren someday."

"I don't have children," Penbras whispered. "I have two cats. And a husband."

"Then this will be a wonderful story for your cats and your husband." Gwydion finished binding the wound. He closed his eyes for a moment, then hummed. And with as much effort as one might pull a dandelion free, he reached down and yanked a root from a nearby tree. It came up easily, curling around his hand. Before Branwen's eyes, the root shifted and changed into a walking stick. "You're going to be a little drowsy. The poppy tincture will make you giddy, but you have to fight through that.

"You are going to go northwest," continued Gwydion. "You hear me, Penbras? You will go that way. Get to Gwynedd." He reached into the hidden pocket of his cloak and withdrew several gold coins. He knotted them into a strip of bandage and tied it around Penbras's wrist. "You use these to pay for a healer. If you go to Caer Dathyl, ask for Eilwen. She'll find you a place to stay while you recover. Tell her the gardener sent you, all right?"

Penbras's eyes were glazed with pain. "I can't outrun them," he whispered.

Pryderi snarled as Cigfa's blades nicked his arm. He whirled, a blur of graceful violence as he struck out. Cigfa was forced to retreat, merriment in her eyes.

It was true. Penbras would never survive Annwvyn so long as he was part of the Hunt. Branwen's mind whirled. If he were taken out of the Wild Hunt, if he was no longer something to be hunted, he would have a chance.

Cigfa did not want Penbras. She wanted the ring he bore.

Branwen leaned over Penbras, brushing the hair from his forehead. "They will not hunt you," she said. "If you give us that ring on your finger. It's not yours, is it?"

Penbras shook his head. "She put it on me," he said. "Two days ago. Said I had to run, to stay hidden."

"All they want is that ring," said Branwen. "Give it to me, and she will have no reason to hunt you."

With trembling fingers, Penbras yanked the signet ring free. It looked to be carved of stone, with a fish etched into it. He held it out to Branwen. There was a trust in his eyes, and it made Branwen think of how children would reach their arms out to adults when afraid. Of how Palug leapt into her arms when he'd climbed too high into a tree. She hoped Penbras's trust was not misplaced.

She took the ring from him.

And in that moment, something thudded to the ground. Branwen flinched, half expecting to see Pryderi fallen, a knife in his chest. For all that he had been raised by a monster, surely he could not win against an immortal.

But it was not Pryderi's weapon upon the ground.

It was Cigfa's.

Before Branwen's eyes, the magic of the forest took hold. Cigfa's wooden ring looked to be made of elder. Roots twined around her fingers, burrowing into her flesh. Sprigs of green twisted around her forearm, small white flowers bursting into bloom.

And that was when Branwen realized what she was holding.

This was Cigfa's ring. She had been hunting her own signet.

"Fallen kings," Branwen whispered.

Gwydion let out his own little curse. He heaved Penbras to his feet and gave him the walking stick. "Go," he said. "Get as far as you can while the pain is gone."

Penbras looked at them both with a wild relief. "Thank you," he whispered. "Thank you, thank you." He turned and hobbled away, leaning heavily on the root walking stick. Gwydion watched him go, then his gaze met Branwen's. She could see the hope and anger churning behind those dark eyes. The Hunt was magic and power—but it was also so much unneeded pain and cruelty. His expression mirrored her own, and in that moment, she felt as connected to Gwydion as she had felt with anyone.

Thank you, she thought, hoping he saw the sentiment in her eyes. Saving that man had been a kindness only he had the skill for. She could not have managed it.

"I've spent enough time with the healers," he said. "Picked up a few things."

She let out a small, jittery laugh. Then they were both rising, her hand in his, terrified and elated, and carrying the signet ring of an immortal champion.

Cigfa stood very still. Along her left arm, the elder flowers shifted in the breeze. They were beautiful—a living armlet of blossoms and leaves. Pryderi was leaning on his spear. When he met

Branwen's eyes, he gave her a nod of thanks. A tremble ran up his legs, and Branwen realized that he would not have been able to battle Cigfa much longer. She returned his nod. He had saved her life in that fight—and she had just saved his. They were even.

"My dear prince," Cigfa said, "you chose your friends well." And without hesitation, she sank to her knees before Branwen.

They all gaped at her.

"Is this . . . what normally happens?" asked Branwen, feeling distinctly uncomfortable.

"How should I know?" said Pryderi.

Cigfa said, "My fealty is yours. Now, what do you command?"

Branwen took a step back. "I . . . I don't know what you mean."

"You hold my ring," said Cigfa. "You hold my fealty until you give it to your king."

Branwen gazed at the woman. The words simply did not make sense. "I hold your fealty?"

Cigfa gave her a level, patient look. The look a parent might give an ignorant child. "My dear huntress. What did you think you were hunting for?"

Unease roiled up through Branwen's stomach. ". . . Rings?"

Cigfa shook her head. "Jewelry is of little use to kings," she said.

Branwen drew in a sharp breath. "What?"

"We do not hunt for rings," said Cigfa. "We hunt for loyalty."

This did not make sense. This was a hunt, just another hunt. A hunt for monsters and creatures and humans—but it was still just a hunt. Branwen felt as dizzy and unsettled as when she'd first glimpsed those hands at Cigfa's belt.

"What do you mean?" asked Pryderi.

"I mean," said Cigfa, "exactly what I say."

And abruptly, Branwen remembered that eerie song—the one she had heard as they entered Annwvyn.

Every fifth year as harvests wane,
Two kingdoms meet in wooded domain.
And those who cannot hunt nor slay
Belong to your lord for a year and a day.
Kings and beggars, trust to your aim—
For in the Wild Hunt, all are fair game.

This hunt—it was no mere celebration.

Which meant—

"The Hunt," breathed Branwen. "We're—we're not just the hunters. To the kings, we're the prizes."

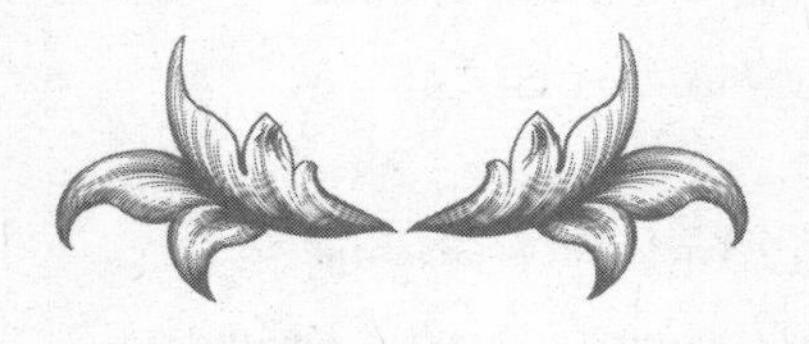

CHAPTER 25

FOR A FEW moments, Branwen could not breathe. She held Cigfa's stone ring as though it might burn her. She did not want this; she did not want anything to do with this.

Her brooch was out there. She had tied it to a lapwing, unknowing of how much she was risking. Her life. Her loyalty. It would belong to whomever found it. She looked down at the oaken ring upon her finger—it bound her to the forest, to the Hunt. Once her own loyalty was caught, that spell would ensnare her. There would be no escaping it. Her brooch would be delivered to one of the kings, and she would be his servant for a year.

The thought made her feel ill.

"The kings divide up the hunters?" asked Pryderi in astonishment. "That's what the Hunt is about?"

"For a year and a day," said Cigfa, painstakingly slow. "Yes."

Gwydion said, "Why?" His voice was oddly emotionless. Perhaps the implications had not sunk in.

"It's a celebration," said Cigfa.

Pryderi took a step forward. "How is trading *people* a celebration?"

"You know the story of how your father and Arawn met, do you not?" asked Cigfa. She sat on the ground, seemingly tired of kneeling. The elder flower armlet rustled as she moved. "Pwyll intruded on the Otherking's hunt. As recompense, Arawn shape-changed them both. For a year and a day, Pwyll ruled Annwvyn in his stead. It was a test of loyalty—one he passed. In doing so, he earned my lord's trust. And now, every five years, they trade hunters for a year and a day. To keep our alliance strong."

"But none of the hunters know about this!" cried Branwen.

"Most of them do not," agreed Cigfa. "But they will serve, nonetheless."

Branwen turned toward Pryderi, naked panic on her face. "Did you know about this?"

"Branwen, I didn't," he said. "I promise you. I thought this was just a hunt."

"How could you not know?" she cried.

"Because all the Hunt's participants are magicked never to speak of it," said Gwydion quietly. "Right? To outsiders, it would simply look as though certain hunters or nobles were on a diplomatic task."

Branwen swallowed. She felt dizzy as she spun around, her gaze on the trees. Some wild part of her thought she might see the lapwing. "We have to find my brooch."

Gwydion put his hands on her arms, steadying her. "We will," he said. "Breathe, Branwen."

She breathed. It came out jagged and shuddering. She had come here for her mother. She could not keep her mam safe if she belonged to a king for a year and a day.

Pryderi squatted down beside Cigfa. "Those hands. They belonged to kidnapped humans?"

"Some mortals trespass," said Cigfa simply. "They serve a purpose."

"They are people, not a purpose," said Pryderi.

"That's exactly what we are," said Branwen wildly. "All of us—in this hunt. We're pieces being moved about a board, to be collected and hoarded. We're just tallies to be counted." Panic rose hot in her throat. The Hunt was not an enemy she could fight, not a beast she could best. The Hunt was a game, and she was not even truly a player. Her fate had been taken from her the moment she slipped her brooch onto a lapwing.

She clawed at the ring around her finger. The oaken ring would not budge, no matter how she yanked at it. Pain flared up her hand as she dug her nails in so deeply that she drew blood. The tendrils of golden magic were embedded in her hand and arm. She had willingly given herself over to the Hunt—and the enchantment would never release her.

She had walked into this trap. Worse, she should have known it was a trap all along. People like her—they did not get to be heroes. They were simply unimportant pieces in someone else's tale.

Helpless.

She was helpless.

Hands settled across her shoulders. She looked up.

Pryderi stood before her. His face was steady, his eyes on hers. "Branwen, I'll get your brooch from my father. I'll take it. If it's delivered to him, I will command you. And I promise, I'll give you only one command—to live your life as you will."

It was a kind promise, but his words rang hollow.

"And if one of the folk finds my brooch and delivers it to Arawn?" she said.

It was Cigfa who replied. "Then you shall be a champion of the Otherking. After all, you bested me. You will take my place."

The thought made Branwen shudder. She did not want to belong to anyone, much less the Otherking.

She looked at the stone ring in her hand; part of her yearned to simply throw it into the woods. But another thought occurred to her.

"This means I can command you?" she said.

Cigfa nodded. "Until you deliver it to your lord. Whoever that might be." Her eyes flicked between Gwydion and Pryderi.

Branwen took a step forward, holding out the ring. Maybe she was not so powerless as she thought. She could command Annwvyn's champion—at least for the moment. "Those hands. Set them on the ground."

Cigfa tilted her head. Branwen expected her to argue, but the champion of Annwvyn merely reached down and began to untie her morbid trophies.

"Pryderi, add those rings to the ones we have," said Branwen. Perhaps it was wrong to steal those rings, but they had been taken already. And all this fear, all this fighting, it could not be for nothing.

If Branwen could wrest a victory from this, then perhaps everything would be worth it.

She might belong to a king, but she would still have the boon.

Pryderi looked a little green as he pulled each ring free. They went into the pouch with the other rings.

Still holding Cigfa's signet, Branwen said, "I command you, Cigfa of Annwvyn. You will return to camp and remain there until the Hunt is ended."

"You could command her to find your brooch," murmured Pryderi.

Branwen shook her head. "No. I won't trust her with that. The folk—they're used to twisting words. If I ask her to find my brooch, she would. She'd also likely whisper its location to every raven, every songbird, and every magical creature she could find."

Cigfa beamed. "Lovely and intelligent. I hope whoever finds your ring understands what a prize you are."

"She is not a prize," said Gwydion hotly. When Branwen met his eyes, he looked away. Shame flickered across his face. *Guilty,* Branwen thought. *He feels guilty for bringing us both here.* But this was not his fault, and she yearned to tell him so.

Cigfa stood. "I will do as you command," she said to Branwen. She turned west.

Before she could go, Gwydion spoke. "That was too easy," he said. "Ask her what she doesn't wish to tell you."

Branwen shot Gwydion a sharp look. "What?"

"Trust me," he said. "Someone like that only obeys orders if they want to, fealty or not."

Branwen stepped in Cigfa's path. The other woman was shorter, with that gleaming afanc armor and dark sea-green eyes. She was so beautiful that Branwen could only look at her for brief moments before she had to glance away. "What are you hiding?" she asked quietly.

Cigfa's eyes glittered. "Many things."

"What are you hiding right now?" said Branwen. Perhaps if she was more specific with her commands. "What do you not wish us to find?"

The corner of Cigfa's lip curled. Then she reached for a chain around her throat. She pulled it free, and with it came a heavy ring. It was crafted of gold and bore the signet of a dragon and seahorse.

Branwen drew in a sharp breath; Gwydion took half a step forward, his fingers outstretched. Pryderi made a strangled noise. "That's—that is my father's ring."

"I tracked it," said Cigfa. "As my king bade. And I was to bring it to him." There was a low note of pride in her voice. "Arawn trusted only me to do so."

"Does that ring hold the same power as the others?" asked Branwen.

"Yes," said Cigfa.

Pryderi sounded appalled. "You mean...you mean that the kings trade power every five years. They do so still?"

"Yes," said Cigfa. "No. Sometimes. Regardless of who holds the fealty, nothing changes in the kingdoms. Pwyll and Arawn would never harm each other. No one even knows the difference. It is why the Hunt matters little to the balance of power. One king will never move against another."

Branwen's mouth felt too dry. That ring was not simply a ring. Not in this hunt. It was a weapon far more powerful than anything she could have ever dreamed. It was a crown, an army. It was the fealty and command of a throne.

It was power. So much power.

"Give it to me," said Branwen.

Cigfa unclasped the chain around her throat and held out the golden ring.

Branwen took it. The gold glittered in the sunlight. She touched her finger to the smooth edge. Then, taking a deep breath, she turned toward Pryderi. If anyone should have this ring, it should be him.

Pryderi's thumb brushed over the dragon and seahorse. He dropped the ring into the pouch at his belt. "It will go with the others."

Branwen nodded. "That's safest." She touched her forehead, rubbing at the headache throbbing behind her eyes. "This ring wasn't on a human, was it?"

"Of course not," said Cigfa. "King Pwyll bound his to a trusted hunting hound and sent it into the wood."

"He does love his hunting hounds," murmured Pryderi. "That makes sense he would entrust his ring to one."

Gwydion's eyes were still intent on Cigfa. "Ask her where to find Arawn's ring," he said to Branwen.

Again, it felt as though the world had been upended. Branwen gaped at him. "What?"

Gwydion's eyes were alight. "If anyone would know the beast he chose, it would be his champion. And it's like that hunter said. Some rings will carry more weight than others. If we possess the rings of two kings..."

"We would win the Hunt for certain," said Pryderi. His fingers tightened around the pouch.

Gwydion nodded eagerly.

"What about our rings?" asked Branwen. "Aren't you frightened? You could be—I mean, if your signet ring falls into the wrong hands—"

This near to Cigfa, she dared not utter her true thoughts: that Pwyll or Arawn may command Gwynedd's trickster. If Gwydion's loyalty were claimed, untold damage could be done to Gwynedd. She would have expected him to share her fears, particularly after their talk last night. He feared powerlessness, just as she did. And having one's fealty at risk...there was no greater vulnerability.

"We'll find it," he said calmly. "But the kings' rings come first." He took a step toward Branwen. "We could win this. Truly win this. The Hunt—the boon. It would all be ours."

"I agree," said Pryderi softly. When she looked at Pryderi, she saw the tentative anticipation in his face. She realized that he had not believed he could win the Hunt, not until this moment. Sudden hope was written across his face, like dawn breaking across the mountains. He looked at her beseechingly.

"What if it's been found?" asked Branwen.

Cigfa made a derisive sound. "Only one mortal has ever managed to hunt Arawn's ring," she said. "And you are not Pwyll."

"Well, if that isn't a challenge, I don't know what is," drawled Gwydion.

Branwen turned to Cigfa, the champion's ring tight in her hand. "First, you will hunt no more mortals for as long as you live."

Cigfa blinked once. Only once.

Branwen said, "And second, you will tell me how to find Arawn's ring."

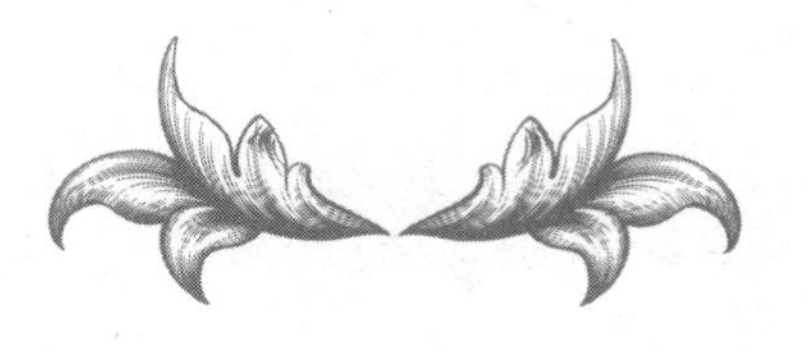

CHAPTER 26

A BONE-DEEP EXHAUSTION PLAGUED Gwydion's every step.

He had spent too much of his power in too short a time. He yearned to stop and find a place to rest, to close his eyes. But he knew his body well enough to realize that to indulge in a short respite would only leave him more tired. So he reached into those reserves of energy he kept for days like this—when rest and care were not options.

They went east, following Pryderi up a steep path. It was only when he heard the sound of falling water that Gwydion realized Pryderi had discovered a waterfall. A creek carved a path down a slate cliff face, descending to a small lake. The ruins of a stone cottage stood near the water. A deer drank from the lake; when she heard the sound of the approaching humans, she lifted her head warily. A crow sat atop the ruins, silent and watchful.

Neither animal bore a ring. They were simply creatures of the forest. "Come," said Pryderi, and he led the way toward the ruins. "You're both ready to fall over. We should rest before we continue the Hunt."

Branwen reached out and caught Pryderi's elbow. "Let me go first."

Her eyes raked over the ruins—likely checking for magical traps or illusions. "It's safe."

Part of Gwydion wanted to keep going. With the knowledge of where to find the Otherking's ring, they were within arm's reach of a prize that even he hadn't dared to consider. To possess the rings of not one but two kings? It would change everything. His victory was only a short distance away…but he knew they all needed rest. He and Branwen were nearing the edge of their endurance.

Inside the stone cottage was an old bed frame. It had not been carved but rather grown from roots. It took only a small whisper of magic for those roots to awaken. An old maple tree overlooked the stone house. It was heavy with winter drowsiness, but maples were kind trees. When Gwydion called, it answered. Roots grew up around the ruins—not thick enough to be a barrier, but so that Gwydion would know if anyone—or anything—stepped on them. He would be forewarned should anyone try to attack.

Pryderi unpacked a meal of half-stale pies and old bread. Gwydion had little appetite, but he forced himself to eat. Branwen drained her water flask, ate an apple, then closed her eyes.

"Willowbark?" Gwydion asked, opening his own pack. "Or poppy?"

Branwen cracked one eye open. "What?"

"How bad is the pain?" he said. He gestured at her eye. "Don't lie. That is my talent."

The corner of Branwen's mouth twitched. "When did Gwynedd's trickster become such an accomplished healer?"

"Probably about the time he realized healers knew nothing about his own maladies," he answered. "They could do little for me, so I learned on my own." He shrugged. "If anyone asked, I told them I was growing and learning about poisons—which is not entirely a lie. Most remedies can be used to harm, if one knows how."

"Comforting," said Branwen. "But I'm not sure if herbs will help." She touched the corner of her right eye. "Iron is the only cure I've found."

"Then let's make something of iron." Pryderi reached down to the pouch at his belt. Gwydion's heart leapt as he saw the jumble of signet rings in Pryderi's palm. There were several of Dyfed nobility. The rings of the tylwyth teg were unknown to him but no less powerful. It was the heavy golden ring that drew Gwydion's attention. The heavy signet ring of King Pwyll was beautiful. Part of him yearned to slip the ring into his own pocket, so that he could be sure it would not be taken.

"I think this is iron," said Pryderi, picking up a small, unadorned ring. "It must have come from a hunter—there's no signet. A wedding ring. Maybe it was the one that woman tied to an otter." He grimaced, likely remembering this ring had come from one of the severed hands. "I hope not."

Gwydion took the iron ring. He folded it into one of his clean bandages, then folded it again. "Here," he said, gesturing Branwen closer. He bound the cloth in place around her head, ensuring the iron ring gently rested against her eye. "It isn't very secure, but as long as you don't thrash around in your sleep, it shouldn't come off. How does it feel?"

Branwen kept her eyes closed for a moment. There were flickers of movement beneath the one visible lid, and a tensing in her jaw as though she was waiting for a blow. Then her shoulders slumped. "Better. It's—better. I'll need a few hours to rest, but after that I can use the eye again."

The relief stripped all the defenses from Branwen's face. Gwydion had never seen her look so vulnerable. With her eyes closed and tension unspooling from her body, she looked less a fierce huntress and more the eighteen-year-old girl.

Gwydion looked away before she could open her eyes and see him staring. He looked at Pryderi instead.

It was a mistake. Pryderi had pulled off his tunic. Shirtless, he was all sun-burnished muscle and sinew. Gwydion gazed at him perhaps a moment too long to be casual, then shook his head and glanced at Branwen. She had seen him gawping at the prince. She winked with her one visible eye. He tossed a bandage at her, and she batted it away, laughing quietly.

"What?" said Pryderi.

"Nothing," said Branwen.

"Then I am going to stand under the waterfall," Pryderi said. "See if it can't wash away what feels like half a mountain's worth of dirt in my hair and clothes. Either of you wish to join me?"

A bath might have been nice, but the thought of undressing sounded like too much work. "Tomorrow," Gwydion said.

Branwen frowned. "We can't stay here that long. We need—"

"Rest," Gwydion said firmly. "Trust me. No one will get to the ring before us. No one even knows where to look."

Branwen arched a brow.

"Well, Cigfa knows where to look," said Gwydion. "But you bound her to silence. I think we can afford a night's rest."

"I, for one, welcome a night when I will not be sleeping in a tree," said Pryderi. He bundled up his dirty clothes, yanked off his boots, and walked out of the stone cottage. Palug curled up in a patch of sunlight where the cottage's roof had given way.

"You know, I'm beginning to think my tree houses are under-appreciated," remarked Gwydion.

Branwen laughed, and there was an adorable snort in it. "He appreciates them. He just doesn't enjoy them."

"All right, I'll accept that," said Gwydion.

They fell into quiet as Gwydion unbound his hand brace. The poultice had helped, but he wanted to wash away the slick oil and herbs and replace them. Branwen watched as he worked. "Do you want help?"

"I have it," he said. He was rather good at tying and untying knots with his teeth and left hand.

"I didn't ask if you needed help," said Branwen. "I asked if you wanted it."

His left hand froze. He had spent so much of his life learning self-sufficiency, ensuring that he relied on no one but himself.

"If you like," he said quietly.

Branwen scooted closer, her hands hovering over the brace. "How do I remove it?"

He talked her through it, and her hands were steady as she

unbound the laces and slid it free. She had an archer's hands: strong and marked with calluses from a bowstring.

His right hand was paler than his left, the first two fingers stiff from lack of use. The pain was subdued, but it throbbed when he clenched and relaxed his hand. There had been a time when he'd considered simply cutting off those fingers and crafting a replacement from living wood. Perhaps he still might, someday.

"Can I ask how it happened?" said Branwen. Her voice was soft, and she held the brace like it needed to be protected.

Perhaps he should not have answered. But after the chaos and exhilaration of the day, he felt disarmed. He was sitting in an abandoned cottage in the middle of a magical wood with a king's signet ring only an arm's reach away. His world had ceased to make sense—as did all the reasons for keeping certain secrets.

"My brother crushed it in a door," he said simply. "For besting him in a game."

Shock flashed across her face. "How old were you?"

Gwydion's lips twitched into a sour smile. "Twelve."

Her eyes blazed with fury. "For family to do that to one another... it seems even more cruel. And over a game?"

Gwydion felt as though he owed her a few truths. "After my mother died, my uncle—the king—took charge of me and my siblings. He did not raise us the way a foster parent might. There was no affection, no love, no trust. Rather, he had us play games. He would ask us to steal something, to fetch a paper or a trinket and bring it to him. Little did we know that he was using us to do spying for him. And testing us to see how we would each play the game. If you won, you had his favor for a day, a week, a month. You could never guess how long. And it would be wonderful while it lasted. But then it would fade, and you would have to fight for it again."

"That sounds terrible," said Branwen.

Gwydion nodded. "In hindsight, it was. But at the time...I wanted the king's favor. I wanted to prove myself. Do you want to know why I became a trickster? Because the only way to survive in a court of games and shadows is to master them both. And perhaps with my power, I can keep my nephews from having the same childhood I did."

"That's why you're trying to win the Hunt." Branwen touched her mouth. "For them?"

"And because it's the only way I can think of to keep Amaethon from the throne," replied Gwydion. He held up his hand. "I have seen what he does to the helpless. I would rather not see what he does to our kingdom."

Branwen regarded him with a bitter little smile. "I understand." She leaned back, her fingers absent-mindedly stroking the brace. "Thank you for telling me."

He shrugged. "You came with me on this impossible venture. I thought you deserved to know why."

A throat cleared behind them. Gwydion and Branwen whirled.

Pryderi stood in the doorway, quaking with cold and slick with water. Embarrassment was written into every line of his face.

"Sorry," he said, his voice chattering a little as he spoke. "Did not mean to eavesdrop. I'd have stayed outside, but it's freezing."

"How long were you standing there?" asked Gwydion dryly.

"Long enough to lose all sensation in my feet and hands," answered Pryderi. His blond hair was soaked, and he carried a bundle of wet clothes in his arms.

Branwen scrambled to her feet. "Get in here."

Together, they hung the now clean but very damp clothes. Gwydion coaxed a few maple branches through cracks in the cottage roof. When they had finished, Branwen made a fire in the cottage's fireplace. "Evening is coming on," she said. "That should hide the smoke."

A fire steadily crackled. Pryderi, wearing his dry cloak and little else, sat nearest the flames. He warmed his hands by the fire. They rested in quiet for a few minutes while Gwydion slid his brace back on and Branwen began brushing Palug's fur. The cat lolled on his back, paws in the air as he closed his eyes in contentment.

Pryderi blew out a breath. "I want you to know that it doesn't matter what I overheard," he said. His voice was steadier as he warmed. "Gwydion, whatever you did in the past—I will not judge you for it. I can't. Not with what happened to me."

Gwydion snorted. "You were kidnapped as a newborn. What do you have to be ashamed of?"

Pryderi shook his head. "You know that I was raised by an afanc until I was seven years old," he said. "Everyone knows that. But what no one knows, what only I know, is—the afanc used me as bait. For as long as I can remember. It would put me at the edge of a river or lake. My crying was the lure. Those who were kind enough to stop were devoured." He turned a faint, greenish color. "But that's not the worst part. The worst—when I grew a little older, I *wanted* to help. Because afterward, that was the only time the afanc was ever kind to me. And I wanted that love and approval. It was a monster in every sense of the word, but part of me still loved it. And I wanted it to love me." He closed his eyes, speaking with a hollow despair. "That's why I fear I'll be an unworthy prince."

Gwydion glanced at Branwen. Her thoughts were spelled out across her face as clearly as pen put to paper. Gwydion knew because he felt the same.

"I'm sorry," said Gwydion, "what part of 'You were kidnapped as a newborn' did you not comprehend?"

Branwen hid a smile behind her hand. Pryderi blinked.

"We were all raised by monsters," said Gwydion. Then added, "No, not you, Branwen, your mother is wonderful. But we did not choose our parents."

Pryderi shrugged. "I mean, I sort of did. I helped kill the afanc and chose a foster family instead."

Gwydion aimed a finger at him. "Stop poking holes in my speech."

Pryderi held up both hands in surrender.

Gwydion continued, "You're not a monster. You're a little irritating, too handsome for your own good, and you will be the best king Dyfed has ever had."

Pryderi went bright scarlet. "I don't know which part of that to object to."

"Then don't," said Branwen. "I agree with all of it, except for the irritating part."

Pryderi laughed. "Well, thank you, both. For everything."

"I didn't do anything," said Gwydion. He reached down to stroke Palug's belly. The cat purred louder.

"You allied with me," said Pryderi. He hesitated. "I am going to ask my father about sending a diplomatic envoy to Gwynedd."

That made Gwydion freeze, fingers stilled in Palug's fur. "What?"

"Even if we lose the Hunt," said Pryderi, "I will ask that of him. You've proven that there are good people in the royal family of Gwynedd. My father won't be happy about it, but I will encourage him to reopen diplomacy. And we will support whoever you think should take Gwynedd's throne."

Gwydion swallowed hard. "That's…more than I ever hoped for."

Pryderi gave him a weary smile. "You've more than earned it." He ran a hand through his damp hair. "And what of you, Branwen? What dark secrets will you unburden upon us?"

She snorted. "What makes you think I have dark secrets?"

"Because no perfectly balanced person would risk her life in the Wild Hunt," he said.

She stuck her tongue out at him. "Fair point."

"I know," he agreed. "Is this all for your mother, then?"

Branwen hesitated. "Yes. And no." She drew a breath, and the amusement vanished from her eyes. "My cousin Derwyn used to live near my home. He and his husband lived near the village. Derwyn was a kind soul, gentle and eager to help anyone who needed it. He had adopted a daughter."

Oh, Gwydion thought, seeing the agony flicker through her eyes. This was her own dearly held truth, one so painful that he was sure she had not told another in years.

She continued, "There were border skirmishes along the edges of Gwynedd and Gwaelod, as I'm sure you know. Poisoned wells, little fights, and mercenaries. The mercenaries were the worst—they would come into a village, take what they pleased, and leave only ashes and tears in their wake.

"When the mercenaries came, they demanded Derwyn's home. 'We need a place to stay,' the leader said. Derwyn had tried to use gentle words to fend off the company. The head mercenary was furious that Derwyn would refuse him."

A painful lump rose in Gwydion's throat. He had heard of those attacks, had learned of them through coded missives and reports from his uncle's soldiers. They had been about lost mills and granaries, farmland put to torch and buildings destroyed. Not once had those reports mentioned the people who were hurt. "What happened?" he asked quietly.

Branwen shivered. "He killed Derwyn's child to make an example. I tried to stop him, but I was outnumbered. We sent word to Caer Dathyl, but Gwynedd wouldn't do anything. So I did." Gwydion flinched. Her gaze was cold but without blame, full of old pain. "I tracked that mercenary for months. It wasn't difficult, as he left a trail of mourners. And finally, when he wasn't with his crew, I challenged him to a fight."

"And you slew him?" asked Pryderi.

Branwen let out a bitter, breathless laugh. "No. He bested me soundly, and I returned home with this scar," she touched her cheekbone. "He was slain by another. I know I should take comfort in that, but it still feels like I failed my family."

"How old were you?" asked Pryderi.

"Sixteen," she said, gritting her teeth. "Derwyn and his husband left Gwynedd after that. They were the last blood family that Mam and I had. Now it's just the two of us." Her jaw clenched, and unspent tears shone in her eye. "The week after he left, Mam had her first forgetful night."

Gwydion gazed at her. There it was—the moment that had defined her. Branwen was fierce, unbending, and practical because she had learned that no one would save her. She hated helplessness because she had tasted it.

"I'm sorry," Gwydion said. He winced—an apology with nothing else attached was merely empty words. He reached down, covering her hand with his. "Things will be different if Arianrhod is queen. She would take care of Gwynedd, I know it."

She looked at him with mingled fondness and rueful hope. "For one with so few friends, you do have a lot of faith in certain people. I hope you're not disappointed."

"I have faith in the two of you," Gwydion replied, with a glance toward her and Pryderi. "And neither of you have let me down yet."

"Perhaps later," said Pryderi, with a wry little smile.

Color rose to Branwen's cheeks. She looked down at their hands, but she did not pull away. "You're a rather disappointing trickster. Your truths are far more charming than your lies."

He laughed quietly. "I'll try to make my lies more charming."

"Don't." Her fingers gently squeezed his. "Please don't."

A shiver of pleasure ran up his arm. He liked the way she touched him—without hesitation or fear. She was so close he could see the flecks of gray in her eye.

It would be so simple to kiss her.

The thought jolted him. It was a wild impulse, likely brought on by the chaos of the day. They were lucky to be alive; it was natural that he yearned for the nearness of another.

Of all the lies he might have told himself, that was the weakest. Because looking at Branwen in the dim light of the cabin, unarmored and half smiling, he saw how easy it would be to fall in love with her.

He could not. She was a weakness he could never afford.

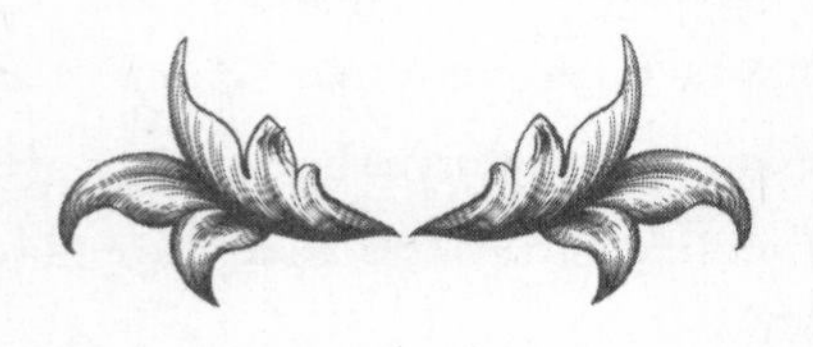

CHAPTER 27

DEEP IN THE heart of the forest, there was a cave.

If she had not known it was there, Branwen would not have found it. Cigfa had told them the paths to walk, the streams to follow, the signs to look for. A large oak tree had grown over the entrance. It was Gwydion who stepped forward, whistling as he approached. At the sound, the roots parted.

Branwen inhaled. The air smelled damp and stale.

"If this is a trap, it's a good one," said Pryderi. He stood with his spear resting against his shoulder. "Once we go in there, it would be a simple matter to collapse the way out."

"Would anyone even know to look for this place?" said Branwen. "We never would have known, if Gwydion hadn't figured out Cigfa was hiding something."

Gwydion gave a humble shrug. "The otherfolk cannot deal in

lies. It made sense if she was unnaturally cooperative that she was trying to hide something."

"It also explains why there is no illusion here," said Branwen. There was no telltale glitter of gold, no spells cast across the cavern. Rather, someone had used the tree's roots and the foliage to hide it. "The folk would notice magic."

"I wonder what kind of game animal Arawn uses," said Gwydion. "What would be comfortable in a cave?"

"An afanc," said Pryderi.

"A llamhigyn y dwr," said Branwen.

Gwydion grimaced. "And here I was hoping it would be an otter."

Branwen took half a step forward. The cave seemed to inspire dread; it looked like a place for dark and crawling things. They would have to venture inside without knowledge of what was awaiting them. Cigfa could not lie, but the folk could mislead through omission. She had said she did not know what creature possessed the ring, but she might have doomed them all by neglecting to mention that there was a secret passage or a lever that had to be pulled, lest a trap kill them all.

Not a comforting thought.

"Who is going first?" asked Branwen.

Before either of them could answer, Palug's tail brushed the inside of her calf. He trotted into the cave.

They stared after him.

"Is the cat braver than all of us?" asked Gwydion.

"Yes," said Pryderi.

"To be fair, I found him in a cave," said Branwen.

"Maybe it's a cavern full of knight-eating cats," said Gwydion.

"I'll risk that." Pryderi set his spear against the outside of the cave, rolled his shoulders, and angled himself sideways to fit into the narrow entrance. He held out his hand. "So we don't lose one another," he said. Branwen nodded. There was no risking a torch in this constricted space, so they would need to take care. He took hold of her left hand and Gwydion her right. It felt a little like a child's game, walking into the unknown, their hands linked.

Daylight struggled to reach more than a few steps into the cavern, and then they were in the bleakest dark. Without torches, the air felt close and damp.

Branwen did not realize how much she relied on her eyes until they were taken from her. The dark was impenetrable, so thick it felt like a physical thing. With every breath, she tasted damp stone and earth. She squeezed her eyes shut and opened them wide again, hoping her sight would adjust. But she might as well have kept them closed.

It was impossible to ignore the press of stone all around her. It felt as though the mountains could come crashing down at any moment, burying them for eternity. The thought made her shudder, and she felt Gwydion's hand squeeze her own. Her boot struck a pebble, and the sound echoed.

No one seemed willing to speak nor break the quiet. Perhaps it was a childish notion, but Branwen was glad for the silence. It felt as though the moment one of them spoke, the darkness might wake up and notice them.

They were intruders in this land, and Branwen had never felt that more keenly. If Annwvyn wished to slay her and Gwydion, this would be the perfect moment. No one would ever find them; no one would even know where to look.

They went slowly. Pryderi was fumbling by touch alone, and Branwen could tell every time he bumped into a stone or tripped over a ledge. The passage was narrow, the stone sharp and unwelcoming. She felt the ridges and breaks against the soles of her leather boots. She hoped that there were no wayward dead ends or they would be lost. If they had brought a long enough rope, they might have tied it to the entrance. But the deeper they went into the mountain, the more certain she became that no rope would have stretched so far.

She was not sure how long they walked—perhaps an hour, perhaps two. Or it might have been half that time. Without sun nor stars, time became irrelevant. There was only the breath in her lungs, the hands in hers, and the darkness all around.

They rounded a corner, and light glimmered in the distance.

They all froze.

"The way out?" whispered Gwydion.

"I think so." Branwen kept her own voice low. Again, she had that horrible sensation of being watched.

"Slowly," murmured Pryderi. He went first, angling his tall form through a narrow bend in the cave.

As they approached the light, Branwen realized her mistake. That illumination was not the warm glow of sunlight—but the flickering of fire.

Torchlight.

Which meant someone—something—was waiting for them. Branwen licked her dry lips. It made sense; Arawn would not leave his fealty unguarded. Her hand twitched toward her knife. As though sensing her intentions, Gwydion pulled his hand from hers and rested his fingers against her shoulder instead. She unsheathed her afanc-fang dagger. The weight was a familiar comfort.

The torchlight grew brighter. Pryderi's shoulders tensed, and Branwen could see how he readied himself: his jaw tight, eyes focused ahead, stride smoothing out. He would go first and take whatever blows would come. Branwen would attack second.

The light spilled through a large crack in the cave. Taking a deep breath, Pryderi stepped through, and Branwen darted after him.

But it was no monster's lair.

She had stepped into someone's home.

There was a wooden door at the back of the cavern, rugs to soften the stone floor, candles merrily burning, and a circular table where someone had set an afternoon tea. Steam wafted from the cups, and the cakes looked fresh from a griddle stone. Branwen's mouth watered, even as her magicked eye warned her that none of it was mortal. Everything in the cave had a glitter of unreality about it—including the occupants.

Three women sat at the table.

The first was a girl with long legs and hair unbound. The second was a woman of perhaps forty, with strong forearms and a keen sharpness to her eyes. The last was shorter than the others: an old crone with a walking stick and wicked smile. There was an eerie symmetry to them—as though a painter had captured the same woman thrice over the years. But even as Branwen gazed at them, her eyes could not seem to focus. One moment, they were beautiful beyond comprehension. And the next, they looked as ordinary as any villager.

Palug sat in the crone's lap. His tail was curled around his feet, eyes half-lidded as she stroked him. The little traitor.

"Look who has joined us for tea," said the middle-aged woman. "A lapwing, a roebuck, and a hound."

"A cat," murmured the girl, in quiet correction.

"Oh no," said the woman, with a glance at Pryderi. "He would make a far finer hound."

Branwen, Pryderi, and Gwydion remained quiet. None of them seemed to know how to speak.

"Has no one told you it's rude to stare?" said the crone. Her voice had a pleasant rasp, as though she had smoked a pipe for many years.

"Sorry," said Pryderi, startled.

The crone laughed, seemingly delighted. "Of course *you* would be the first to apologize."

Pryderi glanced around, as though certain she was speaking to someone else. When her gaze remained fixed on him, he said, "We don't mean to intrude."

"As though you could," said the middle-aged woman. "Not even you, king-born, could find this place without our leave."

Pryderi's mouth tightened. "Have we met?"

"No," said the crone.

"And yes," said the girl. Her voice held all the sweetness of a spring morning. She rested her chin in one hand, leaning on the table. Her hair flowed as though caught in some unfelt wind.

"Which is it?" asked Gwydion.

"That depends on your point of view." It was the middle-aged woman who spoke. "And what a wasteful question, if I do say so." Her attention turned to Branwen. "Now, girl, you are the only one with a question remaining. What shall you ask?"

A jolt of panic went through Branwen. This was some kind of test, she realized. Pryderi and Gwydion had each asked a question—the wrong questions.

Which left her. And she did not know if she would be able to ask twice.

"Can you take us to the Otherking's game animal?" she asked.

"We can," said the crone. She continued to stroke Palug's back.

The woman smiled. "But first, you will pay a price."

"Blood," Gwydion murmured. "Or years of our lives. It'll be one or the other, mark my words."

The crone cackled. "I would take no years from *your* life. That would be far too merciful."

Gwydion blanched.

"No," said the girl, her eyes on Pryderi. "But his would taste so sweet."

"They would," said the woman. "But they're not ours to take." She shifted in her seat, reaching for a pot of tea. The liquid that emerged had a strange quality: thick as oil and a glittering brownish gold.

"Perhaps we should ask them to join us," said the woman. "Or keep one for ourselves. It's been so long since we had a servant."

The crone clucked her tongue disapprovingly. "Because you ate the last one."

The girl sniffed, pouting. "He got better."

The more they spoke, the colder Branwen felt. This cave was a trap. There had been no need to do more than hide the entrance, no need to guard or leave snares to deter hunters. The Otherking had entrusted these three to guard his fealty.

Which meant they were the most dangerous creatures in this forest.

Branwen did not know what they were—monsters, tylwyth teg, ghosts, or something else entirely. But her every sense was screaming to leave, to run, to hide.

"We cannot stay with you," said Gwydion smoothly, but Branwen heard an undercurrent of apprehension. "As lovely as that sounds. We must deliver fealty"—he gestured at the pouch of rings at Pryderi's belt—"to a king."

The crone cackled, her voice dry and mocking as a crow's. "Must you?"

Pryderi said, "We will trade you something for Arawn's ring."

The three women seemed to change. Their gazes homed in on Pryderi, naked hunger on their faces. "Trade?" said the woman as slowly as if she wanted to taste every letter of the word.

"Trades must be fair," said the girl. "If the Otherking's fealty is what you desire, then your sacrifice will be of equal value."

"I don't think I have anything worth a throne," said Branwen tightly.

The woman held out her hand expectantly. "Name yourself."

Gwydion took half a step back. "What?"

"Name yourself," repeated the woman.

Horror rose hot in Branwen's throat. Of all the things they might have asked for, this was the truth she was least inclined to give.

"Name ourselves?" asked Pryderi in confusion. "That's it? How is that a fair trade for the fealty of a king?"

All the women smiled. It was precisely the same smile stretched across three lifetimes.

Branwen swallowed. There was a reason she had forsaken her birth name the moment the tylwyth teg had taken notice of her. The folk could do terrible things with names. There were tales of humans bound by enchantments, lost to their own memories, even vanishing and reappearing decades afterward.

Names were a door. The moment that door was opened, monsters could walk through.

"Wait," said Branwen, a note of warning in her voice. "I think we should leave."

Gwydion looked at her sharply. "What?"

Arawn's ring was not worth this. "Names are powerful," she said softly. "If we give these women—whatever they are—our names, we don't know what will happen to us. Or to our families."

Pryderi raised his voice. "What do you intend to do with our names? Will you use them to hurt us?"

The woman delicately picked up her teacup. "We have never needed a name to harm a mortal."

"How reassuring," said Gwydion dryly. He took a deep breath, turning his head so that he spoke into Branwen's ear. "Perhaps two names will be enough."

It would not be. Branwen knew that as surely as she knew that these creatures were not human. Magical trades required balance. For three hunters to find the Otherking's ring, they would need three names.

"Who are you?" said the girl, crossing her arms. "Tell us before I tire of you."

It was Gwydion who stepped forward, placing a hand across his heart. "I am Gwydion, son of Dôn."

The three women gazed at him, implacable and unmoving as stone. "Who are you?" asked the girl.

"What?" said Gwydion, nerves edging into his voice. "Do you want me to go back further in my lineage?"

The crone shook her head, and her hair drifted like old cobwebs. "We did not ask for your parents' names, boy. Who are you?"

"Gwydion," said Gwydion, sounding out each syllable.

"Who are you?" said the woman.

"My name didn't change in the last moment," said Gwydion, growing frustrated. "I am Gwydion."

"Who are you?" said the girl.

"I'm Gwydion," he cried, "son of Dôn. Of Caer Dathyl. I'm Gwynedd's trickster. Anything else you care to know?"

The three women exhaled in unison. A glance passed between them, and then the crone said, "You have told us all that we need."

"Finally," said Gwydion. He turned, twisting a hand at Pryderi. "See if you can do better."

Haltingly, Pryderi stepped forward. He fidgeted with his hands.

"Who are you?" asked the woman.

"My name is Pryderi, son of Pwyll," said Pryderi.

The girl *tsk*ed chidingly. "Who are you?"

"Oh, good," muttered Gwydion, "it's not just me."

Branwen seized his arm, trying to silence him. His muscles were taut beneath her fingers, and his gaze met hers. He was every bit as frightened as she was. The only difference was that he talked through his fear.

Pryderi cleared his throat. "I am Prince Pryderi, son of King Pwyll."

For a heartbeat, all was silent. Even Palug seemed to be holding his breath.

"Who are you?" asked the crone.

Pryderi's hands clenched. Branwen yearned to reach out and touch his shoulder, to let him know that whatever his answer was, she wouldn't care.

"I was raised by an afanc," he said through gritted teeth. "I am king-born, as you called me. Monster-raised."

"Who are you?" asked the girl again.

"I don't know," cried Pryderi. His voice broke as he spoke the words. "I—I've never known. That's why I came here. To know."

The middle-aged woman rose from her seat. Her dress flowed around her like mist, and she moved with the grace of a serpent. But her hand was gentle as she reached out and stroked Pryderi's hair from his forehead. It was an oddly maternal gesture. "Who are you?" she said. "Truly?"

Pryderi shuddered but did not pull away. When he spoke again, every word was fragile. "Gwri," he said. "My foster parents called me Gwri."

Gwri. Branwen felt her lips form the name. Of course he would have had a different name. His foster parents would not have known his birth name.

"So you are," said the woman approvingly. She stepped back,

returning to her seat. Pryderi's eyes were damp, and he would not look at Branwen nor Gwydion.

And all at once, Branwen found herself standing before the table. She was not sure if the others had taken a step back or if she had taken a step forward.

Palug lifted his head. He had been contentedly sitting in the crone's lap, enjoying having his ears scratched. Now, he let out a meow of greeting. He leapt from the crone, ambling over to Branwen.

She squatted down to pick up the silly cat, painfully grateful to hold him. He felt solid and soft and warm in her arms. He rested his chin on her shoulder and purred.

"Not going to ask the cat's name?" said Gwydion, an edge of challenge to his words.

The crone laughed. "Oh, we know that one's name. All in the forest do. Why do you think the monsters of Annwvyn have given you a wide berth?"

Branwen swallowed. Perhaps it was her imagination, but Palug suddenly felt heavier in her arms.

The crone leaned over the table, tapping a finger impatiently. Her gaze was fixed on Branwen. "Who are you?"

Branwen closed her eyes for a heartbeat.

"I am Branwen, daughter of Penarddun," she said. Perhaps it would be enough; she had gone by that name for so long that the years might have given it the ring of truth.

The middle-aged woman sighed. "Who are you?" she asked chidingly.

Gwydion stepped in front of Branwen, making a shield of

himself. His expression was unyielding as he said, "Ask something else of me. But do not ask this of her."

The girl laughed. It had the tinkling cadence of a bell. "We could never ask more of her than you have."

Gwydion shook his head with such force that his dark hair swung before his eyes. "I will bear the cost of this trade."

The girl replied, "Such bravery. How do you know we won't ask for your nephews' names?"

Gwydion's throat jerked in a swallow. "Would you?"

For a heartbeat, Branwen considered letting him take this risk. It was true that he had drawn her into the Wild Hunt. He had risked her freedom, even if he had done so unknowingly. If she was bound to one of the kings for a year and a day…

If she was bound into magical servitude, then she knew that he would come for her. He would try to find a way to free her.

He was a trickster. He had little love for his enemies, and he would use any means at hand to defeat those who opposed him. But for all his ambition and practiced wit, she had observed the way he treated the helpless. He had seen to Rhain when the older man was dying; he had saved Penbras without so much as hesitating; he carried Palug as though the cat were an infant; he protected his nephews fiercely.

Branwen trusted only a few—but in that moment, she realized that she trusted him.

If he knew her name, he would never use it against her. Nor would Pryderi.

Branwen put her hand on Gwydion's back. With gentle pressure, she pushed him aside. "It's all right," she said softly. "I appreciate your effort, but it's all right."

Gwydion's mouth was set in a hard line. "It's not," he said, his voice similarly quiet. "I've taken too much of you."

"You've taken nothing I wouldn't give," she replied.

And she spoke a name she had not said aloud in years.

The three women smiled together. It was a smile of satiation. "You have all been very pleasant guests," said the woman. "We try to be gracious hosts."

"Tea?" asked the girl, her eyes agleam. "We could give them a drop each."

"Not again," said the woman. "The last mortal who had three drops became such a nuisance afterward."

The crone snorted. "Truth, then," she said, in that dry and crow-like voice. "We will give you each a truth."

"I am not sure that is such a kind gift," murmured the woman.

"Well, you will not let me give them tea," said the girl, pouting.

The women all rose in one movement.

The girl looked at Pryderi. "You will never be a king."

A flicker of shock crossed Pryderi's face.

The middle-aged woman looked at Gwydion and said, "You will break a throne."

Gwydion took half a step back.

Then those terribly ancient eyes focused on Branwen. She felt like a mouse before a cat—waiting for the blow that would shatter her.

The crone said, "You will hunt that which you love."

And with that, the three of them simply vanished.

It was like watching steam evaporate—they dissolved into golden motes, as though they had never been there at all. The cavern's furnishings vanished with them: the table, the chairs, the rugs, even the candles. The door melted away, revealing a passage. Sunlight spilled through it.

Branwen swallowed. They had come this far. There was no turning back. Slowly, she walked toward the light.

The passage led upward, stone giving way to earth, and Branwen climbed out into a meadow. It was beautiful—perfectly green grass, wildflowers in bloom, and a warm breeze. It was a meadow of summer, surrounded by a forest that bowed its head to winter. Behind her, she heard Gwydion and Pryderi make small sounds of surprise. All of the meadow, from the earth to the trees to the water—it was all magic. The golden glow made Branwen's eyes ache.

At the edge of a small pond stood the creature—the one to whom Arawn had given his ring.

It was not an afanc, nor a llamhigyn y dwr.

It was a fallow deer. The buck had enormous antlers and a spotted red-brown coat. The animal was lovely—the curving antlers elegant and full, coat soft as dandelion seeds, eyes large and dark. Tied to the base of one antler was a gleaming gold ring. Branwen slowly reached for her bow, hoping the deer would not run.

But she had forgotten Palug.

The cat meowed plaintively and sidled up to the deer. The buck looked down at the cat with mingled confusion and curiosity. He made a soft, questioning sound. The buck leaned down to sniff him. Branwen stepped closer, trying to keep silent and seem unthreatening.

Gently, she broke the small branch that tied the ring to the antler. The ring fell into her palm. It was far heavier than it looked. Etched into the gold were the sun and moon in perfect balance, circling each other. This was the signet ring of Arawn, Otherking of Annwvyn.

She wondered if the king had given himself a wooden ring. If at this very moment, tree branches were creeping up Arawn's left arm.

The buck stepped away from her. Then, without a backward look, he bounded out of sight.

His leaving seemed to break the spell that had fallen across the meadow. Branwen breathed again and again, feeling the weight of the ring. She had the wild impulse to slip it on, to see if it would fit any of her fingers. A power vibrated through the metal, sending a tingle through her palm. No matter how long she held it, the gold never warmed.

She hoped the ring was worth the price it had cost her.

You will hunt that which you love.

The memory made her flinch.

She would not. No matter what happened, she would never hunt anyone she cared for. Not her mother, not her cat, not—

She thought of the gentle weight of Gwydion's hand in hers. Of Pryderi's warmth and friendship.

No. She would hunt nothing that she loved.

Trying to distract herself from the crone's words, Branwen's gaze fell to the shallow pond. Its surface was clear and still as a mirror.

The woman that stared back had pale hair and sharp features. Her eyes were large and wide-set, and her mouth was set in a line. But that was not what drew Branwen's attention to her own reflection.

It was her eyes. The left was a familiar blue. But the right—

Her right eye was gold.

Branwen blinked. She had seen her reflection before, but always with her iron-stitched blindfold. That woman had been Branwen of Argoed.

The woman reflected in the pond had wild, pale hair and an eye gold with magic. She carried the ring of an immortal king. She was Branwen of the Wild Hunt.

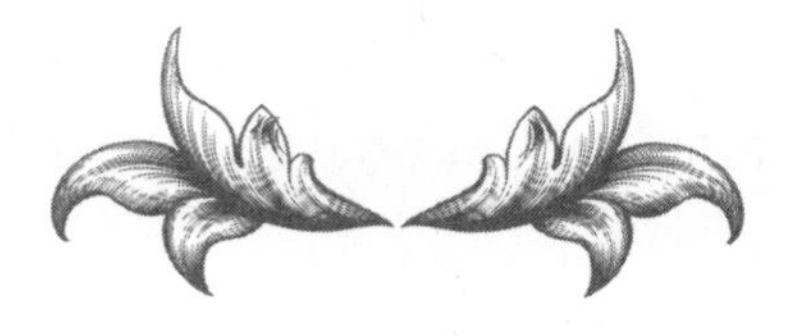

CHAPTER 28

YOU WILL NEVER *be a king.*

Those words might as well have been a knife. They had carved out a hope that Pryderi had cradled near to his heart. He had been afraid of the throne and crown—but amid that fear had been a fragile hope.

He had wanted to do well. He had wanted to be a king that would make a difference. He had wanted to return home and see his foster family beaming with pride.

But he would never be a king.

Which meant—

Which meant there was only one thing Pryderi could be.

Kings and monsters are grown from the same soil.

Pryderi had come to the Wild Hunt to prove himself. And now he knew that he would fail. He almost wished they had never found that cavern; he might have pretended his fate was yet undecided.

Now that he knew, it felt as though an unescapable weight settled upon him.

They returned through the now-empty cavern. All the trappings were gone—vanished with the magic that had conjured those three women. They walked in silence, each lost to their own thoughts. Gwydion's expression was distant; Branwen would not meet anyone's eye. The camaraderie of the night and morning had vanished. A sense of distance had opened up between them all.

You will never be a king.

You will break a throne.

You will hunt that which you love.

Yesterday, they had been friends. Now they were a monster, a throne breaker, and a huntress. If those foretellings had been a gift, Pryderi wished he could have refused his.

Sunlight gleamed through the roots of the oak tree. Gwydion let out an audible sigh of relief as they stepped into the forest. The sun waned, and once again, the air tasted of winter. These lands might not have been mortal, but at least they were familiar.

"I'll find us another tree," Gwydion said, speaking for the first time since the cavern. "Then we can rest. I believe we've earned it."

Pryderi considered protesting. They had the rings; they should have made for camp at once. He yearned to be rid of those wretched things. They were too dangerous, too much a burden. But an exhaustion had taken hold of him, and he had not the will to fight it.

Branwen smiled at Gwydion. "That would be welcome."

"How is your head?" asked Gwydion.

She touched a finger to her right temple. "Once we rest, I'll use the iron blindfold again."

“We should go a short ways from the cave.” Gwydion glanced back at the entrance, as though distrustful of it. “I will not sleep well near it.”

“Agreed,” said Branwen.

They fell into conversation, and Pryderi was glad of it. It meant he was not expected to contribute.

Perhaps, once the Hunt was over, he would return to his foster family. If he would never be a king, he might try to be a farmer again. Let his monstrous instincts grind themselves out against soil and rock. He sighed, forcing himself back to the moment. He would worry about his future once they were safe.

“—think Palug is the reason for it?” Branwen was saying.

Gwydion was shaking his head. The cat rode atop his shoulder, eyes half-closed in the bright sunshine. “He must be. I had wondered why we never encountered any monsters.”

“He doesn’t look threatening,” said Branwen, ruffling her cat’s fur. “Not even with my magicked eye.”

“Perhaps it’s the smell,” said Gwydion.

“Are you saying my cat smells?” Branwen laughed. “Because he might take offense to that and—”

There was a whisper of air, a rustle of leaves.

And then an arrow cut through the undergrowth and slammed into her side.

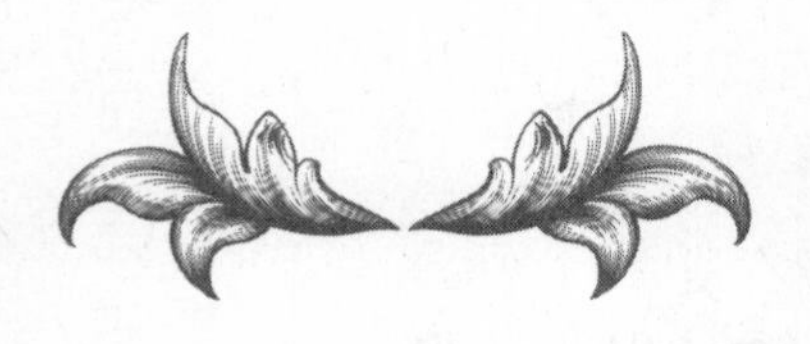

CHAPTER 29

IT HAPPENED SO quickly that Gwydion did not sense the arrow.

One moment they were walking through patchy sunlight, smiling and triumphant—and the next Branwen staggered. Confusion flashed across her face, and she crashed to the ground, an arrow buried in her side.

"NO!"

At first, Gwydion thought he had uttered the word. It resonated through him, a denial that clawed up his throat. But the bellow had come from Pryderi. Spear in hand, the prince whirled toward where the arrow had been fired from.

Fear and fury churning with him, Gwydion fell beside Branwen. She lay on her side, curled in on herself. It had struck her in her right side. Gwydion had spent enough time with the healers that he knew it was a dangerous place for a wound.

"Branwen," he said, trying to keep his voice steady. "Let me." As gently as he could, he rolled her onto her back. She cried out, the movement jostling the arrow. A phantom pain flared in his own stomach, but he ignored it. He used one of his small knives to cut open her tunic.

He remembered that first night, when he used his magic to unbind her dress. He remembered the delicate color on her cheekbones, and the way her eyes caught the candlelight. She had been beautiful in a moss-green gown with her hair bound into a braid. Now, her face was drawn with pain, her fingers digging into the earth as though she needed something to cling to.

There were sounds coming from the trees—the clash of weapons upon weapons, shouts and snarls, and the pained whisper of magicked trees as hot iron sank into the earth.

There was one kind of iron that all humans carried with them. It soaked through Branwen's shirt, warm and sticky against his fingers.

Either Pryderi or Branwen's attacker was bleeding. He hoped it was the latter. Let it be the latter. Gwydion could not fight and keep Branwen safe at the same time. Her lips were pale and eyes glazed with pain.

He should have sensed the arrow coming. He should have deflected it. He cursed himself silently. He should have been prepared for an ambush. He had been too consumed with his own thoughts.

Branwen's eyes slipped closed. "Hey," said Gwydion. "You're going to be all right. That'll hurt for a few days, but you're going to win the Hunt."

She opened them again. "I better," she said hoarsely. "Haven't—haven't said my old name aloud in so long. Has to be worth something."

Branwen—he would think of her as Branwen, even if he had heard her other name. She *was* only Branwen to him. He had spent his whole life as a seeker and guardian of secrets. He would keep her secrets safe.

He would keep her safe.

She deserved more than to be just another fealty to be bartered among kings.

Pryderi strode through the wood, dragging a man by his ankle. Gwydion sat up straighter. He knew that man. It was the red-haired assassin, the one escorting the others back to camp. The one who had looked at Branwen and Palug.

He had shot her.

Tendrils of cold anger wrapped around Gwydion's heart. That assassin was lucky that Gwydion's attention needed to remain with Branwen, otherwise he would find himself devoured by the roots of a tree.

The assassin snarled, kicking out at Pryderi. He managed to free himself and scurried to his feet, knives in hand. He moved with all the grace and ease of a viper.

With a contemptuous snap of his spear, Pryderi knocked him back. Gwydion swallowed hard. There was no mistaking the fury in Pryderi's gait. Even when he had fought Arawn's champion, Pryderi had kept his temper leashed. But now, he had given himself over to the fury.

"Wait," the assassin cried. "I have—I have rings! We can bargain!"

Ice held more warmth than Pryderi's voice. "What rings?"

With a shaking hand, the assassin reached into his shirt and pulled out a small cloth pouch. It clinked with metal.

"Where did you get those?" asked Pryderi.

The assassin said breathlessly, "Took them. From those I was—those going back to camp."

Pryderi said, "You mean those you were protecting. You turned on them, didn't you? Did you kill them?"

The assassin retreated, tossing a knife at Pryderi. The prince sidestepped the blade.

"That's what the Wild Hunt is," the assassin snapped. "You're either hunter or prey. You should've learned that by now."

Pryderi glanced over his shoulder to where Branwen lay on the ground, a bandage against her stomach and Gwydion's hand soaked with blood. Then he looked at the bag of stolen rings the assassin held. Icy wrath stole into his eyes.

"You're right," said Pryderi, and his voice had gone toneless. He slammed the spear into the assassin's wrist, sending that bag of rings flying. The assassin flicked another knife at him, but Pryderi batted the weapon away. Then Pryderi drove his spear into the meat of the assassin's thigh. The scream that ripped out of him was raw and animal.

The man fell, pinned to the ground like a prized insect. Pryderi kept hold of the spear with an almost casual ease.

He was different now, Gwydion realized. Pryderi had changed in the cave—and not for the better. Something had frayed in him. Some crucial part of Pryderi was unraveling. Those prophetic words were swiftly coming to pass.

Cigfa had fought the son of a king.

The assassin fought the son of a monster.

"What—what's happening?" Branwen tried to roll over, but Gwydion kept his hand gently on her shoulder. "Pryderi?"

Pryderi gave his spear a little shake, the way a cat might jostle a mouse in its jaws. "What happened to them? Those you claimed to protect?"

"I—I—" The assassin screamed as Pryderi drove the spear deeper.

"How many did you trick?" snarled Pryderi. "How many did you track and offer protection, only to turn on them when they could no longer hold a weapon?"

The assassin moaned in agony.

"How did you find us?"

"I followed you," the assassin said, when he could speak. "Saw the signet ring on the cat the girl was carrying. It's yours, isn't it? Royal signet and all. It might win me the Hunt. I have to win, don't you understand? I'm dying—there's no cure. Not without magic."

"Then you should have offered yourself up as an ironfetch," said Pryderi. "Traded services for magic. Not killed your countrymen for it." There was a deep contempt in his eyes.

"Be a servant?" gasped the assassin. "I'd rather die."

"All right, then," Pryderi replied, and yanked the spear free.

The noise the hunter made nearly cracked Gwydion's eardrums.

Pryderi leveled the spear at the assassin's chest, resting the tip against his breastbone. "You should never have hurt them," he said quietly. "You should never have hurt her."

"Pryderi," said Branwen. She struggled to sit up. "You don't—you're not this. Pryderi—"

But he was beyond listening.

Branwen panted with pain, and her voice was high and thready as she said, "Gwri!"

It was like snapping a thread on a puppet. The spear lowered, and there was a terrible despair to Pryderi's face. He looked over his shoulder, gaze locking onto Gwydion and Branwen.

"You're only a monster if you choose to be," she said. It cost her to say the words; sweat broke out across her brow, and Gwydion felt a fresh surge of blood against his hand.

There was a long silence, only broken by the hunter's ragged breathing. Then Pryderi stepped away from him.

"Run," he said quietly, "and pray the forest is merciful."

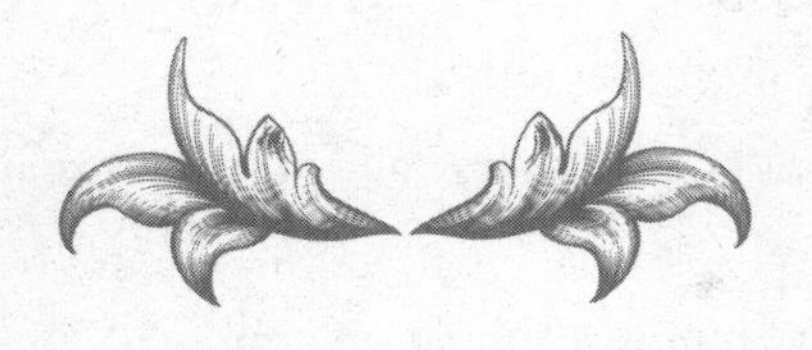

CHAPTER 30

PRYDERI REMEMBERED LITTLE of the aftermath of the fight.

He remembered seeing Branwen fall, hearing that hunter admit he'd killed those he promised to protect, and the last thread of Pryderi's self-restraint had snapped. Falling into that cold rage was almost a relief; he did not have to think. His world had narrowed to blood and bone.

It had taken Branwen saying his old name to call him back.

Names have power, she had told him in the cave. He should have believed her.

Part of him wished she had not managed to draw him back. Because when he returned to himself, he had to face the truth.

He did not know what he was. And the future held nothing but questions.

Gwydion worked over Branwen. "Hold her down," he said to Pryderi.

Pryderi was grateful for the order; it gave him something to do. Branwen made a choked noise as Gwydion pulled away her tunic. Finally, the wound was visible. The arrow had deflected from the hilt of her dagger, sinking perhaps a finger's width into the skin of her stomach.

Painful, yes. But it would only kill her if the wound was not tended to.

Once the arrow was removed and the wound cleaned and bandaged, Gwydion sat back on his heels. He met Pryderi's eyes. "I am going to give her a little tincture of poppy," he said quietly, "and then we'll find shelter for the night."

Pryderi nodded.

They walked with Branwen's arm slung around Gwydion's shoulder. He murmured quiet encouragements as they stumbled along. Her gait was unsteady from pain and the poppy. Pryderi wondered if he should offer to carry her, but the offer felt like an intrusion. Branwen needed a healer—not a monster or a prince.

Palug meowed. The cat had vanished during the fight, reappearing a few minutes later. Perhaps he had gone to hunt for field mice, for he kept licking his whiskers. Pryderi bent down and offered his shoulder to the cat. Palug considered, then leapt atop him and curled against Pryderi's neck, purring. It was a small comfort.

They walked until Gwydion chose an old ash tree. He called to his magic and wove the branches tightly. Then he made a bed of his cloak. The branches lifted Branwen high, as gently as Pryderi could have lifted Palug. When he was certain she was settled, Gwydion turned to Pryderi.

"I'm going to refill our flasks," he said quietly. "She'll need plenty of water tonight. Keep her still and don't let her fuss with the bandage. All right?"

The words seemed to wash over Pryderi. He felt them without truly hearing them. Gwydion had the same decisiveness that he had possessed when fixing that man's knee.

"You should have been a healer," said Pryderi. "Or a farmer. My da would have liked having you around."

A line appeared between Gwydion's dark brows. "Fallen kings, I'm stuck with a wounded huntress and a half-addled prince."

"We aren't the best company right now," Pryderi agreed.

Gwydion took gentle hold of Pryderi's upper arms, forcing the prince to meet his eyes. "Listen to me. Everything I said about you? I still mean it. You're irritating and good-looking, and I still think you'll be the best damn king Dyfed's ever had. But right now, you need to go up into that tree and watch Branwen. And you"—Gwydion looked at Palug—"eat anyone that comes near them."

Palug sat back on his haunches, curled his tail around his feet, and said, "Mreow." To Pryderi's ears, it almost sounded like an affirmative.

With Gwydion heading deeper into the woods, Pryderi mustered what energy he still possessed and climbed into the tree. At least the despair sapped his fear of heights. Branwen lay quietly, her eyes half-lidded. Her hand remained over her wound, fingers fidgeting absent-mindedly with the bandage. "You're not supposed to do that," said Pryderi, gently taking her hand. He guided her fingers against Palug's fur. "Pet him instead."

Branwen obliged.

"You all right?" she asked.

"I'm fine."

She blinked at him.

He looked away. "I lost control. I had hoped it wouldn't happen again."

She exhaled, the sound brimming with exhaustion. "It's been a long day," she said. "And that man did shoot me."

"I wanted to kill him." Pryderi drew his legs up to his chest. "Not only because he hurt you. But because..." He tilted his head back, gazing at the branches. "You heard the girl. I'll never be a king."

"I thought you were a little ambivalent about this whole king prospect." Branwen waved her hand about, as though to convey a ship tossed upon waves.

"I was," he answered. "I still am. But don't you understand what that means? I am going to fail. Something I do, it will be enough to make Pwyll disinherit me." He shook his head, frustrated. "I spent years trying to be good at this. To be the kind of ruler people need me to be. What am I to be, if not a king?"

Branwen patted his hand, and he flinched in surprise.

"Whatever you want," she said. "You get to be whomever you want."

His throat felt too tight. "You think?"

"I think you have a gentle heart," she said, with the earnest honesty of one taken by drink or herbs. "And kindness is rare. Perhaps being a king would force you to become something else."

"Even after I nearly killed that man?" he said quietly.

Branwen snorted. "I may not be able to feel the wound right now, but he did shoot me. He killed others. He ambushed all of us. The only reason I stopped you was because I knew you would blame yourself afterward."

Warmth filled his chest. It was a rare thing to be seen and understood. He had never had anyone like her and Gwydion. They were both stubborn and intelligent and loyal. If nothing else came from the Hunt but this, he would count it as time well spent.

A faint cry made him look up. A second voice joined it, and then a third.

"What is that?" Branwen struggled to sit up, but Pryderi placed a hand on her shoulder. Palug leapt to the edge of their shelter, his green eyes peering into the wood. Pryderi did the same, keeping low enough that he could duck if an archer took aim.

But it was no attack.

Three of the tylwyth teg rode mountain goats. The goats were far too large to be mortal. The otherfolk cried out to one another, cheering as they chased a rabbit. A ring had been tied around its neck.

One of the folk laughed and waved her hand, beckoning her companions to follow. Her goat raced up a sheer cliff, and the huntress leaned low over its neck. She tossed a net at the rabbit, but it darted to the side, and the net tangled around one of her companions instead. He yanked it free, merrily throwing it back to his companion. "Your aim is as dismal as ever!" he called.

The huntress waved him off. "You're in the way as ever."

The third hunter ignored them both, urging his goat mount to give chase. The rabbit vanished into the undergrowth, and the three hunters followed, still laughing.

This was the Wild Hunt. It was companionship and joy as much as it was betrayal and ambition.

"It's beautiful here." Branwen's soft voice startled him. Pryderi glanced over and saw she had managed to sit up. She leaned against the branches, her face exhausted but her eyes alight. "Even with all the monsters and killers and danger. This place"—she lifted a hand to one of the autumn-burnished leaves—"it's still magical. And I'm glad we got to see it."

Pryderi nodded. "Me too," he agreed.

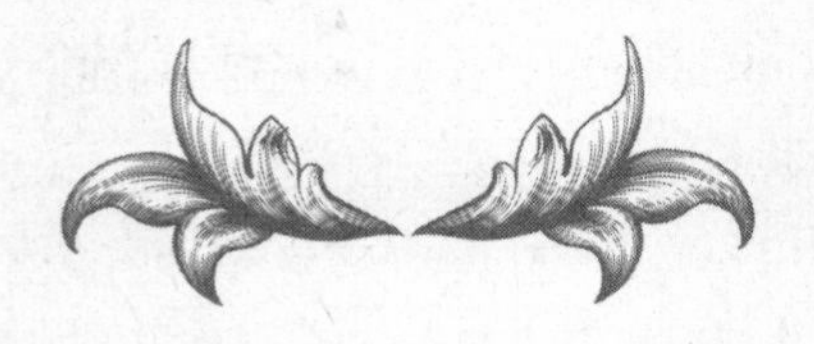

CHAPTER 31

BRANWEN SLEPT THROUGH half the night.

The poppy had kept the worst of the pain at bay. When she awoke, it was to a steady throb in her right side. Irritating, but bearable.

Pryderi was asleep. He snored softly, his cloak drawn up to his chin. Gwydion was on Branwen's other side, sitting with his back to the tree trunk and Palug on his lap. The cat was kneading his thigh, and while Gwydion winced, he allowed the gentle mauling.

"You're awake?" she said softly.

He looked at her. "You should be resting."

She tentatively sat up. Gwydion made as though to help, but she waved him off. She pushed herself slowly so that her back was to the trunk. She dragged her cloak up and over their legs. His own cloak was being used as a bed for Palug.

"One of us should keep watch," he said quietly. "You and Pryderi were half-asleep by the time I returned."

"Well, you should get some rest, too." She patted his arm. "You saved my life back there."

Gwydion looked away. "I hired you. It would have made me a rather bad employer to let you get killed before collecting payment." It was a light answer, and a few days earlier, she likely would have accepted the lie.

Her mouth twisted up at one corner. "Do you ever let your guard down?"

He looked at her sharply. If he had been any less exhausted, he probably would have conjured up a witty reply. "You know why I don't."

"Because your family is terrible," she said.

"Because my family is terrible," he agreed. "And I've grown used to my armor of words and secrets. It is easier to pretend that I love that armor, that I need nothing else."

"You don't need it," said Branwen. "I like you better when you're... you."

And she did like him. She liked his watchful eyes, his laughter, even the conniving edge to his conversations. She understood him now. He was like Pryderi—good-hearted, even if he went about it in an underhanded way.

"I'm always me," said Gwydion.

"You're more yourself right now," she said. Which should not have made sense, but it did. A slight smile flickered across his mouth.

He was so close and yet unreachable.

For a few minutes, they sat in silence. Perhaps it would have been uncomfortable with another, but Gwydion's silences were undemanding. It gave her time to gather her thoughts.

Branwen regarded him curiously. "Can I ask you something?"

"Of course."

"Are you worried about what the woman said?"

He exhaled sharply, his hand still on Palug's back. The cat looked at him in mild irritation.

"You mean the prophecy that I will break Gwynedd's throne?" he said quietly. "Of course it worries me."

Branwen scooted a little closer to him. "She did not say it was Gwynedd's."

"What other throne would I break?" He gave her a bitter smile. "We have the rings of two kings. We could win the Hunt—I am certain of that now. But...what if somehow that is what brings about Gwynedd's destruction?"

"I don't see how it could," said Branwen. "We take the rings to King Pwyll so Pryderi can impress his father. Our team wins the Hunt. Arawn gives us a boon—and you can wish for anything. You could ask for diplomacy, for alliances, for promises to support your sister as queen."

A shadow crossed Gwydion's face. "So we deliver the fealty of kings and knights and hunters to Pwyll," he murmured. "Strengthening Dyfed. One of our kingdom's enemies. Perhaps that is what will do it."

She nudged him with her elbow. "Stop that. Your mind is racing like a hound after a rabbit, and it's getting you nowhere."

He quieted but the unease never left his face. The moonlight seemed to sharpen his features. "If I asked you to leave with me, right now," he said. "Would you?"

She frowned. "What?"

He spoke the words quickly. "If I asked you to leave the Hunt, would you?"

Her brows drew tight. "What about my brooch?"

"We would look for it," he said. "But even if we could not find it, you could come to Caer Dathyl. They would have to fight through armies to take you from me."

Confusion welled up within her. "What brought this on?"

He ran his left hand through his hair. "Just thinking through contingencies."

She reached out and laid a hand on his knee. "If you're worried because one of us got hurt," she said, "don't. I am pretty sure Pryderi is the most dangerous person in this Hunt. Well, except for Arawn. And now, we have the Otherking's ring." She looked at where Pryderi slept. The small pouch full of rings was tied to his belt. "Do you think I could just order the Otherking to find my ring for me?"

Gwydion frowned as though that had not occurred to him. By now both Arawn and Pwyll would know that someone had found their rings. They were out of the Hunt.

"You never answered my question," he said. "If I asked you to leave, right now, would you?"

Her lips pressed together. "I can't. You know I can't. I need the boon."

"If I paid for your mother's care," he said, his voice soft. "If I promised to take care of you both."

She shook her head. "If I am to keep my mam as she is, I need magic. Nothing else will cure her."

He bowed his head. "I'm sorry," he said. "For bringing you into this. For allowing you to be hurt."

"You've nothing to be sorry for," she said. "You brought me to the Hunt. You gave me this chance. If anything, I should be thanking you." She shifted, trying to find a more comfortable place against the tree. She was not sure if it was the poppy that gave her the courage to say, "Are you afraid of me now?"

He raised his brows. "Afraid of you?"

"Because of what the crone said to me," she answered.

"That you're going to hunt someone?" he replied. "No, that does not worry me in the least."

Her forehead scrunched. "I feel as though I should be offended by that."

He laughed lightly. "Not at all," he said. "Rather, she said you would hunt that which you love. Which means the creature in the most danger here is Palug."

At the sound of his name, Palug gently flexed his claws into Gwydion's trousers. He winced and tried to extract those claws without disturbing the cat.

"I'm not going to hunt my cat," said Branwen.

"I assumed as much." Gwydion's smile faded a little. "No. I'm not worried about it."

That made her frown.

He saw it, and he laughed again. "I meant, I am no great wondrous hero of old. I am a liar. I'm not a prince, and I never will be one.

At best, I'm a trickster. At worst, I'm a court gardener. If you were going to love someone, it would never be me."

She gave him a flat look. "You're also a little self-pitying."

"That, too," he agreed.

"You're wrong, though." She leaned her shoulder against his. "You're all of those things, true. But you're also a skilled healer. You're intelligent and determined. You seek power not for your own gain but to protect others. And you're good with cats."

"I do like cats," he admitted. And then, far more quietly, "And you, too."

As Branwen's fingers wove through his, she knew the truth of it.

She did not love him. Not yet. But she could.

She could love him for his wit, for his dry humor, for the way he spoiled Palug, and how he never gave up on those who mattered to him.

"I don't know what's going to happen," she said. "But for now..."

"For now...?" His gaze flicked down to her mouth and then back to her eyes.

And before she lost her nerve, she kissed him.

The kiss burned through her like a hot wine. His mouth yielded to hers, an answer to a question she did not speak aloud. His left hand came up, thumb sliding along the old scar at her cheekbone. She indulged herself and ran her hand through his unruly dark hair. It was soft, curling gently around her fingers. He shivered beneath her touch.

This was unwise, she knew. They lived in wholly different worlds. But for tonight, they were simply together. There were no political machinations, no monsters to be fought, no rings to be found. There was simply the warmth of him, the unsteady rhythm of her breath, and the knowledge that in this moment, she was enough. She was wanted—and so was he.

He pulled back first. She kissed the corner of his mouth, then his cheek, then the corner of his eye. She might have kept going, but she knew they were both exhausted. And this was enough. Truly, it was more than enough. "Branwen," he whispered. "I—"

"Not now," she said. This moment was perfect. She did not want to mar it with talk. "Tonight, we rest," she said. "Tomorrow, we win the Wild Hunt."

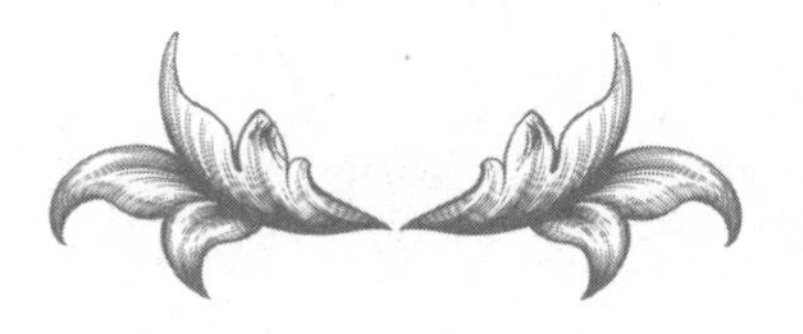

CHAPTER 32

THREE HUNTERS SLIPPED through the morning mists.

They awoke before dawn, ate a hurried meal of stale cheese and old crusts, and left the ash tree behind. Branwen's right side throbbed faintly, but Gwydion packed the wound with herbs and bound it securely. The injury would need time to heal, but for now, she was ready to move.

For there was one last hunt.

She had to find her brooch and Gwydion's ring. Pryderi's would be simple to retrieve, at least. Palug trotted alongside them, tail held high and ring dancing on his makeshift collar.

"How are we going to find two specific animals in all of this?" asked Pryderi, gesturing at the forest. It was a fair question.

"We're heading back in the direction where we first began the Hunt," replied Branwen. "From there...hopefully we'll pick up a trail for the roe deer. Deer tend to keep to the same trails, the same places to graze. They're creatures of habit. The lapwing might prove more troublesome."

"Trust me," said Gwydion. "I'll find them."

They walked for the better part of the morning, diverting when they saw evidence of a recent camp. The ashes were still smoking, and Branwen saw the places where two people had slept.

There were still other hunters. They needed to be wary.

Pryderi carried the small pouch of rings. Branwen found herself glancing at it, just to be sure it was still there. That small bag held all her hopes for the future—and part of her wanted to snatch it and shove it into a pocket so she could be sure it would never be stolen. But Pryderi was unhurt and the most intimidating of their little group. Any hunter would hesitate before challenging him.

They followed Branwen's memory and Gwydion's magical senses. She retraced their steps back to where they had hunted that first night. It felt like ages ago.

She did not know how she would find her lapwing again. It was a single bird in a mountain forest. It might not even have remained in the woods; lapwings preferred open fields. Or would the magic of the Hunt keep every animal contained? She did not know. Her only comfort was that she knew no one had found her brooch. Her oaken ring remained on her finger, the magic sleeping within.

She found the deer trail first. There were a few broken ferns, a trampled bit of moss. This was where the herd had fled from them, where Gwydion had captured the buck with divining and brambles.

"Hold on," Gwydion murmured. He pulled off his boots, settling his bare feet on the earth. Branwen winced, but he did not seem to mind the cold nor the prickle of plants. Gwydion knelt, running his left hand through the dead grasses. Then he closed his eyes and sang a proper tune.

It was a beautiful melody. Tendrils of gold slipped through the earth. It was a gentle pulse of power, a searching. Those golden flickers danced through tree roots, glittered along the canopy, and vanished from sight. Gwydion kept quietly singing, and the trees creaked in answer. Leaves rustled and shifted.

Gwydion was using his power to search for their animals, Branwen realized. He was speaking with the forest in a way that no one else could. Gwydion's head tilted, listening.

Those flickers of gold ran through the ground again—but this time, they returned to him. They flashed along branch and leaf, darting like lightning toward Gwydion. He blinked his eyes open.

"There is a lapwing south of here," he said. "Alone, without a flock, roosting in a maple tree."

"The wood told you that?" asked Pryderi.

Gwydion smiled. "They can feel things, too. Tiny talons, feathers, and they can certainly hear birdsong."

"Could you not have been using your magic for the entire Hunt?" said Pryderi. "It would have made things easier."

"For you, perhaps." Gwydion rubbed at his forehead. "You will not bear the cost."

"What about your deer?" asked Branwen. Her gaze followed the trail.

"We'll find the deer next," said Gwydion. "I'll go after the bird. Yes," he said, seeing Branwen's mouth opening, "I will. Because you're hurt and Pryderi hates heights. I can move more quietly on my own. Birds startle easily."

Pryderi blinked. "True," he admitted.

"You should be resting," said Gwydion. He passed Branwen a water flask. "Drink. Eat something. Pryderi, you stay with her. I'll return in an hour, even if I cannot find the bird. Then we can reconsider our plan."

"I don't need a minder," said Branwen. "And who's going to protect you?"

"I'll take the cat," replied Gwydion. "He's far more terrifying."

Palug looked rather proud of himself.

Branwen snorted. "Are you always this tyrannical in the mornings?"

"Only when someone's snoring keeps me up half the night," said Gwydion, and leaned down to kiss her cheek. It happened so quickly she did not have time to be surprised.

Pryderi cleared his throat.

"Not a word from you," she said.

"I was not going to say anything," Pryderi replied. He was fighting back a grin and losing badly. "Except to say I am a little disappointed that I did not get a kiss, as well."

"Perhaps later," said Gwydion. He leaned down so that Palug could leap atop his shoulder, then sauntered into the woods. Branwen watched him go, her cheeks burning.

Pryderi laughed.

"Laugh all you like, but you're the only one who snores," she said.

"I'll try to breathe more quietly if we have to spend another night in a tree." Pryderi's gaze turned wistfully toward camp.

Branwen took hold of her bow. "You do realize neither of us is waiting here, right?"

Pryderi gave her a little half shrug. "I assumed as much." He hefted his spear across one shoulder. "Shall we go hunting?"

It was a lovely winter day. The air was crisp and sharp against Branwen's tongue, and the forest had an austere beauty. Soon, the winter rains would lash the mountains. She followed the deer trail alongside a small stream and through a thick clot of undergrowth. Crouching, Branwen half crawled and half shuffled into the bushes.

That familiar herd of roe deer grazed quietly among the trees. And upon one of the buck's antlers gleamed something metal.

There it was—Gwydion's ring.

Branwen's heart lurched in relief. Deer tended to remain in the same grazing lands, but she had feared this herd would flee or be captured. The last thing she wanted was for some hunter to capture Gwydion's fealty.

"Do we take the ring?" whispered Pryderi. He had crouched down beside her.

Branwen shook her head. "No," she whispered. "Remember how the Hunt works? If we take that ring, then we own Gwydion's fealty. He won't be able to hunt properly again. We need to bring the deer to Gwydion so he can take his own ring back. The way Cigfa was trying to do with hers."

Pryderi nodded. "Capture? Or . . . ?"

Her jaw clenched. She had hunted deer before, but those creatures had kept Branwen and her mother from going hungry in harsh winters. If she brought down this deer, she knew there would be no time to properly dress it. It felt like a wasted life. But she also knew that carrying or dragging a live roe deer through the woods would bring every hunter within earshot. Roe deer had a shriek that would carry across mountains.

Branwen drew in a breath. For Gwydion, she thought. For the Hunt. For her mother.

She fitted an arrow to the bowstring. The buck was grazing among the herd, his ears twitching—listening for danger.

The buck never heard his death coming.

The arrow slammed home, and the herd scattered in terror. The buck was dead before it hit the ground. A painless end was the only mercy a huntress could offer.

Pryderi pushed free of the bushes, striding toward the deer. "A good shot," he said. "Perhaps when this is all over, I'll hire you as a huntress."

"When this is all over," she replied, "I'm sleeping for a week. And then bathing. And eating a full meal that isn't stale pie."

He flashed a smile at her. "Fair enough." He knelt beside the fallen buck and hefted it over his shoulders. He was strong enough that it looked easy. Branwen nodded, impressed.

"One game animal down," she said. "I hope Gwydion managed as well as we did." She twisted her left arm, gazing at the oaken ring.

They walked back to the clearing in quiet. They both knew how dangerous the wood remained, even if the Hunt was almost over. Branwen looked for traps—magical or otherwise. She kept her bow strung and at the ready. When they returned, Pryderi eased the dead buck to the ground with a sigh of relief. There was no sign of Gwydion.

"You think he was delayed?" asked Branwen, shielding her eyes against the sun.

"It's just been an hour. I'm sure he'll be on his way." Pryderi squatted beside the deer. "Look at this." With care, he took hold of one of the deer's small antlers and tilted its head.

Branwen frowned. "What?"

"This... is this Gwydion's signet ring?" he asked, gazing at the slip of metal.

For one terrible heartbeat, Branwen thought she had shot the wrong deer. "It has to be," she said. "I recognize that deer—the scar along its throat. It's the same animal."

But Pryderi was right. This was not the signet ring she had glimpsed upon Gwydion's left hand. There was no dragon of Gwynedd. This ring was thin and delicate. It looked like an intricate tree.

"That's copper, not gold," said Pryderi quietly. There was a note of disquiet in his voice.

"How can it be the right animal but the wrong ring?" asked Branwen.

Pryderi did not answer. The lines around his mouth deepened, and he sat back on his heels. Unease was written across his face, and Branwen felt it, too. Something had gone awry, but she did not know what.

The undergrowth rustled, and Branwen picked up her bow.

Gwydion strode into the clearing. Between his hands, he held a black-and-white crested bird. Branwen's heart leapt into her throat—it was the lapwing. Her lapwing. He had found it. Palug was trailing behind Gwydion, his attention wholly on the bird. "And here my brother said I would never be a decent hunter," Gwydion began to say. Then he fell into silence when he saw the deer. "What did you...?"

"We went hunting," said Pryderi flatly. "As did you."

And before Branwen could utter a protest, Pryderi yanked the ring free of the roebuck's antler. Gwydion cried out, lunging forward with his hand outstretched, the lapwing gently cradled to his chest.

Branwen drew in a sharp breath. She waited for his ring of roots to spring to life, for it to grow across Gwydion's fingers and up his arm.

It never did.

"Why aren't you out of the Hunt?" asked Pryderi, his voice frozen over. "I captured your ring. Why didn't the spell awaken?"

"Because that's not his ring," said Branwen. She picked up the copper tree ring. "I—I saw his signet ring before the Hunt. It's the dragon of Gwynedd. He hid it before we came here, so no one would recognize it at the revel. I thought he dug it out for the Hunt, but..."

He had not.

"Is this why you did not care if we hunted for the deer?" said Branwen. "Because you knew that it did not matter?"

The blood had drained from Gwydion's face. His gaze jerked from Branwen to Pryderi. "I—"

It felt as though the world had twisted sideways, as though she were scrambling for her feet. Gwydion had given the Hunt a false ring. He had never been in danger of losing his freedom, his fealty.

How had he known—

And a terrible dread swelled in her chest. She knew. She knew even before she snapped at Pryderi. "Give me the rings," she said, holding out her hand.

Pryderi blinked, but he did as she asked. He unbound the pouch from his belt and handed it over.

Kneeling on the ground, Branwen untied the pouch and upended it.

No rings fell out.

Instead, small pebbles and river rocks tumbled to the ground. Branwen stared at them, unable to understand. Her mind simply would not accept it. Perhaps she had grabbed the wrong pouch.

It could not be true.

Please, let it not be true.

She looked up at Gwydion.

"I'd rather hoped," he said quietly, "you wouldn't open that."

The Trickster

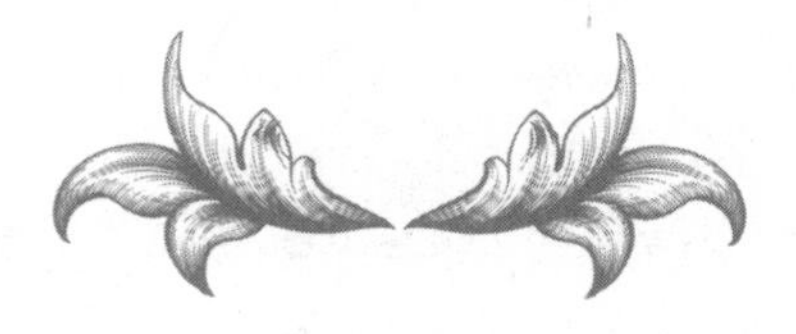

LONG AGO, IN *the kingdom of Gwynedd, there was a woman who should have been queen. Her name was Dôn.*

When she walked, flowers followed in her wake. When she spoke, it was with a gentleness. And when she listened, others felt understood. She should have ruled a kingdom, but her brother was chosen instead. Her brother was colder, cruelly efficient, and he knew the inner workings of a kingdom. So he was given a crown.

Dôn bore five children—each of them with their own gifts. Her twin eldest were born with power over metal; the third forged his own path with cruelty; the fourth found his joy in fire; and the youngest was born to the trees.

The youngest was a tiny little thing, with dark hair and eyes. Dôn had been in a carriage with her ladies when her labor pains began. They took refuge in a warm summer's meadow, and with the help of a royal healer, she bore her youngest child. At first, they thought he would not survive. But then he drew air into his lungs and howled. At the sound, the trees all bent down to meet him.

"There's my boy," Dôn murmured, holding him close. "You will bring down kingdoms with that voice, won't you?"

The lad grew up much like his mother: with a passion for greenery, for open skies and the softness of forests. He loved going out to the gardens and would toddle about the apple orchards for hours. He delighted in his mother's magic, how she could capture a dandelion's seed in her palm and then be holding a flower.

But for every gift came a price. Dôn used her powers freely in the kingdom, keeping the farms fruitful and her own gardens brimming with herbs for the healers. The magic drained her, made her succumb to sickness far too easily.

One of those illnesses took her when the lad was still young.

For a time, he wandered the fields and the gardens, yearning for a connection with his mother. He missed her desperately, and part of him resented her for leaving, for using her magic, knowing what it would cost.

"I don't know why she used her power so much," said the lad's older brother as he toyed with a burning flame. "It is not as though one can win a kingdom with flowers and herbs."

As the years passed, the lad took those harsh words to heart. After all, what good were fields and meadows? Apple orchards and herbs? They had not saved his mother. They did not protect him from his uncle's cruel games nor his brother's violence.

If kindness and greenery would not serve him, then the lad would deny both. He would not be a boy of the forests and fields—he would keep to the cities and become a trickster.

The trickster caged his own heart, ignoring the offers of friendship or love. He became skilled with sleight of hand, with secrets, with power. Soon, the kingdom did not even need a spymaster—it had him. But history had an unfortunate tendency to repeat itself.

When it came time for the king to choose an heir, he ignored the woman who should have been queen. And he chose a fire diviner instead.

The trickster would not let it happen.

He schemed and plotted, and he found his opportunity when the aged king threw out a casual remark: He would only change his heir if a champion from his kingdom won the Wild Hunt.

It was a fool's challenge, a boast that would never come to pass. But the trickster saw the lure of the impossible and rose to meet it.

He went into the city to visit his garden of spies and informants.

For in the tavern there was an old drunk from Dyfed. A man who drowned himself in ale and talked about the time he won the Hunt. He had been there for years, mumbling about his time of glory. The trickster had never paid him much attention—but now, he paid for the man's drinks and asked for details.

The drunken hunter had been name-bound with magic to never speak of the particulars. But if the trickster knew anything, it was that magic was imperfect.

The trickster pierced the man's tongue with iron—for then he could speak of the Hunt.

"It's not like any mortal hunt," the old hunter said, his words coming out half-mangled. "They hunt not for animals but for fealty. For a year and a day, they trade soldiers and nobles. Even thrones. It matters little to Arawn and Pwyll, for they trust each other with their kingdoms."

The trickster drew in a sharp breath. "So the balance of power remains the same."

The old hunter wobbled in his chair, unsteady from pain and drink. "But if someone from another kingdom entered the Hunt..."

The trickster smiled.

"Then he could steal two kingdoms," he said.

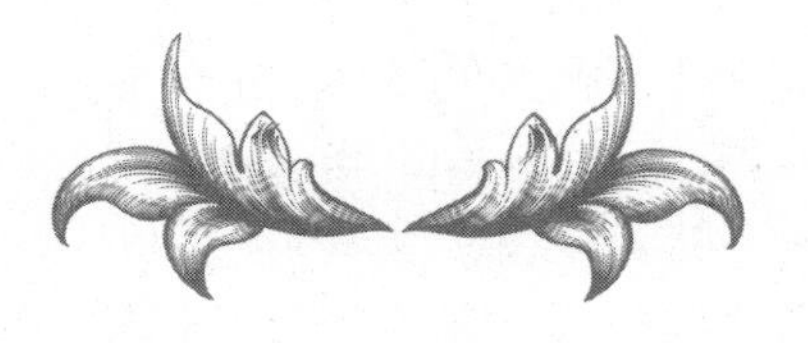

CHAPTER 33

BRANWEN COULD NOT breathe. It felt as though all the air had vanished from the wood.

This could not be true. It simply could not be.

"Do not move," said Pryderi, cold fury simmering beneath every word.

Gwydion was pale but resolute. His gaze flicked toward the woods, as though considering the best way to run. The lapwing was in his left hand, cradled against his heart.

In a moment, Branwen had an arrow fitted to the string. She kept the arrow pointed at the earth—but the threat was there, nonetheless.

Gwydion shook his head. "You can't shoot me," he said. "You do that, this bird flies away. Along with your only chance for freedom."

"Where are they?" said Branwen. Her voice sounded oddly distant. "The true rings?"

Gwydion swallowed. "They're safe."

"With you," she said.

"Branwen, it's not what you think," he said quietly.

She took two steps closer, her fingers tightening on the bowstring. "You stole the rings from us. What else is there to know?"

Pain flickered through his eyes. "I didn't mean to do it this way. I wasn't... You weren't supposed to..." For the first time since she'd met him, his words faltered.

"I wasn't what?" she said. "Supposed to matter?"

He drew in a sharp, pained breath. "Branwen—"

She flung the words at him. "You made me think—you spent all this time getting me to trust you. Playing the part of the wounded royal, the broken little trickster who just wanted someone to love him. Who could be more, if he was just given the chance. Who didn't care that I was a commoner or a huntress. You're a better liar than I thought."

"It wasn't a lie," he said. "I meant it. All of it. I just didn't tell you everything."

"Then tell us what you held back," said Pryderi. If Branwen's fury was molten, his was as icy and unrelenting as winter.

Gwydion's shoulders slouched. Some of the defiance leaked from his face, draining away into unhappiness. "I knew how the Hunt worked," he said tonelessly.

"That's not possible," said Pryderi. "Hunters are magicked never to talk about it."

Gwydion smiled thinly. "There are only two things I excel at: growing plants and finding secrets. I used the latter to give myself an advantage in the Hunt."

Branwen's mind raced, trailing back through her memories. She thought of the first time they met, how he had invited her into his confidences about how they would sneak into the Wild Hunt, how they would infiltrate and win it.

"This is why you gave me a year's pay," she said faintly. "That first day we met, you gave me enough gold to feed a family for a year. A year and a day—that's how long I would belong to someone else, how long I could never go home."

She waited for a denial, but it never came. "You knew the Hunt could kill you," he said. "You accepted the risks."

"I knew I was risking my life," she spat back. "Not my freedom, not my fealty. I told you that's what I feared—being helpless."

"I know that now," he said quietly. "And I truly, truly did not intend to hurt you. That is why I did not simply run off with the rings. I brought you your freedom. Give it to Pwyll. He and Pryderi will never command you against your will."

"What about your own ring?" she snapped. "Did you even bring it with you?"

Gwydion nodded. "It's in a hidden pocket."

"Then whose ring is this?" Pryderi held up the copper ring.

Gwydion met his gaze evenly. "It is mine. Which is why I was allowed to join the Hunt. But it is the ring of Gwydion of the Trees, a Gwydion that might have been." With a twist of his fingers, the root ring slipped from his hand and thudded to the ground. He held up his bare hand. "I admit, I was undecided before. But I know who I will be. I am Gwydion of Caer Dathyl. I am a trickster, not a gardener."

Another terrible thought occurred to Branwen.

"This is why you came up with the idea to put Pryderi's ring on

Palug?" she said. "Because you intended to take it, didn't you? If you couldn't find a king's ring, you would settle for a prince's."

Gwydion simply looked at her. "Of course."

Branwen had opened up to him, told him things she had never told another, and all the while, he had been planning to steal the spoils of the Hunt and deliver them to Gwynedd.

But he had never intended to win the Hunt.

He had never desired the boon.

He had pretended, all this time, when the only thing he cared about were those rings. That fealty. Something he could deliver to his sister. If his sister could command both Dyfed and Annwvyn, nothing would stop her from claiming Gwynedd's throne. It was a cold, efficient plan.

And Gwydion had not cared what it would cost Branwen.

Everything she had felt for him, all the trust and the longing, all the desire and confidences—it had been for nothing. She had been falling in love with him, and all the while, he had been planning to abandon her.

"I changed my mind," Gwydion said. "You should know—after we fought Cigfa, after everything, I changed my mind. I was going to play out the Hunt, let us win it. But...but you heard what the woman told me. I will break a throne. Who is to say my winning the Wild Hunt won't be the thing that breaks Gwynedd?"

Pryderi stepped forward. "I planned to ally with Gwynedd. I told you as much."

Gwydion let out a bitter laugh. "And yes, there is the other stumble, isn't it? What the girl told you. You're never going to be a king.

You will never be able to deliver on those promises you made me. Even if you wanted to ally, you have no power to do so."

He might as well have stabbed Pryderi; it likely would have been less painful. The prince swayed where he stood, fury replaced by shock and betrayal.

"My kingdom is worth fighting for," said Gwydion. "My people deserve better than the prince that will be crowned come spring. And if I have to lie and steal the fealty of two thrones to give them a fair ruler, to give my nephews a chance at a better life, then I shall."

"If you take those rings and deliver them to King Math, Dyfed and Annwvyn will fall," said Pryderi.

Gwydion shook his head. "I'll not give them to Math. He *would* destroy you—but Arianrhod has no desire to conquer."

"You can't know that," said Pryderi desperately. "You can't be certain that Math won't take them. That something won't happen to you. That you don't know your sister as well as you think. If you take those, you take the lives of everyone in two kingdoms into your hands. You could start a war so deadly that it throws all the lands into chaos."

"And if I let you have them," said Gwydion, "how am I to know we won't be on the losing side?"

A long silence drew out between them. Branwen could feel the shift taking place—the change between them all. All the friendship had drained away, leaving only a taut anticipation.

Pryderi's fingers tightened on his spear. "You know I can't let you take those rings, right?"

Gwydion gazed at Pryderi. "If you attack me, I cannot keep

a hold on this bird," he said quietly. "You will cost Branwen her freedom."

Branwen barely heard the words. Her gaze fell upon the lapwing. A gentle bird. They were such beautiful creatures. Her mam loved them.

And without hesitating, Branwen brought up her bow and fired.

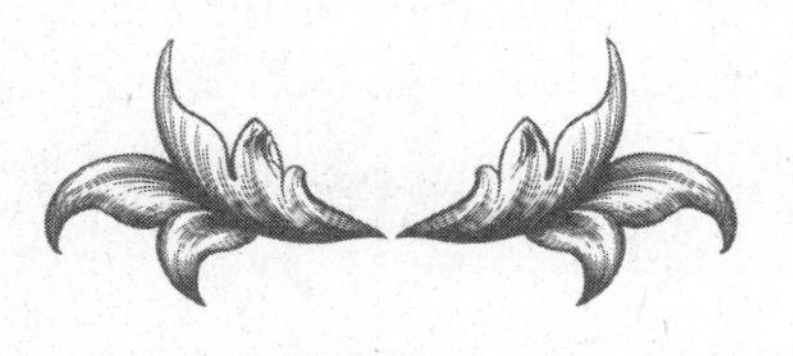

CHAPTER 34

EVERYONE MOVED IN the same moment.

Pryderi knew what he had to do. He had known since he saw that false ring attached to the roebuck's antler. Gwydion could not be allowed to leave Annwvyn, not with those rings. Not bearing the fealty of two kingdoms. Even if it cost Branwen her freedom. Even if she hated him. Pryderi could not let Dyfed and Annwvyn fall.

He lunged, driving his spear at Gwydion.

But to Pryderi's shock, Branwen attacked first. An arrow sliced through the air—toward the lapwing.

The shot would have slain the bird, if Gwydion had not jerked to one side, his braced hand covering the creature. The arrow glanced off the wood-and-leather brace, cracking it. Gwydion cried out in pain.

The lapwing tumbled from his fingers. The bird fell upon the ground, righted itself, and flew into the air.

Gwydion dove for it, but Pryderi gave him no chance.

He attacked the trickster of Gwynedd.

Pryderi had trusted Gwydion. He had offered his friendship—and all the while, Gwydion had been planning to escape with the rings. Not to bring them to Arawn or Pwyll... but to Gwynedd.

It would be the end of two kingdoms.

"Pryderi!"

The name rang in his ears. He chanced a look at Branwen. She had her bow strung, but the arrow wavered back and forth. She had been willing to fire upon her own lapwing, but she still hesitated to shoot Gwydion.

A choice.

Unspoken, unmade.

She would have to choose. Gwydion or Pryderi. Trickster or prince.

Pryderi whirled, striking out with his spear. Gwydion rolled beneath the blow, seizing the obsidian sword at his back. His weapon had less reach, but it allowed him to nimbly dart around Pryderi's blows.

Pryderi had other weapons—a hunting knife at his belt, even his fists—but he knew his strength and reach were the best advantages he had.

That and Pryderi was raised for this.

He let his mind detach from his body, let himself become the creature the afanc had intended him to be. He fought with the spear, keeping Gwydion at a distance, forcing the trickster to react rather than attack. Gwydion wore his exhaustion on his brow; it would not take long to wear him down. When Gwydion dropped his guard, Pryderi would end him.

Gwydion seemed to realize this. He opened his mouth.

Panic flared hot in Pryderi's chest.

He could not let Gwydion sing or speak. It was not only his words that gave him power—it was his divining.

Pryderi lunged at him. It was a mistake—Gwydion darted in close, cutting a shallow wound along Pryderi's arm. Pryderi could not get the spear up fast enough to defend himself. He slammed his knee into Gwydion's gut, driving the breath from him. Gwydion hit the ground, tumbled, and nearly impaled himself on his own sword. Gasping, he touched the grass and hummed weakly.

The greenery around Pryderi's feet suddenly thickened. Roots sprang up, trying to entrap him.

Silence him. That was the afanc's voice in his mind, but it was mingled with the memory of Arawn's words. *Cut out his tongue if you have to.*

He reached down, seized a small rock, and threw it hard. Gwydion's mouth snapped shut, and he struck the rock away with his sword. The distraction gave Pryderi a chance to tear himself free of the roots and grass.

Gwydion's face was set in grim lines. He was outmatched, and he had to know it. He might have been a powerful diviner, but Pryderi was prince-born and monster-raised.

Gwydion rushed him, determined to get in close. He darted around Pryderi's swing and held his sword high above his head. He brought down the sword the way a woodcutter would fell a tree. And in the gleam of its obsidian blade, Pryderi saw his future splinter into two paths.

In the first, he lifted his spear and caught the blade. With the strength of that swing, the blade would bite into the wood and Pryderi could use that to his advantage—twist the spear, wrench the sword from Gwydion's hand, and then shove his smaller knife into Gwydion's ribs. He would kill Gwydion, take those rings, and return to his father and King Arawn. He would deliver the signet rings of two kingdoms. That would be more than enough to win him the Hunt and secure his place at court. He would return not as a monster's adopted son, but as the king's true heir. His loyalty to his home would never be questioned again.

Only Pryderi would know differently. Because he *would* be a monster. He would slay his enemy, slay his friend. This was what the afanc had wanted from him—to be more weapon than man. To wield a blade as easily as thought. To be the shadow that lurked in the minds of anyone that would dare hurt Dyfed.

He thought of Arawn, with a finger-bone crown and a smile on his wine-stained lips.

Kings and monsters are grown from the same soil.

Perhaps it had not been a coincidence that an afanc had come for him. There were tales that said the folk took human babes—and perhaps the king of the folk himself would ask one of his people to properly train his dearest friend's son in the ways of rulers. Perhaps it had been his idea of a gift to a young prince.

Or perhaps none of this had been orchestrated. Perhaps the world was simply chaos and coincidence, and the only way to survive was to ride the waves of chance.

Pryderi could do it. He knew he could.

Be a monster.

Be a king.

Lose himself to the Hunt.

But there was no way to win and remain himself.

He thought of his mam. Not the queen, but the farmer's wife who had washed the blood away when he wounded his knees in a fall, who had rubbed his back when he dreamed of water and scales, who had whispered in his ear that Pryderi was *hers*, that he was good, and he could choose to be good even if the world declared him not.

And he remembered the voice of the girl in the cave.

You will never be a king.

The words had sounded like a curse, but now they were freedom.

He had never wanted to be a king. He had never wanted to be Pryderi.

He thought of his mam, whispering to him when he woke from a nightmare. A chant of his name, to remind him who he was and who he would be: *Gwri, Gwri, Gwri.*

That was who he had wanted to be. He wanted to be a son she could be proud of. Nothing more and nothing less.

He would not be a monster.

He would not be a king.

He had to stop this.

Pryderi caught Gwydion's sword with his spear. "Gwydion," gasped Pryderi. "Please. Wait—"

There was the whisper and twang of a bowstring.

Gwydion wrenched the sword free and stepped back, hesitation written across his face. He opened his mouth as though to answer.

The world slowed. Pryderi turned his head in time to see the recoil of Branwen's bow, the graceful arch of her shoulder and fingers as she fired.

The arrow flew toward Gwydion. His sword was too low to deflect it.

She had made her choice. She had chosen Pryderi, chosen the prince over the trickster.

Panic crossed Gwydion's face. He cried out, deflecting the arrow with a burst of magic.

The arrow wobbled in the air and curved away from the diviner.

Pryderi saw the gleam of sunlight on silver. He heard the whisper of air. He knew. He knew, he knew, he knew.

The girl, the woman, and the crone had told him. *You will never be a king.*

And the arrow sank deep.

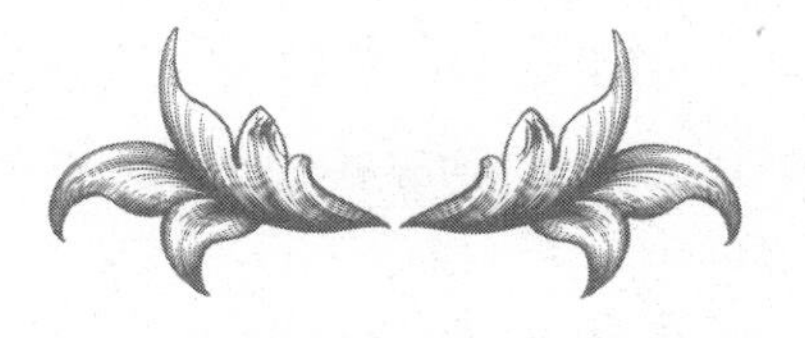

CHAPTER 35

WHEN PRYDERI FELL, Branwen fell with him.

She threw herself past Gwydion, her hands outstretched and seeking. Some part of her thought if she could take hold of him, if she held on tightly enough, she might keep him there. The arrow—her arrow—was buried deep in his chest. Branwen knew better than to yank it free; she had to stem the tide of the blood, push it back in him somehow. Her mind felt as though she'd reverted back to childhood and Pryderi was a broken toy that needed stitching back together. Surely someone could do it—Annwvyn was magic, this whole place was magic, and someone—

"Pryderi," Branwen said, as she yanked her cloak free. She pressed it to his chest, trying not to jostle the arrow. "Hold on, just hold on—"

She should have offered comfort, but the only words to tumble from her lips were pleas.

She pressed a hand to Pryderi's bloodied throat. There was a flutter against her fingertips, like the fading wingbeats of a bird.

This could not be happening. She had fired at Gwydion. It had torn her heart in two, but she had fired at Gwydion. Pryderi could not be dying.

A soft meow made Branwen look up. Palug stood a few strides away.

Something was happening to his collar. Those vines were withering. Tiny leaves browned and shriveled.

And then the collar broke. Pryderi's signet ring tumbled into the grass.

He was gone.

Pryderi, heir to the throne of Dyfed and son of Pwyll, was dead.

In bardsong, he would be the young royal cut down in single combat. But to her, he would remain the kind boy who had saved her, who had only joined the Hunt to make his father proud.

It felt as though an eternity passed. Branwen could not have said how long she knelt there, one hand on Pryderi's throat and the other on his bloodied chest. He was far beyond her reach, but she held on. Her breaths were ragged, her whole body unmoored.

All the birdsong went silent.

Branwen wondered if grief had deafened her. Then she realized the truth of the matter. She looked up and saw the canine silhouette standing between the trees. She should have reached for a weapon, but her fingers would not answer her.

The ci annwn was only a few strides away. It had approached so swiftly that she had not noticed the encroaching quiet.

A hand landed on Branwen's shoulder. Gwydion stood over her, his gaze fixed on the ci annwn. His face was drawn and pale—more skull than human. His obsidian sword remained in his left hand.

The hound looked at them both. It had been drawn by the death...or perhaps it was a death omen come too late.

Branwen waited for the hound to attack. She felt too sluggish to react, too detached to care. If the hound lunged, she would let it.

The ci annwn sniffed the air. Then it lifted its head to the sky, opened its maw, and howled. It was a silent cry, but Branwen felt the echo of her own grief in the dog's stance.

Gwydion's hand tightened on Branwen's shoulder. But before either of them could react, the ci annwn lowered its head. It gave Branwen a steady look, then darted into the bushes and out of sight.

Slowly, ever so slowly, sound returned to her.

Arawn knew of the death. He had likely known about it from the moment Pryderi's blood spattered upon the forest leaves.

He was of Annwvyn and Annwvyn was of him.

Branwen drew a shuddering breath. She and Gwydion would never leave this forest alive. But the thought did not frighten her. There was no fear left in her.

Gwydion knelt beside Branwen. He spoke, but it was as if the words traveled a great distance. Every sound was muddled in her ears, drained of all meaning.

"—wen," came Gwydion's voice. "Branwen, look at me."

He had been speaking to her for some time, she realized belatedly.

Panic had dissolved his surety. Gone was the elegant and self-assured young man, and in his place was someone that looked fearful and boyish. "Branwen, we need to go," he said, as though he had uttered the words again and again. "Word will be traveling to Arawn and Pwyll."

"Go?" she said. She could not imagine going anywhere. It felt as though the world had been cleaved away with that single arrow. All that existed was this clearing, this moment, this fallen friend. "Go where?"

"Gwynedd," he said. His hands came up, cupping her face so that she could not look at Pryderi. "We'll be protected there. When they come for us, they'll have to bring an army."

"When they come for us?" He was not making sense.

"Pwyll," he said. On the surface, his voice was calm, but there was a pressing urgency beneath every word. "Arawn. I know the Wild Hunt is supposed to be that everyone is fair game, but not like this. Not when we infiltrated the Hunt."

"I killed him," she said numbly.

Something between shame and defiance flashed through Gwydion's eyes. "You did not."

"I fired the arrow," she said. "I meant to stop you."

Pain flickered across Gwydion's face. "I know. This is my fault. I didn't mean to—it was an accident. I tried to shove the arrow away from me. I didn't intend for it to hit him." He looked at her pleadingly, as though it was important that she believed him.

She was not sure what she believed.

"We killed him," she said. "He was our friend. He deserved better than this."

"We need to go," he said. "Branwen, please. Come with me. You'll be safe in Caer Dathyl."

Pryderi had been good. He had been kind when kindness was costly. He had been a cornerstone of their little alliance, their little band of hunters. He had wanted to do so much good. He had come here to prove himself...and he had. He had proven himself to be the kind of ruler that Dyfed needed. It had only taken his life to do so.

"No," she said. "We're not leaving. Not like this." It took effort to rise, but she managed it. She feared that if she remained still for too long she would never move again.

"We'll go to Arawn," she said. "We'll make amends. Somehow—we have to. We cannot murder the prince of Dyfed and flee like thieves. Not only would we be hunted for the rest of our lives...it isn't right." She stepped toward him. "We'll tell him and Pwyll that this was an accident." She was pleading with him, but she could not help herself. She wanted him to make amends, to be the person she wanted him to be.

She waited for a reply, but it did not come. Gwydion's hands clenched. Even the right one. Which meant he *wanted* this moment to hurt.

"Branwen," said Gwydion, an ache in his voice.

And that was all the answer she needed.

With a growl, Branwen seized her afanc-fang dagger. "Fine, then. You leave. You go—and I swear if you try and take Pryderi's ring, *I will kill you here*."

Gwydion took a step back, hands held out. "Branwen."

"Just go," snarled Branwen, taking a step forward.

"They'll be coming for you, too," Gwydion said desperately.

She had trusted him. Trusted this beautiful, dark-haired

creature with the smile of a boy and the mouth of a trickster. They had shared blood and secrets, kept each other safe, and hunted through the otherlands. She had told him her name.

And now he stood before her, asking forgiveness she could not grant.

"I know this started with a lie," he said. "I care for you. It's why I tried to bring the lapwing back to you, even if it would have been wiser for me to run. When this began, I just needed a huntress—but I found you. If I had known..."

"If you had known what?" she said, advancing on him. "That I was a person? That I had feelings and family and a life? We're all people, Gwydion. We're not your plants, to be controlled at your whims. But you can't even see that anymore, can you? You've spent so long trying to make yourself powerful that you've armored yourself against what makes you human."

He stopped retreating, and the tip of her dagger dug into his tunic. The fang sliced through the wool, kissing flesh. All she had to do was step forward.

"Do it, if you must," said Gwydion wearily.

Part of her wanted to. Another part of her knew that Pryderi would never have wanted this. He wouldn't want Branwen to become a murderer in his name.

But before she could make a decision, everything changed.

Warmth burned around her finger. Her oaken ring burst into life. Roots curled around Branwen's wrist, caressing her forearm as the magic awakened. Her left arm was snared in a sleeve of oak leaves and branches. All of it was laced with gold.

The spell had taken hold.

Someone had hunted the lapwing.

Gwydion's eyes went wide. He made a horrified little sound, reaching for her. And that was when she understood.

Her fealty, her loyalty, her actions—they did not belong to her. Not anymore.

The dagger fell from her fingers and tumbled into the grass.

Gooseflesh rose along her arms, and she took a step back. She had not meant to take that step—she simply moved. She felt the tug of some invisible cord, the whisper of a command she could not hear. The magic of the Wild Hunt was settling into her bones.

"No!" Gwydion put himself in front of her, hands on her shoulders. "I'll free you, I swear it."

"Why?" she asked. "Why do you even care?"

He looked as though she had run him through with a blade. "Branwen. I cannot lose you to them."

She had no control over her body. The magic of the oaken ring called to her. And perhaps that would have been terrifying if she could feel. The last of her despair had been doused with the capture of her brooch. It was almost a comfort not to feel, to retreat into herself.

"You lost me," she said, "when you led me into this forest under false pretenses. When you looked me in the eye and said that we were equals when all the while I was nothing more than a tool to you."

His hands tightened on her shoulders.

"I tried to take you from this," he whispered. "Last night. Before I took the rings. I tried."

Her body was not her own, but it carried her away. Like a river taking hold of a fallen leaf, she was yanked from Gwydion's grasp.

"You made your choice," she said. Another step took her near Pryderi's fallen signet ring. On instinct, she seized it, holding it against her heart with her unspelled hand.

And then she was running, bidden to flee. Palug was at her side. She chanced one look over her shoulder. Gwydion was reaching for her, one hand outstretched.

It was the last thing she saw before tears blinded her.

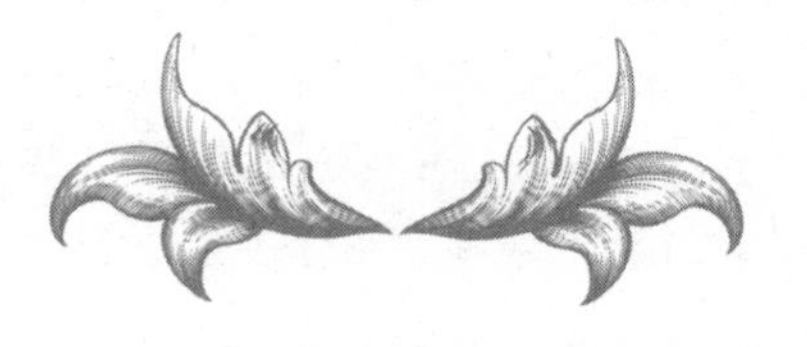

CHAPTER 36

GWYDION RAN.

He ran as though all of Annwvyn were giving chase—because they would be. It was only a matter of time until word reached Arawn and Pwyll. They would be gathering their forces, sending out scouts to chase the wayward trickster.

Every part of him ached. Pain had been a companion for much of his life, but now it nipped at his every step like an overeager hound. He drank his fill at a stream, using those precious moments to catch his breath.

You will break a throne.

Those words echoed within him. He'd always hated tales of prophecies. It seemed a cruel trick of fate to tell a person their future without giving them the tools to avert it.

He remembered Pryderi's prophecy—and then he quashed that thought so viciously that he winced.

He would not think of Pryderi.

He would not think of Branwen.

He would think of Gwynedd. Of the kingdom he was going to build. He would help shape it, grow it as he had grown his gardens. With Arianrhod as queen, they would make a world where villagers did not have to fear mercenaries raiding them or afancs stealing children. He could not change the past. He could only move forward, and he had set out on this path long before he met the huntress.

But it hurt. It hurt so badly he thought he might collapse under the weight of the agony. He could see Branwen's face when she realized the depths of his betrayal, how he had willingly given her fealty to the Hunt.

That was his worst regret. That he had left her behind.

No, he thought. Once the rings were safely with Arianrhod, once her rule was secured, Gwydion would return to the mountains. He did not know what it would take—trickery, fighting—but he would retrieve her brooch. It was the least he owed her.

But for now, all he could do was flee.

As he ran, he reached out to the forest. He went barefoot so that he could feel the breath and pulse of the wood. *Talk to me*, he thought. *Tell me what is to come.*

The trees creaked, shivered, and whispered of an oncoming storm. The forces of Annwvyn were mustering. They would be nimble—immortals could flit through the forest as swift as deer. Even with the trees guiding his way, with undergrowth moving aside for him, the folk would catch up.

And Gwydion could not fight them.

His steps slowed. Every breath felt like fire in his chest, and his legs shook with exertion. His strength was flagging, and he knew he would not reach the edge of the forest before the otherfolk came for him.

As if summoned by his thoughts, he heard the baying of hounds. Shouts rang out, far too close for his comfort.

They were not simply coming—they were *here*.

Gwydion uttered a quiet curse.

This was the true Wild Hunt: a single mortal pursued through a forest by monsters and hunters. A memory flickered back to him—that small gray fox Amaethon had tried so hard to kill.

Gwydion was that fox now. He needed help. But there was no one to turn to.

No.

He would not give up. He had come too far, given up too much, paid too high a cost. He could not fail.

He was *Gwydion*.

He was not just a trickster, not just a hunter, not just the sickly boy with the broken hand.

He was the youngest son of Dôn. He had been born to the most powerful diviner of nature that had ever walked the land. Forests were his birthright. It did not matter to whom the land belonged—everything that grew upon it was his.

This time, he did not sing nor hum. This was no gentle power, no caress of magic to coax a leaf into unfurling or a flower to bloom.

Gwydion fell to his knees and *screamed*.

He screamed his defiance, his anger, his loss. He screamed for the child he had been, for the mother he mourned, for the sister who had tried so hard to protect him, for the nephews he had tried to protect in turn, for the friend he had slain, and for her. For the huntress.

A shock wave rippled through the wood. The trees shivered, and the birds went silent.

For a heartbeat, all was still. Gwydion was on his knees, his chest heaving and throat raw. The world spun around him; he had never used so much power. He could only hope it would be enough.

A young alder tree shuddered. An oak creaked and groaned. A willow branch whipped back and forth, like a soldier loosening their arms before battle. A rowan shivered as its roots curled through the ground.

The magic had gone far deeper than even Gwydion imagined.

Every tree, every bramble, every flower and thorn—they all woke from their winter sleep.

And the forest went to war.

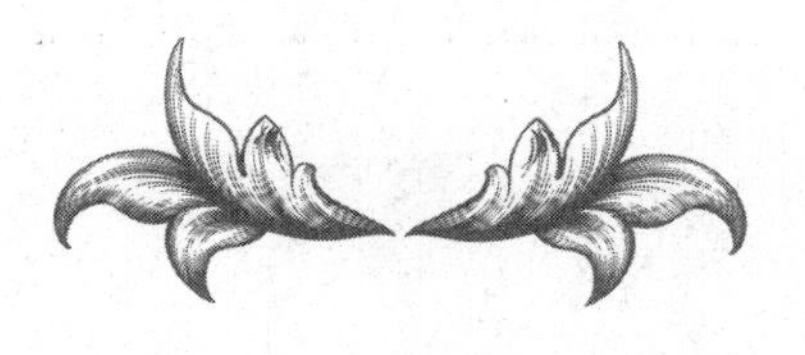

CHAPTER 37

THE WORLD FELT like a fever dream.

Everything was a blur of sounds and sights, the sensation of her feet hitting the ground, branches whipping at her cheeks. It was as though Branwen had died in that clearing and she was a ghost haunting the wood. She could not touch nor affect anything.

There was only the tug of a will not her own. Branwen surrendered to it.

It was a relief. Let someone else have control of her. Let the world carry her away. Perhaps then she would not have to face the death of one friend and the betrayal of another.

She did not know for how long she ran. Her feet ached, and her legs itched with overuse.

Slowly, the world returned to her. She became aware of the smell of woodsmoke and cooking meat, then heard the sound of chatter.

She blinked several times, as though she had surfaced from deep water.

She had journeyed into the camp of the Wild Hunt. Without being told, her feet carried her through the camp, past the watchful soldiers and hunters, past a tent where the wounded were tended, past faces she had glimpsed only a few days ago at the revel. There were significantly fewer than before.

She walked past them all. A guard glared at her but allowed Branwen to pass.

When she finally stopped, she stood in a royal tent. There was a table for food and wines, a desk, and stools for visitors. Sitting on one was none other than Cigfa. Her brows swept upward when she saw Branwen, but that was the only evidence of her surprise. There were a few others, folk and humans, scattered into quiet groups. They stood at the edges of the room, some holding handkerchiefs and others openly weeping.

Branwen wrenched her gaze away.

Two men stood before her. No, two *kings* stood before her. One wore a crown of gold and the other a crown of bone.

Her brooch gleamed between the Otherking's fingers.

And that was it. Branwen would belong to him for a year and a day. She was Branwen of Annwvyn, and her mother would likely never see her again. She would be punished for Gwydion's crimes. Perhaps it would be imprisonment in Caer Sidi or working among the ironfetches for a century. But she would never escape these mountains. Even when the year was ended, she doubted he would release her.

"Tell me your name, huntress," said Arawn quietly.

She did.

"Tell me who killed the prince."

She did. The tale came tumbling from her lips. She could not have held it back if she tried. She told Arawn of her magicked eye, of hunting iron-mad monsters, of Gwydion's offer of work, of their infiltration of the Hunt, of their alliance with Pryderi, of finding Pwyll's ring and then Arawn's, and finally, she spoke of Gwydion's betrayal.

When she finished, her throat was raw. She was so exhausted she might have curled up on that tent floor and slept for a hundred years. But rest was a mercy the Otherking would not grant.

"I did not know," Branwen said hollowly. The room's colors danced around her, a painting smudged at the edges. "What Gwydion intended…I didn't know."

"Why would we believe you?" asked Pwyll. His voice was cracked open by grief. There were tears on his face, and he made no attempt to hide them.

Palug meowed.

She had almost forgotten him. The cat stepped up between her legs, curling his tail around her calf. He looked up at the Otherking, his gaze unblinking.

Arawn's hand curled into a fist. "Where did you find that creature?"

Branwen looked down at Palug. "He's mine. You can't—you can't hurt him." She did not care if he did own her fealty. She would kill him before he touched her cat.

"I could not hurt that creature if I tried," said Arawn flatly. "How did you find him? How did you manage to *keep* him?"

"I don't know," said Branwen. She reached down to pick him up. Every single tylwyth teg took half a step back. All the humans just looked baffled.

Palug began kneading her shoulder, purring.

With her free hand, she held out Pryderi's ring. It had warmed in her palm.

But it was not her ring to keep.

Pwyll rose and took it from her, running his thumb over the golden surface. His eyes welled anew.

"I'm sorry," Branwen said. "For your loss. Pryderi...he was a good man. And he died in single combat against a dangerous foe. You and your wife should be proud."

She could do that much for Pryderi. His legacy would be that of a hero. Of a prince. He would be remembered as a good man.

"So the trickster of Gwynedd has stolen my ring," said Arawn, his golden eyes agleam. "At least now I know who managed to slip past the three. And why I bear this." He held up his left arm. He wore an armlet of yew branches. Pwyll's left arm was ornamented with rowan leaves. They were bound by the rules of the Hunt, just as she was.

"We cannot let him leave the forest." Pwyll slammed a hand onto the table, sending cups and plates scattering. "I will not let him have Dyfed."

Arawn placed his hand on Pwyll's shoulder. "Nor shall he, my friend." Arawn looked at Branwen.

She did not know what he wanted. She had nothing more to give—she had been broken and scraped hollow by the Wild Hunt.

"I shall put together a hunting party," said Arawn. He nodded at Branwen. "Arm yourself," he said. His voice was bone-dry. "My champion was ordered not to hunt mortals. I wonder who might have given such an order."

Cigfa gave Branwen a merry little wave.

"I won't apologize for it," said Branwen stubbornly.

The Otherking exhaled. "You have a fighter's spirit. Good. You shall need it."

He drew in a breath, and in that moment, Branwen remembered the crone's words: *You will hunt that which you love.*

"You," said Arawn, "shall lead the Wild Hunt."

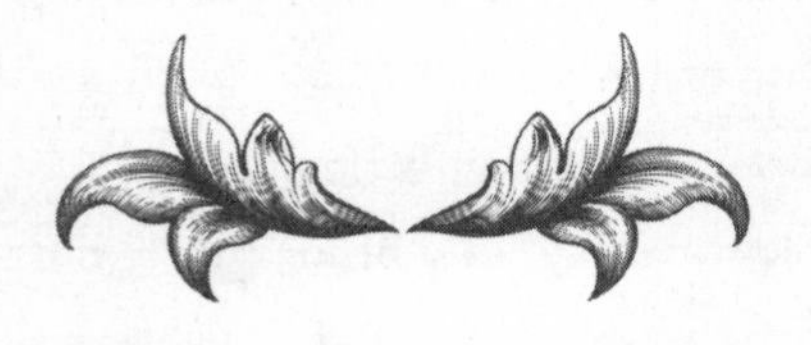

CHAPTER 38

THEY PUT BRANWEN in armor.

The metal gleamed like starlight in deepest winter. Branwen did not protest as a flurry of folk dressed her. One of them fussed over her bandage, but there was no time for healing. Not with two kingdoms at stake.

"Come," said one of the folk hunters. They had gathered as many as they could—humans, folk, soldiers, knights, and hunters. They were armed for battle and waiting expectantly. One of the folk guided Branwen to a horse. "You must lead."

She had little experience with horses, but its saddle and bridle glittered with gold. Magicked, she realized. One of the folk heaved her into the saddle. The horse shifted uneasily beneath her, and before Branwen could steady herself, it broke into a rolling canter.

Gritting her teeth, Branwen tried to hold on to the horse's mane with one hand and the reins with her other. The hunters followed, and hoofbeats rumbled through the woods like thunder.

Branwen tried to remember which direction she had come from and gave the reins a gentle tug. The horse responded to her touch at once, its long strides eating up the ground. It knew the forest, finding unseen paths. She rode out of the camp and deeper into the woods.

Behind her, the Wild Hunt followed.

A black streak of fur kept pace at Branwen's side. Palug was racing alongside the horse, his ears flat against his head as he scurried through the undergrowth.

Gwydion had a head start, but the Wild Hunt had everything to lose.

She would have expected her horse to stumble or trip. The enchantment must have been to prevent that, for the horse never lost its footing. They ran across trails, over streams, through meadows. The horse leapt over a fallen log, sprinted down a game trail, and surprised two gray foxes. They darted from her in a panic. She glimpsed other creatures—deer, pwca, some of the otherfolk. More disconcertingly, some of the cŵn annwn appeared to be following at a distance. She saw their red-tipped ears flashing through gaps in the trees, as they kept pace with the horses. An eerie baying made her shudder.

Finally, she rode into a horribly familiar clearing. Blood spattered the grass, and the earth was torn by magic. One of Branwen's arrows rested amid the leaves.

Her heart lurched in recognition. This had been the place where Pryderi had died. Could it have been mere hours ago? It felt so much longer. She slipped from her horse while the others watched.

She had to look at the aftermath not as Branwen but as the leader of the Wild Hunt. So she inhaled one long breath and let her instincts take hold of her. She was a huntress—she knew how to follow prey.

She found the place where Pryderi had fallen. His body was gone. She hoped he had been found by Pwyll's servants. He deserved a peaceful rest.

She knelt beside the dried blood. Her armlet of oak leaves rustled as she worked.

There were two lines of tracks: one was smaller, leading back toward camp. Her footprints, Branwen thought, seeing the familiar imprint of a boot sole. The other was of a longer stride. Barefoot and sure. Moss had grown up among the tracks. Only a plant diviner could have summoned that trail.

Gwydion had gone northwest. "This way," she said, and mounted her horse a second time.

For all his magic, Gwydion still left evidence of his passing. There were light indentations in the dirt. And even a diviner could not erase every single blade of broken grass. They rode from the clearing, keeping a slower pace for fear of losing the trail.

Branwen followed Gwydion's path. He was headed for the gates of Annwvyn. That made sense—there were few places a human without magicked sight could escape the wood without encountering magical traps or monsters.

She knew they had to be gaining. Even with his head start, he was on foot and they were on horseback. She dreaded the thought of seeing him again; she would have rather squeezed her eyes shut and ridden the horse as far as she could go. But Arawn's orders bound her to this task.

She had to retrieve those rings at any cost.

The memory of last night flashed through her mind—the warmth of his mouth, the way he had looked at her, like she was all that mattered in the world. She did not know if that part had been a lie, too.

They followed Gwydion's trail past a stream, across a meadow, and then into the thicker edge of the forest. Here, the trees of Annwvyn were nestled closely together—likely to keep trespassers from intruding. The canopy overhead twined together, casting the wood into shadow. Fallen leaves crunched beneath the horse hooves.

One of the cŵn annwn let loose a distant howl. "It has the scent," said one of the knights at Branwen's elbow. He rode a white stallion and bore the symbol of Dyfed across his plate armor. His expression was eager, his eyes searching for any sign of Gwydion. He kicked his horse into a gallop and pushed forward past Branwen.

It was what saved her.

For only twenty paces ahead, an ash tree suddenly *moved*.

It snapped one branch downward, catching the knight in the chest and flinging him into the air. *Like a child with a toy*, Branwen thought in wonder as the man flew high. He fell, screaming, and slammed into the ground with the snap of breaking bone.

Every single hunter drew their horse to a halt. The mounts shifted uneasily, tails flicking and eyes rolling.

That was when Branwen heard the silence. The forest had gone utterly quiet. Wind whispered, but there was no birdsong, no rustle of leaves, no murmur of ravens.

A prickle ran up the back of Branwen's arms. And for the first time since she had seen Pryderi die, she felt a flicker of fear. The forest had always been a dangerous place, brimming with magic and wonder and monsters. But now it felt... hungry.

"Something is wrong," said one of the folk.

"What is that—" said another folk hunter in alarm.

Branwen saw the encroaching gold.

Magic crept through the earth. It flickered like a spiderweb growing at twenty times its normal speed, casting out lines of gold. Those magical threads ran along the tree roots, darting from one to another, and the moment the magic connected, the trees glowed with power.

Horror rushed through Branwen. She had never seen magic like this, had never even thought it was possible.

"Fallen kings," Branwen breathed. Then she shouted, "GET DOWN!"

A few of the humans hesitated, but the folk were moving. They had seen the danger just as she had.

Branwen looked wildly at the other mortal hunters. But before she could call another warning—

The screaming began.

Trees slammed their branches into the earth, crushing victims and tossing them aloft. Roots reached from the ground to drag hunters and horses wailing beneath the dirt. Dust flew into the air; Branwen could only see a few paces ahead. She pressed herself low to the horse's neck.

Gwydion had conjured an army from the very forest.

A rowan tree snapped toward her.

Branwen did not have time to make a sound. She threw herself from her horse, rolling out of reach. The rowan struck her horse with all the force of a rockslide. Branwen darted under another branch, hissing as something struck her cheek. Blood welled up, but she ignored it.

She scrambled through the bushes, using her magicked sight to guide her. "Palug!" she cried desperately. She could not lose him.

A black blur leapt through the bushes. Palug kept low to the ground, his fur fluffed so that he looked like a furious black-and-white storm cloud. "Come here," she said. Palug jumped into her arms, and she held him, desperately grateful that he was all right.

Everywhere around her, soldiers and hunters fought the woods. The folk were calling on their own spells, trying to deflect the flying branches and calm the churning earth. Trees crashed into hunters with the force of battering rams, shattering bone and armor in a single blow. Vines curled around wrists and ankles. Roots shifted, making the earth crumble and surge. Brambles snaked around unwary ankles.

It was utter chaos.

The others tried to rally, but they had been caught unawares. They had armed themselves for a hunt, not a battle. Branwen had never wished for her afanc-fang dagger more; the sword in her hand felt unfamiliar as she sliced through briar and branch. A sapling knocked the blade from her hand, and it vanished into the churning earth.

She could see which trees held the battle enchantment and which did not. She followed her sight, trying to find a path through the cursed forest. She ducked under an ordinary oak tree, trying to catch her breath.

An alder root curled around Branwen's ankle and snagged her.

She snarled and reached for a knife. It glittered with the same iridescence as her armor. She swung out, slicing the root apart. It wriggled like a worm. Palug hissed and batted it away.

She pushed herself upright and ran.

Two hunters had lit torches and were driving back the trees with flame, trying to allow for a controlled retreat. One of them snarled as an ash swung at him. He withdrew a flask, scattering its contents across the ground. Then he set the spirits alight. The fire caught in the roots of the tree. The ash writhed, branches clawing at the air in wordless agony.

A folk huntress cast her own spell, murmuring as she tried to calm one tree. That ended when a large root curled around her ankle and began to drag her beneath the earth.

All around Branwen, a battle raged—blade against branch, arrow against thorn, spear against bramble. She could not imagine how much magic this had cost Gwydion.

A vine snagged on her wrist, but she yanked herself free. She could not stay to help the others; she had her orders from the Otherking.

This fight was merely a distraction.

Brambles were growing, creating a wall of thorns. All of it glowed with the same gold magic. Gwydion's magic.

She darted around an oak that swung its thick branches into a human hunter, then around a birch tree that had snatched up several of the folk. There was a break in the magic ahead, and Branwen veered toward it. She was all reaction and instinct, trying to find her way through a chaos the likes of which she had never encountered. She raced beneath the trees and found herself standing on a familiar trail.

It led to the gates of Annwvyn.

Palug wriggled free of her arms. He raced down the path, his tail low to the ground.

She had no time. She hurtled down the trail, heart in her throat. One tree branch fell toward her, and she leapt back, then darted around it. A fallen hunter lay across the path, a sword still in his hand. Branwen snatched up the weapon.

She was so close. She just had to reach the gates before he did.

Brambles closed in around her. She slashed with the sword, cutting through them again and again. Thorns snagged on her clothes, in the oaken leaves along her left arm, in her unbraided hair.

She stumbled, and for a heart-stopping moment, she thought she would fall into those grasping briars. She shoved herself forward, ignoring the flashes of pain as the thorns snagged.

She ran until her lungs were raw, until tears half blinded her. Farther, just a little farther.

She pushed through the briars and fell onto the path. Gasping, her arms stinging from small wounds, she forced herself to rise. Behind her were the sounds of battle: the screams, the clash of weapons, the scent of burning wood. Ahead of her—

The yew-tree gates of Annwvyn.

She saw the familiar shape of the gates: their woven branches, the arch between the two trees.

More importantly, she saw *him*.

Gwydion was half running, half stumbling toward the gates. His cloak had been discarded, and he wore only his tunic and trousers.

Retrieve the rings.

Arawn's command rang through her, and she shuddered. She

could no more disobey than she could have told her heart to stop beating. Her legs lurched without her making the choice, and she bolted after him.

He paused a moment, his head bowed and shoulders moving. As though he were speaking, as though he were singing…

And before her eyes, she saw gold threads leap from Gwydion and flit through the earth. They traveled from root to root, illuminating them beneath the earth. The magic jumped from tree to tree, heading for—

—the gates.

Branwen realized what he was doing. Or rather, what he was attempting to do: close the gates of Annwvyn.

It was impossible. None but Arawn could command those gates.

Gwydion's magic sank into the roots of the two yew trees.

With a hiss of frustration, Branwen forced herself to run faster.

The yew trees were shifting like old warriors after a long nap. Branches creaked as they moved. Slowly, one by one, their branches wove together. Closing the gates.

Branwen tore into a sprint. The space between the two trees was narrowing, growing smaller by the moment. She screamed, knowing that if she was caught in those branches, she would be crushed.

A branch slid across her arm, dragging at the oaken leaves—

And then she was through.

The yew-tree gates of Annwvyn closed behind her. The moment they did, all the sounds of the battle died away. Silence closed in all around her, until the only thing Branwen could hear was that of her own ragged breathing.

She stumbled to a halt.

Gwydion stood in the path. His chest was heaving, face pale and shining with sweat. There was a wildness to him, a ragged energy that seemed to roll off him. There was no restraint to his magic; he had given it free rein for likely the first time in his life.

"What did you do?" she said, her voice a rasp.

Gwydion whirled. When he saw her, his expression crumpled. "No. Not you." The word frayed on his lips; his pleasant voice had gone hoarse with overuse. "Please—just turn back."

"I can't," she said simply.

For a few moments, neither moved. "You unleashed the forest," said Branwen.

Gwydion nodded. "I could think of no other way to escape."

"And the cost?" She thought of how he had spoken of his magic, how every decision had a price. How he had recoiled from using his power too much, lest it shorten his life.

A faint, regretful smile touched his mouth. "It's not the worst cost I've paid in this Hunt."

Palug came up beside her. The cat shook himself, green eyes on Gwydion.

"I'm sorry," said Gwydion. "I'm so sorry."

And perhaps the worst part was she knew he meant it.

Branwen took a step forward. Then another. And another. She could not stop herself, could not even try. "Arawn told me to retrieve the rings."

Sorrow crossed his face. "That's who has your brooch," he said. "I suppose one of his hunters delivered it to him."

It was not a question, but she nodded.

"You will kill me if I refuse," said Gwydion. Another not-question.

"Please don't make me," she said.

He inhaled. Then he turned to run.

She attacked him.

Gwydion darted to one side, avoiding the first sweep of her sword. Before the blade could kiss his flesh, a dagger flashed upward and knocked the sword aside.

He held a dagger. *Her* dagger. He must have retrieved it.

The sharp afanc fang looked crude beside her sword, but it would kill her easily enough. For a few heartbeats, they circled each other. She knew what she had to do, even as she fought against it.

You will hunt that which you love.

Branwen lunged. Gwydion stepped aside, and as they passed each other, she was so close she could feel his breath.

She whirled, bringing her sword down. He deflected the blow, trying to yank her sword from her hands. With a snarl, she cracked the pommel into his side.

Her strength overpowered his. He stumbled, pain flashing across his face as he used his right hand to catch himself. Determination settled across the grim lines of his face.

There was intent in his eyes.

He attacked again, this time spinning the afanc-fang dagger so that she was on the defensive. She caught every slash on her blade, meeting him blow for blow. She was no great soldier, but then again, neither was he. A trickster and a huntress were evenly matched.

But tricksters fought with little honor.

He slammed his elbow into her side, right into her still-healing wound. The pain jolted through her, a spike of unexpected agony that drove her to her knees.

He seized the hilt of her sword, his left hand around her right. She tried to shake him off, the sword dangerously near his face. A few strands of his dark hair were sliced, and they fluttered to the earth. He shoved her sword downward, slamming hand and hilt against the ground and pinning her in place.

She cracked her forehead into his.

Lightning flashed through her skull.

He fell over backward, blood spilling from a wound above his brow. She crawled after, her sword still in hand. In a flash, she was atop him, knee against his breastbone and sword at his throat.

"Give them to me, now," she said. It was not an order but a plea. For whatever had happened between them, she did not want to do this. If she cut his throat, she would never be able to rid herself of this day. She would never be able to look in a mirror, live within her bones, nor forget what she had done.

"I can't," gasped Gwydion.

"Damn it," she whispered. And then she pushed the blade down.

The edge of the blade brushed his throat. Blood welled up, staining the metal.

"Give me the rings," she pleaded.

The resolve in his eyes seemed to shatter. Lips parted, a flush on his cheeks, he looked like who he had been before—her companion. Her friend. And possibly something more.

She sobbed, her fingers tightening around the sword's hilt. The magic of the Wild Hunt pulsed through her, impossible to deny. She was an instrument of the Otherking.

She pressed the blade down.

"Please!" The word ripped out of Gwydion. "Blodeuyn!"

Branwen froze.

That name—the sound of her birth name in his mouth—fractured the magic. For a heartbeat, *just a heartbeat*, she felt herself again. She was no longer Branwen of the Wild Hunt.

She was Blodeuyn.

And then Gwydion was twisting beneath her.

She never saw the knife. She never felt the blow.

All she heard was "I'm sorry."

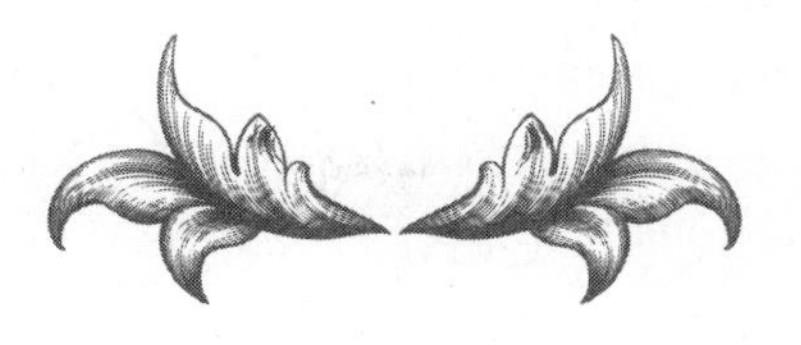

CHAPTER 39

BRANWEN LAY UNCONSCIOUS on top of him.

It was a tricky thing to knock her out. Gwydion had slammed the hilt of the afanc-fang dagger to the back of her jaw. The blow had struck true, and she went limp. He rolled Branwen off of him, settling her gently on her side.

Gwydion pressed his hand to her throat, making sure she had a pulse. It was there, steady against his fingertips. He breathed, sagging in relief. He was bleeding and exhausted, but alive. She was alive. He would figure out the rest.

He had won. He had bested Arawn's champion.

But victory tasted worse than defeat.

He tried to catch his breath. Palug stood a few strides away, glaring at him. "I'm sorry," said Gwydion hoarsely. The cat ignored him; he scurried over to Branwen and climbed atop her chest, as though guarding her.

"I'm not going to hurt her," said Gwydion. "You can—"

A sound made him flinch. It was the creaking of old wood, the whisper of evergreen needles brushing one another. Palug hissed—and Gwydion realized the cat was not guarding Branwen from *him*.

The gates of Annwvyn were opening. Only one person could have enticed those trees to move.

Their twined branches parted, revealing a terrifying silhouette. He stepped through the gates, and they closed behind him. All went silent, save for Gwydion's ragged breathing.

The Otherking approached with the graceful gait of an old wolf. His finger-bone crown was at his brow, and his golden eyes were molten with fury.

"I know you, son of Dôn," the Otherking said. He spoke quietly, his voice deep and soft as distant thunder.

Gwydion had no strength to rise, but he did it regardless. He would not be on his knees before any king.

"You should," he replied, "considering I just won your Hunt."

Arawn smiled with all his teeth. "You have won nothing."

"I have your ring," said Gwydion. "I have Pwyll's. I have several other hunters' signets as well. And considering I just destroyed most of the hunters you sent after me..." He shrugged. "I've not judged many hunts, but I can see only one victor in this."

Arawn tilted his head too far to one side. It was a distinctly inhuman gesture. "You would only speak so if you wanted to die."

"Or to bargain," said Gwydion. "You have something I want. I have many things you want."

The Otherking took another step closer.

Palug hunched over Branwen, hissing at the Otherking. Arawn

spared the cat a swift glance before turning his attention back to Gwydion.

"Give me her brooch," said Gwydion, gesturing at Branwen, "in trade."

Arawn remained still and emotionless as stone. "Explain, son of Dôn."

Gwydion reached into his pocket and withdrew the two signet rings. One bore the signet of Dyfed and the other of Annwvyn. Pwyll's ring and Arawn's ring.

"One ring for another. I'll even let you decide," Gwydion said. "I will put a ring in each closed fist. You choose a hand, and that ring is yours."

"And if I should simply decide to cut you down?" asked Arawn.

Gwydion shook his head. "I hold your fealty. You cannot hurt me. But you may bargain with me."

Arawn stared hard at him. "I can sense lies, you know."

"I know," said Gwydion. "Which is why I am telling you the truth."

There was a long silence. Gwydion counted his breaths, waiting. The moment twisted tighter and tighter, until finally Arawn said, "Her ring for an unseen ring of my choosing."

"Yes," said Gwydion. He tossed the signet rings in the air, back and forth, so quickly that a human might not follow the movement. But Arawn's hard gaze never wavered. He watched as Gwydion passed the rings back and forth.

Gwydion bowed and held out his closed fists.

His heart pounded. This was a risk, such a terrible risk, but he would not leave Branwen to the mercy of Annwvyn. He had lost her already, he knew that. Even if they both stumbled out of these woods, she would never forgive him. At least she would be alive to despise him.

Arawn's attention drifted back and forth between Gwydion's closed hands. "The left," he said.

With a flourish, Gwydion turned that hand over and opened his fingers.

The golden ring of Dyfed sat in his palm.

For a heartbeat, neither moved. It was a loss for Arawn and a victory for Dyfed—but tylwyth teg were bound by their word.

Arawn's lips hardened into a line. He pulled the brooch from his pocket. Gwydion flung the ring at Arawn, who caught it easily.

The brooch thudded into the grass by Branwen. Gwydion dared not reach over and take it, lest he break Arawn's gaze. He had the terrible feeling that to look away was to invite attack.

Arawn shifted beneath his crimson cloak. "You will leave, son of Dôn," he said softly. "Never enter these woods again. I may not be able to harm you, but that cannot be said for the other creatures that dwell here." He turned to go, but Gwydion called after him.

"Wait."

Arawn went still, glancing over one broad shoulder. "What?"

Gwydion held up the ring of the Otherking. It glimmered in the light. "I hold your fealty. I can command you for a year and a day."

"Yes, you could," said Arawn, with a sliver of that wolfish smile. "I would advise against it, however. Unless you word your commands very *meticulously*," he put subtle emphasis on every syllable of that word, "I might prove a less than ideal servant."

Or put plainly, Arawn was sure he could outwit any command

Gwydion might offer. He was probably right. Arawn had centuries of experience with trickery and magic. Gwydion had only nineteen years.

"I have one command for you," said Gwydion. "And it's one you will want to follow."

Arawn's brows swept upward. "Is that so?"

Gwydion gazed at him. "Leave."

Arawn looked at him sharply. "What?"

Gwydion felt as though he were dying on his feet; the world swayed and blood hammered in his head. He had used too much magic, gone too far into his divining. But he managed to stay upright and say what needed to be said.

"Leave the isles," Gwydion continued. "Go elsewhere. I know the tylwyth teg have places that mortals cannot find. There is a war coming. Dyfed cannot let the death of Prince Pryderi go unpunished. They will attack Gwynedd...and King Pwyll will call on you to aid him. The isles will not survive a war between mortal and immortal. Such a conflict would destroy both sides."

Arawn gestured at the woods. "If we leave, so will the magic. Magic, as your kind are so fond of saying, is *other*. When we go, that otherness will fade. In a century, perhaps two, there will be no diviners nor enchantments. No legends nor monsters." He tilted his head. "Are you so eager to usher in an age of iron?"

Gwydion thought of the forest. He could feel its magic throbbing up through the soles of his feet and into his very bones. The magic of Annwvyn was beautiful and powerful—and it could so easily fall into the wrong hands.

"The age of iron has already begun," said Gwydion. "It has soaked into the fields, into the rivers, into the lakes. Humans will never be contained. Monsters cross this land to find sanctuary in Annwvyn, but soon there will be no safety even within these mountains.

"If you stay," he continued, "with your fealty belonging to a mortal... I fear that would be the end of everything. But I am giving you this chance to run. To take your people and your magic and leave. Protect your people. That is the only thing a king should do."

A long silence fell between them.

Arawn lowered his gaze. When he spoke, there was a soft note of regret in his voice. "On that, son of Dôn, we agree."

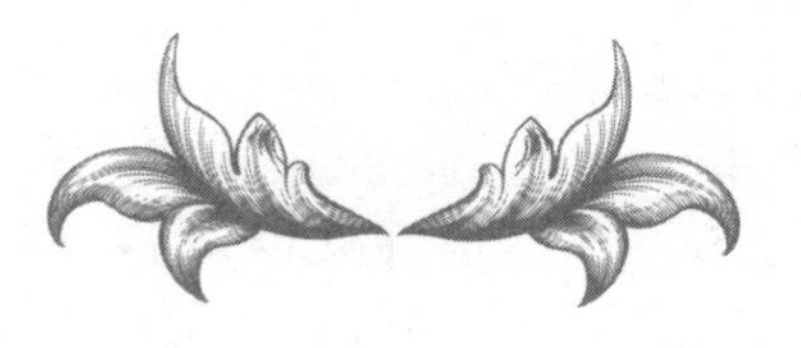

CHAPTER 40

BRANWEN WOKE BESIDE the forest.

The dead grass prickled against her bare neck, and the air smelled of burning. The sky was purpling like an old bruise. Beside her was a black-and-white cat. He mewed softly in her ear, and she rolled over to wrap her arms around him. "You're alive," she whispered. "Oh, Palug."

He head-butted her nose. Which hurt more than it should have.

"You're awake."

A voice made Branwen flinch. She sat up so fast her head swam. The world spun sickeningly, and then there was a hand at her shoulder. "It's all right."

Branwen blinked several times. And that was when she realized—her right eye was covered. The familiar iron-stitched blindfold was tucked around her head. A water flask and a pack sat beside her.

Branwen twisted open the flask and drank, flushing the taste of old blood from her teeth.

A woman crouched beside Branwen, watching her with bird-like interest. "Cigfa?" murmured Branwen. She did not know if she should have been afraid or not. She had bested Arawn's champion. Cigfa might hold a grudge.

"It's me," said Cigfa, smiling. "I know I look different without my magic." She pointed at Branwen's blindfold. "I don't know how you can stand to wear that."

The iron was a relief. There was no flash of gold, no unexpected flare that would scald her sight. Branwen touched the blindfold, then looked around.

They were on the edges of Annwvyn. "How much time has passed?" asked Branwen. "Where—what happened? What are you doing here?"

Cigfa held up three fingers. "It's been a day. I used a bit of magic to keep you asleep and to heal the worst of your wounds." She put one finger down. "We are a short distance from the gates of Annwvyn." Another finger. "And the battle is over. We burned a good portion of the trees, hacked down another, and then it all just went still. Arawn and that human trickster came to some kind of agreement. Arawn sent me to keep you safe until you woke."

"What was the bargain?" asked Branwen. Her head throbbed, but she had to know.

Cigfa shrugged. "Not entirely sure yet. King Pwyll has his ring back, but the rest are gone."

Gwydion had done it. He had escaped with the fealty of hunters and an immortal king. He would be fleeing toward Caer Dathyl with his prize. Branwen closed her eyes for a few moments. He was alive—and she did not know if that was a comfort or not.

"What now?" said Branwen. Surely the Otherking had orders for her.

Cigfa sighed. "We're leaving."

Branwen pulled Palug a little closer. "We?"

"The otherfolk, tylwyth teg, whatever you mortals call us. We can't stay," said Cigfa. "If a mortal can control the Otherking... it's too dangerous for all involved."

"Where will you go?" asked Branwen.

Cigfa smiled. "You would not know the place."

Branwen sat there, holding her monstrous cat, and tried to sort through her muddled thoughts. It felt as though she were trying to find her feet amid a rockslide—every thought sliding away from her as soon as she grasped at it. Her head hurt so badly she wished to lie down and return to sleep. "What about Pryderi?"

Cigfa's smile faltered. "We took his body to his father," she said quietly. "He will be buried at home."

Branwen's heart ached. "I'm sorry."

"Many will mourn him," said Cigfa. "But he will be remembered. It is the best mortals can hope for."

They sat in quiet for a few moments.

"So where do I go?" asked Branwen. She had half expected Cigfa to drag her back into Annwvyn by now. It would be work or imprisonment.

Cigfa looked at her oddly. "What do you mean?"

"I belong to Arawn," said Branwen slowly, trying to make her understand. "For a year and a day."

Cigfa shook her head. "Not anymore. Your fealty changed hands."

Confusion and fear rose within her. What had Arawn done with her brooch? Had he given it to Pwyll? Would she be dragged to Dyfed in chains, to face Pryderi's family as one of those complicit in his death? Perhaps that was the fate she truly deserved.

"Who," she began to say, then faltered.

"You belong to the trickster," said Cigfa. "It was part of the bargain he made with our king." She gave Branwen a curious look. "I must say, you two are far more interesting mortals than I ordinarily deal with."

Branwen closed her eyes. Gwydion. Of course he would have found a way. Somehow he had managed to wrest her free of Arawn's control.

Please, Blodeuyn!

His voice still rang in her ears.

Branwen looked at her left arm. Her armlet of oaken leaves had changed—they had gone golden and brown as a tree in autumn. As she moved, the leaves began to fall.

"What will you do now?" asked Cigfa.

Branwen looked west. "I am going home."

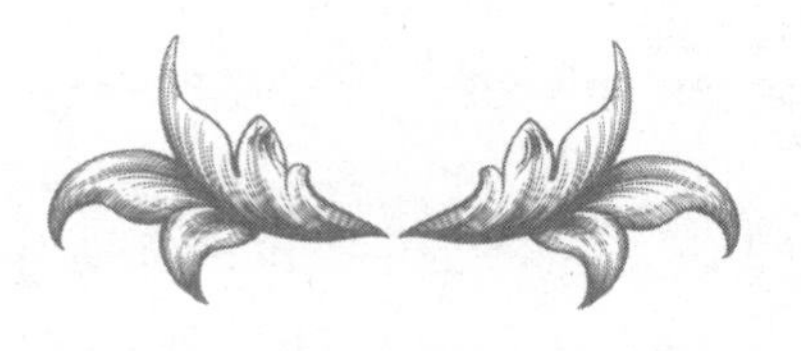

CHAPTER 41

WHEN GWYDION RETURNED to Caer Dathyl, he did so through the main gates.

He rode a stolen horse, wore a cloak of moss and silver, and bore a healing cut along his forehead.

It had taken a week to return. A week of resting in an inn, of trying to recover what strength he had left. He had spent much of that time fevered and half dreaming, his fingers curled around the pouch of rings. When he awoke, he felt thinner and weaker—but he was able to travel.

He strode through the castell, ignoring all who called out to him. He did not waver or step aside for anyone. The main hall was brimming with people. Many who had come for the feast would linger in Caer Dathyl for weeks to come.

At his throne sat King Math, in conversation with a young

woman. Arianrhod sat at one of the tables, the twins on either side of her. When she saw him, her brows drew tight with concern.

Amaethon stepped in front of Gwydion. "Where have you been, dear brother?"

Gwydion did not so much as hesitate. With a murmur, he called to the linen in Amaethon's shirt. The cloth came alive at once, wrapping itself around the would-be king's throat. It was far too satisfying—a cruel little bit of magic that Gwydion had never before turned against his brother.

It would cost him.

All his magic would cost him—but Gwydion had ceased to care about the price.

Amaethon fell, and in the same heartbeat, Arianrhod rose. *Let that be a foretelling,* Gwydion thought to himself.

Conversation died around him, falling into whispers and mutters.

"Get out," said Gwydion. "All of you."

No one moved. No one spoke. The only sound was Amaethon struggling for breath.

"Get," said Gwydion, enunciating each syllable, "out."

He did not raise his voice. He did not have to. He had learned something of power in the last few weeks.

One by one, the nobles and servants slipped from the room. Among them was Arianrhod. She wore an expression of deep concern, and her arms were wrapped around the twins. At her expression, his resolve nearly broke. He had never wanted anything as badly as he wanted to hug her and the twins. To tell her all that had happened. He wanted the comfort of family.

He kept his shoulders straight. When she passed by, he said, "My queen."

She looked at him sharply.

Finally, the last servant drained from the hall. The doors were closed behind them.

"Nephew," said Math, with a glance toward Amaethon.

Amaethon was on his knees, choking and grasping at his own shirt. "Oh, right," said Gwydion. With a hum, he released the hold on his magic.

Amaethon gasped for air and struggled to his feet. When he looked at Gwydion, his anger was mingled with fear.

"Fire cannot be called without breath," said Gwydion. "Harm another innocent, burn another tree, and you will regret it."

Amaethon took a step closer. He looked as though he would have liked to kill Gwydion, but Math spoke. "Leave us."

Amaethon's gaze darted from Gwydion to Math. Then he spat on the stone floor and strode from the hall.

Math sat in his throne, elbow resting idly against his knee. If he was impressed by Gwydion's display of magic, he did not show it. "Where have you been?" he said. "You were missed at the festival."

"I highly doubt that," said Gwydion. "And you know where I was."

Math's eyes glittered. "I could never guess."

"You told me to do it," said Gwydion. "But you assumed I would fail or die. That was your mistake. You underestimated me."

"Did I?" asked Math.

Gwydion reached into his cloak and withdrew a ring. It gleamed in the torchlight. "This is the signet ring of King Arawn. It gives the owner the right to rule Annwvyn for a year and a day."

"And you've delivered it to me?" Math leaned forward, drawn like a plant to sunlight, but Gwydion closed his fingers over the ring.

"No," said Gwydion. "I am giving it to Arianrhod."

"Is that so?" Math said. There was a low edge to his voice, civility receding like a tide. "Then why did you come here?"

"To ask you to name Arianrhod as your heir," said Gwydion. "Politely."

Math smiled coldly. "Strangling your brother and making demands? This is polite?"

"Quite," replied Gwydion. "You have no idea what I gave up to bring this to Gwynedd. The bodies I left in my wake. Far better men than you died so that I could make my sister the queen that our kingdom needs. So you will name Arianrhod your heir. Tonight. This very night."

Math looked nonplussed. "Is there anything else?" he drawled.

"You have not divined in years," said Gwydion. "But you shall do so now. There is a midwife with memory sickness. You will use your magic to help her."

Math tilted his head, an indolent smile on his mouth. "And if I refuse?"

Before the Wild Hunt, Gwydion would have felt a flare of anger. But this Gwydion only felt detached. He gazed at this hall and saw every crack, every flaw—including the man who sat upon that throne.

That *wooden* throne.

A diviner should have known better.

That throne was old and dormant. But it had once belonged to an old yew tree, and even now Gwydion could hear its quiet song.

"I never realized why you did not heal my mother," he said, almost casually. "You could have saved her from that illness, but you did not. I thought perhaps you did not wish to spend your magic in such a way. But it was because you feared her. Dôn's power was far greater than your own."

Math's lips peeled back in disgust. "Flowers? Trees? I fail to see why those things are so frightening."

His throne *creaked*.

Math looked down in surprise. The throne began to sprout. Small tendrils of greenery arose, winding around Math's arms and legs before he could draw a breath. The throne's legs became roots, cracking the stone beneath them. Leaves unfurled from the back, and when the throne stopped moving, it looked like some terrible, deformed tree.

Math made a low, furious noise. He was pinned to the tree throne, his eyes wide with mingled fury and fear.

Gwydion took a step forward.

"Do you know how many plants grow in your castell?" He took another step. "In your city?" Another step. "In your kingdom?" He halted before the broken throne. "Far more than your soldiers or servants. And at my command, they will be my armies. They will be my servants. The roots of the land will answer only to me." He put a finger beneath his uncle's chin, forcing Math to meet his gaze. "As will you."

Math's eyes blazed with resentment. "Who are you to speak to your king like this?"

Gwydion laughed bitterly. "I am Gwydion, son of Dôn, trickster of Gwynedd, slayer of Prince Pryderi of Dyfed, victor of the Wild Hunt, and the one who drove King Arawn from mortal lands.

"In a week, my name will be upon the lips of all those in Gwynedd. In a month, every kingdom will know me. In a year, all those who utter my name will do so in a whisper. And in a thousand years, when all enchantment has drained from this world and all is iron and mortal, children will ask where the magic went. And you know what they will say? It was no warrior, no prince, no king." Gwydion flicked a signet ring into the air and caught it between two fingers. "It was a trickster."

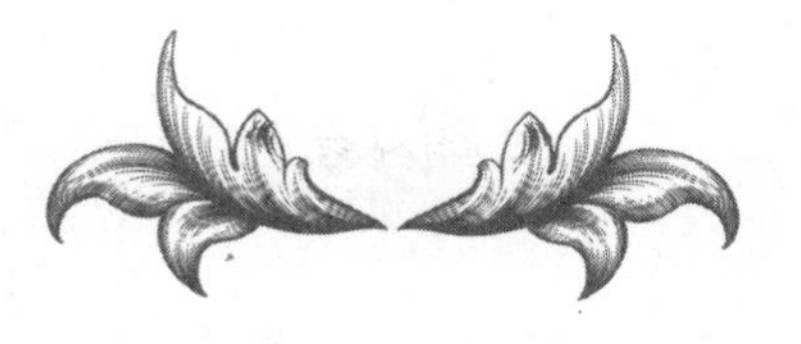

CHAPTER 42

WHEN BRANWEN RETURNED from the Wild Hunt, her mam greeted her at the front gate.

It took her days to walk home. Headaches plagued Branwen. Palug had to meow at her when she accidentally stumbled from the road. Palug ran ahead, scratching at the door until Mam emerged and rushed to greet Branwen.

Glaw's niece, the young woman Branwen had hired, was cooking by the fire. When she saw the state of Branwen's bruises, she rushed to help her. At first, Branwen wanted to protest. But her arrow wound needed tending, and her head continued to throb.

She spent nearly two weeks recovering—sleeping in her bed, drinking warm broths, and allowing herself time to mourn. As far as her mother knew, Branwen had been on a hunting trip with a noble from Gwynedd. Something had gone awry, and Branwen had been injured.

She did not like to lie. But certain truths were too painful to utter aloud.

Time went on, and Branwen went on with it.

She took over the keeping of Rhain's farm. She adopted his chickens and goat. She left flowers on the grave mound beneath the old oak tree. She tended the winter-sleeping gardens, preparing the soil for spring. The work soothed her, reminded her there was a world beyond the magical and the monstrous.

The days were easiest. But every night, she dreamed of a wooded clearing. She dreamed of a bow in her hands, the string drawn taut and her arrow aimed at a dark-haired young man. She dreamed how it felt to release that arrow—the despair and determination—only to see the arrow curve from its target.

She always woke before the arrow struck Pryderi. That was one mercy.

She did not pick up a bow. The thought of hunting turned her stomach. Rather, she spent time with her mother. She chopped firewood and crafted candles and ensured their food was well-secured in the pantry.

A month after she returned from the Hunt, she visited Argoed.

It felt strange. She walked among people she had known her whole life, yet they seemed like strangers. They spoke of local gossip, of small scandals, of the weather. There was no mention of kings nor monsters, nothing about the Wild Hunt. Branwen sat at the tavern, nursing a drink while Glaw told her about the rats he'd chased from his barn.

The stories made her feel both more and less at home.

"I know something happened on that hunt of yours," said Mam one afternoon as they baked bread. Mam's sleeves were rolled up to her forearms, and the house smelled like honey and oats as she warmed the griddle stone. "If you ever wish to speak of it..."

Branwen kept her eyes on the dough. She added another fistful of flour, kneading it. Palug sat a few feet away, watching them work with interest.

Branwen's throat went tight. Part of her wanted to talk to her mother, to confide in her. To tell her all of it.

"I know you think me weak," said Mam, crossing her arms. She regarded Branwen with rueful fondness. "But I am strong enough to carry my child's troubles."

Branwen shook her head. "No, Mam. I've never thought you weak. You're... you're ill sometimes, but that's not your fault." Pain twisted through her. She had come so close to saving her mam. The boon would have cured her... but at least she still had Gwydion's coin. She could afford the sleeping herbs, at least for a year.

"I know." Mam let out a weary breath. "But I promise if you tell me, I will remember. So long as it's in the morning," she added. That earned her a snort from Branwen. It was the first time she had laughed since the Hunt.

"Someday," said Branwen. "I will tell you all of it. When it's less painful."

Mam nodded. They worked in silence for a few minutes until

Mam said, "Derwyn sent a letter. He would like us to visit in the spring."

"Would he?" Branwen looked up sharply.

"He's been taking in some of the orphans from Gwaelod," said Mam. "I think he wants us to meet them."

Branwen thought of her cousin surrounded by children. It made her smile. "We should go. We can find someone to tend to the farm for a few weeks in spring."

Mam nodded. "Something to look forward to."

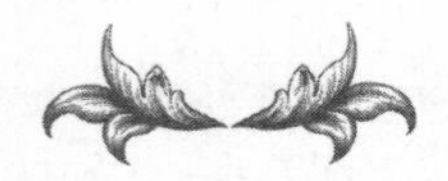

More time slipped by.

As winter deepened, there were rumors that something had changed in Annwvyn. The old sightings of monsters and tylwyth teg were becoming less and less. The villagers spread wildly untrue rumors, but Branwen never argued with them. They would never believe her tales.

And finally, when the first snow touched the land, Branwen ventured out to hunt.

She had to use one of Rhain's bows. Hers had been lost in Annwvyn. She walked through the wilds, snow crunching gently beneath her feet as she enjoyed the quiet peace of the morning. Her mam had gone to the village, so Branwen did not have to hurry home.

When she crossed a hill, she saw three deer. They were clustered together, nosing at a tangle of dead grass. Branwen's fingers went still on her bow, but she did not pull it taut. Rather, she watched them.

One of the deer lifted its head and sniffed in her direction. When she remained still, the deer seemed to decide she was not a threat. They went back to searching for greenery.

Branwen watched them until they vanished into the fields.

When she returned home, Palug was waiting for her. He sat beside the door and howled to be let in. "You wanted to go play outside, you monster," said Branwen fondly. She walked inside, kicking snow from her boots before she pulled off her cloak. Mam's cloak was hanging from its hook, which meant she had returned. She was probably out doing chores.

Branwen strode inside, heading for the fire to warm her hands. As she walked by the kitchen, a gleam caught her eyes.

Sitting on the table was a brooch.

It was a simple circle, light and worn from years of use. She touched it to see if it was real. It clinked gently against her fingernail.

Voices came from outside. Branwen whirled and saw her mam walking through the front door, carrying a basket brimming with fresh herbs. She was laughing. "You'll have to tell me the rest of it someday," she was saying. She stepped aside, and a figure filled up the doorway.

He was thinner than the last time she had seen him. His hair had gone entirely silver. But his eyes were the same—dark and watchful. "I will," he said to Mam. "Let me take that." He took the basket from Mam, hefting it under his left arm. His right hand was in a brace.

Branwen did not move. She could barely breathe.

"Branwen, dear, your friend stopped by," said Mam. "I was just showing him the new chicken coop."

Gwydion, son of Dôn, set the basket of herbs on the table. He wore a simple gray cloak, and his boots were stained with snow from the road.

He was here. In her house.

She had spent nearly an entire season trying not to think about him. Yet here he was.

Palug meowed and walked up to greet him. He did so by reaching up and hooking his claws into Gwydion's trousers, flexing his claws into the man's knee. Gwydion winced, but he did not pull away.

"It was lovely to see you again," said Mam. She poured water into the kettle and hung it over the fire. "I need to finish my chores. Branwen, why don't you offer our guest tea?" And then she was bustling from the house, giving Gwydion a speculative little glance before she pulled the door shut.

Branwen did not speak for nearly half a minute.

Gwydion regarded her softly.

"These herbs aren't in season," she finally said.

If he considered that a strange greeting, he did not comment on it. "No, they're not," replied Gwydion. "I grew them myself." He took a breath. "I know I have no right to ask anything of you, but can we talk?"

Branwen looked at the kettle. "I suppose Mam did offer you tea. You have as long as it takes for me to drink it."

Gwydion smiled. "That seems a fair trade."

She felt his eyes on her as she poured the water and steeped the tea. Finally, she set two cups at the table. He seemed to take that as invitation to sit. Steam danced from the cups, and Branwen watched it in silence. Palug curled up near the fire, licking snow from his paws.

"I met your mother in the village market," said Gwydion. "She was giving a beggar a coin. I offered to escort her home, and we talked a little. You've been having headaches?"

At least this was easier to talk about. Branwen touched her temple. "Yes. Either from using my eye too much during the Hunt or the blow that knocked me out. The village healer isn't sure." She spoke without heat, but Gwydion winced.

"I can make a poultice, if you like," he said.

She wrapped her fingers around her teacup. It warmed her cold hands. "You didn't come here to look at chicken coops and make poultices."

He leaned back in his chair, resting one hand on his knee. "You're right. I came... because I made certain promises. And I needed to be sure they were delivered."

"What promises?" asked Branwen. She had thought it would be something like this. When she glimpsed him in the doorway, she thought he would try to buy her forgiveness with sacks of gold or jewels.

Gwydion drew in a long breath. "Your mam."

Branwen looked at him sharply. "What about her?"

"She met my uncle today," said Gwydion.

Branwen stared at him in bewilderment. "The *king*?"

"It's all right," said Gwydion. "I told him to act like a kind beggar and take your mother's hand when she slipped him a coin." The corner of his mouth twitched. "Seeing him in a beggar's cloak was well worth the trip."

This made no sense. Branwen's fingers tightened around her

teacup. "Your uncle—King Math. He came to my village? He dressed as a beggar to meet my mam?"

"I expect he's riding back to Caer Dathyl," said Gwydion. "He looked as though he wished to remain not a moment longer than necessary. But the divining was part of my bargain with him."

"He divined my mother?" Fear filled her stomach, and she made to rise. She had to be sure Mam was all right, that nothing—

"It was a healing," said Gwydion soothingly. "Nothing more."

She looked at him sharply. "He... healed her?"

"Oh, yes," said Gwydion. He looked down at his undrunk tea. "I'm sorry. He cannot restore memories. She may struggle to remember things that have happened since the illness took hold. But he stopped the deterioration. Your mother will lose no more memories."

The world seemed to freeze around her. Branwen dared not take a breath for fear of breaking this moment.

Mam would lose no more memories. It was a hope she had once cradled near to her heart—and Gwydion shattered it when he lied to her. Now he was here, trying to mend that hope.

"Why?" she finally said.

Gwydion's dark eyes were sorrowful. "Because I spent my life lying to everyone around me. To myself. But I never wanted to lie to you. I meant everything. All of it. My lies were ones of omission, but they were still lies. I led you into that forest knowing what it might cost you. I killed Pryderi, even if I did not mean to. I injured you. And for all that, I am sorry." He swallowed. "I know it means nothing to you, but I am truly sorry."

She did not know what to say, so she kept quiet. They drank tea in silence for a few minutes.

"Your hair," she finally said, gesturing at his temples. "That is new."

"Oh, this?" Gwydion fingered one of the gray strands. "It began to grow in that way after the battle. I was... not myself for some weeks afterward. A cough, a fever. And the hair, of course." He shrugged. "I don't think any diviner has ever done what I did." There was a trace of bitter pride in his voice. "But there's a cost. Always a cost."

"And we all paid it," she said.

"Some more than others," he agreed softly.

She did not have to ask to know he spoke of Pryderi.

She missed him. She missed Pryderi's steady presence, the warm smiles, and the way he seemed to instill everything he did with care. She had only known him a short while, and it had not been enough.

"What will you do now?" she asked.

"I don't know. I can't live at Caer Dathyl."

"You can't?"

"Exile," said Gwydion, with a rueful smile. "A political gesture to appease Dyfed. As long as I keep my head low, I won't be forced from Gwynedd."

"You gave it all up?" she said. From the little that he had told her, he'd spent years building himself a web of informants and spies. His sister, his nephews... she could not imagine him leaving them all behind.

"I did," said Gwydion. "For one thing, I was a political liability. If I stayed, my sister could not create the alliances she needed. And for another . . . when I returned to Caer Dathyl, I could not be myself again. The trickster died that day in the woods, and I have no desire to resurrect him." He sighed. "I'll see my nephews again. They're already sneaking out of the castell. I'm sure they'll find their way to wherever I am. It might take a few years."

She wanted to say she was sorry, but she could not. Somehow it seemed a fitting price that Gwydion lose the home he had fought so hard for. "I'm surprised King Pwyll didn't send assassins after you."

"Oh, he did," said Gwydion, with a trace of a smile. "Four of them. Three were gently extracted from the city and returned to Dyfed. The last was burned alive. He climbed through the wrong bedroom window, and Amaethon has been bad-tempered of late. Being rather publicly humiliated and then stripped of his throne . . . well. After that, Pwyll had to grudgingly accept that the only way he was getting recompense was through official means. Hence, the exile." He spread his hands, gesturing at himself. "I have no title. No kingdom. No friends anymore."

"You had friends?" she said. She meant it as a jest, but it came out too flat.

He looked at her, all the sadness in the world in his eyes. "Once."

As he was leaving, Gwydion hesitated near the front gate. "I almost forgot," he said, and dug into his pack. He came up with a familiar knife. "I hoped to return it."

It was the afanc-fang dagger. When she took it, there was a

slight shake to her hands. She had never thought to see this again. Her fingers settled around the hilt. It felt like a piece of herself had returned.

"Thank you," she said.

He nodded. "You're welcome."

"Where will you go?"

"I have a room in the village," he said. "I can stay there for a while. After that..." He looked at the rolling fields. "I might try farming."

"You, a farmer?" she said skeptically.

"I think I'd be good at it," he said.

"Can you last a day without tricking a rabbit? Or magicking a barley stalk?"

A full-fledged grin broke across his face. "I suppose we'll find out." He sobered a little. "I was thinking...and you may refuse, if you like. I might take up the farm near you."

"Rhain's farm?" she said in surprise.

"Yes." He tapped his left fingers against the fence post. "The barwn will grant me the land if I ask it. You said Rhain had no heirs, and I don't want you to be responsible for it unless you want to."

She thought of that old house. Of the dust collecting on the shelves, of forgotten cups and plates, of rooms that would need airing. "Rhain wasn't sentimental," she said. "There isn't much there anymore."

Gwydion shrugged. "I could refurnish the house a little. Maybe buy a goat or three. You could show me how to feed chickens."

She did not answer.

She knew what he was asking, even as he did not say the words. She looked at him. At the trickster who had lied and stolen and killed. She knew what he had done; she couldn't even deny he had good reasons. But some part of her still shied away from the memory of that betrayal.

"I don't know if I can ever forgive you," she said.

He nodded. "I know. But I have a year and a day to try."

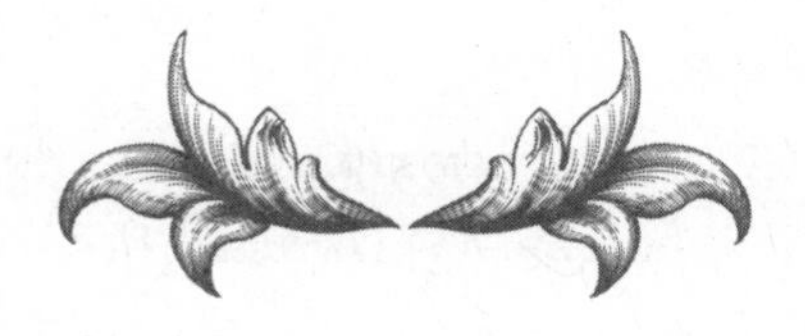

IT WAS SAID *that the otherfolk stole children, but that was before they left the mortal lands.*

They are gone now—vanished to a place where humanity cannot reach.

It was because of a man called Gwydion. He was a trickster and diviner from Gwynedd. Some tales say that he slipped into the wood and stole a roebuck, a hound, and a lapwing from Arawn. For this, the Other-king waged a war to retrieve his lost animals. He sent his champion, a hunter of renowned strength, to retrieve them. The champion was magicked so that none could slay him, and it was only when Gwydion spoke the name "Bran" that the hunter's magic was broken.

Other tales whisper that Gwydion went to that forest to meet with a woman he had fallen in love with. But when Arawn stole her, Gwydion brought a forest to life to win her back.

Another tale says that the trickster stole into the Wild Hunt to assassinate a prince, and the prince's lover—a huntress—chased Gwydion to avenge him.

No one knows the truth of it.

But this much is certain: In the spring after the tylwyth teg vanished, Queen Arianrhod took the throne of Gwynedd. The city of Caer Dathyl became Caer Arianrhod, a home where smiths and tradesmen flocked. It was said the queen was a kind and fair one. Her two sons were good-natured, and they were seen flitting through the city.

As for the trickster Gwydion, he vanished. There were whispers that Arianrhod banished him as a favor to Dyfed. Other rumors swore that the young man had ridden from Gwynedd to find his own fortune. He was the most powerful diviner in the lands, villagers whispered. He could have gone anywhere.

The legend of Gwydion ended there.

But there are other stories.

There was a huntress. She had pale hair and scars across her face, and she hunted monsters. The tylwyth teg had gone, but not all of their beasts went with them.

A young man moved into the farm that neighbored the huntress. He grew fields of crops that fed many that might have otherwise gone hungry. He sold herbs at the village and worked with the healer to keep her stocks full. He was rumored to be of ill health; he grew tired swiftly and wore a brace around his right hand. But he was well liked among the village, where he spent good coin and told the children stories.

When iron-mad monsters were seen, the huntress vanished from her farm for days or weeks, with her black-and-white cat at her heels. She returned with a new bruise or a scar, but she always returned. She helped her mother with the chickens, kept her cat from stealing goat milk, and rested when her head began to throb.

As for the midwife, she grew older. But her memories remained intact. She smiled when the village children brought her freshly picked berries, and she sat with the black-and-white cat on her lap, watching travelers pass by. Trade routes had been opened by the new queen, and Gwynedd invited merchants from other kingdoms to visit.

The world changed, as worlds were wont to do.

But some things remained the same.

There were whispers in the village that the young man was trying to court the huntress. For a year and a day, every evening he left flowers at the huntress's door. They were living things, to be planted and tended, and they flourished in pots on her windowsill and rows along the house.

On that final day, the young man walked to her door. It was the second day of winter, with frost-edged mornings and cold starlit nights. As the sun waned, he placed a wreath of wild roses on her door.

The huntress watched him from within. Broken things could not always be mended, but sometimes, they could be forged into something new.

She thought of what her mam had always said: Evenings were a time for magic.

The huntress opened her door.

ACKNOWLEDGMENTS

In the summer of 2022, I was interviewed on the local radio to promote *The Drowned Woods*.

"I have to ask," the interviewer said. "What happened to Blodeuyn?"

I sat there, confounded by the question. I was working on my next book proposal, cobbling together ideas from three of my favorite Welsh myths: the Wild Hunt, of the Battle of the Trees, and the tale of the midwife. But I hadn't found the thread that would bind them together.

Then I thought of Blodeuyn. Of the fierce fighter with a sharp tongue and sharper attention to detail. What *did* happen to her?

So the first acknowledgment has to go to Michelle Blackwell. Thanks for asking that question.

To my wonderful agent, Sarah Landis—thank you for always being in my corner, for your expertise and guidance, and for always making me laugh on our phone calls. My gratitude goes out to the entire Sterling Lord Literistic team. To Berni Barta at CAA, for your encouragement and passion.

I'm so grateful to the entire crew at Little, Brown Books for Young Readers. To my fabulous editorial team, Alex Hightower and

Crystal Castro—if I ever did have to compete in the Wild Hunt, I'd want you both on my side! To Marisa Finkelstein, Kelley Frodel, and Rina Guo, for all your hard work and attention to detail. To Sasha Illingworth and Jenny Kimura, for turning this book into a work of art. To Savannah Kennelly, Stefanie Hoffman, Alice Gelber, and Sadie Trombetta, for your excitement and enthusiasm in getting my books into readers' hands. To Victoria Stapleton, for all the hard work in school and libraries. And of course, I am very grateful to Megan Tingley and Jackie Engel, for building my career as an author.

I am incredibly lucky to have Moira Quirk bringing these characters to life again and again in the audiobooks. This world would not be the same without her voice.

To Kathleen Jennings, for the absolutely gorgeous map. As a fantasy nerd, having maps in my books has always been a dream. And now if anyone asks where Colbren is, I can finally point to it!

To everyone at the Books Council of Wales, thank you for championing my work.

The biggest of hugs to all my author friends—there are too many to list, but you know who you are. I am fortunate to be surrounded by talented, kind, supportive individuals. Thank you for reviewing my book proposals, for commiserating when the words are being stubborn, and for sharing in my joys and sorrows. This journey would not the same without you.

For this book in particular, I owe thanks to Rosiee Thor, Livia Blackburne, and Jessica Burkhart for looking over this book when it was little more than an outline and a handful of chapters. To Dawn Kurtagich and Kat Ellis for showing me around one of the coolest Welsh castles I've ever seen. (And for the blurbs, of course!) To Kalyn

Josephson, Jessica James, and Mary Elizabeth Summer for the lovely Oregon writing retreat. To Lyndall Clipstone for saying such nice things about my writing and for being an awesome author. And to E. K. Johnston for the wonderful blurb and for answering my morbid questions about Cigfa's belt trophies.

To the booksellers and the librarians who have supported me over the years—you are the best. Shout-outs to Gabrielle Belisle, Jessica Hahl, Emma Theriault, D. Guthrie, Kel Russel, Shelby Escott, Mike Lasagna, Amanda Quain, Tegan Tigani, Toni Wheeler, Kailey Steward, Lily Tschudi-Campbell, Alysha Welliver, and Molly Ashford.

To the Bookstagrammers, BookTokers, BookTubers, and anyone else who has been kind enough to recommend my work, you have my gratitude.

To my family—both the one I was born into and the one I've found along the way.

And lastly, to the readers. Without your support, I would not be able to write these books.

Diolch!

© Tammie Gilchrist

EMILY LLOYD-JONES

grew up on a vineyard in rural Oregon, where she played in evergreen forests and learned to fear sheep. She has a bachelor's in English from Western Oregon University and a master's in publishing from Rosemont College. She currently resides in Northern California, where she enjoys wandering in redwood forests. Her young adult novels include *Illusive*, *Deceptive*, *The Hearts We Sold*, *The Bone Houses*, and *The Drowned Woods*. She is also the author of the middle-grade novels *Unseen Magic* and *Unspoken Magic*. Emily invites you to find her at emilylloydjones.com.